TIE MY BONES TO HER BACK

G·K
Hall
&Co.

This Large Print Book carries the
Seal of Approval of N.A.V.H.

TIE MY BONES TO HER BACK

Robert F. Jones

G.K. Hall & Co.
Thorndike, Maine

Published in 1997 by arrangement with Farrar, Straus & Giroux, Inc.

G.K. Hall Large Print Western Collection.

The text of this Large Print edition is unabridged.
Other aspects of the book may vary from the original edition.

Set in 16 pt. Plantin by Al Chase.

Printed in the United States on permanent paper.

Library of Congress Cataloging in Publication Data

Jones, Robert F., 1934–
    Tie my bones to her back / Robert F. Jones.
        p. cm.
    ISBN 0-7838-1986-2 (lg. print : hc)
    1. Frontier and pioneer life — Great Plains — Fiction.
2. Indians of North America — Wars — Fiction. 3. Women
pioneers — Great Plains — Fiction. 4. Large type books.   I. Title.
[PS3560.O526T54   1997]
    813′.54—dc20   96-43983

FOR ANNIE PROULX

In our intercourse with the Indians it must always be borne in mind that we are the most powerful party . . . We are assuming, and I think with propriety, that our civilization ought to take the place of their barbarous habits. We therefore claim the right to control the soil they occupy, and we assume it is our duty to coerce them, if necessary, into the adoption and practice of our habits and customs . . . I would not seriously regret the total disappearance of the buffalo from our western prairies, in its effect upon the Indians, regarding it rather as a means of hastening their sense of dependence upon the products of the soil.

— Columbus Delano
U.S. Secretary of the Interior (1873)

Acknowledgments

I would like to thank the Ucross Foundation in northern Wyoming and its executive director, Elizabeth Guheen, for providing me with a residency during the month of April 1993, while I traveled and researched a small part of the Great Plains. Thanks also to Claire Kuehn, archivist-librarian of the Panhandle-Plains Historical Museum in Canyon, Texas, for granting me access to invaluable material on commercial buffalo hunting in western Texas during the 1870s. The custom gunmaker Steven Dodd Hughes of Livingston, Montana, an expert on nineteenth-century firearms who is familiar with most of the weapons mentioned in this book, read my manuscript for accuracy; I'm grateful for his time and effort. My editors at Farrar, Straus & Giroux, Margaret Ferguson and John Glusman, demonstrated great patience and a willingness — above and beyond the call of duty — to deal with obscure and violent subjects. To both of them my utmost gratitude and respect.

Introit

The virgin prairie: no wheel ruts, no chimneys, no spiders yet — the bison in his plenitude. No history here, no numbers, not even the resonance of place-names. No villains, no heroes. And if once the land had them, who knows what they signified?

Just the land, flat, empty, endless and timeless, cut to the bone by the rare run of water, pounded by the sun.

The wind blows steadily, night and day, driving men and animals wild.

Then it stops.

The heat builds.

Buffalo gnats swarm everywhere, fleas and lice, the stench of rotting meat. The seasons swing through impossible arcs, heat and cold, sunglare, starglare, frostbite, flood and snow, mirage. Black, dry tongues in skulls that still breathe; a herd of elk frozen in place, standing; mummified antelope withering within their sun-parched hides; frost-puckered men losing toes and limbs to the cold. A couple of newcomers frozen by the norther; other wayfarers come upon them, look down from their gaunt horses; the weather's victims snowblind and helpless, begging for mercy, just a bullet or two, for pity's sake; they ride on, but one goes back and shoots them — is it mercy?

No, he merely wished to see if his rifle would still fire in such a frost as this. Scarce time for pity here.

When horses are starving, men will feed them meat and the horses will eat it as readily as hay. You'll see them now and then, hobbled beyond the firelight, gnawing the bones of long-gone way-farers, whether frozen to death or baked alive matters not to your pony.

The Indians believe there was a time when all animals, even buffalo, preyed upon men and de-voured their flesh. But that was long ago.

The buffalo herd moving through time: big ugly shaggy smelly louse-ridden powerful animals, black-humped, black-horned, huge heads and tiny feet, bellowing, roaring, grunting, pursued by wolves, ridden down by Indians, gunned in their milling millions by hide men, shot and puk-ing blood, hundreds of them pouring into rivers and over cliffs, breaking their bones and dying, or drowning and dying, or doomed to starve with broken backs and legs, and the rest running right over them, through them, with no compassion, no concern, driven mindlessly, as are we, by their nature, our nature.

These lives, our lives, are merciless — they will make you cry out for emptiness — cry out for a single redeeming message.

You'll not get it here, unless . . .

The Human race is vile, unthinking Nature best, and Prayers won't help us anyway.

The plains go on forever.

PART I

1

The Panic of 1873, precipitated by the failure of Jay Cooke's banking house in New York, spread rapidly from east to west. Armies of tramps and incendiaries moved through the land that fall, jobless, roofless, hopeless men, hamstringing blood horses in their anger, burning barns, grabbing broody hens and cooking them — barely plucked, still quivering — over smoky fires made of planks they tore from the floors of chicken coops, wolfing down the red-veined meat half raw. Smoke rose thin in bitter blue-gray columns through the autumn woods and the stench of house fires lay heavy on the land.

In any switchyard along the North West Railroad's right-of-way through Wisconsin, wherever the cars were going slow enough, you could see the tramps drop from the freight cars like ticks from a dead dog's belly, swollen in the wrappings of their filthy rags, shuffling off through the dead-fallen leaves with an ominous whisper, some with shiny new boots, cocksure for the minute.

A farmer residing near Clyman went out to his pigsty one morning and found two dozen saddleback porkers lying dead with their throats slit. He could see from the tracks in the jelled purple blood that the other eleven had been carried away.

In the silent woods near Rhinelander, the bodies of unidentified men are found dangling from tree limbs. A tramp falls from a freight car on the outskirts of Butler, the wheels nip the top from his skull. Tramps turned away from a farmhouse door not far from North Prairie go into the barn, cut the throats of three cows, leaving a card spiked on a bloody horn: "Remember this when next you refuse us."

Suicide takes many forms. Paris green. Carbolic acid. The noose. The revolver. One man beats himself to death with a hammer. Another, demented, eats a dozen cigar butts and chokes to death when he vomits them back up. Yet another lashes sticks of dynamite around his torso, caps them, lights the fuse . . .

A troop of fifty hoboes invades the town of Bad Axe. They terrorize the citizenry and burn the county courthouse. Others occupy Peltier's Store, break into the wine cellar, and devour the sausage and crackers and all but three of the dill pickles. An affray ensues, in the course of which one tramp shoots another over the division of spoils. More gunshots follow. When the smoke clears, the sheriff counts nine dead bodies. Another four hoboes seriously wounded, three not expected to live.

A plague killed many children that year — "the black diphtheria" — infants mainly, though older children, too: a lovely girl of seventeen in Kewaunee, whose picture ran in the paper; and every day the bells tolled another dozen funerals. In some families, two or three children died in a single day. A sore throat at first, a slight fever, then the bacillus raging out of control — throat tissue eaten away, replaced by a tough gray membrane, the telltale sign of imminent death. Suffocation swiftly ensues. (Or worse, prolonging suspense because it is slower, the infection leaches downward through the esophagus, finally inflaming the walls of the heart.)

The babies looked lovely in their embroidered burial gowns: their sightless glances half lidded, blue eyes and silky blond hair, a bit of rouge on their plump smooth cheeks, their bottoms scrubbed clean, held upright, in tiny pine coffins lovingly sawn and tacked together, on hooks implanted in their backs by the town photographer. Family mementos. Many mothers went crazy with grief. Women walked the streets of Wisconsin — the entire Northwest — with their eyes deranged and dead babies in their arms. They walked into stores the way they had when their babies were alive, then sat in chairs before the cast-iron stoves and rocked until the babies began to stink. No man dared approach them. Some women felt so guilty about the deaths of their infants that they cut their own throats with case knives or sheep shears, some threw themselves into cisterns, others laid their heads upon the railroad tracks and allowed the thundering wheels to shatter their skulls. One woman near Eau

15

Claire was chopped into three pieces by the wheels.

Yet the *Badger Banner* reported: "More poetry is written in Wisconsin than in any other state in the Union."

A hard frost that morning, the morning that changed her life, and Jenny Dousmann snug in her bed. It was cold in the loft, warm under the goosedown comforter. She said a little prayer.

Lieber Gott, mach' mich fromm, dass ich in dein Himmel komm'. Amen.

Dear God, make me pious, so that I go to Heaven . . .

She waited until she heard her father rattling in the kitchen, firewood snapping in the stove, then threw back the cover, jumped out of bed, hiked her nightgown, squatted over the chamber pot, and dashed for her clothing. She was a strongly built girl with fair hair and fair skin, large green eyes, and freckles — faint ones — on her cheekbones. The coffee was done by the time she came down the ladder. Vati was out in the barn milking the cows. She punched the air from some bread dough left to rise the previous evening, shaped it into the pans, and set the dough to rise a second time. She covered the pans with damp towels. When she had finished, she went out to the henhouse to gather eggs. She heard her mother stirring in the big bedroom as she closed the kitchen door. Mutti would put the bread in the oven when it was ready. That was their daily routine.

A bright blue morning, frost glitter in the trees, roosters singing all through the valley. Woodsmoke rose in a ruler-straight line from Wielands' chimney half a mile down the road. She noticed that their own rooster was silent, the hens as well. None of the usual *Jammer* that greeted her arrival with a sack of cracked corn and barley.

There were few eggs in the henhouse, just over a dozen. She went across to the barn to tell her father. Perhaps there'd been another fox around during the night. She found Vati hanging from a noose tied to a rafter. His handsome face was dark with constricted blood. A dreadful stink. She saw that he had *beschmutzt* himself. It was dripping from the cuffs of his overalls onto the toes of his boots. His tongue stuck out, dark blue. His eyes bulged. Jenny yelled toward the house for her mother. Mutti came on the run, barefoot over the frosty ground, her yellow-white hair flapping. She stood breathless at the barn door. Jenny pointed. Her mother stared but did not scream.

Jenny dragged a ladder from the side of the barn, propped it against the rafter, and climbed up to her father. She used the blade of a scythe to saw through the rope. He thumped in the mud. She pulled down his overalls to clean his bottom and his legs, using fresh hay from a new bale.

In the bib pocket of his overalls she found a notice from the Heldendorf Mercantile Bank advising Herr Emil Dousmann that full payment of the outstanding amount of his mortgage, $938.55 in toto, was due on the twelfth of October 1873, and that if said payment was not forthcoming by said date, the bank would have no choice but to take over the farm. Below this cold, formal statement, the bank's president, Herr Jochen Sauerweiz, had written in pencil: "Sorry, Emil, but business is business, and it's bad everywhere right now." The Sauerweizes and Jenny's parents had come to America on the same ship from the Old Country.

Today is the twelfth, she thought. *Sakrament!* He hadn't been happy for a long time now. No music in weeks from his fiddle. Too sad; I should have known.

Jenny felt like weeping, but thought of her mother. I'd only get her crying along with me. Mutti is too *zartfühlend,* too sensitive, too soft for this land. She cries at nothing — wind ruffling the water on the stock pond, cold light on the hills at sunset, a kitten suckling on its purring mother. I suppose it reminds her of her innocent childhood in Germany. She never left Deutschland behind. Oh *ja,* she cries plenty when Vati plays his fiddle . . .

Mutti had gone back into the house. Jenny went to comfort her. She found her mother on the floor of the kitchen, her mouth leaking blood. The bottle of carbolic acid stood on the kitchen counter, still uncapped. Jenny screwed the cap back on, its threads crusty on the brown glass. Skull-and-crossbones on the red-lettered label.

18

Jenny knelt beside her mother and tried to wipe away the slippery foam, but it just kept bubbling from her nose and mouth. She was not breathing. She was dead. *Selbstmord.* An ugly word: suicide . . .

Panic thumped Jenny's heart clear up to her eardrums. Her mind leaped away from the horror. My apron's all bloody and stinking, she thought, suddenly short of breath. And my dress, too — filthy! And what's that? — the bread's risen too far! Mutti forgot to put the pans in the oven. Jenny sprang upon the offending loaves and punched them flat.

Outside, the frost was melting under a cheerful sun, dripping from the roof and the trees, black splats in the barnyard dirt, and now finally the rooster was singing as if there were no tomorrow.

I must get word to Otto . . .

After she had cleaned up, Jenny walked over to the Wielands' place. She found Herr Wieland mucking out the cow stalls. Andres Wieland was a tall, big-bellied peasant from Hesse with an uhlan's mustache brindled by tobacco juice, merry blue eyes, and a wart on his right nostril that looked like dried snot. She told him what had happened.

"Du lieber," he said, the smile of greeting frozen at her words. "How? Why? You poor child . . ."

Then she saw the initial shock in his eyes replaced by a look of calculation. All that land now, right next door. Those fine cows . . .

19

He said he would send his wife to help.

He himself would go into town to report the tragedy. He would wire a telegram to Jenny's older brother to return quickly home.

Otto Dousmann was in Kansas, near Fort Dodge, hunting buffalo. A wire might reach him care of the Fort. Or perhaps through the railroad, the Atchison, Topeka & Santa Fe — they now had a station at Dodge City.

The Wieland boys, Friedl and Willi, were still out in the pasture with the cows. Frau Wieland drove Jenny back home in her buggy; she wept silently all the way. Vroni Wieland had been Minnie Dousmann's closest friend in America. They often helped one another with their housework, singing songs from the Old Country as they cooked or cleaned or ironed or beat carpets or washed windows or waxed one another's floors, even out in the garden chopping weeds. "Du Bist Wie Eine Blume," "Der Schwartze Zigeuner," "Am Brunnen Vor dem Tore" — they had sweet voices, Frau Wieland a husky alto, Frau Dousmann a soprano. Jenny had loved to hear them harmonize, their chubby wet red faces streaming with tears and sweat, their eyes laughing as they cried and rolled out strudel dough, the tears turning the flour on their cheeks into white runnels that ended in little lumps of salty pastry dough that almost cooked from the heat of their homesickness.

Those were warm lovely evenings in the kitchen, with the cold black American night wrapping itself around the house, the mothers with their sweet voices, cheeks wet with tear-shine. The men came back from barn or field, clumping mud off their boots on the back stoop, and sometimes there was the bang of a shotgun off in the distance as Willi or Friedl or Otto, when he still lived at home, shot plump prairie chickens, and later the birds coming brown and hot and gleaming with fat from the oven, with bread and apple and onion stuffing, and potatoes and red cabbage, strudel with *Schlagsahne* — what the Americans called whipped cream — from our own sleek cows after, and then Vati playing his violin . . .

Later that night, after Frau Wieland had returned home, Jenny prayed for Otto's swift return. He's a soldier, she thought, familiar with death and decisions. He'll know what to do. But she had to make some decisions of her own, she knew. Frau Wieland had been kind, offering to take Jenny into her household "like a daughter of my own." The Wielands had had a daughter once, named Hannelore, but she had died at the age of eight. They had buried her at the foot of a big red oak at the top of the hill behind their house. The sun set in winter directly behind that oak, and every evening Frau Wieland watched it go down and wept a little. Jenny had seen her tears often.

Herr Wieland had always wanted this farm. A frugal, penny-pinching man, he had plenty of money now and he might very well buy it from the bank for the price of the outstanding mortgage.

But I don't want to live with the Wielands, she thought. Even if Otto had enough money to pay off the bank, she knew she couldn't keep up the farm all by herself. Yet her father had worked so hard to build it. He was an educated man, not an *echt Bauer* — a true farmer, like Andres Wieland. Emil Dousmann had grown up in Kassel and attended the Technische Hochschule there. His own father was a draper, a member of the Bürgerstand — the bourgeoisie — but Emil Dousmann had joined the Socialist Party. After the '48 revolution failed, he and his wife came to America. At first he had worked as a printer in New York, played violin with the Liederkranz, and written for socialist newspapers in Milwaukee. His dream, Vati had always said, was to build on his own acreage and farm "scientifically," following the precepts of his heroes, Thomas Jefferson and Alexander von Humboldt. With the money saved from his newspaper work, he'd bought this land near Heldendorf, west of Milwaukee, and made it into a small but productive farm. He had borrowed money from the bank only to improve his herd and his orchards, and to send his daughter to the Heldendorf Academy.

Otto never attended the academy. He went off instead to fight in the war with the 2nd Wisconsin Regiment of the Iron Brigade. Wounded twice,

22

at Antietam and Chancellorsville, he came home a sergeant. Jenny didn't recognize him when he returned. He was pale from the hospital, his pallor accentuated by his big black mustache and the black slouch hat of the Iron Brigade, and he walked with a limp. But he smiled and slapped her hard on the shoulder, and then she knew him as of old.

That fall he took her on hunting trips. They camped out up north in the big woods and slept under a canvas tent from the war that still smelled of old gunpowder and the red Rebel mud that had stained it. They ate rabbits and squirrels and deer meat fresh killed from the woods and speckled trout from cold black streams that smelled of iron. Those were good days, Jenny recalled now, without the sour stink of the dung heap behind the barn and the clamor of hens waiting to be fed, only the drumming of partridges in the pine woods, the ice like a mirror on the water kettle in the morning . . .

But Otto had contracted the wanderlust from too many years on the march. Like so many veterans, he could not stay at home. So he went West. Mutti had cried and pleaded, but Vati said he couldn't blame Otto, for hadn't he himself gone West at the same age? It's in the blood, her father said, this chasing the setting sun. Mutti had cried even louder.

America is hard, Jenny thought.

It tried to kill my brother, and when it couldn't kill him, it killed my father and mother instead.

I'm sure it'll try to kill me, too, sooner or later. May all bankers burn in hell. Especially Herr Jochen Sauerweiz of the Heldendorf Mercantile Bank.

2

Otto arrived three days later, in time for the funeral. Jenny walked into town to meet him at the railway station. He was tanned as dark as an Indian, with sunbursts of white wrinkle lines fanning outward from his grave blue eyes, and he did not look as large as she remembered him. He still wore the black slouch hat, dusty from the war — or perhaps merely from the train ride, she realized — but with the same bullet hole through its battered crown, not yet patched ten years after a Rebel minié ball had perforated it somewhere along the Rappahannock. He was thinner, too, and as he walked unsmiling toward her, she noticed flashes of gray in his mustache and at his temples. The limp, though, had vanished, except for a slight hunching of his left shoulder as his weight came down on the opposite foot. An almost imperceptible wince, perhaps habit now after all these years of pain, tensed his facial muscles as a spasm of toothache might have done.

"Na ja, du Hübsche," he said — Now then, pretty one. And smiled finally, a sad smile but a warm one, revealing a gap where a shell fragment had extracted his lower left molars, both top and bottom, in the cornfield near the Dunker Church

at Antietam eleven years earlier. The exit wound had left a knot of scar tissue in the center of his left cheek. It was shaped, she suddenly realized, like a gnarled heart. The small piece of shrapnel must have entered through his open mouth, for there was no sign of an entry wound. He could not remember just how it had happened, there had been so much tumult in the cornfield that day.

"Ah, dear one, how did they die?"

"*Selbstmord*," she said. He winced again, and his eyes slipped out of focus for a moment.

"*Ach*, Christ, Hanna! How? Why?"

She told him as they walked uphill from the station to the Lutheran church on the ridge above town. The day was cool and bright, and overhead ragged wedges of geese flew south, their high, distant cries sounding festive. She spoke of the bank's foreclosure, of rope and acid, her tone cold with the ugliness of it. He stopped to look down at the Heldendorf Mercantile Bank, a solid, solemn structure built of gray limestone from the local quarry, with heavy wrought-iron grillwork over its windows. A fortress of financial integrity. Not even Jesse James could rob this bank. It would turn him to stone before he set foot inside the door. Most of the buildings in Heldendorf were built of stone or brick, many of the larger homes as well. It looked foreign to him after the raw-plank architecture of the West, where sudden towns bled sap all summer long and warped the winter through.

"How much was left to pay on the mortgage?"

"Less than a *tausend* dollars — nine hundred and a bit."

"I'll pay it off." He slapped the new carpetbag he had carried from the train. "When the wire arrived, my partner and I were in Dodge City selling a load of hides. Twenty-four hundred dollars' worth." He smiled.

She frowned. "Are you coming back? I'll not work the place by myself."

"No, but you could hire help. I'm sure there must be some strong young backs looking for work. Maybe two or three?"

"And how would I pay for their *Arbeit,* in buttermilk and manure? Vati couldn't even meet the loan payments, with the price milk is bringing these days — even buttermilk. There's no money anywhere."

"*Doch zwar,*" Otto said. "Too true — except on the Buffalo Range. But might you not marry, Hanna? Have no lads come a-courting?"

"*Keine,*" she said firmly. "Not a one, thank God! And by the way, my name is no longer Hanna. I call myself Jenny now — proper American."

"Tschenny?" He laughed. "No wonder the local boys aren't coming round. To them you're a 'Yenny.' And don't stare daggers at me that way. Why are women always so serious about their names? Why have all the girls I've ever known felt bound and determined to change them?"

He looked at her and laughed again, winked

27

and composed his face in mock seriousness.

"Well then, with no marital prospects in sight, you could sell the herd and rent out the pastureland. Or keep the herd — fine stock it is — and make an arrangement with some good farmer in the neighborhood to go shares with you on the milk, in return for his labor. Wieland always had his eyes on our herd, as I recall."

"*Ja sicher*," she said. "True indeed. Frau Wieland has invited me to move in with them, and in return allow Herr Wieland to work our herd. But I won't live with the Wielands. I won't be a replacement for her dead Hannelore."

"Then perhaps we might sell the place," Otto said, "even at a loss, if necessary — I want no money from this farm, it would all be yours — and you could move to town." He glanced at her quickly, striding along beside him, and saw the hard set of her jaw.

Suddenly he knew what she wanted.

She wanted to go West with him.

She must be thinking that it would be like those hunting trips they'd made together when he got back from the war. Another lighthearted outdoor adventure. Or perhaps she wanted to be with him wherever he went — after all, she was his little sister, she loved him as dearly as he loved her, and now, with Mutti and Vati gone . . . She was only sixteen, after all. But the West? The only women there were whores and outlaws.

"It's not like up north, Jenny," Otto explained quietly. "It's different out on the prairies. An alien

28

world — there are no trees, only grass. Little or no water, and what you do find is bitter or full of buffalo dung. Rattlesnakes everywhere. Wolves as big as yearling calves. We sleep on the ground most of the time, and the ground is hard. And the wind blows always, always, day and night. Sometimes it's so cold that mules freeze stiff, standing up. Sometimes so hot and dry that your eyelids crack just from blinking, so hot and dry that your nose bleeds. Often you can't bathe for weeks on end, out in those badlands where the buffalo are today. You can't even wash your face or brush your teeth. And nothing to eat but buffalo hump and hardtack, day after day after day."

"I know."

Christ, she was stubborn! She *didn't* know. She'd only read newspapers, or maybe some silly dime novel about valiant, handsome, devil-may-care buffalo runners. If only she could smell one.

The funeral service was short but solemn, Pastor Koellner's words heartfelt. He had stretched the rules concerning suicide, making it sound as though Vati had died in a farm accident and Mutti, in her grief, had returned to the house distraught, grabbed a bottle she thought contained Himbeerschnaps, and taken a fatal draught before realizing it was carbolic acid. No, the Dousmanns were not the first suicides the pastor had buried. America was a hard place.

Otto hadn't been in the wooden church since before the war. He had gone then only to please

29

his mother, as had Jenny. He recognized many faces in the congregation, but had difficulty at first putting names to them. Herr Albrecht, the stone mason, with his ruddy, wind-scoured face and hands hard as horn. Beside him Mrs. Obst, the schoolteacher — old now and, though dressed in her churchgoing finest, still smelling of chalk dust and India ink. Ursula Frischert, the love of his youth. Beside her stood two sturdy children, redheads both, a boy and a girl, and her husband, Otto's marching *Kamerad* from the 2nd Wisconsin, Lud Nortmann, balding, he saw, with the stooped shoulders and spidery, ink-stained fingers of a bookkeeper. And when Ursula — whose waist Otto had once been able to span with both hands — turned sideways to whisper something in Lud's ear, Otto noticed that she was with child once more. With sudden clarity Otto recalled a morning in the autumn of 1861 when Lud Nortmann, younger, slimmer, untried in battle, had been splattered with the brains of a comrade — was it Sergeant Houghton? — on a dusty road in southern Maryland and, while a volley of musket shots sought the Rebel skirmisher in the trees beside the road, had collapsed against Otto, weeping hysterically. They hadn't killed the Johnny, either.

Ein' feste Burg ist unser Gott . . .

Later she stood beside him, dry-eyed, the grief leached out of her. All that remained now was the graveyard. She'd weather that. Then Otto would go down to the bank and speak with Herr Sauerweiz. He would gladly accept Otto's money in payment of the mortgage. Why, he must have dozens of farms on his hands by now, what use would another be to him? Otto would make some kind of arrangement regarding the farm with Herr Wieland. He was an honest man, Herr Wieland, and he knew as well that if he cheated the Dousmanns, Otto would simply return and thrash their money out of him. There were advantages to a soldierly reputation. When those matters were out of the way, along with her packing, Otto and Jenny could depart for Milwaukee, Chicago, St. Louis, Kansas City, Topeka, and the Great West. Otto had said that the buffalo herds should be moving by now. There were "shaggies" to slaughter, money to be made, a whole new direction to her life. She had known her brother could not refuse her, no matter how grimly he described the West. For the first time in days she felt hopeful again.

Two days later they were on a train. Jenny sat in the swaying car, her arms crossed beneath her breasts, jaw set, eyes hard, so firm in her childish convictions, Otto thought — so clean and sure in her crisply starched shirtwaist, her neatly pleated wool skirt, her pert little cap with a stuffed bobolink perched on top. The true West would be a rude awakening.

They had left Chicago that morning and now the train was rolling through rich Illinois farmland. Cow corn stood tall in the fields, hardening off for the silos, pumpkins bright between the rows. Big red slate-roofed barns and trimly painted white houses rested content beneath the shade trees, elms and oaks and chestnuts, and tall, sweet grass surrounded the farmhouses, with herds of fat Holsteins and Guernseys grazing knee-deep in it, staring mindlessly at the passing train. Look at this, Jenny! he wanted to say. This is *your* America. Brooks and creeks and rivers full to overflowing with clean, cold, fast Midwestern water. Towns clicking past the train windows, the glint of plate-glass windows, righteous women walking the streets, shopping baskets on their arms, their children trailing obediently behind. Schoolhouses built of brick. Prosperous farmers coming to town with hayseed in their beards, their wagons drawn by matched pairs of glossy draft horses. Tall-steepled churches. Paved streets and sidewalks. How could she want to leave all this for the stink of the Buffalo Range?

"It's not adventure, Jennchen," he told her once again. "It's not even hunting, not the way we did it in Wisconsin when you were a girl. That was sport. This is business. It's ugly."

He thought of the skinned, raw carcasses of buff so thick along the Arkansas River and the Pawnee Fork, where they'd shot them when they came to water, that a man could hop from carcass to carcass for a mile without touching the ground. Rattlesnakes coiled in buffalo skulls. Buffalo putrid on the Smoky Hill River, or the Solomon, or

32

the Platte when the skinners were finished with them, shining on the sandy slopes like the windows of a great city reflecting the sunset. Poisoned wolves bloating in the sun, skinned out and reeking to high heaven. The stink of arsenic and strychnine and rotten meat.

"The whole damn prairie stinks," he said. "Here, you can still smell it on me, smell it — and I've been away for more than a week."

He thrust his hand under her nose. She turned away, silent, obstinate.

"And the redskins, there's the Hostiles to worry about, too. Constantly. Cheyenne, Arapaho, Shoshone, Satanta's Kiowas sometimes, up from Texas, young bucks out for ponies and scalps and some fun. Or Comanches — even worse. They'll take a man's pizzle for a trophy."

"Oh, please!" She turned to stab a look at him, grimmer still. Then she laughed. "And anyway, I have no pizzle to worry about. *Nein*, Otto, you can't frighten me with Red Indian tales."

"*Das ist nicht komisch*, Jenny. Not funny at all."

He rose to his feet and shrugged his jacket straight on his shoulders, hitched up his trousers, and grabbed his hat. He felt himself reddening, with anger or perhaps with shame.

Pizzle!

He'd been too long in the Army.

"I'm going for a smoke," he said.

3

He walked to the rear of the train and stood on the platform in the cold rushing air. He lit a cheroot and drew the smoke deep into his lungs. The bite of the smoke felt good.

Well, it was done; he had tried his best. There was no dissuading her. He'd better learn to live with it. After all, she was a good, strong, tough-minded girl. He doubted he could have handled the death of their parents as well as she had. Not the way they died. She wasn't struck helpless in the face of blood or death, so far at least. Anyone could handle its ugliness, he'd learned that in the war, but those who were queasy took longer to learn. The fearful, after they had mastered their fear, often became unnecessarily cruel, or took too many heedless risks.

He'd been a good soldier, and he was proud of that. But it had ruined him for real life. He couldn't abide a farm when he returned to it. Nor a town, for that matter. He couldn't abide the rootedness of it. He had to move, to march, to shoot.

The Great West suited him, with its alkaline water and searing winds, buffalo grass and sandstone buttes, its promise of challenge over every horizon. Even its cheapjack towns and pox-ridden

34

women, the wasted drunks pissing their lives away in some rat-squeaking, flea-bitten road ranch. The brash young drovers up from Texas, pistoled down in honky-tonks and brothels from Abilene to Ellsworth. Dodge would no doubt be their next slaughterhouse. Saddest of all, the failed homesteaders who'd come West with dreams and returned East, penniless and broken, as if fleeing a nightmare. "No place for a white man," they said.

Strangely enough, though, he had prospered in the Great West. At first when he left the farm he'd been content repairing farm machinery in western Minnesota, but the work got too steady, so he sold shoes door-to-door for a while in Iowa, then cut firewood in bulk near Omaha, drifted north one winter to run a trapline on the Niobrara River, and finally landed a job with the Union Pacific, bossing a gang of Irish, Norwegian, and German gandy dancers laying steel for branch lines along tributaries of the Platte. The U.P. was organized on military lines and its officers liked his soldierly bearing. But when the railroad advised him, as a salaried employee, that he must vote for Grant in '68, he quit. He would have voted for General Grant, his old commander, in any event. But not on the railroad's orders.

With the $373.68 he'd managed to save on the U.P., Otto bought a five-year-old chestnut mare named Vixen; an elderly mule named Zeke, whom he knew to be steady in the traces; a light spring wagon with outsized iron-rimmed wheels; a stew kettle, frying pan, coffeepot, and tin cup;

35

five pounds of coffee beans, twenty of flour, another ten of dried fruit (apples, apricots, prunes), thirty of soldier beans, a slab of fatback, two fifty-pound kegs of rock salt, a small bottle of arsenic with which to rid the hides he took of vermin; a pewter spoon, a butcher's knife and sharpening steel, four woolen blankets that still bore a faded U.S. Army stencil and the stench of Southern dirt upon them; an ax, pick, and shovel, bar lead, a bullet mold, a swage, a primer punch, a wad cutter, and a cast-iron pot in which to melt the bar lead for bullets; a large round carton containing a thousand Berdan primers, four dozen reasonably new $1^3/4$ -inch brass cartridge cases in .50 caliber, a twenty-five-pound keg of Du Pont Fg-grade black powder, and a Model 1866 .50-caliber Sharps military rifle, modified to accommodate center-fire cartridges, whose full stock had been cut back to 10 inches, then capped at the end in German silver. The barrel had been shortened as well, to 29 inches from its original $30^1/4$, thus improving the rifle's balance as well as its appearance. A tang sight was mounted on the wrist of the oiled walnut stock, just behind the sidehammer. Its vernier elevations were graded out to 1,300 yards, but that was sheer vainglory. With 72 grains of Fg loaded behind the 457-grain grooved ball, it shot accurately at ranges only slightly in excess of 400 yards, and the big, slow bullet tended to drift quite atrociously in a crosswind even at that piddling range. Yes, he thought, I love rifles, perhaps too well.

Vixen had a split in her left hind hoof, but it hadn't yet reached the frog. Because of that fault, which Otto knew he could quickly heal with the application of warm tar and tender, careful handling, he was able to talk the seller –– a meat hunter for the railroad who was going back East soon to marry his childhood sweetheart — out of a Texas stock saddle as part of the deal.

It was late autumn then, with inklings of sleet on the wind. Otto headed southwest from Fort Kearney after Vixen's hoof had healed. He wanted to find good game country quickly so he could lay in a supply of meat for the winter and build a dugout within which to weather it. He found his country in the rolling grasslands along the Smoky Hill River in western Kansas, after a long and difficult journey across the Republican, Solomon, and Saline Rivers. It was just what he was looking for — a country black with buffalo.

The herds were still moving slowly south for the winter, but once they were gone he would have abundant blacktail deer, elk, and pronghorn antelope to hunt along the river bottom and in the brushy draws of the hills rolling up behind it. There were plenty of wild turkeys, partridge, and prairie chickens, while out on the grasslands flocked sicklebills, doughbirds, and upland plover. Otto wished he had brought a shotgun for the smaller game birds. The big Sharps would tear them up too badly if he shot them on the ground, and he much preferred wing shooting anyway.

He excavated a dugout on a south-facing slope well above the Smoky Hill's high-water mark, roofing it over with a weave of hardhack poles, themselves covered with a layer of dirt and sod a foot and a half thick. He chopped wide, deep ditches around the soddy that would bleed rain and snowmelt downhill to the river. He had learned to do that in the Iron Brigade. Nothing was more uncomfortable than a wet camp in winter.

On the dugout's back wall he built a hearth and chimney of stones carried up from the river, chinking them with clay from its bank. The clay hardened quickly to the heat of a fire. He extended his crude flue a couple of feet above the sod, then added two feet more of stone when he pondered the winter snows to come. Beside the fireplace he constructed a bunk of roughly squared timber. With a buffalo robe as a mattress, a flour sack stuffed with the curly black hair from the topknot, beard, and mane of a stub-horn bull as a pillow, his Army blankets and perhaps another brain-tanned robe to cover him, and the fireplace at his back, he knew he could survive the worst that a prairie winter might offer.

A rough-hewn table and stool completed his furnishings.

Downriver one day, hunting buffalo, he found an outcropping of sandstone. On his next visit to what he called the Quarry, Otto brought his pick and set to work "making little ones out of big ones," as they said in the Army. He built a travois of popple poles, stretched a green buffalo hide over it, loaded it with flat slabs, and that evening laid a reasonably smooth floor within his dugout, complete with a sandstone "stoop" at the doorway so that he would not drag mud into the soddy with him every time it rained or snowed.

Ach ja, bin echt Deutsch, he told himself with a wry grin. A true German . . . Everything clean and in order.

A buffalo hide served for his door. Hollowed stones from the river, filled with elk or buffalo tallow, were his lamps, cotton cords his candlewicks. A nearby blackjack oak stood him as a drying rack, and on it at all times hung strips of buffalo, elk, or deer meat, drying in the wind and sun, along with heavy, tapered cuts of buffalo "hump," which, though delicious enough fresh, underwent an ambrosial metamorphosis when subjected to a few days of cool windy weather. Each piece was as long and thick as a grown man's leg. As it crusted over, the fat-marbled meat aged evenly and sweetly. Otto could believe the tales he'd heard of mountain men devouring ten pounds of lightly charred hump at a single sitting, then loosening their belts and crying for more. Later he'd grown tired of it — too much of a good thing — like those indentured servants in New England he'd heard about who rebelled at being fed salmon at every meal and demanded that it be served no more than three times a week.

A small stable dug partway into the hillside just beside the soddy provided shelter from wind and weather for Vixen and Zeke, with a corral of popple saplings surrounding it. He did not peel the saplings. His animals would see to that, munching on the sweet bark as a person would nibble an apple. In the Niobrara country he had fed his horses through the grimmest part of the winter on shavings of popple bark. Otto could not allow Zeke and Vixen to graze tethered to picket pins or in hobbles at night for fear of the big gray lobo wolves that followed the buffalo herds. Their howling at first spooked the animals, setting them to rearing against their halters and whinnying in terror, Vixen more so than the old veteran Zeke. After Otto had shot a few of the wolves and left their hides nearby, moving them closer and closer to the corral over the course of the next few days, both horse and mule lost their native fear of wolf scent. Anyway, most of the wolves would soon be gone south with the shaggies.

He remembered how he had missed them when they were gone. Their singing had lulled him to sleep during those first nights alone on the Smoky Hill River, while he was still adjusting to the solitude. He had never been alone this long. At home there'd always been Mutti and Vati, then Jenny growing up. In the Army there were his tentmates, messmates, marching comrades. On the hunting trips up north, he had brought Jenny — mainly for her company, he realized, though ʰad been enjoyable teaching her how to shoot, ʼo skin and butcher and cook what they had

40

killed together. Now he had only himself for company, and until he realized what was bothering him, the loneliness had been hard to bear.

Vixen and Zeke were some comfort, but it was the wolves that really saved him. Their voices, combed by wind and grasses as they echoed through the empty hills, sounded to him like some alien choir — remote and ancient, untranslatable, like the Gregorian chants he'd heard one Sunday morning in Fredericksburg while walking past a church where the Catholics were burying their dead.

Late one night, awakened by wolf howls and the panic of his beasts, he had taken his rifle and gone into the hills determined to find them. He stalked quietly into the wind toward their chorus. The moon was just rising, and by its cold light he saw them outlined in silver on the crest of a ridge. Half a dozen at least, maybe more in the shadows. He lay on his belly for a long while, watching them circle, sit, scuffle with one another, raise their muzzles to the moon and sing their baleful song. Then he elevated the sights to 350 yards and proceeded to kill them. He dropped three before the rest ran away. When he went up to skin them, he found that the largest wolf was still alive — a scarred and grizzled male, taken through the shoulders, who stared up at Otto with slanting yellow eyes. Otto stepped back quickly. The wolf's gaze was like a match to his heart. The wolf was unafraid. Otto cocked the hammer of the Sharps and finished him.

After taking their hides, Otto dragged the skinned carcasses down the riverbank. By the next morning, nothing remained of them but splintered bones. The rest had disappeared into the bellies of their kinfolk. That helped somewhat to ease his sense of guilt.

There were catamounts in the hills along the river, too. Otto saw their signs on the mudbars and heard their occasional screams at night, loud and shrill as a woman in terror. But the big cats never ventured near his camp. He wished he had a few dogs to run the panthers with, and for companionship through the long nights. Panther meat was good, light as veal. He'd eaten it that winter on the Niobrara.

Each morning he rode out to hunt and to explore the country. He wrapped burlap sacks around his calves for leggings, securing them with wraps of rawhide. The bottomland was thick with ripgut cordgrass and sunflowers, ten feet high, wind-dried now as winter came on. It was impossible to see more than a few feet ahead, even on horseback. The rattle of the sunflowers in the constant wind and the sudden spatter of their falling seeds unnerved him at first, as did the unexpected flush of migrant birds feeding in the brakes — warblers and goldfinches, sparrows, blackbirds, and jays. War nerves, Otto thought. With me forever, I guess. How silly, expecting any movement to explode into screaming Secesh . . .

places, though, the buffalo and elk had

beaten a labyrinth of trails through the sunflowers. He and Vixen rode the trails slowly, always hunting into the wind. Sometimes they came face-to-face with buffalo at a bend in the trail. Most of them fled instantly, spinning on their spindly legs and crashing away with the speed of cavalry ponies. But Vixen was quick off the mark and in a few jumps was alongside, allowing him a heart-lung shot behind the shaggy's shoulder. He learned how to drop them when he was on foot, too, as they were going away. The surest shot was low down in the flank, so that the bullet raked forward through the paunch, striking the heart. Almost as good but not as certain was a ball placed behind the huge, bucketing head, in line with the base of its horns, which would pierce the brain for an instant kill. A ton of buffalo made quite a thud.

Twice he had killed charging bulls at close range with shots to the forehead. He suspected that the buffalo's small brain sat very high in its head and split open a skull to confirm his guess. He was correct.

Vixen proved staunch. She never flinched when he shot, always stood her ground, rock steady. She was a good pony, he'd known it from the start.

The simple routines of his life pleased him profoundly. Returning from the hunt, he would clean his rifle: pour scalding water through the barrel first, swab out lands and grooves with a wiping stick, using a swatch of buffalo hair for his patch, then scrub the gummy black-powder residue of the day's shooting off the dropping breechblock, before reassembling the Sharps and brushing it with a fine, clear oil he had extracted by boiling down the plucked carcass of an eagle. Next he pegged out the day's hides, stretching them taut, flesh side up, to dry in the wind and sun. In four days they were hard as flint. Then he turned them hair side to the sky and sprinkled the wool with a dilute mixture of water and arsenic. This discouraged the big gray moths that laid their eggs in the hides.

After supper — usually hump steaks, flour gravy, beans, bannock bread, and coffee — he reloaded cartridges. It was a soothing ritual, rather like prayer in its rote repetition. He removed the expended primer, inserted a fresh one, filled each brass case nearly to the top with gunpowder, slammed the butt end of the cartridge on the tabletop to settle the powder grains, thumbed in a cardboard wad, added a pinch of powder on top of that, wrapped a small, carefully cut trapezoid of high-bond notepaper around the bullet and seated it. Paper-wrapped bullets kept the lands and grooves of the rifle barrel from fouling with lead, and the high-grade paper burned completely when the shell was fired. No tiny, smoldering surprises waiting to go off with a bang if a leaking cartridge entered the breech.

These chores completed, Otto usually ate a few slices of dried fruit for roughage and took another of coffee as a nightcap. Regularity in the field was important. A costive comrade in the 2nd Wisconsin, Phineas Babcock, had learned that to his momentary but eternal regret: squatting over-long to relieve himself one lovely fall day in the cornrows off the Sharpsburg Turnpike, he had been shot dead by a Confederate rifleman.

Otto's last task before rolling into his blankets of an evening was to apply a fresh coat of buffalo tallow to his boots, then set them near the fire so the grease would soak into the leather overnight. He slept too soundly for war dreams to awaken him.

All told, it was a good life up there on the Smoky Hill River. He saw no reason why it couldn't last forever. The buffalo were infinite in number, and it was from the buffalo that all else followed — ease and abundance for every living creature on the Buffalo Range, from the lobo wolf and the Indian to the coyote, the eagle and the raven, even down to such creatures as the line-back louse, buffalo gnat, and the myriad fleas that thrived, like the others, on the blood of their shaggy host. Songbirds built their nests of buffalo wool, as he'd seen on the Niobrara. Harvest mice and kangaroo rats lined their nurseries with it. The buffalo wallows, scrubbed out when the huge beasts rolled in the dust of prairie-dog towns to scratch their humped backs, later filled with water and thus afforded drink to antelope, elk, blacktail, lobo, coyote, badger, swift fox, and even the dry-mouthed two-legged pilgrim. The flooded wal-lows served as convenient way stops for the ducks and geese and cranes and herons that twice a year traversed the skies of the Great West. Buffalo birds — magpies, merles, redwings, and cowbirds — snapped up insects kicked out of the grass by the hooves of the migrating herds, picked lice and flies off the buffalo's back in summer, and warmed their toes in its wool in freezing weather. Otto had seen a dozen cowbirds perched in a row on a single bull's back, as on the ridgepole of a slowly ambulating barn. It was the buffalo in its millions that kept the prairie fertile and growing, by cropping the curly buffalo grass back to its roots and enriching the soil with dung. Otto was farmer enough to see that. The only thing that could threaten the ageless rhythms of the Buffalo Range was civilization. But these badlands were too poor, too dry for farming, as many home-steaders had learned to their sorrow. And high plains winters were too severe to support cattle without costly supplementary feeding. What's more, the Great West — thank God — was too remote from the cities of the East to ever attract industry. At least in the opinion of Eastern editorial writers.

The door banged open behind Otto, and the conductor stepped onto the rear platform of the train, a portly, prune-faced man.

"Did I get your ticket?"

Otto showed him the punched stub. Took another drag on his cheroot.

"Kind of chilly back here, ain't it?" the conductor said, reluctant to return to his duties.

"I'm used to it."

The conductor studied Otto's face and attire. "You one of them Westerners, hey?"

"Of late," Otto said.

"Too bleak a country for me," the conductor said. He pulled a big silver watch from his vest pocket and consulted it with an air of self-importance. "Well, you'll be back in it right quick now. We're almost to the river."

Otto stared at him, silent, and then turned his back on the man. A moment later he heard the door slam shut. Too many people back East, he thought, and all of them want to make conversation. Yet he had to admit that there were times on the Smoky Hill when he'd found himself longing for the sound of a human voice.

One day, hunting elk in the timber above the sunflowers, Otto had found a stand of cedars. Returning with his ax, he split out a buckboard load of fragrant red shakes from the stumps of wind-felled trees. With these he shingled the roof of Zeke and Vixen's stable, and the sloping roof of a porch he built out from the entrance to the soddy. He made a large smokehouse of cedar slabs, where he brined the tongues, hams, hump steaks, and tenderloins of young buffalo in a pit vat lined with a green hide and smoked them over a slow, cool fire of damp alder and cedar chips until they were cured to his taste.

He had seen the smoke of many small fires up

the valley of the Saline, where it entered the Smoky Hill River, and knew that a settlement lay under the pall. He scouted a bit and found a well-traveled wagon road, the hoofprints of iron-shod horses. White folks for sure. On a sunny, lazy day when he had nothing better to do, he drove up the Saline with a load of flint-dried buffalo hides, robes, smoked meat, and split cedar shingles.

It was a town called Hell Creek. At the general store he traded his goods for coffee, dried fruit, tins of canned peaches, a crock of molasses, gunpowder, bar lead, a bag of birdshot, priming caps, and a double-barreled shotgun — an English-made 12-bore by Westley Richards. Though the scarred walnut stock and the bluing on the tubes, worn silvery in places, attested to hard service, the insides of the barrels were unpitted and the vents in the nipples looked free of rust. With the permission of the storekeeper, he took the shotgun out to the street, capped it, and fired it, uncharged and unshotted, into the ground.

The dust jumped.

"You want to do some serious bird hunting, that's your gun," the storekeeper said. Otto closed the deal.

He went across the road through dust and skittering chickens, past a gaunt, three-legged dog, and into a dramhouse, where he ordered a beer. There was only one patron at the bar, a husky fellow about his own age, clean-shaven, with long ɪd hair. He wore a heavy gray Confederate officer's greatcoat and a straight-brim gray hat. His boots had seen some wear.

He would prove to be Raleigh McKay.

He was drinking red whiskey. He looked at Otto's slouch hat. "You're one of them black-hat fellows," he said. "Iron Brigade, wasn't y'all called?"

Otto nodded.

"I was on the other side," the Rebel said. "Eighteenth North Carolina. We bumped against y'all a few times, you Black Hats, don't know who got the best of it, though. South Mountain. Brawner's Farm. Second Manassas and Fitz-hugh's Crossing — suchlike places. Dutchmen mostly, wasn't you?"

"Not all of us." Otto finished his beer. He was unarmed.

The Rebel wore a holstered pistol beneath his unbuttoned greatcoat. It looked like a Whitney five-shot rimfire. He had it rigged for a left-handed cross draw.

"A silent Yankee, ain't you just? No need to be unneighborly, though, not because we fought once in the 'way-long-ago. Hellfire. I don't harbor grudges, and it weren't a personal thing, not for me anyways." He frowned, then smiled suddenly, bright as a sunrise. "Say, Black Hat, I'll buy you a beer!"

He pushed a cartwheel dollar toward the bar-man. Then he took off his hat, combed back his hair with hooked fingers, and smiled again at Otto, a boyish grin empty of guile. He drew his pistol slowly and sent it skidding across the smooth wet wood.

"I'll let the gentleman behind the bar hold on to this for a while," he said. "I see you're not carrying one, or at least I trust you aren't. Now we're on even terms, I'd be obliged if you'd accept my hospitality. Fact is, I haven't talked to another white man in a good long spell. Hey, what say ye, let's tell us a few war stories? And have you a whiskey instead of that swampwater they sell for beer in these parts. Hell ain't half full yet, or so they tell me . . ."

That was the beginning of his partnership with Raleigh Fitzroy McKay, Esq., late Captain of Infantry, 18th North Carolina regiment, C.S.A.

With a sudden, clattering change in the roar of its wheels, the train rolled onto a trestle. They were crossing the Mississippi River. Otto gazed down at the coiling, dun-colored Father of Waters and suddenly felt sad. No, perhaps only apprehensive. This is truly the Great Divide, he thought. The nation east of the Mississippi was now the country of comfort, or at least what passed for it in the America of that day — a land of farms, towns, homes, jobs, libraries, newspapers, churches, schools, a country suited to sensible men, level-headed women, and their gentle children. West of the river lay wilderness, dry plains and bleak mountains, wolves and buffalo and wild Indians, a vast reach of country nibbled nly feebly by the main-chancers and the desperate — railroads, mountain men, hide hunters; soiled doves, homesteaders, gamblers, and cowboys.

He felt at home in that far country, but he feared that Jenny would not. Her presence alone would change things for him, he was sure. The joy he'd felt in his solitude and self-sufficiency along the Smoky Hill River would now be diluted by his concern for her welfare. And how would his partner, McKay, react to her presence? Raleigh was ostensibly an officer and a gentleman, if only by act of the Rebel Congress, but he was also a hot-blooded Southerner and a damned handsome man. Women melted in his company — even tough old horn-hided hookers turned giddy as schoolgirls when McKay switched on his charm. Otto had seen it happen again and again in bawdy houses and honkytonks from Abilene to Hays City. Well, he'd have to ride herd on Raleigh, that was for certain sure.

With a frown and a sigh, Otto took one last drag on his cheroot and flipped the stub into the river. He watched it fall, spinning on the wind, tumbling, sparking, until it blinked out in the muddy waters.

PART II

4

The bones began a mile east of town. They were piled in ricks, twice as high as a man is tall, overarching the tracks on both sides of the right-of-way. The steel rails ran straight through them, as if diving into a skeletal mineshaft that shut out the light of the prairie. High-angled hipbones, bracketed ribs, the concave graceful plates of shoulder blades, skulls gaping empty-eyed with the black sweep of horns hooking up, down, sideways, black splintered hooves, leg bones knobbed like giant clubs, the shallow, knuckled curve and recurve of spinal columns. All tumbled together in the ricks. Some were whiter than others, some tan, some moss green or the hectic pink of diseased gums. Some were a dark, sickly brown, like rotten teeth.

And the straight lines of the steel heading West, right through them.

The train slowed, chuffing, and clouds of steam billowed up through the bones, ghosting out through eye sockets. It was getting on toward dark now and the headlight of the locomotive reflected off the steam.

Otto and Jenny stepped down out of the cars, knocked cinders off their shoulders, and there it was: Buffalo City, Kansas, as they used to call it, now Dodge City. They might have named it Golgotha, Jenny thought, if they'd had any imagination.

"Pfui," she said, and wrinkled her nose.

"I told you so. It isn't called the Land of the Stinkers for nothing," Otto said. "You'll get used to it, though. The whole West smells like this now, from the Platte and the Republican clear on down to the Cimarron."

They walked past the bone ricks and the new frame stationhouse, past the yards of the big hide dealers — Rath & Wright, Myers & Leonard — where the stacks of stiff, flint-cured hides loomed twelve feet high. Smell of hair, dead meat, arsenic. Out onto wide-open Front Street — no blue laws in Dodge.

Otto carried the carpetbag and Jenny's small trunk along the wooden sidewalk past the lighted saloons with their breath of stale beer cutting sharply into the buffalo smell, the quiet gaming hells, festive honky-tonks, and F. C. Zimmerman's dry-goods store. Otto stopped to look at the new rifles in the window, a sidehammer Sharps in .44 caliber that took a bottlenecked, $2^5/8$-inch cartridge packing 90, 100, or 105 grains of powder, and a .44 Remington rolling-block Creedmore that fired a slightly shorter 90-grain cartridge. Both rifles would throw a heavy, 550-grain bullet with great accuracy, but the Sharps allowed more latitude in terms of powder loads, and certainly it possessed greater range. On the other hand, the Remington looked

56

tidier, racier, more "modern," with its small center-mounted hammer and sleek, neatly checked pistol grip.

The weapons leaned behind the window against the glass-eyed head of a buffalo. The stubborn bull stared out into the street. Not mournfully, Otto thought, but resignedly, almost philosophically. As if it knew its days were numbered, as were those of all its kind. Sure, he thought. Philosophically. But at least it made him feel better to think so.

They passed a dovecote. The girls, some of them older than Frau Wieland, looked out the door and giggled as Otto and Jenny walked by. The soiled doves made little O's of their painted mouths, and one of them flipped her skirt to display her unclad nether parts, grinning and saying, *"Whoops!"*

They hurried on, Otto glaring back at the fallen women, Jenny a bit flustered by the display. No girl in Heldendorf was that brazen, not even Gretel Schlimm, who had been known to flirt in church.

"Where are we going?" she asked.

"To the livery stable. Then camp — about an hour west of town."

"Can't we eat first? Or anyway, get something to drink? I've got coal smoke in my *Kehl'*."

"Plenty of coffee out at camp. Clean, cold water. And buffalo steaks. Over at the Cox House they'll give you thin, lukewarm coffee, canned pork and beans, yesterday's bread with pepper sauce to disguise it, and then charge you six bits for your supper. A man would have to skin out three buffalo to pay for a meal like that, though he'd still be wolf-hungry half an hour later."

He walked on glumly, his back stiff with suppressed anger. At what?

"Another thing," he said, "you've got to stop talking half Deutsch, half English. You sound like some Dutchy peasant fresh off the pickle boat."

"I'll try," Jenny said as humbly as she could. "But at least let's stop for something cold and wet right now. Even if it's *nur ein Bier* — sorry, just a beer. *Bitte,* Otto, please, it won't take long."

"I hate this town," Otto said gruffly. "All towns, for that matter."

But he was unstiffening a bit. She vowed to speak only English from now on, if it would make him happy.

Ahead of them a man strode along, slow and full of himself. He was tall, pigeon-chested, with a wide black flat-brim hat, a tailored broadcloth suit of pinstriped gray, hand-tooled boots with high heels, and when he turned quickly to look at them they saw a ruffled white shirt with a black silk string tie. His flabby upper lip stuck out, sparsely mustached, under a long, sharp nose. His eyes, close-set, were rheumy but quick. The ivory grips of two Colt pistols stuck out of his waistband, sharp-curved against the dark figuring of his waistcoat.

"Why, Otto, you old sausage stuffer!"

"How's you doing, Jim?"

"Just fine, feller. How were things back East?"

"Crowded. They're all still talkin' about you, though."

"Sure," the man said in a scoffing tone. But he laughed in his long nose nonetheless, pleased, for all his self-deprecation.

Then the tall man tipped his hat politely to Jenny, spun on his heel, and walked on, mournful and sudden as his earlier smile.

"Who's that?"

"Duck Bill Hickok."

"*Wild* Bill?"

"So they call him," Otto said. "His real name's Jim."

The barman sliced the head off two lagers with a single slash of his spatula, then topped the schooners. He slid them over, along with the free-lunch bowl. A drunken teamster was weeping at the end of the bar. Six cowboys played poker at a corner table, but quietly. The evening was young.

"You got you a ladyfriend," the barman said to Otto, smiling. "Don't believe I've had the pleasure."

Otto took a long pull at his beer and wiped his mustache with the back of his hand.

"This here's my sister, Miss Jenny Dousmann," he said. "Jenny, meet Fred Peacock." They nodded across the bar, peacock still smiling playfully. "Jenny's going to hunt with me and Captain McKay this winter; she'll rustle for the

59

outfit, maybe skin some."

And shoot, too, Jenny added silently.

"You look for a good season?"

"Good as last year, anyway," Otto said. "We sold Rath & Wright about three thousand hides all told, and McKay figures this year to be better."

"Not around here," Peacock said. "They're mighty thin on the ground up along the Arkansas, I hear. Say, I can remember when Bob Wright and me shot buff from his corral, to feed his pigs with. Down at the feedlot they had to hire guards to keep them durn shaggies away from the haystacks in the winter, right here in town, and that's not long ago."

"We'll probably hunt farther south this fall," Otto said. "Plenty of buff down toward Indian Territory. McKay's scouting the Cimarron country right now. He'll sniff out them shaggies wherever they are."

"And you want to skin a few, do you, young missy?" Peacock asked. "Well, I hope you've got a strong stomach, I do. And a itchproof hide. I wouldn't stick a butcher knife into one a them stinkers again for love nor money." He reached both hands across his chest and clawed at his shoulders. "Why, just the mere idea of it gives me the rampagin' *ek*-zeemer."

"Miss Dousmann has skinned pigs and sheep and steers on the farm back home," Otto said. "And plenty of deer, too; even a bear once, when we were hunting up north."

"A pig comes close to a buffalo for tight," Peacock said. He leaned his elbows on the wet, dark wood, smiling at Jenny with a teasing look and moving his mouth around playfully. "And a bear for smelly. But there's nothing like a shaggy for bed rabbits."

He was flirting with her, Jenny suddenly realized. "*Bed* rabbits?"

"Yes, missy. Linebacks, some fellows call 'em. Graybacks? Lice."

Jenny took a sip of her beer. Felt the fizz tickle her nose.

"And buffalo gnats? And fleas? And the maggots come later." Peacock shuddered. He reached under the bar and brought up a water glass half full of whiskey. "Nope," he said, "I done it one whole winter, that's enough." He drank off a big swallow of the whiskey. "Here, missy, have a plover egg."

He forked a small egg out of a jar filled with brine and peeled it. Jenny ate it. She was hungry. Then she forked herself another from the jar, peeled it, and popped it in her mouth. The eggs lay like pale pink, bloodshot eyeballs on the grainy rock salt at the bottom of the jar. She chewed down the second egg and forked out a third.

"Well, Otto, she sure eats for a buffalo runner," Peacock said. He laughed loud and approvingly, then reached under the bar again and brought up a bottle of whiskey. He winked at Otto. "Would you care for a sip of Old Baldface, ma'am, to settle your stomach? Or p'raps a proper cocktail — I do a nice Citronella Jam?

61

It's on the house."

"Thank you, no, Mr. Peacock. This beer suits me nicely."

When they left the saloon Otto led them back to Zimmerman's. The shop was still open.

"I need a new rifle, and that .44 Sharps looks just fine," he told Jenny.

"What about me? Something to fight off the bed rabbits?"

"Oh," he said, smiling, "you can use my old buffalo gun on those fellows." A thought occurred to him. "No, it's .50 caliber. Probably kick too hard for you, and it's only a single-shot rifle. You might need something faster than that."

"For what?"

"Well, camp meat for one. Unwelcome visitors for another."

"Are there likely to be bandits?"

"Always a possibility, though a slim one, but it was Hostiles I had in mind. You never know when redskins are likely to go on the warpath."

Jenny laughed, but Otto remembered the Santee Sioux uprising in Minnesota back in '62. During the course of it, the Indians had attacked a small German community called New Ulm, where the Dousmanns had friends. The militia finally fought the Santees off, but not before they'd killed or wounded nearly a hundred townsmen and burned all but a few of the houses. A childhood friend of his had written to Otto about it, just after Antietam, reporting in shocked words that more than seven hundred whites, many of them women and children, had been slaughtered before the uprising was suppressed. The atrocities were too horrible to relate in detail, the friend wrote. Otto had been scornful at the time — at Antietam, the single bloodiest day of the war, some 23,000 men had died or been wounded on both sides. But now, visualizing Jenny as the victim of an Indian attack, New Ulm seemed horrible enough.

"How's about that little repeater there?" she asked, pointing to a rifle in the window. It was a lever-action carbine, an improved model of the Henry with a loading gate on the side of the receiver.

"*Ja,*" Otto said. "Just the thing. Holds seventeen bullets, .44 rimfire — the same round I use in my pistol. We can share bullets for economy's sake. You wouldn't want to use it on buffalo except up close, it doesn't pack much punch, but for antelope it'll work just fine. Come on, we'll go in and buy it. Then we've got to get packing for our rendezvous with McKay down toward the Cimarron."

Good, Jenny thought. He's willing to let me hunt. She had worried that he would keep her campbound day and night, cooking and cleaning.

Later, at Durgen's Livery, she waited outside with the bags and the newly purchased rifles, humming happily to herself while Otto settled his bill. He led out a pair of mules and she helped him harness them to a light wagon parked in the corral. He tied his saddle horse, Vixen, to the tailgate.

"So I *may* hunt?" she asked as they drove out of town. She wanted confirmation, his word on it, so that he couldn't change his mind.

"*Ja sicher,*" he said, "certainly. Not buffalo, or at least not at first, but camp meat surely. There are always prongbucks or turkeys to be found in the country we're headed for. They'll make a welcome change from a steady diet of buffalo meat. And I want you to keep your rifle close at hand." He turned to look at her. "My partner and I will be out all day, along with our skinner, scouting or shooting or working the hides, and there are dangers. Wolves or bears, you know, attracted to the smell of meat. And snakes. And always the chance of, well, Indians."

"Who's the skinner?"

"His name's Tom Shields, a good worker. You'll meet him tonight if McKay's found buff."

Otto's camp was a few miles west of Dodge. They saw the looming light of its fire in the dark hills along the Arkansas River and the mules pulled for it at an eager trot. Jenny was chilled and weary by the time they arrived. A man rose from beside the fire, a rifle in his hands, and stepped back into the shadows as they approached.

"It's all right, Tom," her brother shouted, "I'm home at last."

The man stepped into the firelight, lowering his rifle. Jenny jolted wide awake, her shivering stopped. Tom Shields was a red Indian.

"Any word from Captain McKay?" Otto asked.

"He's found 'em, sure enough," the Indian said. "He's still out there with 'em. And he wants us to come quick, while the killing's good."

That morning Raleigh McKay was standing on the bales of hides piled in the wagonbed, scanning the horizon with field glasses. No buffalo in sight. Not even a tree. There was no horizon. In the middle distance, sky and grassland blended to a pale tan monochrome. To the east, low, the morning sun glinted like the stud of a silver finishing nail tacked to the wooden sky. He lowered the glasses. They were excellent, long and heavy, made by B. H. Horn of Broadway, New York City. He had taken them from the body of a dead Yankee major, eleven years earlier, near White Oak Swamp on the way to Malvern Hill. The brass was scratched in places, the blacking rubbed through with use, but the lenses were still clear. McKay could never have afforded them himself back during the war, much less before it. Even now, when he found himself rich beyond counting, he would hesitate to lay out the gold eagle necessary to buy even these battered binoculars. Hell, and he had all of five thousand Yankee dollars in the bank back at Leavenworth.

He raised the glasses again and swung them slowly in a full circle. Still nothing. Not a dot of movement, no dark wavering line wriggling like a worm through the far frost haze. Squinting from the lens-gathered glare, he decided that perhaps the haze was a bit thicker to the northwest. Maybe they were coming from that direction. Even here, standing on the thick bed of hides, he thought he could feel the tremor of their movement.

It was that faint quivering of the ground which woke him before dawn, a subtle vibration, directionless, almost imperceptible, as if the atoms of earth and sky were shivering together ever so slightly, colliding like the shoulders of an anxious crowd. Soldiers awaiting the first bugle calls to battle. It had jostled him out of an uneasy sleep into the cold dark, from another dream of the war. He had been in the woods again, at dusk, with the gunfire growing louder as it neared. Scrub oaks and pines. They lay or knelt behind hastily felled tree trunks, in a semicircle, waiting for whatever was coming up the line to reach them. From off in the murk came rebel yells, rising and falling in counterpoint to the spurts of musketry. Now and then the far thump of cannon. Harsh, indecipherable cries at a distance, an order edged in hysteria, its meaning swallowed by distance, and the thud of his own fast heart. Then the louder, slower thud of hooves through the earth, tiny, palpable punches in his chest and belly. Stronger as the horses neared. They heard the whistle of horse breath, a nicker, the clank of a brass-tipped scabbard against a stirrup. Dim, tall forms moved toward them in the dusk. Swaying. Lumpy. Greasy glint of steel.

Must be the same damn Dutchmen back again, that wild-eyed screaming Christ-forsaken pig-fucking 8th Pennsylvania Cavalry outfit who'd rid through us half an hour ago. . . . *saberswinging-pistolsbanging . . . boys knocked right and left by the knees of horses . . .* And were gone, leaving plenty of dead behind them. Both horses and men. They learned the outfit's number from looting the bodies.

Blood drips in the leaf mold.

A sudden spatter of musketry, not far off.

Panic.

"Cease firing, you are firing into your own men!"

"It's a lie!" in a Tarheel accent.

A Tarheel accent . . .

"Pour it into them, boys!"

He hears the hammers click back all up and down the line . . .

No don't! he cries . . . *They're ours! Cease firing!*

But his breath stalls again, as always, in his dry throat. He kneels in the chill. His own thumb is steady on the splayed tang of the Enfield's hammer. He feels the growing tension of the spring, the click of the locking sear. He sees the barrel, brown and oil-dim across the tree trunk, leveling out into the darkness, the faint evening star of the front-leaf sinking low between the unfocused limbs of the rear sight. The touch of his trigger finger on the curved new moon of steel. The horsemen clatter near, dim forms, then clear in the last, lost radiance of daylight as they enter the open wood, uniforms dark, wide hats; one officer twists in his saddle to talk with the lean, long-bearded officer in a raincoat and scruffy forage hat trotting beside him, starlight on hair; the bead of the Enfield sensing how the junior officer defers to the other and, following in suit to the higher rank, settles square on his chest.

Squeeze now, squeeze off . . .

No — not again! Not now! Old Jack — Old Blue Light! Not ever . . .

The roar and kick of his rifle.

My God, you've shot the general . . .

It was then that he'd wakened to the tremor of the buffalo. Always the same dream woke him in times of tension. The memory of killing Stonewall Jackson. Raleigh McKay would never live that memory down. In his mind, it had cost the South the war.

But now he was out to kill buffalo. Finally, they were here. While Otto was away in Wisconsin, McKay had hunted south and west between Crooked Creek and the Cimarron, looking for the main herd. He'd killed a wagonload of hides just picking off the early arrivals, the scouts of the main herd. Never more than fifteen or twenty in a bunch, but they added up. He had sent Tom Shields to town earlier, after hearing the buffalo coming over the horizon somewhere.

Get Dousmann, if he's back. Have him hire another cook — a decent one this time, goddamnit, and make sure the cook don't bring no popskull with him like that damn Harvey Logan — then rendezvous at our old camp on Crooked Greek. Quick as you can get there.

McKay stayed with the wagon. He had lead and powder enough for the Sharps, so he wasn't afraid of Indians. Too early yet for Comanches, though maybe a few hunting parties of 'rapahoes might be down this way, killing along with the herd. But whatever their tribe, they'd be back toward the rear of it, and it went north for miles.

An hour later he saw them, first the frost cloud of their hot breath crystallizing in the cold morning like the smoke of a distant grass fire, then the wormlike wiggle dark under the thickening cloud. He heard them, too, the rumbling minor thunder of a thousand hooves on the hard earth, the roaring of the rutting bulls. It always took him aback, this first sight and sound of buffalo. As if they'd emerged suddenly, full-grown, from some fissure in the prairie, a kind of smelly, dusty, woolly afterthought to a volcanic cataclysm, stupid-eyed, the long curls of their dung-caked hair swaying rhythmically beneath their clumsy humps, horns poking spikes at a sky obscured by their dust. All of them covered with dollar signs.

It would be hot work for the next month or so.

He watched them just long enough to ensure they were definitely headed south, then hitched the team, checked the lashings on the load, and lined out toward the rendezvous.

For the moment, at least, the dream and the war forgotten.

5

Jenny drove the spring wagon behind the mules, Zeke and a more recently acquired animal named Zebulon. Otto said the mules seemed no older now than when he'd bought them. "That's mules. Probably looked ancient when they were foaled."

Vixen, his chestnut mare, trotted along behind the spring wagon, hitched to the tailgate by a braided rawhide lead shank. She was Jenny's horse now. Otto had a new mount he'd bought in Dodge that morning, a tall, lightly dappled gray named Edgar. He rode ahead, swinging in wide sweeps from one side of the trail to the other, scouting the landscape. Jenny noticed that he never skylighted himself for more than a few moments on the crests of the rolling prairie swells, merely peeking over the tops to see what lay beyond. He always took his hat off before peeking.

"They're out there," he told her. "And they'll see us before we see them. Count on it."

"They," of course, were the Hostiles, a term Otto seemed to use for all Indians except Tom Shields. Sometimes he called them "Mister Lo" or "Poor Lo," which puzzled Jenny until he told her it was a sarcastic play on the phrase "Lo, the poor Indian!" — often quoted by the Eastern

70

newspapers in their naïve laments over the treatment Indians received at the hands of Westerners. Mister Lo had been making trouble lately, he said, burning out a road ranch between Dodge and Fort Hays to the north, killing four workers on the A., T. & S.F. just west of Granada, Colorado, the railroad's current "head of track," and only a week ago waylaying, murdering, scalping, and mutilating a solitary buffalo runner who had been transporting a load of hides back to Dodge along the well-traveled road from Camp Supply in the Indian Territory.

Before they'd left Dodge City that morning, Otto gave Jenny a "parting gift," smiling sardonically as he handed it to her. It was a .50-caliber brass cartridge case plugged at the open end with a piece of cork. Within it reposed a glass vial filled with a viscous blue fluid. He showed her the vial, then replugged the case.

"This is the best I can offer you by way of an insurance policy," he said. "It's hydrocyanic acid. If you're about to be captured by Poor Lo and his brothers, one sip of this is a far more certain means of escape than that 'last cartridge' the dime novels talk about. They never tell you what happens if the last cartridge is a dud. But this works every time, instantly. All you need do is 'bite the big bite.'"

Now she understood his ironic smile.

In German, *"Gift"* means poison.

Tom Shields brought up the rear with the Murphy hide wagon, which had been parked at Otto's camp until Captain McKay found buffalo. It was drawn by eight spans of oxen. Tom's pony, a pretty pinto mare, trotted behind, unleashed but never straying. The wagon wheels were seven feet tall and nine inches wide, which made for easier rolling in the prairie's loose sand. Its bed and treads were made of iron, like those of the trailer it towed behind. Both were painted blue, as were the oxbows and yokes of the huge steers that pulled it. Tom Shields had decorated the sides of the bed, Indian-fashion, with the tails of many dead buffalo, and painted the horns of the oxen red. Fully loaded, wagon and trailer could carry up to five hundred sun-cured "flint" hides — six tons of them.

Captain McKay had the third wagon, another light one similar to Jenny's, which Otto said could carry an additional thirty or forty hides. Each of the smaller wagons could carry a ton of dried hides apiece. Jenny did the arithmetic in her head as they rumbled slowly along. Let's make it 580 hides at an average of $2.50 per hide. . . . That's $1,450 a load — a small fortune.

She looked back at the hide wagon, which followed about fifty yards behind. Tom Shields was a *Halbblut,* Otto had told her — a half-breed. He was older than Jenny, but not much — maybe twenty or twenty-two. Tom told her he didn't know when he'd been born. His mother, a white captive, had died when he was not yet a year old. His father was a Cheyenne named Oh-kóhm, which meant either Coyote or Little Wolf, Tom wasn't sure which, but anyway, they were the same animal. He, too, was now dead, Tom added, avoiding her eyes. Having been raised and then orphaned among the Sa-sis-e-tas, as the Cheyennes called themselves, he had now cast his lot with his mother's people.

Tom was a strong, wiry, rather handsome fellow, Jenny thought. His raven-black hair was cut short in the white man's style. He had the long, slightly bowed legs of an Indian who has spent most of his life on horseback. He wore white man's clothes — a tan, wide-brimmed hat, a hip-length drover's coat of rough brown wool, and faded denim trousers. Only his feet, shod in calf-high moccasins, remained Indian. He tucked his trouser legs into the moccasins as if to show off their elaborate beadwork. Yet his eyes were a white man's eyes, startling green, and he spoke good English, but grudgingly, as if from a reluctance to waste words unless spoken to.

So far, the country they passed through was as bleak as Otto said it would be, no trees save a few dusty, discouraged cottonwoods, post oaks, and box elders along the rare watercourses, but the rest of it just grass, grass, and more grass, running off to the horizon in undulating waves. You could see the wind working its way from southwest to northeast, over the grassland, like wind over water. The wind never let up. She could feel her skin turning to leather under its constant push. It was a warm, dry wind right

73

now, smelling of dust and distance. When it worked to the northwest, Otto said, it would smell of rock and snow from the faraway mountains.

The sky overhead was huge, far broader than in hilly Wisconsin. Its size made Jenny feel like a mouse being watched by an invisible hawk. Tall, shape-shifting clouds sailed across it, swift as the freight schooners she'd seen plying Lake Michigan from Green Bay to Milwaukee to Chicago. Once, she looked up to spot a buzzard circling high on tilted wings, far to the west. When she searched for it again, a minute or two later, it was almost directly overhead — blown downwind that fast without a flap of its pinions.

The prairie seemed empty of life. Only buffalo skeletons dwelt here, as yet uncollected by the bone pickers from Dodge. Once she saw a small flock of prairie chickens skitter across the trail ahead of them, and later, in the distance, so faint and far that at first she took it for a mirage, a band of pale-tan deerlike animals that must be antelope. But they turned immediately at the sight of the wagons and fled, their white rumps flashing as bright as heliographs. After them loped some animals that looked like gray dogs, but bigger and heavier, with huge heads and jaws. These must be the infamous buffalo wolves Otto talked about, the lobos. Fallen on hard times, now that the buffalo had been killed off hereabouts. It struck her that the wolves, nearly out of provender, were not unlike the nation itself, with the

74

Panic raging. True Americans, these lobos.

Otto had said that the distance to Crooked Creek and their rendezvous with Captain McKay was only some thirty miles from Dodge City, half a day's ride for a man on a swift pony. But it would take them longer. The oxen were slow. They could have made better time staying on the Camp Supply road, but Otto was fearful of Indian attack. Hostiles. She thought again of the poison he'd given her. She could never "bite the big bite," as he put it. What would the Indians — Mister Lo — do with her if indeed she was cornered? She was young and not bad-looking. He wouldn't tomahawk her or scalp her or torture her, he did that only to old women and men of fighting age. Didn't he? The young, especially those of the feminine gland, Mister Lo took captive. He would rape her probably, but rape wasn't fatal, and perhaps he'd then claim her for a bride. It happened, you read about it all the time. It had happened to Tom's mother. What killed her, anyway? Probably pneumonia or smallpox or something even worse; the sanitation in their camps was said to be dreadful.

She reached into her blouse to withdraw the poison capsule from between her breasts, where, lacking a reticule, she'd placed it for safekeeping. In the sunlight she saw that the brass was tinged with verdigris. She threw the horrid package away into the prairie grass, not looking to see where it fell.

Whatever happened, she could never bring her-

75

self to use it. Jenny Dousmann would be no martyr to virginity.

That first night they stopped to make camp with an hour of daylight left. Otto led the wagons to a shallow coulee he knew not far off the trail. Here they would be out of the wind, with water close at hand. A seep spring flowed year round at the head of the coulee. After they had unhitched the horses, mules, and oxen, Tom and Otto rubbed them down with gunny sacks while Jenny filled two camp kettles with spring water. Then they led the animals to water. Tom gathered dried buffalo chips from the surrounding grass and started a small, nearly smokeless cookfire. There was no firewood to speak of, just saltbush, prickly pear, and a scrubby chokecherry or two growing along the seep as it ran down the coulee to disappear in the sand.

"Perhaps there is some good to this slaughter of the buffalo, after all," Otto said. "If they were still here in their millions, our pleasant little spring would be a stinking bog filled with their dung, the grass trampled and cropped so short that our stock couldn't feed."

He laughed, slid his new Sharps from its leather case in the smaller wagon, and threw a loaded belt of cartridges over his shoulder.

"I saw some prongbucks a while ago," he said. "Maybe I can kill one for supper, spare us eating bully beef."

Jenny watched him out of sight, heading back

the way they had come. Then she, too, went to the wagon and removed her Henry from where it lay wrapped in some sacking.

The Henry was a slim, beautiful, lever-action rifle with an oiled walnut stock and a steel-blue octagon barrel. On its brass receiver a previous owner had engraved a melodramatic etching of a frontiersman shooting two Hostiles. About a dozen more Indians lay dead in the background. One of them reached an arm skyward as if to touch it one last time. Poor Lo! On the other side was a scene of a mighty stag's death leap at the sting of the fatal shot, its long-tined antlers laid back in graceful agony, with the same bold frontiersman standing off at a distance in the forest primeval, his rifle at his shoulder, dribbling gunsmoke.

In the wagonbed Jenny found the box of .44-caliber rimfire bullets for the Henry. She began pushing the flat-tipped rounds through the loading gate on the forward right-hand side of the receiver, as Otto had showed her. They made a snicking sound going in. Tom Shields looked up from where he was feeding buffalo chips to the fire, saw the rifle, and smiled widely — the first genuinely joyous smile Jenny had seen on his face so far. A white man's smile.

"You got you a Yellow Boy," he said.

"Yellow Boy?"

"Yah, that's what we — ah, the Indians — call that make of rifle, for the brass frame, you know?"

77

It gleamed like gold in the low sunlight.

He got up and walked over to her, still smiling.

"My father had one, not as good as this, though. You had to fill your cartridges from the top end of the tube, not by sliding them into the receiver there. You had to tilt the barrel up to drop the bullets in, and that wasn't good in a fight. Someone might see your hand in the air and shoot it off. But it was a fine rifle anyhow, you could shoot it nearly all day before you had to reload. My father got it up by . . ."

He stopped, suddenly shy again, and looked away. This was the longest speech Jenny had heard him utter since they'd met. He had a pleasant voice when he was happy about something, the harshness gone, and his eyes sparked pure green delight.

"Where did he get it?" she asked, not wanting him to stop talking.

"Well, up north there in the Big Horn country, near the Pineys and what we, uh, they call Crow Standing Creek." He still couldn't meet her eyes.

"In the Fetterman Fight, you know?" he explained.

She didn't. She would ask Otto about it later. For the moment she just nodded and gave up trying to draw Tom Shields out further. He'd fallen back into his customary watchful silence.

"I'm going to hunt down this gulch a ways," she said to his back as he went over to the fire. "Maybe I'll see something to shoot for the pot."

He turned to look at her. "Watch out for . . .

stuff," he said, his brow furrowing.

"What, snakes?" She laughed.

"Yah," he said, his eyes popping wide, surprised but dead serious. "Snakes." He made a sinuous move with his wrist at waist height, his hand extending slowly, fingers and thumb touched together to represent a snake's head. She would later learn that this gesture was Plains Indian sign language for the Snake tribe, traditional enemies of the Cheyenne. Right now, though, it was just another indication of Tom's odd behavior.

She walked down the coulee in the rapidly fading twilight, past the horses and mules grazing knee-deep in bluestem on their picket lines, past the oxen lying farther on, boxlike, chewing their cuds. The oxen were free to roam, but they wouldn't wander far. The herd's leader, a phlegmatic old bullock, would not let them, Otto had said. She stopped near the oxen to pull the forward hem of her ankle-length skirt up between her legs and tuck it into the back of her belt, converting her skirt into a baggy culotte for easier going.

She began to hunt as Otto had taught her in the Wisconsin woods, walking a few quiet steps, then pausing for an equal length of time to scan the country around her. Carefully, slowly, watching for the least flicker of an ear or tail, the subtlest hint of an animal silhouette hidden in the maze of grass. Slowly, slowly . . .

As she eased her way around the gentle slope of a rise, something sprang away from her, startlingly swift, right from under her feet.

A jackrabbit.

She had the rifle to her shoulder in a flash, following the bouncing hare along the gun barrel, and hit the trigger.

Nothing happened.

She'd forgotten to cock the hammer.

She did so now, feeling her cheeks burn with shame. Then she reconsidered: if she tripped and fell, the rifle at full cock might go off, scaring away all the game in the country. She eased the hammer back down to half-cock, holding it with her thumb as her forefinger released the trigger. She would remember to cock it next time. Some Diana she was proving to be. Thank God, no one was watching. She pressed on, her knee-length boots — the ones she'd worn to muck out the barn at home — admirably silent in the dry prairie grass.

Farther ahead, in the last of the day's light, she stopped again. Something ahead, up on the far slope? A hundred yards away, maybe a bit more.

Something brown, no, tan. Tan and white.

She watched it until her eyes began to slip out of focus, then looked away and tried to catch its outline from the corner of her gaze, as Otto had taught her.

Ja, definitely something there! A *Rehbock?* No, not a deer, not in this dry place. It stood stock-still against the hillside.

An antelope?

Yes.

She suddenly saw the erect black horns, hooked backward in semicircles at the tops, and the big triangular prongs lower down, pointing almost directly at her. She began to raise the rifle . . .

The antelope bounded away, twisting and leaping in the same fluid motion toward the top of the hill. The rifle was up, hammer cocked. She whistled sharply. Just as the buck hit the crest of the hill he halted, turning to peer at her over his shoulder. He was outlined perfectly, as if cut from cardboard, black against the paler sky. She held the sights on the white patch behind his shoulder and squeezed . . .

Whack!

For an instant she lost the pronghorn in the rifle's recoil, the gout of white gunsmoke. When it cleared he wasn't there.

Did I miss? *O lieber Gott, bitte — nicht!* Let him be there, please! *Ich bin klein, mein Herz ist rein* . . .

Then she saw the antelope's hind leg sticking up at an angle, outlined against the sky, shuddering slightly. Her heart was shuddering, too, thudding in her throat. She was very happy. She levered another round into the chamber, seeing the empty cartridge case spin off into the grass. Better retrieve it — Otto says we must reload all our shell cases. No gun shops on the prairie. She groped in the grass, found it by its heat with her fingers, and stuck the warm brass casing between her breasts, where the poison capsule had rested earlier in the day. Then she hiked up the slope to gut her antelope . . .

She was nearly finished, concentrating intently on the work, when Tom Shields spoke quietly not far behind her.

"Don't shoot, Mr. Dousmann. It's just your sister and me. She killed a nice little prongbuck for our supper."

Jenny spun around. Tom Shields was ten feet behind her, a rifle in his hands. Her eyes jumped to Otto, skylighted on another ridge across the draw, the Sharps at his shoulder. He put it up and came striding toward them, his boot heels angry in the dry grass. When he reached her, she saw his face was stiff, bone white behind the black mustache.

"Jennchen," he said, quietly and in German so that Tom Shields could not overhear what he said, "*das war ja dumm*. Stupid. You must never ever do that again without telling me first. I heard your shot. It was not the sound of a buffalo rifle. The Hostiles shoot lighter calibers, rifles like yours. Hearing it, I thought you were under attack. Maybe dead. Or worse, taken. I ran back to the camp. You were gone. Tom was gone. I followed your tracks down this way, saw you in the dark, and Tom behind you. In this light I could not recognize you. I was just about to shoot when he spoke. *Gott sei Dank!* But you must never do that again to me. *Das war wannsinnig, stumpfdumm.*"

Only much later, when her shame had burned away, did Jenny realize that Tom Shields must have shadowed her all the way.

When they finished supper — broiled antelope tenderloin, potato dumplings, soldier beans stewed in molasses, and hot black coffee — Otto and Jenny turned in. They unrolled their blankets in the spring wagon. Tom Shields took his rifle and walked out to check on the livestock. He brought along a bait of oats in his hat crown and went from one horse to the other, giving them each a mouthful while he checked their picket pins. His own pony nickered softly when he came to her.

He always fed her last, so he could talk to her without the other horses getting jealous. She was a spotted-rump pony who had come to him from the Nez Perce country by way of the Yellowstone — an Appaloosa, the white-eyes called her breed. He had stolen her six years ago from a hunting camp of the Absarokas, those wicked Sparrow Hawk People the white-eyes called Crows. He and his friends had taken many horses that night, but of them all he had picked her as his prize. He had watched her running buffalo that afternoon. He had to crawl into the Absaroka camp to get her. Her owner had picketed the spotted-rump pony beside him while he slept, so greatly did he value her. Tom had lain within ten feet of her for a long time, perhaps an hour, looking up into her eyes and thinking hard, "Come with me, Pony, and I will love you always, but do not make any noise when I cut your picket line." Over and over. She did not nicker but only stood watching him, her ears pricked forward. When her ears relaxed and went back to scanning the night for random sounds, he knew she was ready. He cut the rawhide and crawled away into the darkness. She followed him silently, her unshod hooves making no sound in the damp, sandy soil.

The Absarokas had pursued them, and in the running battle she'd done all that his knees had ordered. She loved gunfire. It made her think of hunting. He had killed two of the Sparrow Hawk People and taken not just their scalps but their war shields as well. He and his pony bore them back home. He won a new name that day, Two Shields. More important, he had won her. She was long-legged and heavier than most Indian horses, but she ran and turned quickly, and she was tireless. She could run buffalo all day with him on her back. She had a sweet, forgiving disposition. Now he spoke to her in a soft, low voice as her velvet lips nibbled the last of the oats from his cupped palms.

He spoke endearments in Sa-sis-e-tas. *My good little Pony Woman, did you miss me this evening? I had to follow that ugly white-eyes girl down the gulch to make sure she had no trouble. There are Snake People nearby. I saw three of them today, out on the horizon, riding parallel to us. But never fear, maybe they are only our friends the Crazy Knife People, the*

84

Kiowas. It was too far to see clearly. This is far south for the evil Snake People to be, so early in the Deer-Rutting Moon. The white-spider girl threw her poison away. I picked it up and am keeping it for her. She is afraid to die but too ignorant yet to fear the Snake People. Perhaps they will come around here tonight and try to steal you both! But I will not let them. We will kill them all and take their scalps and ride back north across the Greasy River to our Cut-Arm People and gallop into camp the way we used to, with you prancing proudly and tossing your tail and I swinging the scalps on high, and all the girls will come running, the men, too, to praise you for your valor. The old women will sing the Scalp Songs and we will have a big Scalp Dance to honor the Medicine Arrows. We will run races against those weak, puny little Indian ponies, you and I, and win all the bets. Maybe we will bring the white-spider girl with us. She knows how to hunt and cooks good food. You could carry her on your strong back along with me, couldn't you? Or maybe we shall steal these white-eye horses. And my uncles will give us more horses for you to run with when we get back, and a big, strong stallion to give you babies. All will honor Two Shields and his brave buffalo pony. I will feed you apples and oats and the sugar we take from the wagon trains of the spiders when we kill them, and the girls will play their hands over you and sing your song and weave primrose and desert plume into your mane and tail. All that we will do when the Snake People come!*

He walked back up the side of the coulee, well out of the light of the dying campfire, and squatted with his back to the wind, leaning forward on the butt of his rifle. It was a U.S. Cavalry Springfield carbine, a .50–70 breechloader whose stock had been split in the fight where he won it. He had mended it by sewing a strip of green deer hide around the stock. When the deer hide dried and shrank, it closed the split better than glue. He had decorated the stock with brass-headed tacks in the shape of two shields. He could sit this way until sunup, motionless, recalling the battles of the past, and he would do so this night. If the Snakes came skulking around, his pony would warn him. Many thieves had tried to steal her in the past. None had succeeded. He kept the scalps of the failed horse thieves hidden away in his war bag. It would not do for Mr. Dousmann or Captain McKay to see them. His other scalps he had burned in a medicine fire when he went to live among the white eyes. Some of them were white-spider scalps. But to throw away the scalps of the horse thieves would be unlucky; it would be asking for trouble.

He watched his pony moving gracefully through the darkness. He had untethered her from the picket pin. She did not need to be held by a white-eyes rope. He could tell by her ears what was out there in the darkness. If they flicked and went every which way, it was only buffalo or wolves or coyotes. If they pricked forward and remained there, she was listening to enemies. She would make no noise but stay near, waiting for the fight, and come when he whistled. She loved war as much as she loved running buffalo. She loved them as much as he did. He would rather fight mounted if many Snake People came. His pony was fast and brave. Sometimes up close she nipped at the men he fought, or at their horses. Her name was Wind-Blows-Snow-over-Bare-Rock. He called her Wind Blows, or sometimes simply Wind.

Otto woke suddenly.

He looked up at the sky. The Dipper had clocked itself most of the way around the North Star — an hour shy of dawn. Jenny breathed steadily, deep asleep. Otto slid his hand under the rolled jacket he used for a pillow and withdrew the .44 Smith & Wesson revolver. He sat up, reached for his boots, and was just pulling one on when the first shot was fired. He heard a whoop, then two more shots. Another whoop. Some horses whinnied. Jenny sat bolt upright. Otto pushed her down again, then crouched in the wagonbed, peering over the top in the direction of the gunshots.

"It's all right, Mr. Dousmann," Tom Shields said. He was standing at the far end of the wagon, behind Otto. With him stood his pony. He smiled. "Just Poor Lo trying to make off with the stock."

"Well, Christ, Tom — let's get after them!"

"No need," Tom Shields said. He raised a hand black with blood. "I got 'em. Now I'll kick up the fire again and start us some coffee."

Tom sent his horse back to the herd and went over toward the pile of buffalo chips, where a few coals still glowed. Something limp dangled from his belt. No, three things, swinging wet and loose as he walked away.

"What's he got there, by his hip?" Jenny asked.

"Nothing," Otto said. "Get back to sleep, Jenny, it's still a ways to go until morning."

6

When Jenny woke again, the sun was up. The hide of her antelope lay draped over the wagon's gate, near her feet. Tom must have completed the skinning last night. She saw that he had fleshed the skin side, too. Neither Tom nor Otto was in sight. They must be down seeing to the stock, she thought. A pot of coffee seethed beside the fire. She was just pouring herself a cup when Tom Shields came up the draw. His face, as usual, was expressionless.

"Thank you very much for the skin, Tom," she said.

He grunted and kept on walking, back to the hide wagon.

Well, she thought. You're welcome, I'm sure.

Now Otto appeared, looking even angrier than he had the previous evening. He grabbed the coffeepot and poured a swallow directly from the spout into his open mouth. He winced, swilled the mouthful around through his teeth, and spat it into the fire. She saw that his hands were shaking.

"What's the matter?"

"That *verdammter* red devil," he said. "He killed those horse thieves last night, all three of them, and . . ." He was speaking in German again. She answered in kind.

"And what? He saved our livestock, didn't he? And maybe our lives as well. Shouldn't we be grateful?"

"It's not that." Otto glanced at her, then looked away. "It's what he did after."

"Scalped them? I saw those scalps hanging from his belt last night. I know it's barbaric, Pastor Koellner most certainly wouldn't approve, but don't white men take scalps, too? What's . . ."

"No, not just the scalps. It's what he did after that." Otto put an arm around her shoulders. "Look, Jennchen, these people are beasts. They don't think the way we do. Not even when they've got good white Christian blood in them, as Tom does. They have no sense of decency, of pity, or of kindness. And none at all of guilt. They are heathens, barbarians, plain and simple. The men Tom killed last night were Shoshones, some folks call them Snakes. But these Indians weren't even men yet, they were only boys, about your age. No, probably younger. Out on a horse-stealing expedition. Out for a little fun. To make names for themselves among their people. Most of the so-called wars between these Plains tribes are nothing more than minor raids like this, a few young bucks sneaking in at night to steal horses or women, maybe lift some scalps while they're at it. But the Shoshone and the Cheyenne are long-time enemies. They've been raiding, raping, burning, scalping, killing, and thieving from each other for ages now. Don't bother to ask them why, they don't know, nor do they care. They just love to do it."

He drank some coffee and sighed.

"This is the ugly part," he said. "When an Indian kills another Indian, he goes the whole hog. He not only ends the man's life in this world, he makes sure the poor blighted heathen won't have much fun on the Spirit Road either. After he's scalped his enemy, if he's got the time, he'll gouge out his eyes, slice off his nose, knock out his teeth, yank out his tongue, cut off his hands and feet, take out his brain and lay it on a rock. They do tricks with other body parts as well. That way, when the dead man gets to the Happy Hunting Ground, he can't see, smell, or talk with his comrades, eat buffalo meat, or even make babies. More important, without hands or feet or a brain to plan it with, he can't take revenge on his killer when that unfortunate finally shows up in the sweet by-and-by. It has a warped sort of logic to it, I guess, if you believe in an afterlife, but the worst part is that after all this jolly whittling is finished, he'll leave those items standing around on rocks or logs or on the victim's body, to taunt the fellow's friends when they find him later. The more grotesque the array, the better."

He put both his hands on Jenny's shoulders, stepped back, and looked her in the eyes.

"Don't go down by the horses, Jennchen. Take my word for it. Our Tom has a fiendish sense of humor when it comes to the human anatomy. Let's just pray that he never takes a notion to practice his heathen folkways on us."

Snakes, Jenny thought. She recalled the hand sign he had used. When Tom warned me to look out for "snakes" yesterday, he must have known those Indians were around here. That's why he followed me with his rifle.

"What was the Fetterman Fight?" she asked.

Otto looked at her in surprise. "Why do you want to know?"

"When Tom saw my rifle last evening, he said his father had had one like it, an older version, that he'd come by at some battle called the Fetterman Fight, up north of here somewhere."

"The Fetterman *Massacre*," Otto said. "Up in Wyoming Territory, about six or seven years ago. You never heard of it? Out here folks can't forget it. Some young bad faces of the Oglala Sioux under a chief called Red Cloud, along with a few Cheyennes, lured eighty-one men — U.S. Army troops and a couple of civilians — into an ambush, killed the lot of them. Just before Christmas, it was, in '66. The Army was building some forts along the Montana Road, what some call the Bozeman Trail. It runs smack through the Indians' sacred hunting grounds. The forts were supposed to make it safe for the miners heading to the goldfields around Virginia City. The government was trying to negotiate a right-of-way through the Big Horn Mountains and the Indian Territory beyond, and most of the Sioux agreed. But Red Cloud and his Oglalas, along with some of Tom's people, wouldn't allow it. They kept sniping at the Army work parties, didn't want the white eyes, as the Sioux call us, cutting their sacred groves, or some such thing. At any rate, there was this hotheaded captain named William Judd Fetterman, bragged that if the Army'd just give him eighty men he'd ride clear through the whole Sioux nation. So one day, when the Hostiles were acting particularly stroppy, the commanding general gave him eighty men and he rode out. But he didn't ride through the Sioux nation. The Oglala branch of it rode through him."

"Killed them all?"

"Every last one, and in only about half an hour. Then they did to the bodies what our Tom did to those Snakes last night."

"Could Tom's father have gotten a rifle like mine there?"

"Certainly. The two civilians, Jim Wheatley and Ike Fisher, had Henry rifles and apparently they did the only real damage to the Hostiles. The Army troops were armed mostly with single-shot Springfields left over from the war. Slow-loading, no match for arrows and lances at close range. I was up that way when they brought Ike Fisher's body back to the fort, he looked like a porcupine. Had 105 arrows in him. Tom's father could have recovered one of those Henrys. Hell, Tom could have been there himself, for that matter. He's old enough. These boys start on the warpath when they're fourteen or younger."

He looked over at Tom Shields yoking up the oxen. A good hand with draft animals. Very patient. Gentle and sure with his voice and his movements. Viewed from behind, he might have been any Western stockman, perhaps even a Wisconsin farmhand preparing for a trip to town on market day. A good-natured country yokel — you'd enjoy drinking a lager with him down at the local tavern. Maybe even spin a yarn or two. But turn him around and you'd see the face of a killer.

"The only way to make a Cheyenne quit the warpath," Otto said dryly, "is to shoot him off of it."

Despite Otto's admonition, Jenny could not resist having a peek at Tom's handiwork. She waited until the men were busy rearranging the loads in the wagon, then slipped down to the streamside meadow, where the horses still grazed. The hum of a thousand flies led her to the bodies. They hung over the scene like a blue-gray cloud. She edged closer, fearful of what she might see. It wasn't as bad as she had feared. The blood had dried and blackened by now, and the mutilated corpses, despite their fearful wounds, looked like strangely painted wax mannequins, certainly no worse than the freaks of nature she'd sneaked in to see at a raree show near Heldendorf — she still had occasional nightmares about the Lipless Woman.

A footstep sounded behind her. Turning, she

saw it was Tom. He stood there staring at her, his face impassive, and for a moment she felt a tingle of fear.

"Don't worry," he said. "You're not my enemy."

"How could you do this?" she snapped, angry that he had seen her fear.

"They'd have done the same to me," he said. "To all of us, if they'd had the chance. They were brave boys. Especially that one." He pointed to an emasculated body whose head stood eyeless on a nearby rock. "Even with a bullet in him he came at me with his knife. I had to club him down with the rifle butt." He swung the Springfield to show her. "He was still alive when I took his hair, his eyes open, looking up into mine. He knew he was finished, but he smiled. He never cried out. He never begged for mercy, even when my knife went into his heart. He was a *man*. By-and-by, if I ever get back to my people, I'll tell them this story. I shall dedicate the Scalp Dance to his memory."

They reached the rendezvous shortly before noon. McKay wasn't there, but his hides were. He had left them, neatly baled and covered with a tarpaulin, beneath a lightning-blasted cottonwood where Otto and Raleigh had made their camp most of last spring.

"How come he left the hides behind, unguarded?" Jenny asked.

"Well," Otto said, "he'd probably killed all the

shootable buffalo in the immediate vicinity and thought it best to hunt on elsewhere, to make the most of his time. He couldn't carry all these hides in that light wagon he's driving, so he left them here until we arrived with the big ox wagon. He knew Tom and I would be coming soon. And there's not much danger of the hides being stolen. All of us hide men in these parts know one another. We're friends. Honor among thieves, and all that."

Under the tarp was a note in the captain's spidery Rebel scrawl.

Am running buff on down toward the cimaron You know the alkaly flat near where Gramm was kilt We campt ther a short wile last winter? Look for my outfit thare. Go to the sound of the guns Thers others down this way. Wright Moores crew B. Dickson Wm Tilman Mastersons Billy Og. Ile borow a extra skinner from them til you com. Hurry! RFMcK. pS Hope you got us a good sheff *i'm sick of my own dern cooking!*

Good, Otto thought. There'll be plenty of rifles if the Hostiles come looking for trouble. Old Raleigh. No wonder the South lost the war. Most of Lee's officers couldn't spell to save their souls, much less write a clear battle order.

They pounded south for an hour, two hours more. The country was all creosote bush and dust. Odd-shaped clouds boiled over the plain.

The wind had died a slow death through the morning, working gradually toward the west, then a bit north of west. A great blue-black cloudbank that looked like a range of mountains reared slowly behind them. At the top of a swell, Otto reined in. He signaled the wagons to halt. He wanted silence, no squeaking wheels. He looked to the south and listened.

There it was. The sporadic thud of buffalo rifles, far off through a yellowish haze of dust that thickened to tan on the horizon. Within the haze he could make out a blurred snaky line, vague, almost ephemeral, that would be the Cimarron River . . .

At the base of the rise, Tom Shields had dismounted from the hide wagon and knelt with his face near the ground.

"Listening for buffalo?" Jenny asked him.

"No, looking," he said.

"What do you mean?"

"Come over here, I'll show you."

She climbed down and walked to where he knelt in the dry grass. He pointed to a dull black tumblebug that stood rigid in the turf, its quivering antennae angled forward.

"Buffalo beetle," Tom Shields said. "Where he points, that's where the buffalo are. I don't know, maybe he feels them through his feet or those twig things on his nose. But when he finds them, he goes over there. He and his tribe. To make balls out of the buffalo's shit, you know? Whenever you see an Indian climb off his pony and put his face sideways to the ground, he's not listening, he's asking this fella for directions."

They found the alkali flat easily. Otto would never forget it. A hunter named Tobe Graham and his crew — two skinners and a cook — had been slaughtered here last winter by Comanches. The Comanches had tied Graham and his men alive and naked to the wheels of a wagon and built a fire at their feet, feeding it with flint hides and corncob-sized chunks of tallow. But not before scalping them. Graham was from Chicago, where he'd been a streetcar conductor. He had a wife and half a dozen children and couldn't support them with what he earned on the cars. At least not in any comfort. His wife, he said, had prayed and pleaded with him not to leave her for the Buffalo Range, she couldn't stand it all alone with the babies in that cold, cruel city.

"She's just a little wee lass, from near Belfast," he had told Otto. But Graham had promised her it would be only for the winter, no more, no more, and when he got home they'd be rich as lords. Five bucks a hide for shaggies . . .

Raleigh had pitched his big white canvas Union Army supply tent, purchased last fall from the sutler's store at Fort Dodge, under a stand of cottonwoods half a mile from the alkali flat. Buffalo hides lay pegged out all around it. Tom Shields wheeled the big wagon in a tight circle and parked beneath the trees. Jenny reined in beside him. They set about unloading gear, racing

98

against the coming storm. Already they could hear a sullen cannonade on the horizon and see ragged, dirty-white whorls of storm wind careering along the tops of the blue-black thunderheads, and occasional flashes of lightning.

Raleigh rode in before sunset, just as they finished.

"Huzzah, the late arrivals!" he bellowed. "Whatever become of that far-famed Dutch punctuality? We've killed all the shaggies in these parts, so you might as well pack up and get back to town, old hoss."

His white teeth gleamed within a dry, dusty, wind-burned face. Jenny watched him from the mouth of the tent. He had a wide smile, and eyes that crinkled around the edges as he grinned.

Raleigh swung down from his horse — a tall sorrel stallion — and turned it over to Tom Shields for unsaddling, along with his buffalo rifle. He walked across to Otto, still smiling widely. He was shorter than Otto, but of a heavier build, with wide shoulders and a deep chest. He wore an unfringed doeskin hunting shirt and bandoliers across his chest, tightly fitting sky-blue cavalry trousers striped yellow down the sides, knee-high black boots, and a blue bandanna knotted loosely around his throat. The blue matched his eyes, Jenny thought. His dusty hat was cocked back on his forehead. A sheath on his belt held two long-bladed skinning knives and a sharpening steel. She noticed that dried blood caked his hands and wrists, disappearing up his forearms into his shirt-sleeves.

"Where's the other wagon?" Otto asked.

"Should be right behind me," Raleigh said. "I hired a spare skinner from Billy Ogg's crew. Milo Sykes — you know him from up on the Pawnee Fork."

As if on cue, Sykes and the wagon rattled out of the sunset, the mules in a stiff-legged canter. *"Racing to Beat the Storm,"* Raleigh said. "Make a nice study for Currier & Ives." Tom ran over to help unload the fresh hides. They would have to be protected from the rain.

Raleigh McKay turned toward the tent and noticed Jenny for the first time. He nodded gravely and doffed his hat to reveal an unruly mop of wavy blond hair burnished almost red in places.

"Well, I see you took my note to heart and hired us a real live professional to be our chief cook and bottle washer."

"More than that," Otto said. "Pending your approval, she's a full partner in this enterprise — my sister, Miss Jenny Dousmann."

Raleigh wiped his fingers carefully on his shirt, took Jenny's hand, and kissed her fingertips lightly. He smiled into her eyes. It was a formal gesture, but his eyes belied it.

"Most pleased and honored to make your acquaintance, ma'am."

"If it's all right with you," Otto told McKay, "I figured we'd cut my sister in for a quarter of what we earn on each wagonload of hides, less the skinners' pay. You and I will split the remainder, fifty-fifty."

"Sounds fair enough," McKay said, smiling. "Though the mere presence of such a charming feminine soul in our rude camp is of course beyond price."

A great rattling boom of thunder exploded above and around them.

"Here she comes," Raleigh said, looking skyward. "A right gullywasher, I'd guess. We better be getting inside . . ."

Then he sniffed himself, looked over apologetically at Jenny, and smiled once again.

"Or maybe not. I'm afraid, at the moment, I don't quite rival the prairie rose for fragrance."

A cold rush of wind enveloped them. Then the rain swept down in a gray roaring blur that obscured the world from horizon to horizon. As Jenny peered out from beneath the canvas, she saw Raleigh McKay barefoot and shirtless cavorting in the slashing rain, his cavalry britches plastered to his legs, scrubbing himself with a bar of fancy store-bought soap and whooping a joyous rebel yell. He applied the suds most assiduously to his hair — of which he seemed inordinately proud, Jenny thought.

Tom was shirtless now, too, lugging a barrel of molasses to the tent, the rain pelting his hard tan chest and shoulders. He had white, mouth-shaped scars on his ribs — old arrow wounds? How dark he was. How pale, almost marble-smooth, was Raleigh McKay.

She wished she could join them in their dance, peel off her stale, sticky clothing and pirouette naked and clean beside them in the downpour.

7

The line storm blew through after dark. McKay and Otto walked out to survey the damage. Stars had broken clear, spread cryptically across the night sky in a great frozen matrix — here comes Orion slouching toward the zenith. Prairie wolves yipped up at the moon from the east. The drying hides lay sodden between their pegs. Gray moths swarmed, flapping damply in the gloom. Fresh arsenic was indicated. The cavvy had weathered the storm in good fashion, as always. Indeed, the horses and mules, even the drowsy-eyed oxen, looked cleaner and sprightlier than they had before it struck.

It hadn't been much of a supper. Cold hump steak. Cold beans. Stale ship's biscuit. Impossible to start a fire. The buffalo chips slumped in a soggy pile beside the tent, Jenny grim-faced with frustration. She must have had such plans, Otto thought.

"Keep away from my sister," he said to McKay.

"Why, *I've* got no designs on her, hoss."

"Like hell you don't. You may not know it now, though. I've never seen men alone — in war or peace — who didn't have designs on the first woman they saw, once they'd been in the field a few weeks."

They walked out onto the prairie. Not a fire in sight.

"Any sign of Mister Lo?"

"Not for a while," Raleigh said.

"We had some Snakes up the line. Tom took care of them."

"He's a good 'un."

"Too bloody, though, too much the savage."

"You know the Cheyenne. Just like Bill Sherman. Make war so terrible that no one wants to fight you." Raleigh laughed. "Old Bill, he sure showed all us Southrun folks — from Georgia to the sea. The whole damn nation, for that matter. 'War is hell.' As you Yankees are only too glad to remind us."

They walked on.

"What are the buff doing?"

"Not much. Thinner on the ground than I hoped they'd be, just like last winter. Maybe we've shot 'em out in these parts, like the do-gooders back East say we have. I came on a herd last week, thought they might be the vanguard, as of yore, but they blew right through with nothing followin' along behind. Not all that many of 'em, really. Headin' to join their kinfolk across the Red. All noses pointin' southwest for Texas — the Yarner. There's still plenty of shaggies down that way, for sure."

The "Yarner" was what Texicans called the Llano Estacado, the Staked Plain of the Texas Panhandle. Southerners like Raleigh were

104

damned if they'd wrap their tongues around foreign words.

"But Texas is way across the Dead Line," Otto said. "The government says we can't hunt them down there. The Army will stop us."

"No, it won't, old son."

Raleigh turned in the darkness and smiled at Otto. His teeth looked luminous in the brittle light of the stars.

"Wright Mooar and John Webb went down below the Cimarron to the Yarner this summer, or early fall, it might of been. They went right across the Dead Line, through the Indian Territory, and clear to the North Fork of the Canadian, then west across Wolf Creek. Nary a soldier boy interfered with 'em. They saw buff like in the old days. There's another whole herd down there, big anyways as the Republican River herd we've been killin' these past few years. By treaty it's Lo's herd, I guess, but what the hell. The Medicine Lodge Treaty's goin' to get broken just like all the rest of 'em. Mooar and Webb went back up to Kansas and talked to Colonel Dodge at the fort. Asked him straight out, they did, asked what'd happen if the bluelegs caught buffalo runners south of the Deadline. The Colonel, he just looked out the window. Said, 'Boys, if I was huntin' buffalo, I'd hunt where the buffalo are.' "

He slapped Otto on the shoulder. "How do you like that, Black Hat?"

"I like it fine," Otto said. "I just have to

wonder how old Satanta's going to like it. Or Quanah or Tall Bull or Whirlwind, for that matter. There's Apaches and Kiowas, Comanches and Cheyennes and Arapahos galore down there, all on the prod, not to mention the so-called Civilized Tribes. If we start on their buff, it'll be hell to pay and the pitch not hot."

"You worry too much, old son. What the hell, we're here to make money, aren't we?"

At dawn McKay and Otto caught their horses and rode out to kill buffalo. The horses puffed smoke as they trotted away and a thick hoarfrost rimed the prairie. Milo Sykes, a wiry, sour-mouthed Georgian with muddy eyes, rode after them in the skinner's wagon. Deep pockmarks on his cheeks gave his face the texture of a walnut. A strange old coon, Otto thought. Skinny as a skeeter hawk, his chin hobnobbing with the tip of his pointy nose, Milo always walked or rode with his head bent forward, looking at the ground. When he spoke, which was rarely, his voice had a high, dry, whining quality, like fingernails on slate.

Tom Shields stayed in camp to poison and repeg the damp hides and help Jenny through her first morning. The sun rose white in the east, promising a fair day. Jenny straggled out of the tent and collected what dry sticks she could from under the cottonwoods. Not many.

A number of trees had been snapped off at their boles by last night's storm. She went to the tent

106

and found the ax. She began splitting spear-shaped slabs of heartwood from the cottonwood stumps, carrying them back to the tent in her apron. She kindled a fire with her few dry twigs and quickly piled thin slivers of heartwood upon the flames. In a short while she had a good blaze crackling. The heat of the fire felt good. She clapped her hands and said, *"Juch-he!"* A whoop of triumph.

"My mother used to say that."

She turned and found Tom Shields behind her. He was smiling his nice smile again.

"Well then," Jenny said brightly, "she must have been German! *Kannst du Deutsch,* Tom?"

"Oh no, just a bit. *Nur a' bissel?* I understand it better than I talk it. She used to speak that lingo to me when I was very small. Before she died, you know."

"You can't have been that young, if you re-member some of it."

"Well, I was little then," he said, suddenly embarrassed. "You remember a lot from when you're little." He turned and walked away to busy himself with the hides. Jenny wondered what had set him off this time. Perhaps his mother had died when he was older than he said. Maybe it was too painful for him to think about her and that's why he pretended he couldn't speak German. Perhaps she's still alive and he's afraid that if the Army finds out, they'll go and rescue her . . .

Two magpies swooped down from the cottonwoods and began squabbling over a chunk of buffalo suet she had placed by the fire. They leaped in the air in a flurry of white wing patches and struck at each other like gamecocks, screaming indignantly. She ran to shoo them off, but they'd ruined the suet anyway. She threw the battle-scarred remnant after them. Who knew what those filthy beaks had been into last — probably a rotting buffalo carcass. She placed a fresh piece in the sunlight, next to the fire, and covered it with a large curl of cottonwood bark. That should keep the pirates off. She was softening the suet to make dough. It would be saleratus bread, because she hadn't had a chance last night to mix up a batch of sourdough. She had brought along from Wisconsin the family "barm," which Mutti said dated back to the dawn of time, there in the Old Country, perhaps (Vati added sarcastically) to the days of the Nibelungs. Jenny carried the fabled starter West in a patented Mason jar, a big one. But today she would merely bake bread and hard rolls, and perhaps a pie with some of the fresh apples she'd bought before they left Dodge.

But what for meat? The antelope was finished and she was sure that Raleigh and Sykes were tired of buffalo hump.

After setting her dough to rise and rigging the sheet-metal reflector oven to heat over the fire, she tidied up the tent, then placed a tub of water beside the oven to heat. Tom showed her where a spring lay hidden in the jumbled rocks near camp, so she needn't use the water they'd brought along in barrels. She found a lopsided square of hard, dry, homemade soap, took her vegetable grater from the big wooden crate that contained the cooking utensils, and grated the soap into flakes, catching them in an empty hardtack box. She would wash the men's clothes later. She liked washing. The smell of it, the soft feel of hot soapy water. Her mother had hated washing clothes. Perhaps she would, too, in time.

Jenny had noticed Otto's shotgun case lying in the tent. Maybe she'd mosey out through the grasslands beyond the alkali flat and try for a few prairie hens. They would make a nice change from buffalo for the men. She could hear Raleigh and Otto shooting now, not more than a mile or two from camp, it sounded. The chance of Hostiles nearby was remote, Raleigh had said. But Tom insisted on coming with her anyway on her bird hunt, just to be on the safe side.

It was a fine morning, crisp and bright, and beyond the alkali flat the prairie seemed to roll on forever. Small birds sang and flittered through the swaying grass. An animal she recognized as a badger shuffled away on short, bowed legs. It was paler than the badgers she'd seen in Wisconsin, with an upturned snout and small, beady black eyes, dirty white stripes down its sides. She thought that badgers came out only at dusk, and perhaps that was true in populous Wisconsin, where the beast was hunted mercilessly for its stiff, thick bristles, which were used to make shav-

109

ing brushes, but apparently on the Buffalo Range, where they had little contact with men, they roamed around in daylight as well.

Well, they would learn better.

"Why didn't you shoot it?" Tom Shields asked.

"What for?" she said. "You can't eat them."

He laughed, puzzled, and shook his head. Apparently her way of thinking was as indecipherable to Tom as his was to her.

"Indians eat 'em," he said finally. "At least the Sa-sis-e-tas do. They're not bad. But the badger is very powerful, too, very wise. You can use him as a looking glass, to see the future."

"How do you do that?"

"Well, if a war party comes across a badger they'll kill it and take its guts out, then lay it on its back in a bed of white sage. The blood pools up inside there, you know, and come morning, they go by the badger and look at their reflection in the blood. If they see themselves white-haired and wrinkled, they'll live to be old. If they see themselves skinny and pale, they're going to die from some sickness. If they're going to die in this raid, their eyes will be closed. If they're going to be scalped, their heads will be bald and bloody. You know, like that."

"Did you ever try it?"

He looked at her and smiled a little, then nodded.

"Well, what did you see, Tom?"

He laughed and would not tell her, and they walked on.

"There they are," Tom said quietly, crouching suddenly beside her. She followed suit.

"Where? What?"

"*Wikis,*" he said. "Birds. You stay here, I'll sneak around behind them and make them come to you."

He disappeared on his belly into the grass, quiet as a housecat. She waited. She could hear rustling ahead of her, then saw some movement — quick forms like elongated chickens, barred brown and white, scuttling through the dense stems. She cocked the double hammers of the shotgun. She thought of shooting into the flock while it was still on the ground, but realized she might hit Tom where he crawled somewhere behind them. Then the birds rose with a loud, slurred rattle of wings, pouring toward her low and fast over the waving seed tops. She stood and swung with the lead bird, leaning into the weight of the gun the way her brother had taught her with partridges back home, swinging on with the leader until he was abreast of her, then she pulled the forward trigger. The gun bucked tight against her shoulder   that pleasant solid thump she'd grown to enjoy, clear down to her toes. She continued to swing around through the billowing white smoke, the momentum of the heavy barrels carrying her around smoothly, following two birds close together toward the rear of the flock. Fired again as they went away . . .

Tom whooped. It was the same whoop she'd

heard when he killed the Shoshone horse thieves.

"You shoot good!" he said. He came toward her with a wide, happy, white man's smile. "Two shots, four birds! I never seen a woman shoot so good." He held two of them aloft, then stooped to pick up the remaining pair. "I can't shoot 'em that good, not when they're flying."

"The shot pattern must have spread just right," she said, pleased at his praise. "I only fired at two. But Otto taught me how to swing with them, and he must have taught me well. Up north, you know."

Tom carried the gun on the way into camp. He killed two more prairie hens, but only as they were running on the ground ahead of them. Back at the tent, he cleaned the gun while Jenny plucked and drew the birds. She hung them head down in the shade of a giant gnarled cottonwood. Remembering the magpies, she covered the grouse with burlap sacking. Tom ate some cold hump and hardtack, swallowed the last of the morning's coffee, then hitched up the ox team and rolled out to help with the day's skinning.

Jenny saw that the water in the washtub was steaming now. Big, fat bubbles seethed and sucked as they rolled from the bottom. She poured in some soap flakes, then threw the foul clothing after them. She stirred the noxious stew with a long, broad spear of cottonwood. Left it to boil. Her greased pans of dough were ready and she put them in the glowing oven. She sat back by the fire, humming to herself, satisfied with the morning. Let the wash cook for a while, then I'll start scrubbing. This afternoon I'll do the pie.

For an instant she had an image of her class at the academy, parsing Latin phrases as Dr. Williams looked on, frowning. *Et ego in Arcadia . . .*

She laughed out loud.

Indeed she was there.

Otto and Raleigh rode in just shy of sunset. Jenny had water on the boil, ready to clean their rifles. Her apple pie stood cooling near the fire. Raleigh bent down to whuffle up the sweet steam rising from its crisp brown crust.

"Unless my nose deceives me, that ain't no dried apple pie," he said, winking at Otto. "You know the old ditty we used to recite in the Yadkin?"

> *You can spit in my ears*
> *And tell me lies,*
> *But don't give me none*
> *Of your dried apple pies!*

He turned to Jenny with his wide smile and dropped to one knee.

"Miss Dousmann, will you marry me?"

"You'd better ask me first," Otto said, unsmiling.

Raleigh laughed. "Now why would I want to marry you, old Black Hat?"

The wagon followed soon after. Tom and Milo

Sykes saw to the horses, then began stretching and pegging the hides. Jenny helped them. When she lifted the first limp, rolled-up hide from the wagonbed, her knees nearly buckled. It must have weighed sixty or seventy pounds. She stiffened her spine and carried on. When she finished half an hour later, her back was sore. It's not quite like hanging out the wash, she thought. She went to the fire, where her birds were roasting in a slow oven. The hens were stuffed with crumbled hardtack, onion, and wild Mexican plums Tom had found growing near the spring. Her baking had turned out nicely. On the dropped tailgate of the spring wagon she had tin plates, spoons, and forks arrayed, along with a crock of salted buffalo tallow, a plate of hard rolls, and a loaf of bread with which to mop up the gravy, five tin cups (clean for a change), a full, steaming coffeepot, and two flower-patterned china bowls she had brought from home, one filled with sugar, the other with salt. There were no napkins. To make up for that shortcoming, she had picked some blackfoot daisies and purple prairie asters near the spring, arranging them neatly in an empty Mason jar.

"Quite a picnic," Raleigh said, coming up behind her with Otto and the skinners. "If it all eats as good as it smells, you'll have done us proud, Miss Black Hat."

They helped themselves and dug in. Ten minutes later all her day's work was undone. What remained of it were gnawed chicken bones, bread crumbs, grease spots, and a pile of dirty dishes.

Milo Sykes belched, sprawled on an elbow in the grass, and began picking his teeth with the point of a boning knife. Otto loosened his belt a notch, wiped his mustache with the back of his hand, and sighed heavily. Tom Shields, who had hunkered on his haunches away from the firelight as he ate, rose and slipped quietly into the darkness after scraping his plate into the coals. Raleigh lay against a wagon wheel, feet to the fire, and sipped a mug of coffee, watching the stars pop into being.

Jenny gathered up the plates and went to wash them. They heard her rattling and splashing at the tub behind them, singing some German ditty.

"Scarce thirty hides between us in a whole damn day," Raleigh said. "It don't shine, old son."

Otto grunted.

"Let's go down to the Yarner," Raleigh said.

Otto looked over at Jenny. He looked down at his feet. He grunted noncommittally once again.

"What's that mean, yea or nay?"

"I don't like it, Cap. Not with a woman along. Especially when she's my own flesh and blood."

"We can't make money up here. Face it, Black Hat, this here now herd is finished. Shot out."

"He's right," Sykes said. "But they're thick as fleas on a spotted pup 'twix the Cimarron and the Lodge Pole." Lodge Pole was another name for the Washita River, where the 7th Cavalry had wiped out a village of Cheyennes five years earlier.

"We've never been there," Otto said. "We don't know the country."

115

"Tom does," Raleigh said. "He's got Southern Cheyenne kin in those parts. And Sykes was down that way in '68 with Custer, weren't you, Milo?"

"Right down on the Lodge Pole," Sykes said, nodding. "In Black Kettle's very camp. November it was, just like now, only colder: we rode through 'em at dawn with the whole damn regimental band playing, b'God. 'Gary Owen,' can you believe it? Lifted some hair that day, b'God." He spat in the fire. "Them Dog Soldiers won't be bothering us no more."

"B'God," Otto said.

Raleigh laughed, then said, "Aw, Black Hat, your sister will be safe. Tom knows the lingo, Milo knows the country, and you and I know how to shoot. Hellfire, I'll look after your sister myself, her personal bodyguard, with your say-so, of course. I'll vouch for her safety, on my honor as an officer and a gentleman." He winked, then continued more seriously. "If anything happens to her, you can lift my own hair and I won't even whimper."

Otto laughed and shook his head. "No, thanks. Some redskin will lift it first."

He rose and stretched. "But you're right, there's no money to be made hereabouts. And we're here to make money. Okay, let's do it. Tomorrow we'll find someone to take our hides back to Dodge, or failing that, we'll cache 'em. Then on to the Yarner it is."

8

The wagons rolled at noon. They hauled the hides over to Wright Mooar's camp a mile or so to the west and left them with that trustworthy Vermonter. Mooar said he thought that Charlie Rath might be down to the Cimarron soon with a wagon train to buy hides on the spot and agreed to sell theirs to the trader along with his own. "Soon as Charlie shows and I sell our hides," Mooar said, "I'll be headin' down Texas way myself. Probably a few other outfits will come along. Ayuh. More of us the better."

From the way Tom and Raleigh spoke of him, Jenny had expected Mooar to be a crusty, grizzled old-timer. Instead, she saw a young, blond-bearded, sour-mouthed fellow with close-set, pale-blue eyes, stingy with his speech, a veteran of the Buffalo Range though only in his twenties. Not much older than Tom. He never even looked at Jenny.

"Mooar wandered West in the late sixties like so many of us," Otto told her as they headed down to the Cimarron crossing. "Worked the wheat harvest in Illinois at first, carpentered a bit, I guess, later chopped firewood in Kansas over by Walnut Creek, south of Hays. He and his partner sold to the Army for two dollars a cord,

117

about what I got up in Omaha. Then they switched to buffalo, shooting meat for the Eastern market at three cents a pound."

He laughed.

"Doesn't sound like much, does it?" he said. "But I did it, too, on a smaller scale. It adds up. There's lots of meat on a buffalo — a big bull will weigh nearly a ton, a cow about six or seven hundred pounds. Cows taste better, more tender. The saddles alone, hump and tenderloins, weigh up to two hundred pounds apiece. We were earning $90 or $100 a day, when you average it out. Hell of a lot more than for firewood, and a lot less work."

There was no market for the raw, untanned hides back then, Otto said, though some fellows traded with the Indians for their soft, brain-tanned robes, laboriously scrubbed and thumped and worked up by squaws. These elegant robes brought from eight to sixteen dollars apiece in the cities back East. The Indians would trade a dozen robes for a pint or two of rotgut whiskey. This whiskey, of course, had been diluted by half with creek water, then fired up with ample doses of paregoric and red pepper.

"The tanneries back East said raw buffalo hide was too thick and spongy to make good leather. So we usually left the skins on the prairie, or sold the butchered meat unskinned to middlemen at the railheads. We'd chop a buff in half lengthwise after gutting it, sling the halves on the train just that way, hair and all. But market hunting's a seasonal trade. In the spring and summer the buff are out of condition and the meat tastes awful.

"All that changed in the spring of '71. A hide dealer in Kansas City named DuBois sent out circulars all across the range, offering to buy flint hides for good money, any time of the year. He'd found some tanners in Germany who had a process for making good leather out of them. Lobenstein in Leavenworth jumped on the bandwagon right away, along with a slew of other dealers, and the big-time killing began. Wright Mooar sent some hides to his brother John, in New York, and he found takers, too. Suddenly everyone wanted buffalo hides — for everything from leather drive belts in factories to saddles and harnesses and furniture upholstery. I hear the swells in New York and Philadelphia even paper the walls of their parlors with it."

He laughed again, shaking his head. They were into the stink now. Dead buffalo lay all around them, on the hillsides and in the muddy wallows, some still pink, others going black or green with rot. Vultures on the carcasses bated at them as the wagons passed, hissing and flaring their wings. Tendrils of intestine festooned their hooked beaks. Bluebottle flies hummed everywhere. Coyotes slunk away, and a pack of fat lobos lolled on a nearby ridge, sated.

"You're seeing the results today. Buffalo hammered year round, all ages and sizes of them, anywhere they run. They're gone from the Republican clear down to the Cimarron, and now we're going South to do the same to the Texas herd. It's worse than the war. In the war at least we buried the dead. The whole West is a *Schlachthof*, a slaughterhouse. But more wasteful by far than a slaughterhouse. Nobody gets to eat the meat."

"Why don't you quit?"

He looked at her, his eyes sadder than she'd ever seen them.

"What else could I do?"

"Farm. Open a shop somewhere. A business, you have money enough now to start one. Or maybe study the law, or go to Deutschland and practice medicine. Get married to some nice girl and raise a family, like most people do!"

"I'm not cut out for that kind of life, Jennchen."

No, she thought sadly, you're *schwach* — a weakling, like Vati. Brave only against nature and other men. Soft, though, when it comes to complex things. More meaningful things. A household. A woman who loves you. Children, no matter how foolish they seem. *Ach,* men — you cannot endure!

Yet you mourn for the buffalo, when any fool can plainly see that they're doomed.

"Vati didn't have to kill himself," she said abruptly. "So what if the bank took the farm? We could have moved back to Milwaukee, where he certainly could have written for the German newspapers again. I could have found work, too. It would have been enough. He let the bank beat him, he let it kill him."

Otto stared at her. "Jennchen . . ."

She halted the mules, handed Otto the reins, unhitched Vixen from the lead shank, and mounted the pony.

"You drive," she said. "I want to ride for a while."

She chucked the mare into a canter, on past Sykes's wagon and up toward McKay, who pranced ahead of the column on his tall, fiery-eyed stallion.

Their way from Mooar's camp to the new hunting ground led now through bur oak and sage, over loose wet soil deposited by the river. Through it the Cimarron swung red with the line storm's runoff, roiling upon itself in glutinous coils. Filthy clots of foam skittered crazily across its surface, driven this way and that by the wind. They forded the river with difficulty. The hide wagon bogged twice in quicksand. The men had to unhitch the mules from the lighter wagons and add them to the ox teams to pull it free. Jenny watched from a bluff on the far bank, the Henry resting crosswise on her pommel. She had braided her hair. A kerchief knotted in pirate fashion covered the top of her head clear down to her eyebrows. Her lips were dry, cracked, and bleeding from the wind. Raleigh was up to his chest in the rushing water, his clothing plastered against his taut muscles, blond hair wet and wild.

The country rose slowly as they climbed away from the river, heading southwest along an old wagon track grown over with prickly pear and bunchgrass. When the wagon track suddenly stopped, she and Raleigh swung out in circles. They found a few pieces of burned wood half buried in the drifting sand. The partial rim of a wagon wheel protruded from a dune. Raleigh dismounted and kicked at the soil. He turned up a bone, a large one, then another. A few big yellow teeth, immensely long.

"Mule or horse, one," he said. "This is about as far as they got." He looked around in the distance. Nothing but prairie. Jenny hoped he wouldn't dig further. He might turn up human bones as well. He kicked over one of the charred boards and wrenched something from it, held it up for her to see. A rusty iron arrowhead, broken off short on the shaft.

"Arapaho," Tom said when they rode back to show it to him. "Pockmark People." He cupped his hand and tapped the center of his chest with the fingertips. "See the binding?" He pointed to the translucent leathery wraps that secured the arrowhead to the shaft. "They use rattlesnake gut, supposed to be more deadly, you know?"

"How old?"

"From the rust, maybe two years, or less. Hard to say. More if it's been dry down here."

"You talk 'rapaho?"

"Little bit," Tom said. "We can always talk signs, though."

"The Cheyenne and the Arapaho are pals," Raleigh said as they rode away. "They don't speak the same lingo, but they camp, hunt, and make war together, have for ages. Anyway, whatever the 'raps did to that wagon happened too long ago for us to worry about it."

But for the rest of the afternoon Jenny imagined Arapahos over every rise.

Toward evening they began to see buffalo, scattered bands at first that fled on sight of them. Then larger gatherings, mostly cows and ungainly, half-grown calves. The calves were a dirty yellowy-red color, like cinnamon, their humps already forming, tiny black horns just beginning to sprout. The farther southwest they rode, the calmer the buffalo seemed. At one point Jenny topped a rise to find a small herd standing not three hundred yards away. She reined Vixen in and waited, watching them. Raleigh, who had been riding behind her, now came up quietly on foot. She saw that his horse stood, its reins dropped on the grass, just under the reverse slope of the swell.

"Ease on back," Raleigh whispered, placing his palm over Vixen's muzzle. "Down out of sight behind the hill." He walked them both to cover, slowly and quietly. She slid out of the saddle.

"Just about time to make camp," Raleigh said softly. "This bunch looks good for a stand. Wind's right, from them to us. Come on up with me and see how we do it." He smiled, close beside her. "Maybe I'll let you shoot one, Miss Jenny."

They slipped up to the crest again through the blowing grass, crouched low in the dusk. Raleigh had his rifle and shooting sticks in one hand. With the other he held Jenny's. His palm and fingers were hot and damp. Or maybe hers were. In a little sag of the hilltop, he pulled her down and lay there beside her. The buffalo still seemed undisturbed, some lying catlike on folded fore-legs, some grazing quietly. One larger cow looked up now and then to scan the grasslands and sniff deeply.

"That's the leader," Raleigh whispered. "An old cow, as usual. They're the wariest. If I can drop her, first shot, we might could do it."

He laid his cartridge belt in the grass close at hand, then slowly sat up to spread his shooting sticks, secured near the top with a wrap of raw-hide to form a V-shaped bipod. He eased the barrel of the Sharps out into the V, cocked the hammer, and leaned forward, kneeling, to snug the sights on target. His finger closed on the trigger . . .

Whump!

Jenny saw dust puff from the old cow's side, about a handspan behind the shoulder. The cow jumped forward a step or two. She coughed. Gagged. Stopped abruptly as bright ropes of blood spilled from her mouth and nostrils. Then she stepped back a pace. She stepped forward again and leaned to sniff at the curious stuff, pawed at it tentatively. More blood poured from her mouth and nostrils.

The rest of the herd had looked up at the shot, watching her, prepared to run if she ran. Now they, too, walked over to sniff the blood, which still poured from the cow's nose with every breath. She stamped impatiently. Two young bull calves started hooking her with their spike-like horns, then suddenly turned on one another in mock combat. The stricken cow went to her knees. Her haunches gave way, her head swayed slowly to the ground. She seemed to fall asleep.

Raleigh had quickly worked the lever that formed the rifle's trigger guard, ejecting the spent case. He threw a fresh shell into the breech and closed the lever with a sharp clack.

Whump!

Another cow leaped at the shot, spewed blood, then dropped to her knees. The herd wheeled in disorder, confused, leaderless. Too much, all at once. A younger cow suddenly came to her senses and started to run.

Click, clack.

Whump!

Raleigh stopped the fleeing cow in her tracks with a quartering shot that knocked her sideways. She skidded on her nose through the grass. Flailed around for a moment. Tried to rise, then collapsed.

"Your brother showed me that shot," Raleigh said. "Pretty, wasn't it?"

When all were down but one of the bull calves, which stood gazing in wonderment at the carnage around him, Raleigh turned to Jenny.

"Your turn?"

"*Lieber Jesus, aber nein* — no!"

She rose stiffly to her feet and started downhill.

"Well then, it's the lobo's night to howl, for sure," Raleigh said. "No mama to protect him, that poor little feller's a goner. Just as you wish, ma'am. You just ankle on back to the horses. Don't pay it no heed. I'll pop the little chap, save him havin' his guts tore out when the wolves catch him."

Jenny stopped.

"I'll do it," she said.

He rolled to one side and Jenny slipped in behind the Sharps. She knelt on one knee. The bull calf went over to one of the cows and began to bawl. He hooked at her and tried to wedge his head under her flank, to get at her udder. But the cow lay dead and heavy. Jenny's throat caught. She felt tears sting behind her eyelids.

She had killed many farm animals — chickens, ducks, sheep, pigs, steers — all of them without a qualm. That was their *Schicksal,* their fate, what *Herr Gott* intended for them. To feed men and women. Yes, she had killed grouse, wild turkeys, many deer, and once — in the autumn beech woods, and unforgettable, a great black bear — but that was in the heat of the chase. This was different. It was murder. Worse yet, the murder of an orphan . . .

The cinnamon calf butted and bawled. He was getting angry at his mother for ignoring him. He knew nothing of death.

Jenny lifted the butt of the rifle to her shoulder. Heavy, heavy. The bipod was set too high for her, so she adjusted it, inching the sticks through the grass. Then she looked through the tang-mounted peep sight. The cinnamon calf stood behind the cow, half obscured by its mother's body.

Jenny steeled herself, took a deep breath, and whistled, once, sharply, through her teeth.

The bull calf looked up.

She saw his face through the peep sight, eyes wide.

She held her breath. Laid the sights on the base of his throat.

She neither heard nor felt the shot, nor did she look to see where the bullet hit. She opened the breech, threw the spent case clear with a musical *ting,* and left the rifle resting in its bipod, muzzle pointing aimlessly into the red westward sky. She walked back down the slope.

Tom Shields was on his way up, whetting the edge of a skinning knife against his steel. He smiled and raised his eyebrows.

"You get one?"

She grunted and walked on past him, not meeting his eyes.

In camp that night she sorted through her clothing. Selected an old ankle-length gray woolen skirt. Cut gores from it, front and back; then, with a needle and heavy thread from her housewife, stitched it into a pair of loose-legged

127

trousers. She was long at her work, beside the fire. Otto and Raleigh turned in early. Tom was out watching the horses. Milo lay in his blankets, watching her with blank, mudpie eyes. They made her feel — *ja, schmutzig.* As if she needed a bath. Then Milo, too, fell asleep, snoring lightly and grinding his teeth with a sound like an emery wheel.

9

Raleigh poured some more whiskey into his tin cup. It was a good, smooth, red Kentucky bourbon; he kept a keg of it in his wagon, usually having just a drink or two at the end of a hard day's killing. But this night, camped among buffalo on the headwaters of Wolf Creek between the North and South Branches of the Canadian, with Milo Sykes on watch, Tom Shields and Otto reloading cartridges, and Jenny knitting quietly beside the fire, he had had more than one or two belts. These recriminatory binges — "high lonesomes" Otto called them — occurred, as best Otto could tell, about once every couple of months, Raleigh drinking himself ever deeper into guilt. Imagined sins . . .

"I can, too, be sure," he said now. "I had him square in my sights. That old .577 Enfield shot true. Have you ever known me to miss, especially at such a range as that? Bead right smack on his chest; then just as I touched off, he twisted to his right, pulling back on that hammerhead pony. His left shoulder took the shot."

"You sound almost proud of it," Jenny said.

"Huh?"

"Proud of killing Stonewall Jackson, the South's greatest general, proud of losing the war.

129

Why else do you go on about it so?"

"Like hell, if you'll pardon me, ma'am. I never was proud of it . . ."

"Then why?"

Silence. Raleigh reached for his cup, drained it, went over to the tent, and drew another dram or two.

"We could of won," he said, when he returned.

"I don't think so," Jenny said. "Mere generalship . . ."

"You don't know the first thing about war," Raleigh said. "Do you know maneuver? Do you know surprise? Do you even know how Blue Light brought it off there at Chancellorsville? Here . . ."

With the haft of his skinning knife, he sketched the battle plan in the dirt beside the fire ring. The coiling Rappahannock. Hooker's Union line deployed near the hairpin of U.S. Ford. Lee's main body a series of dashes in the dirt, facing Hooker, pinning him in position. Then the sweeping arc of Jackson's long march from Catherine Furnace to Dowdall's Tavern around Hooker's right flank, following farm tracks and an unfinished railroad-bed through the Wilderness on out to where Oliver Otis Howard's Hessian division was digging in "with its bum in the air," as Raleigh gleefully put it — a drove of Dutchmen from New York and Pennsylvania dangling out there all by themselves, with no single feature of terrain, neither river nor hill nor swamp, to anchor their vulnerable flank. The mortal sin of defense.

Worse than a mortal sin, for that can be absolved with adequate penance. The *unforgivable* sin. Then Jackson shaking his corps out into line abreast, there in the woods, as the sun sank ever closer to the horizon.

"By God it was great," Raleigh said, his eyes electric beside the fire. "Here's us hid in the woods" — he thumped the dirt with his knife haft — "with the Bluebellies down there below us — no offense, Black Hat, but you boys called us Graybacks, didn't you, like unto some lowly vermin? — their rifles all neatly stacked, you see, Miss Jenny, the mess sergeants gettin' their cookfires goin', big Dutch butchers with their shirts off slaughterin' beeves to fry up for supper, other Dutchmen choppin' trees for breastworks, still others playin' cards or smokin' or singin' songs of home and mother, one gang on toward the back just lazily knockin' a baseball around, and couriers gallopin' hither and yon, and work parties diggin' latrines like as if you Bluebellies was there to stay. All convinced Bobby Lee was retreatin'. But we was all set, near on twenty-six thousand of infantry in butternut and gray, stacked in a line two miles wide, astraddle the turnpike, everyone locked and loaded, bayonets bristlin', and we moved out. *O grand, grand!* Deer and rabbits spooked out ahead of us, warblers and sparrows and a flock of wild turkeys even, out of the cat briars and the steepletop brush. When the Yankees seen the animals come into your lines, some of 'em whooped and hollered, runnin' for their ramrods, lookin' for to pot a nice bit of meat, others wavin' their caps like they was spectatin' at a parade. Hah! they shut up, though, soon as they seen us, you bet you — skedaddlin' hell-for-leather away as we come a-crashin' down the hill. Some of 'em slashin' the knapsack straps off their backs as they ran, I seen it. And all of us comin' on, bayonets flashin', barefoot and awful and whoopin' that grand old caterwaul . . ."

He gave a joyous, drunken rebel yell, which startled Milo Sykes and set the horses and mules all a-flutter. Then Raleigh drank off his cup once more, grinning awfully and wonderfully, whiskey trickling down his chin.

Jenny felt a stab of fear. Not from the rebel yell, but from the wild look of him — a vein pulsing thick on his forehead, his hectic cheeks, the palpable heat pouring off him in waves that matched his rapid pulse. He was living it all again. His blood was up. He had ignited. Now she knew how men looked in war. She had seen the same fire in the eyes of a pair of battling bulls, at home in Wisconsin, slamming and hooking into each other even as their lifeblood flowed away, unheeded. Vati could never have felt that hot. Had Otto lit up that way in his battles? *Herr Gott,* but of course . . .

The fear she felt transmuted itself subtly into . . . what?

Excitement.

Tom Shields sat at the edge of the firelight,

listening. He liked to hear Captain McKay speak of the war. Captain McKay fired up like a Cheyenne Elk Soldier. Tom could feel, even at a distance, the captain's joyous love of combat. The tactics and strategy, though, made no sense to him. He and his friends, if they were to attack an enemy, would have gone straight for him. Spent that joy directly at close quarters. Honorably. Not sneaking like cautious prairie wolves around the enemy's rear to hit him from behind. Those tactics were better suited to stealing horses or women. Tom had heard massed gunfire of the sort the captain mentioned only once, at Sand Creek in Colorado. He had been just a boy when Chivington and his Volunteers hit the Cheyenne encampment. The spiders were likkered up plenty that morning, you could smell them coming. They fired a lot of bullets, but few of them hit. Their big weak horses charged wheezing through the village, knocking lodges askew, trampling some of the older people who could not dodge them. Recalling his own emotions at the time, Tom could honestly say he was not frightened. Cautious, yes, and quick to take cover under the bank of the creek. But not frightened. A spider trooper had ridden at him as he ran for the creek, tried to ride him down, swinging a saber at Tom's head. Tom had calculated the horse's approach, ducked easily under the clumsy swing, then picked up a rock and bounced it off the trooper's head as he galloped away. It was like counting a coup. What he regretted about

133

that morning was that he had not had the presence of mind, after dodging the saber, to leap up and snatch the reeling trooper from his horse by his long, greasy hair, then brain him with another rock and lift his scalp. It was reddish-yellow hair, rather like Captain McKay's, and though the Cheyennes rarely took spider scalps, because white soldiers wore their hair too short, this one would have looked good on a lodgepole. Perhaps one day he'd get another chance.

Often at night, while Jenny was washing the dishes and Tom was out checking the stock, Otto and Raleigh would sit beside the campfire, sipping tin cups of whiskey from Raleigh's jug and singing old, familiar songs from the war. Milo didn't sing — *Gott sei dank,* Jenny thought — but accompanied the others on a harmonica. He surprised her with his virtuosity. These songfests often turned into friendly musical duels, the two Southerners needling Otto with spirited renditions of "Dixie" or "The Bonnie Blue Flag" while her brother countered in kind with "John Brown's Body" or "Hold On, Abraham" or, best of all, "Marching Through Georgia." That song really burned Sykes up.

Raleigh had a strong, sure baritone voice, a far better sense of pitch and key than Otto. Jenny liked to watch him from the safe precincts of the dishpan. She liked the way his blue eyes sparkled. She liked the winsome twist that came to his lips, the playful lilt to his words that subverted the

proud, high-flown sentiments of the more patri-
otic songs. His parody of "Yankee Doodle" always delighted her.

> Now Yankee Doodle had in mind
> To whup the Southern traitors
> Because those Rebels wouldn't eat
> His codfish and pertaters.
>
> Yankee Doodle, fa la la,
> Yankee Doodle dandy,
> So keep your courage up, my boy,
> And take a drink of brandy . . .
>
> I've shot a pile of Mexicans
> And kilt some Injuns, too, sir,
> But I never thought to draw a bead
> On Yankee-Doodle-doo, sir.
>
> Yankee Doodle, fa la la,
> Yankee Doodle dandy,
> And so to keep his courage up
> He took a drink of brandy.

She wandered over to the fire one evening as
he was finishing the tune. Looking up, Raleigh
winked at her and offered his cup.

"No, thank you," she said, suddenly stiff and
flustered. Then chided herself. He certainly
meant no harm by the gesture. You're acting like
a silly schoolgirl, she thought. Well, of course —
until recently that's just what you were.

135

Raleigh grinned, asked Milo if he knew a song called "The Southern Soldier Boy." Sykes nodded. "Miss Jenny might like this one," Raleigh said. "I've changed the words some, but that's a soldier's due." He took a sip of whiskey, cleared his throat.

> *Raleigh is my sweetheart's name,*
> *He's off to the wars and gone.*
> *He's fighting for his Jenny dear,*
> *His sword is buckled on.*

He winked at her again, then put on a solemn face.

> *He's fighting for his own true love,*
> *His foes he does defy.*
> *He is the darling of my heart,*
> *My Southern soldier boy.*
>
> *Oh, if in battle he were slain*
> *I'm certain I should die . . .*

Then in a deeper voice, his eyes twinkling —

> *But Milo here will come, my dear,*
> *To dry your weeping eye.*

Raleigh guffawed, Milo cackled, and even Otto joined in. Jenny felt herself blushing. She pulled herself together. "All right, now it's my turn," she said. She stood beside Otto and took his hand in hers. "I'm sure Mr. Sykes knows this tune, it was popular on both sides during the war. 'Was My Brother in the Battle?' And I'll take a sip of that 'brandy' now, Captain McKay, just to warm my throat."

Milo tried a few bars, knocked the spit out of his mouth harp against the palm of one horny hand, then nodded his readiness. Jenny's sweet alto sounded in the darkness. She stared straight into Raleigh's eyes.

> Tell me, tell me, weary soldier,
> From the rude and stirring wars,
> Was my brother in the battle
> Where you gained those noble scars?
>
> Was my brother in the battle
> When the noble highland host
> Were so wrongfully outnumbered
> On the Carolina coast?
>
> He was ever brave and valiant
> And I know he never fled.
> Was his name among the wounded,
> Or numbered with the dead?
>
> Was my brother in the battle
> When the Black Hats boldly came
> To the rescue of our nation
> And salvation of our fame?
>
> Did he struggle for the Union

Midst the thunder and the rain
Till he fell among the bravest
On that bleak Virginia plain?

Tell me, tell me, weary soldier,
Will he never come again?
Does he suffer with the wounded
Or lie silent with the slain?

Raleigh watched her intently as she sang, his eyes misting slightly at the sentimental words, then brightening to the barbed humor of the "Black Hats" reference. "Just beautiful, Miss Jenny," he said, applauding. "Though I do believe you got the words a bit wrong. Those were *Rebels* fighting for *Old Blue Light*. Ask your brother."

Milo Sykes rose to his feet. "I'll go out and check the hides one more time," he said. "Can't trust that redskin to do it proper."

"Sho'," Raleigh said. Then to Otto and Jenny: "How's about 'Lorena'? That's a song we can all agree on, not a danged word about the war in it." Their three voices joined in harmony . . .

Oh, the years creep slowly by, Lorena . . .

Milo walked out into the dark. His eyes, too, had filled at the words of Jenny's song. *Damned Yankees. You bet my brothers were in the battle.* Two of them, Hod and Virgil, dead at Chickamauga; Cyrus — the youngest and most promising —

blown in half by a cannonball on the slopes of Kennesaw Mountain.

Wolves were singing in the hills to the east of camp. The music attracts 'em, Milo thought. They'd sung like that near his camp in the Bayou Salado every night when he played his French harp. He liked to hear them. That meant more hides. He'd been wolfing then, right after the war. Every evening he shot an antelope or a buffalo, laced the carcass with strychnine, which he carried in a little blue bottle around his neck, and then in the morning went out to skin the dead wolves that had fed on the meat. Stiff, snarling faces. At night he'd play the harmonica, more wolves would be drawn to his camp, and the next day he'd start all over again. Good wages, wolfing. But it was too dangerous now, Injuns on the warpath. A man alone in the mountains wouldn't stand a chance.

10

They hunted their way to the Yarner, taking their time, gathering hides as they traveled. Near the headwaters of the Prairie Dog Fork of Red River they saw the Llano Estacado rising ahead of them from horizon to horizon as if the earth had suddenly broken on a north-to-south line, one part of it rising like a cracked china platter half a thousand feet above the prairie floor.

They made their way slowly up the escarpment and found buffalo beyond counting. Jenny had never seen a bigger sky, or a bleaker one. The winds, even on warm days, blew cold and steady from the northwest. She expected to see the ghosts of Coronado's conquistadores trotting on horseback over the prairies in casques and breastplates, their bones shivering. Raleigh had explained the plateau's history to her. "It's so big and flat that Coronado's men had to drive stakes every few miles so that they could find their way back. That why it's the Staked Plain."

Otto and Raleigh called a halt two days later. They had swung north along the Yarner and made a semi-permanent camp near Palo Duro Creek, a small dribble that assured them a permanent though muddy water supply. From here, if the Indians made trouble, they wouldn't be too far from Camp Supply or even Fort Dodge to make a successful fighting retreat.

Each evening when Tom and Milo rolled in with the day's take, Jenny walked over to what they called the hide yard — a level, stoneless patch of sunny ground selected by the men to peg the skins on — and stood in the wind to make notes in her ledger. She wrote down the numbers and size of the buffalo Tom and Milo had skinned that day. Some days they managed only twenty or thirty between them, some days twice that, one very long day (and well into the moonlit night), in excess of 120. She wrote her totals in a very precise hand and showed the figures to the skinners when she was done and asked them to make their marks in the margin. That way there could be no arguments later.

The agreement Otto and Raleigh had reached with the men called for Milo to receive thirty cents for each buffalo skinned, Tom twenty.

"But that's not fair," she protested to Otto, out of earshot of the skinners. "Tom's faster than Milo, and he never tears a hide."

"*Ja, doch zwar,*" Otto said. "True enough. But Milo has a wife and five children back East. Tom isn't married and he doesn't really need the money. What would he do with it? Just drink it up or gamble it away, like all the red devils."

"Have you ever known him to drink or gamble?"

"No, but they all do. Ask anyone. Ask Tom."

Jenny thought privately that it was foolish for Otto and Raleigh to pay the skinners at a fixed rate per hide. Jobless men were now pouring onto the Buffalo Range, killing buffalo right and left. Because of the Panic the railroads had ceased laying track. Farms and small businesses were failing across the nation. Those who were out of work looked increasingly to the West for a chance to scratch up a living. At this rate the hide market would soon be glutted. The price paid by the big buyers in Dodge City, from $3 to $5 per hide, was bound to decrease. It was probably falling right now. Better to pay the skinners a percentage — say, perhaps, 5 percent — of the price received for their hides.

Otto and Raleigh also allowed the skinners to keep the meat not required for camp use. Each evening when he returned to camp, Tom Shields had a pile of choice tongues, hams, loins, and humps stowed beneath the rolls of hide in the wagonbed. These he brined in a pit he'd dug, lined with green hide, then cured slowly over a cool, smoky fire enclosed by a hood of tightly woven willow withes overlaid with bull hide. Milo Sykes left his tongues, hams, loins, and humps to rot, even boasted about it.

"Nigger work," he'd say, watching Tom busy at the brine tub. "A white man oughtn't be eatin' that buffler tongue anyways — why, he'd start jabberin' Injun talk."

But Jenny's thrift could not abide the waste. One morning after cleaning up around camp, drawing water from a small creek a quarter of a mile back in the cottonwoods, baking the day's bread, setting a pot of stew to bubble slowly near the fire, roasting green coffee beans and then cranking them through the patent grinder, she saddled Vixen to ride out in the direction of the guns. By now she could distinguish the heavy boom of Raleigh's Big Fifty from the more rifle-like crack of Otto's .44–90. Milo skinned with Raleigh, so she rode for the sharper sound. She was looking for Tom Shields.

She found him hard at work in a little swale where more than a dozen gigantic black bulls lay slain, all in a heap. The spring wagon was off to one side, the mules cropping dried grass, oblivious of the dead buffalo. Otto was nowhere in sight. She looked at the buffalo. She had never seen full-grown bulls before.

"*Herr Gott,* these are the biggest we've shot so far!"

"Yah," he said. "We found 'em just this morning. Been looking for the grown-up bulls all along, but they keep away, out in the hills. From the Deer-Rutting Moon until a few weeks after the Hard-Face Moon, these big bulls, what we call scrub-horns, they hang by themselves. Like a war party. Only come to the cows again when they want to make some babies."

"What are those months in American, that Deer-Rutting thing and the other one?"

"Cripes," Tom muttered, looking away. "I never can remember the English words. Uh —

143

November, yah! That's when the deer fuck. To maybe February?"

"Rut," Jenny corrected him, feeling suddenly prissy and schoolmarmish. Yet the simple, unaffected way he had said the ugly word, without leering or sniggering, made it not quite so shocking.

"Well, they certainly are big, much bigger than the cows and kips we've been killing," she said. "But what I wanted to ask you, would you show me how to butcher out the choice cuts? Milo leaves all those buffalo to rot. Doesn't even take the tongues or humps."

Tom nodded. White spiders waste everything, most of them. There had been times, in the Moon of Hard Faces, when he and his family would have given their rifles, probably even their ponies, for a single rancid buffalo haunch. But this white-eye woman, maybe she understood. Maybe she wasn't a waster.

"Tongues are easy," he said. "I once seen a greenhorn try to cut one out by reaching down the buffalo's throat." He shook his head. "Took him forever, and he cut his hand about ten times doing it. Here's the right way."

He stuck his knife hilt-deep beneath a dead bull's chin, slit back toward the throat, reached in with his free hand to grab the base of the tongue, then slid the knife blade in below the grasping hand and sliced across the tongue's root. He withdrew the heavy piece of meat. He laughed, delighted with himself.

"You get you a good edge on your knife and keep it that way," he said. "That's all there is to it."

"What about the hump?"

Tom went over to a bull he'd already skinned. The naked hump stood pink and solid, marbled with white tallow. He slapped it and grinned.

"All muscle, sweet meat," he said. "There's ribs that stick up along the center of it, inside, like the spines on the top fin of a catfish, you know? Here, you do it like this."

He sliced deep along the lower edge of the hump, to where it sloped down and disappeared into the line of the buffalo's wide back. Then cut down vertically from the top, along one side of the upright ribs. A thick slab of meat fell off into his hand, about three feet long and the diameter of a man's thigh at the front end. He laid it across the buffalo's skinned flank.

"You want to cut out this hunk here." He pointed with the tip of the knife. "It's all gristle." He whacked it away.

He repeated the process on the other side. Jenny looked at the exposed dorsal ribs. They were about ten inches high at the top of their curve, tapering down in size as they went back along the spine and disappeared. Like a catfish, all right, she thought. A one-ton catfish.

"You can take out the backstraps, too," Tom said. He showed her how. Then he showed her how to section each haunch into three hefty hams, by separating the meat at the seams

145

between muscle groups.

She thanked him and stood her horse.

"When you got you a pile of meat," Tom said, "cut a travvy. Then horse your whittlins back to camp. Ol' Vix here ought be able to pull about three hundred pounds on the travvy poles, maybe more. Put your meat in my brine tub if you like. We'll sort it out later, and I'll show you how to make your own tub if you want." He smiled up at her, holding Vixen's curb rein. "Or we can do our meat together. We can smoke it in my little smoke tepee. You'll get good money for that meat back in Dodge, six or seven cents a pound for humps and hams, but it adds up. For tongues, if they're pickled and smoked good, you'll get eight or nine buckskins a dozen, 'specially now, just before Christmas. Charlie Myers tells me all the folks back East eat buffler tongue for Christmas dinner. Good money. Buy you some pretty foo-faraw, you know."

She neck-reined Vixen around, then turned in the saddle to look back at him. Foofaraw? That meant girlish fripperies.

"By the way, Tom," she asked sweetly, all innocence but suddenly seething, "what do you do with *your* money?"

He laughed again, his bitter laugh this time. He'd caught the nuance.

"What else? Get drunk. Play faro or monte. Maybe go on the warpath a bit. I'm half Indian, ain't I?"

He turned and walked back to his skinning. He

was actually using his money to buy guns, new Winchesters, the 1873 model. He cached them, well coated with buffalo tallow and wrapped in oiled rawhide to preserve them from rust, in a cave near the Pawnee Fork. He had purchased eighteen of them so far. But it was none of her business. No white spiders would know of it, none except the merchant, Herr Zimmerman, and he didn't mind so long as he got his $45 for each rifle. If he ever talked about the matter, Tom would cut his throat. Herr Zimmerman knew that.

Jenny followed the sound of Raleigh McKay's rifle and found his killing ground about a mile to the south, on the edge of the Palo Duro breaks. He, too, had located the big scrub-horns. Milo had skinned out about twenty of them so far, and she paused on the rise to watch him. Unlike Tom, who skinned entirely by hand, Milo used his mule team and wagon to help. After slicing the hide with the point of his ripping knife along the insides of the legs, around the tops of the hooves, and again around the neck just back of the ears, he worked it free near the slices. Next he pegged the head down with a long steel spike, using a heavy oak-headed mallet to drive the spike through the buffalo's nose and into the hard earth. He tied a rope, secured to the rear axle of the wagon, around a knot of gathered neck hide, then chucked his mules forward.

The tow rope tautened, the bull lurched a bit,

and the hide slowly peeled away with a sticky, sucking sound. Like pulling off a wet union suit, Jenny thought.

Now and then Milo halted the team, leaped down, and helped the hide along with his crescent-shaped skinning knife, working the adhesions loose as the mules pulled. But still the hide tore in places. Jenny could see that such a short-cut method really required three skinners, one to drive the team and the other two to help the hide come loose with their knives. No wonder so many of Milo's hides were ripped when he brought them in. Each careless rip, Otto had told her, meant ten or twenty cents off the price they'd get for the hide back in Dodge City.

So far Milo hadn't noticed her, but when he straightened to rub his back after peeling a hide, he did. He dove without hesitation for the leeside of the wagon, grabbed his Army Springfield musket from where it leaned against the bed, and crouched behind the wheel, peering out like a frightened muskrat.

"Mr. Sykes, it's me — Jenny Dousmann!" she yelled. My God, he must have taken me for an Indian, she thought. Not a hundred yards away. Must be nearsighted. Blind as a bat. That's why he doesn't shoot buffalo, only skins them. He can't see far enough to shoot a shaggy.

He was fiddling with a wheel nut when she rode down, pretending nothing had happened. He looked up, more sullen than usual.

"What do you want?"

"I want to take the humps, hams, and tongues from Raleigh's buffalo," she said. "I plan to smoke them and bring them back to Dodge with us."

"Them aren't the captain's buffler no more," he said. "Not after he shoots 'em. Moment they hit the ground, they're mine. That's our contract."

"But you've taken the hides," she said. "You never bring in the meat. It just lies out here to rot, or to feed the wolves and buzzards."

"It's still mine. I can do with it what I please, jest like that red nigger Two Shields does with his. Keep 'em or let 'em rot, it's up to me. Cap'n said so. It's in the contract."

His eyes narrowed shrewdly, mud in the cracks of a sidewalk.

"But I reckon I could sell the meat over to ye, if ye want it that bad."

"And if I don't want to pay you?"

"Well, leave it rot, then," he said. He turned his back on her and snorted.

"Mr. Sykes, you said it was *nigger* work to cure and smoke that meat, that's why you wouldn't do it. Well, I want to do some nigger work. You won't be losing any money by letting me take that meat, which would otherwise just go to waste. You're already getting half again as much per hide for skinning as Tom Shields, who's a far better skinner than you are. What's more, while you're out here in our employ, your room and board come free of charge. Perhaps in return for your generosity I should start charging you for the meals I cook and serve to you, and the filthy clothes I wash. I'm not only your landlady, Mr. Sykes, I'm also a partner in this corporation. And I *will* have that meat."

She rode to the farthest skinned carcass, dismounted, and pulled her butcher knife. Just as she was about to make her first incision, Sykes came stumping up at a run. He grabbed for her shoulder, his face working, white as a bleached skull as he wrenched her around.

"You nigger-lovin' honyock bitch . . ."

He raised an arm to swat her.

She wrenched herself away, crouched, and flashed the butcher knife. Held it low, point first, toward his belly.

"Keep your hands off me or I'll cut you. By God, I will. I'll rip you like you rip those hides."

"Hey-hey, what is this?" Raleigh yelled. He trotted down to them on his sorrel. "What'sa matter here, Miss Jenny? Milo?"

"This bitch tried to steal my meat," Milo said. "It's in our contract . . ."

"Enough about that *verdammter* contract," Jenny said. "This meat's just going to waste, and this redneck skunk . . ."

"An' you wanna make some Christly money off it, you cunt!"

"Easy now," Raleigh said. "Put that knife away, Miss Jenny. Let's not be cuttin' anyone. Now, Milo, you ease up on the profanity and leave her have that meat if you got no use for it. I'll give

150

you a nickel more a hide to make up for it. Thirty-five cents a shaggy. How's that?"

"Well . . ."

"*Das stinkt,* Captain McKay," Jenny said. "He's already being paid too *verdammt* much, and you're skimming part of that extra nickel from my share of the profits."

"Now, now." Raleigh smiled, eyes twinkling. "You just go ahead and take your meat, Miss Jenny. Milo, come over here with me."

They went toward the wagon.

Jenny bent to her work. Her heart was pumping hard. She would have cut him, *ja* sure. Like butchering a hog.

By the time she was finished, Milo and Raleigh had hunted on, out of sight. She straightened, stiff, and held her hands to the small of her back. She stretched. This wasn't like doing dishes. It wasn't even like kneading bread dough. Yet it had seemed so easy when Tom did it.

She was just looking around for the nearest stand of trees, figuring to chop poles for a travois, as Tom had suggested, when she heard the squeak of wagon wheels. Tom came over the rise.

"Thought I'd take your meat back to camp in the wagon, if you were still here," he said. "I'm going over to help your brother with his skinning and then head in — save you a bit of heavy hauling."

"Appreciate it."

151

He studied the pile of tongues, humps, hams, and backstraps. "You did pretty good, first time."

"Thanks."

He hadn't laughed. Perhaps she *was* doing well.

"But that's a lot more than three hundred pounds," he said. "Good thing I come by."

When he finished his killing for the day, Raleigh left Sykes to skin out. He rode northwest toward where he'd last heard Otto's shots. He had tried to soothe Sykes's ruffled feathers, but the cracker-eater was still all swole. Angry words had passed, and finally Raleigh had been forced to conduct Sykes through a brief but strenuous exercise in military discipline. He'd knocked Sykes on his ass and taken out a tooth with the punch. It was the only form of instruction his kind would understand. Raleigh knew this type of man. Deep down he was one of them himself — a hardscrabble Southern plowboy raised on red dirt and hookworm, grits and greens.

Not anymore, though. By Act of Congress he'd been pronounced an officer and gentleman of the Army of Northern Virginia, Confederate States of America, and though he often made light of that fact, he still carried in his war bag the parchment to prove it, with Secretary of War James Alexander Seddon's signature across the bottom, dated June 16, 1864. Sure, he thought, but no Congress left to vouch for its validity, no C.S.A. left to defend, in gentlemanly fashion or otherwise. His commission was worth no more than a bankroll of Confederate shin-plasters. Good enough to patch bullets with, or perhaps start a fire.

He found Otto and Tom on a windy slope, skinning the last of their buffalo. The spring wagon sagged with the weight of the day's hides. Big scrub-horns, all.

"We near got enough for a run to Dodge," Raleigh said. "I tumbled more than seventy today, and it looks like you did just as well."

"Sixty-eight," Otto said. "This new rifle shoots true, even in a wind, but only for the first couple of hours. Then it starts fouling something fierce. I think it's these damned bottleneck cartridges, make the bullet fit too snug on the lands, and they scrub the soft lead right off it."

"Go back to your old Fifty."

"Too much drift in this wind," Otto said. "I haven't got your eye for Kentucky windage. Maybe I'll get me a Ballard next time we're in Dodge, or one of those new Remington rolling-block .44s, see if it shoots any cleaner."

"Anyways, we ought to send some hides back north," Raleigh continued. "You and Milo could go up there, get you that new rifle while you're at it."

"I don't need one *that* bad."

"Well, one of us ought to go along with Sykes. He had a little run-in with Miss Jenny this afternoon, she wanted to save the meat from his buffalo and he got all hot about it. Though the dim redneck bastard won't stir his bones enough to butcher it out, let alone brine it himself. I tried to calm him and he got sassy with me. Had to knock him down, finally. Skinned my knuckles on his rotten teeth, hope I don't get poisoned." He showed Otto the barked fist. "Anyways, I can't ride north with him, the mood he's in, and if we send him alone he might make off with the money once he's sold our hides. I suppose Tom could go along, but he couldn't stop Milo from swipin' our money, not in Dodge he couldn't. Mister Lo don't swing much weight in that town."

"*Ja, doch zwar.*"

"You could leave here tomorrow, head up north-by-east past Owl's Head Butte to the Cimarron, then cut the road from Camp Supply. Ought to make Dodge in a long three days, if it don't rain none."

Otto scanned the sky. "Doesn't look like anything's coming our way. Hey, Tom — is it going to rain or snow in the next few days?"

Tom didn't even look up from his skinning. "Nope," he said. "You never know with a norther, though."

Raleigh said, "When you get to Dodge, why don't you fire Sykes and sign us on a new skinner? Maybe two. We're into the big bulls now."

When Otto told Jenny that he'd be leaving for Dodge with the hides the following morning, she felt a momentary qualm. "I'll be gone only a week," he reassured her. "And I'm taking Sykes with me. Heard about your run-in with him to-day, so he won't be here to make trouble. Tom's a good lad, though, and Raleigh — as he never tires of telling us — is a Southern officer and a true gentleman. He'll take care of you."

"Don't worry about me," Jenny said blithely, but she was embarrassed that her concern had shown.

11

Raleigh sat by the fire, sipping bourbon again. He had been careful not to pay too much attention to Miss Jenny while her big brother was around. Though the men were friends and partners, Raleigh knew that even Yankees could prove murderously protective of their sisters. He'd seen his partner in enough fights, in saloons or out on the Buffalo Range, with fists or with guns, to know that the Dutchman was no coward, even if the regimental hat Otto wore hadn't told him so. He also suspected that in a fistfight Otto might get the better of him. The Dutchman had a longer reach and moved fast as a striking blacksnake. Otto was strong, too. Raleigh had seen him sling three rolled bullhides in one armload onto the wagon. Green hides, at that. A green hide weighed anywhere from eighty-five to a hundred pounds.

But now Otto was gone. For at least six days, likely a week or more. Raleigh knew when a girl was interested in him. You can tell it by the way she moves and watches you, he thought, the way she talks to you. If you were a man like Raleigh McKay, you saved time by noticing these things. You didn't waste jaw on ladies that showed no interest. Consolidate that interest, win Jenny firmly to his side, and perhaps by the time ol' Otto gets back we might could show him a full-blown, honorable courtship.

He swallowed some whiskey, leaned over to the keg, and drew some more.

Raleigh's intentions — strangely enough, he suddenly realized — extended beyond a quick roll in the hay, nice as that would surely be.

Oh yes, there's a long, cold winter coming, on up to the Yarner, where the northers, by all accounts, roar ice-blue clear through the Fourth of July. But Jenny can cook, too, and I've seen her shoot. She's passable for pretty, if you liked 'em a bit on the gristly side, all muscle, no fat. I sure don't mind. She's clean, she's not a boozer, but no Christer either. And she sings good, at least for a Dutch girl. Almost good as an American. Why, come to think on it, she's downright intelligent. Wish she wouldn't wear them pants, though.

What the hell was he tryin' to argue himself into? Or out of. An armful of warm girl was the best bedwarmer he knew, and if she was a good catch to boot . . . hell then, why not marry her?

He had enough money now to marry. A few more years in the hide game and he'd have even more. Maybe him and Jenny could stake some land somewheres, up in the Smoky Hills. Prove it out fast, with her bustlin' ways. Say, that's pretty country up there, we'll run beef critters, maybe buy a bit more land later. A thousand acres at a time dependin' on how the prices go. Otto can come visit. We'll go huntin' together, the three of us, antelope and blacktails. Jenny likes to kill prongbucks, Tom Shields says. We'll kill off all the lobos, though, first thing; a little strychnine will do it, and good money to be made off their pelts. Poor Lo ought to be tame by then, with the shaggies gone, tied to the rez by the government beef-and-blanket allotment, troops nearby to chase his sorry ass back if he gets uppity. Maybe me and Jenny'll have young'uns, too. Why not? Name the boy for me, the girl for her. She can name the second pair. Or maybe I'll call the second boy after my daddy, the second girl after Mother. We'll name one for Otto, too, one that comes later. Ottoline if it's a girl. That's a pretty name, Ottoline.

"Otto-*leen?*" he asked the stars. The stars had no answer.

He walked out from the fire and looked up at the sky.

Cold out here in the Indian Nations. All them dead Cheyennes on the Washita. Black Kettle's ghost . . .

Why sure, that's what he'd do — marry Miss Jenny Dousmann. Otto had been gone a day now and he'd better make his move quick if he wanted to be sure of her by the time Otto got back. He went to the fire and rolled himself in his blankets. That's what he'd do, he'd woo her. Soon he was snoring.

Maybe I'm getting too white, Tom Shields

thought. You hang around with the spiders long enough, you begin to think like them. Take the simple matter of bathing. As a boy, growing up Indian, he had bathed in a cold stream every morning of his life, winter or summer alike. Sa-sis-e-tas lodges were always near water. White spiders didn't live that way, not the hide men anyway. Now weeks often went by with no running water. At least in this camp there was the creek nearby. He felt human again only if he had his morning wash. The spiders were happy enough to survive on the stale water in their barrels. They usually camped on the buffalo grounds, where there was no water, only muddy wallows. At those times Tom couldn't bathe if he wanted to. He had tried to sneak water from the barrels and wash himself, but Captain McKay caught him at it once and scolded him. "Don't waste the water," he yelled. "Our lives may depend on it. What if the Indians come and besiege us?"

If the Sa-sis-e-tas come, there won't be any siege, Tom thought. You'll all be dead before you can wake up.

Then there was this question of killing. No, not exactly killing, all spiders were natural killers, but what came after the killing. Mr. Dousmann had gotten angry at what Tom did to those Snakes, the horse thieves. Tom had only been protecting himself, all of them actually, from the revenge of the Snake ghosts. A blind ghost cannot see you, and even if it could, a ghost without hands or feet

159

could not get close or do harm.

But then, in the middle of Mr. Dousmann's sermon, Tom had suddenly seen what he was getting at. Yes, they were just boys, no older than he had been the night he stole Wind Blows, clumsy boys who knew little of war. Killing them was no more of a challenge than killing the yellow calves of the buffalo, and among the Sa-sis-e-tas only boys killed calves. There would be weeping in the lodges of the Snakes when those boys did not return. Mothers would cut off their hair, gash their heads, and if one of the sons was a favorite, his mother would chop off a joint of her finger. His own mother would have done so.

Too much white spider.

But the girl was pretty. She reminded Tom constantly of his mother. Especially when she talked Dutch words. His mother would do that when she was angry, or when she felt sad and homesick for her spider people. She would croon him a little song in Dutch, when he was small. Something about *das Veilchen,* the violet . . . When he was sick she made him soup from plump young prairie chickens and wild leeks, no other woman of the Sa-sis-e-tas did that. They made blood soup. Her hair was yellow, too, like Jenny Dousmann's. Some of the other boys said his mother looked like E-hyoph-sta, the Yellow-Haired Woman in the old tribal stories, the woman who had brought buffalo to the Sa-sis-e-tas.

Long ago, that was. The Cut-Arm People were

starving, eating only skunks and turtles and bitter roots. Yellow-Haired Woman came from beneath a spring on a magical mountain and brought buffalo galloping after her. She showed the People how to kill them and eat them, make lodge skins and shields and bull boats from their hides, scrapers and shovels and knives and needles from their bones, thread from their sinews, rope from their wool, water buckets from their stomachs, glue from their skins and hooves. The last thing she said was that when the buffalo were gone, the People would soon follow. The Cut-Arm People begged her to stay, or at least to return if ever the buffalo disappeared. She had only smiled at them. She went back to her spring on the mountain.

When Tom was very young he had asked his mother if she was Yellow-Haired Woman. His mother said she wasn't. Then she started crying.

Tom rolled out of his blankets, under the spring wagon. The fire was down to embers. A half-eaten moon lay low in the west. He pulled on his coat and hat, slung Wind's apishamore over his shoulder, and picked up the Springfield. The rifle was cold in his hands. There was already a round in the chamber. He walked silently to where Wind Blows stood grazing in the flat beyond the cottonwoods. She heard him coming and tossed her head. He placed the soft, tanned, buffalo-hide apishamore on her back, smoothed it, vaulted onto her back, and with his knees guided her southwest, first at a fast walk, then, when they were far enough from the camp, urged her into a gallop.

He rode fast for half an hour, to the spot where Raleigh had killed his last buffalo the previous day. There he stopped, near the top of a prairie swell. Tom took two bones from his war bag. One was the sinuous antler of a young spikehorn elk, with a snake's head carved at the thicker end. The antler had forty-five notches carved into its back, which was painted blue. The belly of the snake bone was painted yellow. It was a ceremonial rattle, and it represented a snake revered by the Sa-sis-e-tas, the blue racer, which came from the sun. The other bone was from the shank of a prongbuck. Tom ran the shank bone along the notched back of the snake. The rattle sounded loud and ominous in the quiet prairie night. An answering rattle came from just beyond the crest of the swell. Tom rattled twice in reply. Three horsemen topped the rise. Tom took off his hat so they would recognize him.

They were young men of about Tom's age, two of them naked except for breechclouts and knee-high leggings. They all wore their hair in braids adorned with the tail feathers of an eagle. The two bare-chested men carried cased bows, with quivers of arrows across their backs, and led a string of three tall horses. The third man, who preceded them, wore a tattered blue U.S. Cavalry blouse and carried a lance which was shaped at the butt end like a shepherd's crook. The shaft of the lance was wrapped in strips of otter skin, with pairs of bald-eagle tail feathers attached at four places. A long-barreled rifle rested crosswise on his pony's withers. It looked like a Sharps, Tom thought. The horses they led were not Indian ponies.

"Two Shields," the man with the crooked lance said.

"Crazy for Horses," Tom answered in Sa-sis-e-tas. "Elk Soldiers. What news of the People?"

Crazy for Horses leaned from his pony and punched Tom lightly on the shoulder. "Bad since you left us. But it shall be better now that I have counted coup on you." They both laughed, and the others joined in.

They were Tom's comrades of many battles from his soldier band, the Him-o-weh-yuhk-is, or Elkhorn Scrapers, commonly called Elk Soldiers, as the Dog Men were called Dog Soldiers and the Red Shields called Bull Soldiers. There were seven traditional soldier bands among the Sa-sis-e-tas. The Elk Soldiers were also called Blue Soldiers, for the U.S. Army jackets they sometimes wore. They had killed sixty white-spider troopers near Fort Phil Kearny and taken the clothing from the dead. Crazy for Horses had been Tom's best friend since that fight. Cut Ear and Walks like Badger were younger, but good soldiers.

Crazy pulled a redstone pipe from his war bag. Tom produced a tobacco pouch of antelope hide from his coat pocket. They filled the pipe and lit it, offering smoke first to the earth, then to the east, to call the blessing of the Medicine Arrows

163

on their meeting, all still on horseback as they puffed and blew. Then Crazy dismounted and the rest followed suit. They squatted by their ponies as they refilled the pipe and passed it around, smoking now for pleasure while they talked, as the white spiders did. The talk was of births and deaths, ponies stolen, buffalo hunts, love affairs begun and ended, of raids on enemy camps, and of the four beautiful *noot-uhk-e-a*, the girl Elk Soldiers of the band — in short, Tom thought, what comrades-in-arms of every nation discuss, wherever they meet.

"When did you spot me?" he asked.

Crazy gestured with his thumb toward his chest, then toward Wind Blows, pointed to his eye, and made the sign for "night laid aside," meaning "yesterday."

"That is when you allowed me to see you as well," Tom said.

"And you signed us to meet you at this place," Crazy agreed. "That was wise of you. When we saw your pony we thought a white spider had killed you and stolen her. We were going to kill her rider and lift his ugly hair and take your pony back to her People. We did not recognize you in your spider costume, which is truly very ugly. And your hair — you had such beautiful long braids before you joined the spiders. Then you saw us and made the signs."

"It's good you came," Tom said quickly. He, too, missed his braids. "I have rifles for you. Not here, though. Two days' ride to the north, beyond the Buffalo Bull, even beyond the Flint River."

The Buffalo Bull was the river the spiders called Cimarron. The Flint River they called the Arkansas. He told Crazy how to find the cave on the Pawnee Fork where he'd cached the rifles.

"They are Yellow Boys," he said, raising an imaginary Winchester to his shoulder and working the lever. Then he made the sign for "eighteen." "Bring them to Oh-kóhm, my father," he said.

"Your father said we should seek you down here," Cut Ear said. "During the time you've been gone, he has been on a great journey of his own — with the other Old Man Chiefs to the big camp of the spiders. What they call Washington. There they heard nothing but lies, of course. He wishes you to continue on your mission, learning the spiders' true intentions, and getting more guns for us. Your mother still mourns your leaving . . ."

"I've told the spiders I hunt with that they are both dead."

"Your mother says you must dress warmly, even here in the sunny South," Cut Ear continued, grinning openly now. "You must also avoid being killed by the Apaches, who are very cruel. And you must under no circumstances marry a woman of the Hev-a-tan-iu, the Rope People of the Southern Cheyenne, for their girls are all horse thieves and have the spider pox."

"Why did you tell the spiders your parents were

dead?" Crazy asked.

"Oh-kóhm wished it so, my mother also," Tom said. "The spiders would take pity on a boy whose parents are dead, she said. They call these boys 'orphans.' The spiders have soldiers with no honor who go into the enemy's camp and pretend to be relatives of the enemy. That way they learn what the enemy plans by way of battle. I am to be one of these, but for the Sa-sis-e-tas. The spiders call these soldiers 'spies.'"

He said the last word in English, there being no equivalent in Sa-sis-e-tas except for the word "wolf," which meant "scout." Walks like Badger guffawed, since the English word "spy" sounded like a Sa-sis-e-tas obscenity. Tom frowned at the boy.

"It was my mother's idea," he said. "At first I refused. It hurts worse than a scalp knife, dishonor. But Oh-kóhm thought long and said that it was a greater honor to swallow one's pride for the sake of the People than to count even many coups in battle. 'The information and rifles you bring us will help us to defeat the spiders,' he said, 'for we must defeat them before they kill all the buffalo, or we go under.'"

"He speaks truly, the Little Wolf," said Crazy for Horses. He got to his feet and tapped the hot ashes from the red pipe into the palm of his hand. They sizzled. Tom knew he was showing off his scorn of pain. But then Crazy mashed the hot coals against Tom's forehead, grinning. Tom refused to flinch. "This to remember us by, Elk

Brother," Crazy said. "We will retrieve your rifles from the cave and bring them to Little Wolf. Do you remember the Yellow Boys when we killed Fetterman? They are good rifles, and now we will turn them on the spiders, kill them all, young and old — men, women, and children."

Tom thought again of the dead Snakes. Yes, he was getting too white.

"Tell my father the buffalo killers are now all hunting below the Flint and the Buffalo Bull," he said. "I'm sure you've seen them, having come this far. They plan to hunt the Staked Plain of our friends the Crazy Knife People, the Kiowa, until they have killed all the buffalo in the south, just as they have already done between the Shield River and the Buffalo Bull. It is more properly the fight of the Crazy Knives and of our southern brothers, the Hev-a-tan-iu in particular, but perhaps Little Wolf could send some soldiers down to help them."

"We will tell him," Crazy said. "And yes, we have seen the buffalo killers you speak of." He reached into his war bag and withdrew three fresh scalps. He laughed. Tom checked the scalps to see if Mr. Dousmann's was among them, or perhaps Milo Sykes's, but they weren't. They belonged to other hide men — strangers. He wouldn't have minded seeing Sykes's hair. Crazy would have gotten the new Sharps rifle, and the three white-spider horses, too, when he took those scalps.

"Hang these from your lance," Tom said, re-

turning them. "They'll stink up your war bag."
He slapped Crazy on the shoulder and stepped
back quickly to remount Wind Blows. He jumped
her away and curvetted her.

"My luck will improve, now that I have counted
coup on a brave Elk Soldier of the Sa-sis-e-tas,"
he said, grinning.

"*Piva!*" yelled Crazy for Horses as Tom galloped away. "It is true!" Crazy held the crooked
lance high over his head, the eagle feathers swinging wildly as he pumped it up and down. There
were only two such lances among the Elk Soldiers, and they were carried only by the bravest
soldiers in the band. If a battle was going against
the Elk Soldiers, the man with the crooked lance
would plant it point first in the ground. No one
could retreat beyond the lance without incurring
shame and dishonor. The lance was a rallying
point, like the regimental flags the white-spider
soldiers used in battle to stem a rout. A crooked-
lance soldier fought to the end. He could relin-
quish his lance to another soldier only when he
tired of taking risks with his life, or when he
wished to marry and not go so often on the war
trail. Or in rare cases, for other reasons.

Tom Two Shields had once carried this very
lance. He had relinquished it to his friend Crazy
for Horses for one of the other reasons, and he
had not liked doing it.

12

At the buffalo camp that evening, Raleigh waited until Tom Shields was out visiting with the horses. Jenny was cooking supper, singing one of her German songs. He ladled some hot water from the kettle into a copper bowl, carried it to the tent, and shaved for the first time in a week. He lathered up with soapsuds before applying the horn-handled straight razor. He walked over to the water barrel, stripped off his shirt, and washed his armpits. He looked back over his shoulder and, when all was clear, dropped his cavalry britches and washed his crotch. He went in the tent, rummaged around in his gear, and came up with a red wool shirt that Jenny had laundered. He rummaged further and found a vial of cologne, applied a splash to his raw, stinging cheeks, and rubbed the rest into his armpits. Then he put on the red shirt. It was faded from two years of washing in lye water slaked with ashes. Kind of a dark, mottled pink. He was about to exit the tent when he looked at his legs. The cavalry trousers were splotched black on the thighs with dried buffalo blood and smelled to high heaven. Thank God, I noticed, he thought. Been livin' on the plains so long I've got used to my own stink. He went back to his trunk, felt around in its jumbled depths, and pulled out a pair of canvas shooting pants, stiff and baggy — but at least clean.

Christ, it was troublesome, wooing a serious woman. He needed a drink.

"You smell nice," Jenny said after Raleigh had been lurking around the fire for a while. "Or is it the cinnamon in these potatoes I'm frying?"

"I took a bath," he said. "Seemed about time." He had also applied a fragrant pomade to his hair. She had noticed him brushing it vigorously, then shaping his waves with an elegant ivory comb.

"I wash every day," Jenny said, turning the potatoes in the skillet. "So does Tom, for that matter. There's always plenty of water hot on the fire, Captain, if you want to make use of it."

"Aw hell, don't call me Captain, call me Raleigh," Raleigh said.

Jenny stirred some more.

"That's a nice name," she said. "What does it come from? Is it some kind of a family name?"

"Well, no, it's the name of the capital of my home state, the Tarheel State, North Carolina, and it's also the name of a man who was a captain of the Britishers when they first come over here. To Virginia, they come. Sir Walter Raleigh was a great soldier and explorer, and he founded a colony called Roanoke there. But he got his head chopped off later, I'm told."

"How awful!"

"He, like, *overreached* himself. He was the Queen's boyfriend, they say, but he wanted to be King. Too ambitious, I guess. Got chopped for it, he did. You gotta wonder what he thought while his head was a-tumblin' into the basket. Was it really worth it, after all? Sure hope it was. That Queen must have been one tough lady."

He stepped in close to her nigh shoulder. Nearly as tall as he was. She was wearin' a shirt she had sewn from sun-bleached, brain-tanned antelope hide, with Tom's guidance, Raleigh remembered. Tom had shown her how to bead it, too. She was a little sweaty, but Raleigh liked the smell of a sweaty woman. Brought out the aroma of her soul, some fellows said. You could always whiff a whore, for instance, and if you had your doubts, just put her near a fire. The whore smell would come out. Whores try to make themselves smell good and end up smellin' like a mixture of sweat, stale booze, high-summer roses, and marsh-rat musk. Jenny was no whore.

Make your move, son . . .

He slicked back his hair, then leaned over and kissed her on her sweet, salty neck.

Jenny turned at Raleigh's kiss. One of his hands cupped her buttocks, squeezing hard, and the other came around under her armpit to grope at her right breast. Even through her clothing his hands felt rough as dried corncobs. "C'mon, Jenny," he breathed sweetly into her ear, "let's do it." His breath smelled of booze. The cast-iron skillet of cinnamon potatoes, fried in buffalo tallow, tilted just a bit.

She was shocked, suddenly very disappointed — and very angry.

He had *overreached* himself!

Hot tallow from the skillet spilled down the front of his stiff canvas trousers.

Milo rode hard through the sunset, heading back south toward Captain McKay's camp. He didn't dare ride north for Dodge, it was too far, too risky. Too great a chance of running across more Indians along the way. Every few jumps he lashed the horse hard across the neck with the reins; it was Dousmann's horse anyway, and if he ran its heart out, it was no skin off Milo's hinder. The bluebelly bastard had gotten them into this. He hoped the red devils took their time killing the damnyankee, skun him out on a wagon wheel and burnt the fucker. Black Hat should of told me he'd seen Injuns, he should never of gone to take a potshot at 'em. Brother and sister, shee-it. They're alike no good. That bitch. Try to screw me outta my meat, will she? I'll fix her fuckin' wagon yet or my name ain't Milo Aurelius Sykes.

He pounded into camp from the north the next morning, while Tom and Jenny were turning dried hides. Her Henry lay on one of the hides and she grabbed it when she saw the rider. Then she saw who it was. Milo was riding Edgar, she saw as he got closer, and the horse was lathered near white. Their eyes looked wild, both horse and man alike.

Raleigh was out killing buff, having said not another word to her after she poured the hot grease on him. He'd gasped at the pain, nearly

172

as loud as she had at his words and actions, but then merely turned his back and stalked over to the tent. He ate no supper that night. She could hear his tin cup clanking whenever he refilled it with whiskey. She'd be damned if she'd go over there and apologize to him. He was crude, and he was the offending party. In the morning he was gone before she got dressed, out to the Buffalo Range. He'd calm down, though, or at least she hoped he would. Still, she didn't know — that damned Southern pride. If only he hadn't rushed things so fast . . .

And now here came Milo. Suddenly she was alarmed. No sign of Otto.

"Where's Cap'n McKay?" Milo panted as he reined in the horse.

"Where's my brother?" she asked, frightened. "And the wagon?"

"Injuns jumped us. Kioways or Comanch'. They kilt him an' burned the wagon. I seen the smoke behind me as I rid in here. Now, where's the cap'n, you goddamn honyock?"

"Out there somewhere shooting more buffalo," she said, waving vaguely west, not even responding to the insult. She couldn't think straight. Milo kicked up the exhausted horse and rode west, toward the distant sound of Raleigh's rifle.

Indians? Killed him? Otto dead? Her knees went weak and she sat down on a stretched hide. Tom walked over to her. He sat beside her, folded his arms across his knees, and leaned forward.

"I heard him," he said. Her mind thinned out

173

and started spinning. She leaned over and rested her head against his near arm. It was hard and warm and smelled of woodsmoke. Her throat choked up and she closed her eyes. Flashes of light cascaded down the insides of her eyelids. I won't cry, she told herself desperately, *I won't. Noch nicht,* not just yet . . . Then she was crying.

Raleigh McKay topped the rise just before entering camp, Milo trailing well behind him on Otto's winded horse. A storm was building to the north. Appropriate, Raleigh thought. He was still seething from the girl's rebuff of the previous evening. Sure, maybe he'd been too abrupt with her, but he was horny, too long without a woman. In his experience some women appreciated bluntness, directness, not enjoying the coy dances and wordplay of dalliance any more than a real man did. Time enough for that stuff after the first hot fires had started to burn low, when you'd gotten to know a lady a little better, in intimate terms.

He didn't believe Otto was dead — Milo had refused to look him in the eye when Raleigh asked if he'd actually seen Otto go down — but now he figured maybe he could make up for his bad mistake last night by being comforting and gentle in this her time of grief. Naw, Black Hat couldn't be scragged by any gang of young Hostiles. Not a man who'd survived the best Bobby Lee and Old Blue Light could dish out. Old Blue Light . . .

As he reined in at the crest of the rise, he couldn't believe his eyes. There in the hide yard, not two hundred yards away, Tom Shields was hugging Miss Jenny. His arms were around her, her head on his chest. The goddamn redskin had stolen his play. Raleigh kicked the sorrel in the ribs and poured down the reverse slope toward them at a raging gallop. Off to the north, thunder boomed, but nobody heard it.

Milo, riding up moments later, watched as Captain McKay pulled Tom to his feet, smashed him in the face with his right fist, and clubbed him hard behind the ear with the other hand as he spun and fell. The half-breed dropped and McKay kicked him in the ribs. Tom's eyes were glazed and blood ran from his nose and mouth. The captain had caught him completely by surprise, yanking him away from Jenny by the coat collar and punching him in the mouth. Mess with a white woman, would he? Even a ugly honyock bitch like the Dutch girl was white. Rape her, that's what the breed had in mind. Milo dismounted and grabbed from the ground a mallet used to peg down dead buffalo hides. He stepped up as Tom tried to regain his feet. Milo cocked an arm to hammer him full swing from behind. Finish the fuckin' red devil . . .

From behind him, Jenny slammed the brass-shod butt of her Henry into Milo's right kidney, hard, then swung it low and upward into his ribs as he spun around. "Stop it right now, the both of you." She levered a round into the Henry's

175

receiver and pointed the rifle at Milo. "I swear by the *allmächtiger Gott* I'll kill you!" She swung the rifle next to cover Raleigh. "You too." Then she glanced briefly at Tom, who had sunk to his knees. Blood dripped from his mouth and lay in red loops on the matted grass.

"Tom, wipe that blood off your face."

Tom didn't look at her. He climbed to his feet, swaying, grabbed his hat, and then, still not looking at anyone, walked down to the campfire. He gathered up his war bag, his bedroll, and his rifle. He whistled once, off-key through broken teeth, and Wind Blows came at a canter, her ears pricked forward in question. Tom grabbed her mane and pulled himself onto her back. Kneed her into a gallop and headed north, toward the weather. He was still swaying as he rode off.

Jenny watched him go. Then Raleigh grabbed her from behind, wrenched the rifle from her hands, and threw her to the ground. He slung the rifle aside. He stood spraddle-legged over her as he undid his belt and trousers. His face paled beneath its tan, his hair was wild, and his eyes looked crazed.

"Hold her down, Sykes," Raleigh said. "Pin her arms with your knees, that's right, and sit on her head if you have to. We're gonna show her a little Southern hospitality. Don't worry, old son, you'll get your turn." He yanked down Jenny's pants and placed the palm of his big, horn-calloused hand flat on her white belly, then looked at her with a vicious grin. "Goddamn Injun lover."

"About time we taught her a lesson," Sykes said.

An hour later, in the dead, loud dark, Jenny slipped away from the camp. Once clear, she galloped north after Tom Shields, her mind awhirl with shame and anger. She had left Raleigh and Milo sitting around the whiskey barrel, getting drunk fast. They had both had their way with her, outraged her most vilely. Her mind skittered from the memory. She had to find Tom. Together they'd follow the hide wagon's tracks to where the fight took place, see if Otto was really dead. If he was, at least they could give his bones a decent burial.

She had taken only Vixen and the Henry from camp. All she wore was what she'd been wearing that morning before Milo rode in — her boots, longjohns, makeshift trousers, a heavy wool shirt of Otto's that was too big for her over the antelope-hide blouse, and a wool stocking cap she'd knitted for herself. It was getting quite cold out here, with this snuffling roundabout wind. One blast would blow warm as summer, from the south, then the next, straight out of the north, would be bone-chillingly icy. She pulled the cap down over her ears. Looking ahead as she topped a rise, she thought she could make out Tom in the distance. Then his horseback figure disappeared in a dirty yellow-white blur of dust and

— was it snow? It was snow.

She urged Vixen into a gallop and headed as fast as she could into the building storm, toward where she'd last seen him.

13

Otto had become aware of the Indians the evening after they'd left camp. He couldn't make out what tribe they were, but by the way they trailed the wagon, keeping low on the crests of the swells, he knew they were Hostiles. Jenny had kidded him about branding all Indians he saw as hostile, but in his experience they were. Even the tamest, most "civilized" of them, a lowly Ponca or Chickasaw or Choctaw, would shoot you in the back and loot your quivering body, then lift your hair for a trophy. He'd spotted this particular group of red devils yesterday afternoon as he and Milo crawled past Owl's Head Butte. First just a glimpse of a buck peeking over a hilltop, eagle feather wagging in the wind. The eagle feather caught his eye. Otto kept guard that night.

The following morning as the oxen plodded northeast over a frosty plain toward the Cimarron, he had seen five of the murderous bastards for nearly half a minute, exposing themselves contemptuously to his sight, but just out of rifle range. Clearly they wanted a fight. Then they disappeared again into a swale. This time he saw them long enough to notice that their skulls were shaved bald on one side. The hair on the other side was braided into scalp locks. Red or blue fabric wraps, not otter skin, tied off the braids. That could make them "tame" Comanches or Kiowas or Kiowa Apaches, probably living off government beef at the Wichita Agency in Texas when they weren't out raiding. "Tame" was hardly the word for these reservation bloods — they were as murderous on government beef as they'd ever been on buffalo. Ungrateful sons of bitches. We're only trying to civilize them, can't they see that?

Then he stopped himself. I'm sounding as bad as Milo, he thought, or Raleigh, for that matter. Actually, if I were a red devil like Tom, grown up on the wild roaming life of the plains, I'd bite the hand that fed me, too, if it insisted on keeping me in one place for the rest of my life.

The war party showed itself again an hour before sunset, at least a dozen strong this time, and all of them wearing paint. Now they were truly redskins. Mister Lo always painted before battle. They must have waited for reinforcements to make sure of their attack. Nearsighted Milo hadn't spotted them yet, and Otto hadn't told him. He didn't want to get into a futile debate over what they should do. Now he had no other choice.

"We've got company, Sykes," he finally said. "You see 'em out there, just over the top of that ridge to the right?"

Milo squinted and turned white.

"Let's leave the hides and ride for it, back to camp," he said. They had Otto's horse, Edgar,

180

and Zeke, the old riding mule, tethered and bridled behind the Murphy wagon. "Let the red fuckers burn the wagon and eat the damn oxen. It'll give us a good lead on 'em. An Injun can't pass up a chance at fresh meat and a nice warm fire."

Goddamn quitter, Otto thought.

"No," he said. "There's only a few of them, probably just young bucks off the reservation for a little sport. Next time we spot 'em, I'll give 'em a shot across the bows with the Sharps. If they see we're willing to fight, they might think better of it and go away. You know what Mister Lo calls the Sharps. 'The gun that shoots today and kills tomorrow.' I can drop 'em at half a mile, and they damn well know it."

The Georgian steadied down. I should have told him sooner, Otto thought, let him get used to the idea.

"If it does come to a fight, we'll get in among the hide bales," he said. They had compressed the bales tightly, wrapping each bundle of hides with a rope and using a wagon wheel for a winch, but leaving a hidey-hole in the center. A man could shoot safely from the hole even if Mister Lo got within bow range. It was a leather fort.

"We probably ought to go watch-and-watch tonight," Otto said. "One of us sleep in the wagon while the other keeps a lookout."

Milo made a face.

Herr Gott, I shouldn't have mentioned it, Otto thought.

"All right," he said, trying to regain lost ground, "let's stop now while we've still got good light and I'll go out with the Sharps and see if I can't knock over a couple of 'em."

"You gonna take the horse?"

"No, I'll leave him here, I'm better off on foot. They're less likely to see me."

Otto crouched as he neared the top of the rise. There was always this anticipation on the plains, sometimes eager, wanting to see what lay beyond, but just as often reluctant. It could be the death of a man. He got down on his belly and snaked to the top, the Sharps nestled in the crooks of his elbows. Its weight reassured him. He peered through the grass stems.

Yes, there they were. Ten, twelve, no — fifteen of them now. Seated on their scrawny ponies in conference. Not more than five hundred yards away.

He studied them for a moment, then eased the Sharps forward, elevating the tang sight to "500" as he did so.

How fast could their ponies cover the intervening ground?

Very fast.

He looked for the leader of the group. It was an older man, of course. His face was painted black on one side, red on the other. Otto saw gray in the leader's scalp lock. Three eagle feathers. He swung the Sharps to cover the man, hanging him on the crosshairs of the peep sight just in the middle of his naked red-and-black chest. He cocked the hammer . . .

A ratcheting clack, but the forgiving prairie wind obliterated it before it reached the savages.

He squeezed the set trigger to arm the hair trigger that nested just ahead of it. A sweet, quiet, oily click. He nestled his shoulder snugly into the rifle's curved butt, his cheek tight on the smooth, oiled comb. Refined his sight alignment. Moved his forefinger up to the hair trigger, barely grazing its familiar, cold, smooth arc. Took a deep breath and then released it in a sibilant hiss, slowly, slowly. Just like killing buffalo.

I'll roll the bastard . . .

The smoke spurt nearly obscured the leader as the bullet took him, but Otto saw him launched miraculously, horrified, off his pony's back. Before the leader hit ground, Otto had twisted sideways, downhill. He ran for the next ridge. He levered the spent case out of the breech as he ran, took a loaded cartridge from between his left thumb and forefinger, and fed it into the breech, closed the lever but kept his right thumb on the cocked hammer of the Sharps in case he had to dive for cover in the grass. He didn't want the rifle going off without him aiming it. He had run this way before, many times, during the war, but then he was pulling a paper cartridge from his flapping leather bullet pouch, biting off the bitter end of the case, inserting it with difficulty into the muzzle of the Springfield, ramming it home and trying as he ran to jam a copper cap onto the nipple of the rifle without dropping it. This was

183

certainly simpler. Hurrah for progress.

He hoped the young bucks would be delayed by the death of their chieftain, but as he reached the top of the rise he saw a painted rider galloping toward him, bow in hand and an arrow nocked. Otto knelt at the ridge top, watching down the octagon barrel of the Sharps as the Indian neared. He looked no older than a drummer boy. Braid flapping to the gallop, eyes hot and close-set, his jaw working in rage. A lightning flash of yellow ocher zigzagged down his blue-painted face from brow to chin. Lather blew from the corners of his pony's mouth. A bold horse and rider. Otto blew him off the pony with a bullet through the chest at a range of no more than fifty yards.

Then he stood and ran for his life.

When Otto topped the ridge, rifle reloaded, sprinting back to the safety of the wagon, he saw immediately that his horse was gone. Milo had run for it. The oxen milled and plunged where they stood on the trail. Two of them were down with arrows in their sides. Another arrow protruded from old Zeke's shoulder. He was worrying it with his long yellow teeth. Zeke saw Otto and brayed once, like a jackass. His eyes rolled wildly in his long, knobby head.

Otto grabbed the last belt of cartridges out of the wagonbed. Each belt held forty-two rounds. He'd shot away two from the belt he'd carried up the hill. That left him more than eighty shots. He pressed his fingers hard against the sides of the mouth-shaped wound the arrow had kissed in

Zeke's shoulder. The shaft looked as if it was buried three inches deep.

"Easy, old boy," he whispered in Zeke's gyrating ear. "You're the best mule in the world."

Pressing hard, he yanked the arrowhead loose from the muscle. Zeke shuddered and raised his hammer head. He shuddered again and brayed. Otto untied the reins.

No time for the saddle. He jumped once to get on Zeke's tall back. He failed. An arrow whipped past. On the next leap he succeeded. Zeke needed no urging. They galloped off toward the southwest, toward Owl's Head Butte, which reared black and crooked against the fading red glow of the sunset.

They reached it in the last of the daylight. He urged the mule partway up its steep slope and looked to the north. Behind them he could see the dull, flickering, red-and-yellow glare of the burning wagon. Vagrant gusts of a cold, fresh wind carried the stench of burning hides to their nostrils. Zeke snorted repeatedly at the smell. The wind had swung around to the northwest and Otto thought he could smell snow on it when the gusts weren't clotted with hide fumes. Weather coming on.

He dismounted and led Zeke in a scrambling climb to a tall, pointed boulder near the top of the butte. From a distance the butte resembled the head of a great horned owl, and this would be one of its ears. Old Zeke had outrun the Indian ponies. Otto led the mule behind the boulder,

185

out of the way of future arrows, and knotted the reins to the bole of an oak sapling growing from a crevice. He could hear hoofbeats approaching and turned to lay the rifle over the sloping side of the owl's ear. Three horsemen galloped toward him, well ahead of the other Indians. He took a quick sight and dropped one of their ponies. Reloaded. Knocked an Indian from the back of his horse. Reloaded. Killed the third devil with a lucky head shot as he whirled his pony and tried to race out of range. Then he searched the grass for the man whose pony he'd dropped. Spotted him crawling away. Killed him. That's five of them down, he thought. Only ten to go.

But the remaining Indians reined in at extreme rifle range. Knotted up to confer. He elevated the tang sight to 1,000 yards, added a bit more by raising the muzzle, and fired into the group. A pony whirled and dropped. An Indian howled. The rest then galloped away.

They'll be back, Otto thought. Where the hell do I go from here?

During the night he made up his mind.

He crept down to one of the dead ponies before dawn, removed the apishamore from its back, and, bending low, hurried back to Zeke. He cut the buffalo-hide saddle blanket into four pieces and, with thongs sliced from one of them, bound them tight to Zeke's hoofs. That way the mule's iron shoes wouldn't ring on the rocks as they sneaked away.

He didn't know where the remaining Indians

were. Maybe they'd only sent one of their number back to wherever the main body was camped, to get more reinforcements, or maybe they'd all gone. He knew he'd killed the leader of this band, and he'd probably killed the next oldest and most experienced warriors with his sundown fusillade. He had to head south, back to McKay and Jenny. Milo had certainly gone that way, and more than likely, to cover his sorry performance, had told them that Otto was dead. Jenny would be grieving.

No, he couldn't expect help until morning at the earliest, and maybe they wouldn't come at all, certainly not if McKay believed he was dead at the hands of a large band of Hostiles.

He led the mule back down through the dark, taking his time, making sure of every step. "Don't worry, old fellow," he whispered in one tall ear, "we're going to be all right come sunup."

Walks like Badger had heard the shots Otto fired the previous evening, when he killed the three front-running Kiowas at Owl's Head Butte. Crazy for Horses led them in the direction of the gunfire, though it meant hooking a bit south again rather than onward to their destination. Halfway to the butte they met the ten surviving Kiowas. They were just boys, and frightened, though they refused to show it. A white man had killed five of their party, they said in sign language, for no good reason. By surprise. From a distance with a rifle that shoots today and kills tomorrow. Like the one Crazy was carrying. The spider had killed their leader, Bad Pants, who in his dying breath had ordered them to return to the main camp of the Kiowas and make medicine for his soul. They were obeying his orders as fast as they could. They were good soldiers.

Walks like Badger had also been the first to cut the spider's trail, in the half-light of early morning, as they circled the butte shaped like an owl's head. Walks didn't speak much, but he had sharp ears and eyes.

Not to be outdone by a youngster, Crazy had sharpened his own senses then, and he was the first to see the spider far ahead of them soon after daybreak. The spider was riding a mule. Following a low meander of the prairie, the three Elk Soldiers kicked their horses into a gallop and tried to cut him off. But the spider had outsmarted them, cutting to his right as part of a zigzag pattern. Crazy had loaded the big new rifle and tried three shots at him, at a range of about half a mile, as the mule topped a ridge. He had not hit the spider, but he hoped he had frightened him. The mule walked steadily onward, yet it looked as if it was weakening. Perhaps the Kiowa boys had wounded it yesterday. Walks found blood in the mule's dung a few minutes later, confirming Crazy's guess. Black blood. The mule must have a wound in its belly. Soon it would die. Then they would kill the spider. In the storm that was coming, it would be easy.

The norther struck when Otto was within ten miles of the camp. The Indians were close on his trail. At least one of them had a rifle, a Sharps Big Fifty by the sound of it, and had tried a few ranging shots from a long way off. One bullet threw dust not far to his right. Where had the rifle been earlier? Why hadn't they used it in their attack on the Owl's Head, or even earlier? They could have killed oxen, mule, and horse at their leisure, or killed him and Milo just as easily. No, they wouldn't have wanted to hurt the horse. He had seen no sign of firearms, though, and certainly not heard any shots. Maybe these weren't the same Indians. He could make out only three of them this time, and their hair seemed braided on both sides now. A Cheyenne or Arapahoe hairstyle, possibly Sioux, though they weren't likely to be this far south.

He saw the dirty line of the snow scudding toward him on the edge of the wind, wriggling like a bone-white sidewinder, moving with incredible speed. Then the wind's sound came to his ears, a steadily increasing roar that became, as it neared, louder even than the nonstop artillery barrages at Gettysburg. Oh yes — a norther was indeed blue, he thought. The sky above the snow snake was almost the color of a brand-new Army uniform.

The Indians would make their move under cover of the storm. As soon as it hit and obscured him from their vision, he must break off to the right or left, sharply, and get Zeke into a gallop. The old mule was about blown. The blood he'd lost from the shoulder wound must have drained him more than Otto realized.

When the snow hit, Otto kicked Zeke in the sides, and the animal galloped a few hundred yards. But Otto could feel him faltering at every jump. Then Zeke threw up his head, blew bloody froth from his nostrils, and rolled his eyes backward in his head until he was almost looking at the man. Zeke stopped and fell forward to his knees. Otto slid from his back. Zeke rolled weakly onto his side. Only then did Otto see the broken-off shaft of an arrow protruding from Zeke's side, low on his belly. Tears suddenly stung his eyes. Every time Otto had kicked him to get him galloping, his boot must have hit that arrow shaft. Zeke vomited black blood into the snow. His eyes stared up into Otto's, and it seemed to the man that the mule was begging for something.

He drew the revolver and cocked the hammer. He imagined an X drawn from the animal's right ear to left eye, then from left ear to right eye. He aimed at the spot where the lines crossed and pulled the trigger. At the buck of the shot, gunsmoke bloomed and blew away on the wind. The mule's head fell, squarely brainshot. Didn't feel a thing, Otto thought. Wish I could say as much.

Then he ran. The footing was already miserable, snow piling fast and slippery underfoot, half blinding him when the wind swirled around to the south. It nearly knocked him down a few times. He couldn't see three feet ahead. He blundered into a thornbush, almost dropped the Sharps, recovered his balance, and pushed on. He smelled sage underfoot, sharp through the snowy wind. He thought he could make out a bluff through the sheets of horizontally blowing snow and he ran for it. Get to the top of that and make your stand, he thought. He staggered forward, but immediately the bluff was obscured by another sheet of stinging, blinding sleet that turned the whole world white to within an inch of his eyeballs.

Then, as suddenly, the air was clear.

The bluff was a horse with an Indian on its back. The Indian was coming toward him.

Fast.

The Indian had a long-handled war club in his right hand and was swinging its polished stone head counterclockwise in great circles as he galloped. Two braids, no warpaint on his face, only intense concentration. Otto raised the Sharps to his hip. The Indian was close. He fired.

Walks like Badger flew from the pony's back.

Otto took refuge just below the lip of the wide, deep coulee into which he'd tumbled. Thick brush grew there. He nestled into it and let the snow build up on his back, head, and legs. The Indians couldn't find him here without dogs, and even a foxhound would be hard-pressed to take a scent in this blowing hell of a weather. He

191

tucked the Sharps under his body to protect the action from freezing. *Christus,* it was cold! Christ, that was a lucky shot. He couldn't have been five feet from me when I fired. Didn't have time to get the rifle to my shoulder. He'd have taken my head off with that damned club. *God but it's cold!* Maybe the snow will insulate me some. I might lose a couple of toes, though. Frostbit already, feels like. I'm all sweated up from the run. Should be moving, so my longjohns don't freeze from the sweat. Can't, though. They're out there.

Twice in the next hour he thought he saw one of them, moving wraithlike through the billows of falling, blowing snow. Never for long enough to take a shot, though, even if he was willing to risk one. The cold's got to be getting to them, too, he thought. Indians are tough, but not that tough. Remember those poor hide men in the blizzards last winter. First one started in mid-December and blew for eight days. Two more storms in January. Major Dodge at the fort said more than a hundred buffalo hunters died along the Arkansas alone. Mules froze standing in their traces. The sky was a solid blast of ice particles. Bob Wright had to burn his wagons for firewood. Sawbones at the fort performed seventy amputations. Some fellows lost arms and legs, both. Washtub cases, they called them. Otto had talked to one of them, an old skinner named Josh Beasley. Beasley told him how it was, freezing like that. He begged Otto to shoot him, there in the fort's infirmary with the stink of bedpans and gangrene all around. Shoot me, for Christ's sake, or give me some cyanide, how can I live like this? I can't shoot myself with no hand nor no feet, the frost even took my pecker off me. Tears in his eyes. Otto didn't shoot him, though. But he told the sawbones. The sawbones said he'd maybe give old Josh a long, long pull on the laudanum bottle. And then a few more. It's a pleasant way to go, he said.

Otto was shivering nonstop now, muscles out of control, great convulsive shudders that he knew would go away soon, leaving him incapable of movement. After that he'd go to sleep, like as not, and wake up a block of ice. You've got to move, he told himself. You've got to move — *now!*

"*Haáhe,* Two Shields." It was Cut Ear. "I almost shot you for a spider." He looked at Tom's face. "What tried to eat your head, a white bear or a wolf?"

Tom merely grunted. "Have you had a fight with the spiders?"

"One of them," Cut Ear said. "We hunt him even now. His mule died. He shot Walks like Badger through the shoulder. Tore him up pretty bad." He told Tom about the Kiowas and the burned wagon. "The Kiowas said another spider ran away, on a good horse."

"Do not kill the spider if you catch him," Tom said. "He is my friend."

"Crazy for Horses wants him badly. I said we must get out of the snow and the wind, but he wants this spider's scalp."

"Where is Crazy?"

Cut Ear made the sign for "Who knows?" Then he said, "Out there," and swung his arm to indicate just about everywhere.

"We will find him," Tom said.

During a brief lull in the storm, Otto saw a figure on horseback making slow progress in his direction through the snow. It was nearly three feet deep now. He had passed a small group of buffalo standing in the bottom of a draw, out of the wind. The buffalo stood like snow-crusted black boulders, with their heads down, facing into the wind. They hadn't even raised their heads when he passed them, not fifty feet upwind. They must certainly have smelled him. But the storm had declared an armistice.

The figure he saw was no Indian. Then he recognized the horse. Vixen! It was Jenny out there. He ran toward her, stumbling through the drifts in nightmare slow motion. The wind hit again with renewed strength, almost toppling him into the snow with its sudden force. Blowing snow obscured her from his sight. He slogged forward, hoping he was headed right. He couldn't see more than a foot or two in front of him now. But he knew the horse would not move far during the height of the wind. A horse's instinct is to turn its tail to the weather in a storm like this. It will not walk happily into the teeth of a blizzard. Only a human being will do that. He pushed ahead.

A few minutes later, or perhaps they were hours, he banged into something large, hard, wet, and warm. He looked up, into the muzzle of the Henry. Heard the hammer snick back.

"*Nicht schiessen,* Jenny!" he shouted. "Don't fire!"

She raised the muzzle of the rifle as suddenly as she'd aimed it, then slid from the saddle and clutched him. Vixen turned to run away from the storm, but Jenny was still holding the reins. They huddled in the horse's lee, hugging each other. Jenny was weeping with relief. The tears cut runnels through the sleet on her cheeks. She shivered violently.

"*Wir müssen Schutz suchen vor'm Schneesturm!*" Otto yelled in her ear. "Got to get out of the blizzard!" He remembered the buffalo back in the draw. "Bring the horse, we'll need her when the blizzard blows out. Come on, we're going this way." He pulled her by the hand, back toward the buffalo.

They were still there, or at least a few of them. He counted five. The others must have walked around a bend in the draw, where they hoped to find more shelter from the icy wind. There were no tracks in the snow to indicate where they had gone. The tracks had drifted in already. He raised the Sharps and, from a range of no more than fifty feet, killed the closest buffalo with a brain-shot through the back of its head. At the shot, the others started down the draw. He tried to work the lever for a second shot. It was frozen

195

shut. He fumbled at it, but his fingers were stiff from the cold.

"Quick — *mit dem Henry,* shoot another! *Schnell, schnell* — we need two of them!"

Jenny raised the rifle. It wobbled in her numb hands. She couldn't hold it steady. She pulled the trigger vainly until she nearly bent it. Then she saw the rifle was still at half-cock. It couldn't fire no matter how hard she pulled. She withdrew her finger from the trigger, leaving a ragged strip of skin annealed to the brass.

Verdammt, Otto thought. "It's all right," he said. "One dead buff will save us."

He led Jenny and Vixen down into the draw and with his rip knife quickly opened the dead buffalo. It was a cow. *Verflucht noch einmal!* He should have picked a big bull, they'd both fit. But this band was all cows and calves, he now realized. The blowing snow had left him no way to gauge their size, or even their sex. He reached deep within the body cavity and pulled out the paunch and the intestines, heaping them beside the belly. Sweet steam boiled into the air from the empty body cavity. He reached up into the chest and pulled out the lungs, one by one. He rummaged in the hot gut pile and found the liver. He sliced off a long, bloody strip, then a piece of white tallow.

"Eat this," he said. "It'll warm you. And stick your hands in here, like I'm doing." She obeyed. When Otto's hands had warmed again, he sliced off a strip of liver for himself. Jenny chewed the slippery liver, swallowed, almost retched at the sharp, metallic taste of it, but kept the rich organ meat down.

"Now get inside the buffalo, where its innards were."

"Da drinnen?"

Steam continued to boil from the gaping stomach walls, carrying with it the hot, strong, sickly-sweet stench of blood. She could see more blood pooled deep in the bottom of the cavity.

"Ja, schnell, sonst frierst du."

She stared blankly up at him.

"You must, Jennchen," he said more gently. "If you don't, you'll surely freeze to death."

"What about you?"

"I'll stay close to the body; the hair will keep me warm enough, and I'm out of the goddamned wind."

"Shoot Vixen. I can fit inside her, and you in the buffalo."

"We'll need her when the storm blows over. With redskins hunting us, we wouldn't stand a chance afoot. Don't worry about me, I'll lie up against the buffalo's side; it'll keep me out of the wind and warm enough when the snow drifts over."

"Take this shirt, anyway," Jenny said. "It's your old one, good warm wool." She pulled it off, shook the snow from it, and handed it to him. Otto cut the buffalo liver in two and gave Jenny her portion. Then she crawled into the hot, rank carcass. It was like descending into a steaming

197

red cavern, a sudden gateway to hell. At once she was soaked in blood, hot, slippery on her bare hands and face, sticky in her hair. She gagged involuntarily, gulping for air. But at least I'm finally warm, she thought, and with that realization her body began to relax.

Otto pushed the body cavity closed as tightly as he could, sat against the buffalo cow's warm belly, and stuck his booted feet under the gut pile for whatever warmth it could afford. He sliced off more liver, chewed it, and swallowed.

He had cinched Vixen to the dead cow's horns. He couldn't bring himself to shoot the mare, he had known that all along. Zeke had been bad enough. Now he got up, untied the mare, and led her down the draw, around a corner where he had noticed a small stand of blackjack oaks growing. The trees provided a lee beneath the bank. He knotted her reins to a lower branch, unsaddled her, took the horse blanket off her back and folded it over his arm, patted Vixen on the rump, and hiked back up to the dead buffalo. He hunkered in the lee, out of the wind, pulled the wool shirt up over his ears and face, threw the saddle blanket over his back and shoulders, wrapped it tightly, tucked his hands into his crotch, and tried not to shiver.

Already, he noticed, the blood on his wrists was frozen.

The wind howled like a pack of white buffalo wolves. He settled back and waited for morning . . .

14

The storm blew out by noon of the following day. As the wind died, the temperature dropped below freezing. From the draws where cottonwoods grew came sharp explosions as the sap in their trunks expanded and split the boles at their weakest places.

Tom and his Elk Soldiers had found a deep, hard-packed drift on the lee slope of a swale and with knives and rifle butts had excavated a snow cave for themselves. Crazy for Horses had cut some poles from a clump of Osage orange saplings and spent much of the night making two pairs of snowshoes from the limber wood. He bent the poles into circles, tied them with rawhide thongs sliced from his apishamore, and webbed them with more of the leather. Walks like Badger's shoulder wound was ugly but would not kill him. The big bullet had nicked a bone but passed completely through the right shoulder, so that Tom could poke a stick in one end and feel nothing until it emerged from the other side. Walks felt something, all right, but did not complain. Cut Ear built a fire of tinder he kept in a parfleche bag, feeding it with small sticks of wind-brittle Osage orange, then later with buffalo chips he'd dug out of the snow and dried beside the fire. The ceiling of the snow cave glazed over from the fire's heat and reflected it back on the Elk Soldiers. They ate pemmican and talked and smoked from Crazy's red pipe. It was warm. Tom slept.

Jenny was warm, too, at least far warmer than she had been outside the buffalo. After a while she no longer gagged on the bites of raw liver and tallow she sliced and chewed. Nor could she smell the rank blood reek that had nauseated her at first. She worried about Otto, out there in the cold, until at last she, too, fell asleep.

When she finally awoke, stiff from her cramped position and with shards of horrid but fast-fading nightmares still bucking through her mind, the wind seemed to have gone silent. She called out to Otto. Silence. She called again, louder, and tried to push open the cow's belly. She couldn't do it. The carcass was frozen shut. Panic . . . she had to get out. She could see sunlight, blazing white, through a few small crevices in the slit. She drew the skinning knife with difficulty from where she'd stuck it between two ribs and inserted the point in one of the crevices. She used it as a pry bar. She got to her knees, agony in the restricted space, and pushed upward on the rib cage with her shoulders and back, still prying with the knife. Then the knife blade cracked off near the haft. The steel was too cold, too brittle. Her breath caught in her throat and for a horrible moment she couldn't inhale. Her heart hammered wildly.

She inhaled.

Sei ruhig, Mädl, she thought. Calm yourself, girl! Take a slow, deep breath. And *think!*

Three ravens in ragged formation flapped over the ocean of snow. Their sharp eyes searched for breakfast. Instinct told the birds that many animals must have died in the blizzard. It was only a matter of finding them under the white blanket, a rump or hoof or horn poking out, and they would begin feeding.

Tom had been watching them for twenty minutes now as he and Crazy resumed their hunt on snowshoes for Otto. The snow was blinding and both Elk Soldiers had smeared soot from the fire on their cheekbones and eyelids. We look like raccoons, Tom thought. One of the ravens suddenly swerved in midair, croaking to its partners. They all peeled off and dove for something at the bottom of a draw. Crazy grunted as he watched them. "Over there," Tom said. Crazy smiled. They slogged through snow that came halfway up their shins even with the big bear-paw webs on their feet.

As they neared the draw, they saw the hoofprints of a horse leading into it, almost filled now with blowing snow, and then the fresher hoofprints of two horses leading out and to the south. A man on horseback had gone down into the draw and fetched out a horse that had been hidden there. Tom reached into the bottom of one of the holes the horses had left in the snow and felt carefully around the hoofprint. The animals had worn iron shoes. White-spider ponies. The tracks had been made no earlier than two or three hours ago, just about an hour after first light.

Tom and Crazy paused at the lip of the draw and studied it carefully. Tom saw the carcass of a buffalo cow three-quarters buried in the snow. That's what the ravens had seen. The meat-eater birds were perched now in some oaks a short distance down the draw, where the horses had emerged earlier. That's where the second horse must have been hidden. Tom's eyes shifted back to the buffalo carcass. It seemed to him that the dead buffalo was moving. Crazy saw it, too. His eyes widened.

The sun had been beating down on the black buffalo hide for a couple of hours now, with ever-increasing heat. The frozen buffalo was out of the wind and the reflective snow had helped the sun to thaw it. Tom and Crazy watched the buffalo's ribs heave, once, twice, three times. They heard an icy, crackling sound. The buffalo cow's belly split open. A human figure, armored in blood-red ice, stepped out. Staggered, reeled around, stretched its arms. The human pulled a cap from its head. Long yellow hair cascaded to the human's shoulder, and it shook its head, breathing deeply through its wide, bloody mouth.

"E-hyoph-sta," Crazy said in a trembling voice. "Yellow-Haired Woman."

"Jenny," Tom said. She looked up.

"So you found her horse," Milo said. "What about the bitch herself?"

Raleigh leaned over and backhanded Milo across the mouth. "Goddamnit, I told you not to call her that, you cracker piece of shit!" He pulled the Whitney from his belt and thumbed back the hammer.

Milo shut up. He spit a mouthful of blood into the fire, took another swallow of whiskey, and sulked. The barrel was running low. Raleigh let down the hammer and reholstered the pistol. He was glad to see that the Georgian had at least made a fresh pot of coffee. He poured himself a cup, drew half an inch of bourbon into it, and slumped by the fire. He had hunted for Jenny since noon the previous day, more than twenty-four hours of arctic cold and howling wind and near-blindness, stopping only briefly to sleep huddled beside his horse in a hollow under the buffalo robes he'd brought along in anticipation of saving her from the storm.

He'd resumed the search at first light. When his sorrel horse suddenly threw up its head to the north wind and whinnied, and he heard Vixen whinny back, his heart had soared. He gave the sorrel its head and the horse led him to the mare. He couldn't see much, from snowblindness. His eyes felt full of gravel. He found Vixen but not Jenny. He called her name, bellowed it into the dying wind, but heard no answer. He'd dug through the drifts around the blackjack oak stand, searching for her. Found nothing. He didn't see the dead buffalo cow only a hundred yards up the draw, or the long hump beside it that was Otto, buried under a blanket of cold white snow.

Was she dead? Somewhere out there on the prairie, under three feet of snow, waiting for the spring thaw to reveal her to the waiting ravens and coyotes? All his fault if she was. For drinking too much, for losing his temper, for not apologizing to her right off like a gentleman would of if he'd got carried away like that, and then . . . later. He couldn't believe what he'd done. His mind shied away from the word. But he'd lost his head when he saw Tom with her. He should have . . . What?

Of course it was understandable — she was in shock, having just learned that Black Hat was dead. Her brother. Her only living relative. Tom was probably just trying to comfort her. What does a half-breed know of gentlemanly behavior? He must figure he's all white, anyway. Might not even know that it's wrong for the lesser races to comfort the white man. Or woman. But Raleigh knew that he himself was an even worse offender of the proprieties. An officer and a rapist. He was no better than this white-trash Georgia cracker feeding booze into his fat-lipped, knuckle-cracked mouth and wincing at the sting. How could he have let Sykes even touch her? He should have shot the bastard, and shot himself as well. He had to get out of this godawful place.

204

"Grab your gear and load the wagon," he ordered in his best Southern officer's voice. "Strike the tent and pack it. All the camp gear, too. Get the mules and hitch 'em up."

"Where we goin', Cap'n?"

"Over east to Camp Supply. Now hump your sad excuse for a butt or I'll put a pistol ball through ye."

"What about the other wagon? And the rest of these hides?"

"Fuck 'em. We'll come back for the wagon in the spring. The hides can rot along with the stinkers they came from."

Tom and Jenny spent that night with the Elk Soldiers in the snow cave. Crazy had found Otto buried in the snow beside the buffalo. He was still alive. Just barely. Tom built a fire beside the carcass and placed Otto near it, rolled him in the saddle blanket, and, after skinning the cow, wrapped the stiff hide, hair side down, over that. Then Tom and Crazy built a travois and pulled Otto back to the snow cave, with Jenny following in the trail they had broken. Jenny made hot broth from pemmican and chips of fresh buffalo meat hacked from the icy carcass of the cow. She fed it slowly to Otto until his eyes came back into focus. His hands and feet were badly frozen.

The next day they pushed north, across deeply drifted prairie. They pulled Otto on the travois behind a pony. There were plenty of ponies. The Indians still had the horses they'd taken from the hunters they'd killed. Jenny rode one of them. Tom said that someone, a white man, had stolen Vixen during the night. Probably Raleigh, she thought. Milo was too yellow to have gone out into the blizzard after her. But Raleigh would do it, for revenge. If the storm didn't kill her, he probably figured, then leaving her afoot on the snow-covered prairie would finish the job.

She had to reach Fort Dodge as quickly as possible. Maybe the post surgeon could save Otto's hands and feet. She was worried about gangrene. Already his toes and fingers were going dark. If they hurried, maybe something could still be done. And she had to report Raleigh McKay to the authorities for attempted murder. Horse theft as well.

Don't be silly, she told herself. They won't do a damned thing. What could she prove, anyway? She had only Tom's word for it, and even he hadn't seen the thief. What if Vixen had just broke loose and drifted off in the storm? And would a U.S. marshal or an Army officer believe the word of a half-breed Cheyenne?

They reached Fort Dodge two days later, having made good time north of the Arkansas River, where the snow hadn't fallen. The three Cheyennes had left them, riding on to the Pawnee Fork of the Arkansas on some mysterious mission of their own. After Jenny explained their situation, the officer of the day escorted her to Colonel Dodge's quarters.

Colonel Richard Irving Dodge was a bluff, red-faced man, but understanding. He called in the post surgeon, Dr. Wallace. It was clear to Jenny from the major's tone that there was no love lost between the two officers. The surgeon was a gray-whiskered, potbellied gentleman with a whiskey tan and small blue eyes as hard as tin-alloyed musket balls. He had served with Sherman during the war. "Mr. Dousmann suffers severely from frostbite," the major explained in Jenny's presence. "He is a veteran of the Iron Brigade, a former sergeant, 2nd Wisconsin. You will do your best to see that he recovers with the *full use of all his limbs*. Save every finger, every toe if you can. Don't just break out your bone saw because it's easier, Doctor. And that's an order."

Dr. John Wallace amputated Otto's right arm to the elbow. After long consideration, he took the thumb and first two fingers of his left hand and the toes on both feet. It was the best he could do.

"Gangrene," he told Jenny when he came out of the operating room. "Once it starts, it never stops, unless you amputate. Skin, muscle, bone, blood — they all die, and finally the patient himself. I saved as much of the man as I dared. If only you'd brought him to me sooner."

She glared at him and he looked away, brushing nervously at the blood that was drying on the backs of his hands.

"How could I have brought him any faster?"

she said. "We'd been attacked by Indians, betrayed by our friends, we were down on the Buffalo Range in Texas and there was a blizzard — three feet of snow on the ground."

"I'm truly sorry, miss," Dr. Wallace said, still avoiding her gaze. "But these things happen. I've seen a lot worse. Your brother will live, he's a strong man. Oh, certainly, he won't be able to shoot a buffalo rifle any longer, or even handle a knife and fork, and perhaps for the rest of his life he'll walk with a severe limp from the loss of his toes. But that's better than no limbs at all. I saw many such cases during the war. He'll suffer awhile from the megrims — melancholia, lethargy, dejection — but I'm sure that if you'll try your jolly best to cheer him, perhaps read to him from the Good Book, soon enough he'll be right as rain. Now, if you'll excuse me."

He hurried back to the bottle of rye that awaited him in his quarters.

The first word that came to Otto's mind when he awoke from the Lethean anesthetic was "Beasley." I'm a washtub case, he thought. Though it seemed that he could feel his fingers and toes throbbing under the wire-mesh baskets and sheets that covered his extremities, he had talked with enough sawbone victims during the war, in one field hospital or another, to know about ghost limbs. They would be with him for a long time, itching where he couldn't scratch — even if he had fingers left to scratch them with.

Reminders of what was gone.

No more walking, he thought. No more riding, no more shooting. No more . . .

But then as his mind cleared he grew hopeful, finally certain, that at least his legs and his left arm were still with him. He flexed his knees and saw them rise beneath the blankets. He could feel the weight of the lower legs beneath them. But when he flexed his elbows, only his left forearm moved. And though he felt certain that his fingers and toes had been amputated, at least he would still be able to ride once his strength returned to him.

He called for an orderly. Dr. Wallace himself entered the ward.

"What's the trouble?"

"You know what the trouble is. I make my living by hunting. Couldn't you have saved me just one goddamned finger to pull a trigger with?"

"No. Quite frankly, my good man, if this had been a field hospital during the war, with a battle raging, I'd have had no choice but to take off both your legs to the knee and both your arms to the elbow. You should be grateful to me for my solicitude."

"You bastards and your bone saws."

"Call me what you like, soldier," Dr. Wallace said. "It's water off a duck's back. If I had a penny for every time I've been called a bastard by an awakening amputee, and another for every limb I've hacked off, I'd be richer than Astor. I saved your life with what I did. You still have your legs and one arm. Now just take a slug of this and stop feeling sorry for yourself."

He pulled a medicine bottle from his hip pocket and unscrewed the cap.

"What is it?"

"The Waters of Lethe," Dr. Wallace said. "More prosaically known as Wallace's Cordial. My own special concoction to alleviate the pain and worry of human existence, replacing it with the warm, bright fizz of forgetfulness. It's a variant on the world-famous Godfrey's Cordial, popularized by the Philadelphia College of Pharmacy. I dissolve $2^{1}/2$ ounces carbonate of potash in 26 pints of water, add 16 pints of molasses, heat them together over a gentle flame till they simmer, remove the scum, and, when sufficiently cool, add a half ounce of oil of sassafras dissolved in two pints of rectified spirit, and 24 fluid ounces of opium. I'll give you my recipe. The concoction contains about 16 minims, more or less, of pure laudanum — rather more than a grain of opium in each fluid ounce. A slug or two will, I assure you, alleviate the mischief of your post-operative humors."

With raised eyebrows, he offered the bottle to Otto.

"No thanks, I'd rather you brought a pistol next time."

"Without fingers you'd have a hard time using it."

"I'll find a way."

15

By order of Colonel Dodge, civilians — especially Indians — were allowed within the gates of the fort only during daylight hours. But the colonel had been kind enough to let Jenny use a suite of vacant rooms — kitchen, parlor, and bedroom — in the bachelor officers' quarters, since she wished to be close to her brother during the critical period following surgery. It would be at least two weeks before he could be moved. Tom Shields was required to sleep outside the fort with the rest of the Indians. Half Indian is all Indian, she thought, as far as the U.S. Army is concerned.

Her rooms were on the ground floor at the far end of the B.O.Q. A coal stove stood in the parlor. On the night following Otto's surgery she could not sleep and sat up, wrapped in a blanket, on an ottoman beside the stove. She had borrowed a book from the post library, one volume from a set of six of the works of an English poet she'd never read, John Donne. Poetry always settled her when she was worried. She found the verses hard going, written in antique English, and looked at the title page. The book had been published in 1839, she saw, which should have made the writing sound normal. But then she noticed

211

that Donne had lived more than two hundred years earlier, his dates being 1572–1631. She was about to close the book when it fell open on her lap to an obvious favorite of the original owner. It was titled "On His Mistris." Jenny knew what a "mistris" was.

She read on. It seems a woman wanted to accompany the poet, her lover, on a long trip through Europe — there was mention of France, Italy, and either Holland or Germany — maybe to war or maybe just on a business trip. But she wanted to go disguised as a boy. Donne discouraged her. All Frenchmen are fops and lechers, he said, while Italians love boys. The "Dutch" (and Jenny bristled at this, since it was what Germans were often called in this country by people too ignorant to know the difference between a Hollander and an *echt Deutscher*) were libeled as having "spungy" wet eyes.

But there was a nice sentiment, nicely put, right at the end:

When I am gone, dreame me some happinesse,
Nor let thy lookes our long hid love confesse,
Nor praise, nor dispraise me, nor blesse nor curse
Openly loves force, nor in bed fright thy Nurse
With midnights startings, crying out, oh, oh,
Nurse, o my love is slaine, I saw him goe
O'r the white Alpes alone; I saw him I,
Assail'd, fight, taken, stabb'd, bleed, fall, and die.
Augure me better chance, except dread Jove
Thinke it enough for me to've had thy love.

She flipped to the flyleaf to see who had owned the book before donating it to the post library. The name, written in a gentlemanly hand, was "George Frederick Ruxton, Lieutenant, H.M. 89th Regiment." The "H.M." stood for "Her Majesty's," Jenny knew, so George Ruxton was a Britisher. She wondered what had brought him to the Great West.

Next morning at breakfast in the officers' mess, she asked Colonel Dodge. "Yes, Ruxton," he said. "A great adventurer and explorer, he was. An Englishman who'd fought as a mercenary in Spain during the Carlist Wars, decorated there by Queen Isabella II, later tramped around in the wilder parts of Canada and southern Africa. He'd been to Sandhurst briefly, bought a commission in an English regiment, but peacetime Army life was too quiet for him and he sold it. He traveled alone through Mexico, riding up clear into Colorado, where he made many friends among the mountain men — Old Bill Williams, Joe Walker, Black Harris, and William Bent, among others. Hunted the Bayou Salado, traveled the *Jornada del Muerto* when the Apaches were making it truly a Journey of Death. Later he wrote a fine book about his time in the mountains, *Life in the Far West*, that was serialized by *Blackwood's* magazine. It was published in this country, in book form, three or four editions, I believe. I think we have a copy in the library. Some say he was an undercover British intelligence officer, sent to map the southern approaches to the United

States. He could have been. It was just after the Mexican War that he came over here, after all, and the British were certainly worried about American expansion."

"What happened to him?" Jenny asked.

"Went under," the colonel said.

"Indians?"

"No, dysentery," he said. "In St. Louis, back in '48. Indians alone couldn't kill a fellow that tough. Took a bug to do it."

And a blizzard to destroy my brother, Jenny thought. She excused herself. It was all too sad.

The fort was busy preparing for an inspection by Lieutenant General Philip Henry Sheridan, the hero of Winchester, Cedar Creek, and Yellow Tavern during the war and now commanding officer of the Military Division of the Missouri. A dinner for officers and their ladies would follow, and Jenny was invited as the colonel's guest.

"The general is particularly fond of buffalo hunters," Dodge told her, "and the fact that your brother served during the late war will make him even happier to meet you."

The adjutant's wife, a kindly woman named Abigail Augustine, provided Jenny with an exquisite dress of strawberry-colored *poult-de-soie* shot with white for the occasion, along with a lace cape and appropriate shirtwaist, shift, and pointy-toed white pumps that pinched horribly. She felt rather silly in the outfit, but pleased nonetheless. It seemed like years since she had dressed as a full-blown, out-and-out woman, though never as elegantly as this. It felt . . . luxurious.

She studied herself in Mrs. Augustine's mirror. Apart from the darkening of her skin to a rich golden tan from exposure to wind and sunlight, and a rather unfeminine strength to her neck and arms from all the lifting, pulling, and cutting she'd been engaged in for the past few months, she thought she looked rather good. Her freshly washed blond hair, blanched even paler by the weather, hung nearly to her shoulders, secured in artful swoops and swirls by mother-of-pearl barrettes. A hint of lavender rose from her warm flesh, courtesy of Mrs. A's bath oil. The *moiré antique* cape was secured across her bosom by an ivory brooch into which was etched the profile of Queen Victoria (a sour-faced prig, she looked, like so many German widows Jenny had known in Wisconsin), the only jarring element in Jenny's borrowed ensemble.

General Sheridan, at the age of forty-one, was a stouter, shorter man than Jenny had imagined, not even five and a half feet tall. Actually, he would have been quite tall had his legs been in proportion to the length of his upper body and the size of his large, fierce-looking head. But the muscular legs were short and, like Tom's, slightly bowed from too much time in the saddle. She recalled a remark of Abraham Lincoln's she'd read somewhere. In a classic case of pot and kettle, Lincoln — no Adonis himself — had described Sheridan as "a chunky little chap with a long body, short legs, not enough neck to hang him by, and such long arms that if his ankles itch he can scratch them without stooping." Yet there was something compelling about the man. Dark-haired and highly colored, he had immense, wild, dark eyes, like those of some great war hawk, she thought. He exuded an aura of what the romances called "animal magnetism" that she found faintly exciting. She was seated on his left during dinner, across from Colonel Dodge, and found herself watching the general's every move.

"Miss Dousmann has only recently returned from the Texas Panhandle," Colonel Dodge told him when they had finished the soup course (a somewhat acrid consommé). "She was down there hunting buffalo." The great man's shaggy brows arched as he focused those fiery eyes on her. She soon found herself relating the story of the hunt. General Sheridan wanted to know details of the routes they had followed, available forage and waterholes found along the way, Indians encountered, the shape of the terrain, the strength of rivers in spate and at normal levels, the makeup and consistency of their bottoms at the fords — more questions than Jenny could imagine being asked on any subject. When she got to the norther and Otto's misfortune, he frowned.

"Ah, Miss Dousmann, what a pity," he said. "A brave man maimed, as so many were in the war. For this, too, is a war, you know. Yet there are persons in this great nation of ours, mainly in the cities of the East, who are demanding that the Congress pass laws to prohibit the hunting of the buffalo. These foolish gentlemen, knowing nothing of the West or of the hostile, uncivilized savages who infest it, call the buffalo hunter a vandal and a profiteer. A criminal, if you will! On the contrary, Miss Dousmann, I believe that instead of prohibiting such hunts, the Congress ought to vote all buffalo hunters a hearty and unanimous thanks. In fact, it ought to appropriate sufficient funds to strike and present to each hunter — yourself included — a medal of bronze showing a dead buffalo on one side and a discouraged redskin on the other."

Officers within hearing said, "Hear, hear!"

He raised his voice and his wineglass in response, warming to his audience. "By God, Miss Dousmann, the buffalo hunters have done more in the past few years to settle the blamed Indian question than the whole damned Regular Army has in the past thirty years! Why, they're destroying the very *commissary* of the Indian nations. And as Napoleon so wisely put it, an army fights on its stomach. We should be sending the buffalo hunters *free rifles and free ammunition*, not mealy-mouthed complaints from a gang of limp-wristed Eastern fops who never skinned so much as a jackrabbit!" He emptied his glass, as did the whole table. Colonel Dodge signaled a steward to bring more wine.

"Believe me, Miss Dousmann," the general continued in a quieter, more reasonable tone, "if we want lasting peace on these prairies — if we want to see great towering cities and hives of industry humming on the plains, which of course we do — we must allow the hide man to kill, skin, and sell until the last buffalo is slain. Only then can these grasslands — the greatest, richest, finest pasturage in the world — be covered with speckled cattle and what the Eastern fops so cynically call 'the festive cowboy.' For civilization truly follows the hunter, as surely as rain follows the plow."

The officers and their ladies rose spontaneously as one and cheered. Huzzahs and loud hand clapping, tears, spilled wine, heaving bosoms. Jenny remained silent. She wanted to object, so many thoughts raced through her brain — the aridity of the Great West, painfully obvious to anyone who had traveled it, would alone prevent the growth of great cities or any sort of civilization worthy of the name. And the incessant wind — what white woman could consider living permanently in a world where dust crept into everything? And the cold, the numbing, nerve-killing cold, always waiting to leach the very life from man, woman, or child? Only Indians could live happily in this world of the Great West, and a few like-minded whites who might as well themselves be Indians. But they had to keep moving to do it — they had to follow the herds.

She realized, just then, that she was becoming one of them.

The following morning, before he returned to his headquarters in Chicago, General Sheridan stopped at the infirmary to visit Otto. "How are you doing, son?" he asked after he'd seated himself beside Otto's cot.

"About as well as can be expected, General." Though he was awed by the presence of the great man, Otto had never had more than grudging respect for him. "Little Phil" Sheridan was a bulldog of a fighter, but his willingness to kill his own troops in the furtherance of his career was legendary in the Union Army. In that respect he was the equal of Grant and Sherman, now President of the United States and overall commander of the U.S. Army, respectively.

"That's good, that's good," Sheridan said. "No complaints, no whining. What I'd expect of a Black Hat soldier. Tell me, was you at the Wilderness?"

"Yes, sir, I was."

"A grim fight, that," the general said, shaking his massive head. The dark hair shot with gray was cut so short it looked as if it were painted on. "My cavalry didn't see much action there, thanks to the terrain and the timidity of George Meade. But we more than made up for it later in the campaign — at Yellow Tavern."

"That's where you killed Jeb Stuart."

"Yes, it was, that damned Rebel poseur, with his yellow sash and his ostrich-plume hat and his goddamn cape lined with red satin. It was one of

George Custer's men put a pistol ball through Stuart's miserable guts. John Huff was his name, an elderly private of the 5th Michigan Cavalry. A satisfying day, that one was."

"General Custer's making quite a name for himself out here in the West," Otto said.

"Yes — as a butcher." The general laughed. "If you're to believe the Eastern papers, that is. He did too good a job for me down on the Washita. But you're an Indian fighter, your sister tells me. You understand that this is total war. The only way we can hope to put an end to all this rape of our women, this burning of homes, this hit-and-run warfare at which the redman excels, is to burn him out of the West, root and branch. Or starve him into submission. You buffalo boys are doing just that, destroying his means of livelihood. Why, take the Cheyenne, just one tribe — though, granted, the cruelest of the lot. No better than Mosby's or Quantrill's banditti — sneaking in when we're not looking, pretending to be what they ain't, coming up to a farmhouse door and begging for food; then when a soft-hearted farm wife fixes 'em a hot meal, what do they do? They throw it in her face and rape her before ripping off her scalp. They kill all her children and livestock, and burn the place down. But you know that, I'm sure."

"I have good friends among the Cheyenne," Otto said. "But yes, they're bloody-minded."

General Sheridan frowned and rose from his chair. "I must be moving on," he said. "Duty calls, alas. I told your sister last night at dinner that the government ought to strike a medal for you buffalo hunters. I doubt it shall ever come to pass, but I would like to reward you personally with this."

He bent down to place an ugly, double-barreled revolver on the cot beside Otto.

"This was Jeb Stuart's pistol," he said. "It's a nine-shot, .42-caliber LeMat — ten shots if you load the 20-gauge underbarrel — and no doubt it's killed many of your comrades in years past. Perhaps you'll never be able to use it on redskins, and more's the pity, but you can leave it to your heirs. There are still thousands of red devils left for us to kill."

The general leaned over and patted Otto on the shoulder, then turned on his heel. He had purchased dozens of these revolvers after the war and passed them out regularly to men like Otto — brave soldiers of the Union who had fallen on hard times. It was a heartfelt gesture.

Tom Shields stood quietly in a corner of the infirmary, having come in to visit Otto, as he did every morning. He had heard Sheridan's words and recognized the man. The spider war chief passed within ten feet of him as he left. It took every bit of willpower Tom Shields possessed not to draw his knife and kill this enemy of his people.

Jenny came to the infirmary every day, bearing trays from the mess hall to feed Otto. At first he hardly acknowledged her presence, taking the food off her fork or spoon and chewing embarrassedly, refusing even to meet her eye. She prattled on about the affairs of the day — more gunfights in Dodge City, an elegant new restaurant opened on Front Street, wagonloads of hides arriving in droves from the new hunting grounds down in Texas — but he rarely so much as grunted in reply.

"Why don't you talk to me?" she burst out one evening. "I know you must blame me for . . . this" — she gestured at the wire cage that still protected the stump of his arm. "But can't you see that I'm sorry? It really wasn't my fault."

Finally his eyes looked at her. And darted away again. He shook his head and blushed.

"No, no, Jennchen," he whispered. "I don't blame you. I don't blame anyone. It's just . . ." Tears leaked from the corners of his eyes and he took a deep breath. "It could have happened a thousand times in a thousand ways, at any time during the war. It could have happened — maybe it should have happened — before Mutti and Vati died, when I was alone on the buffalo ground. Yes, I should have been dead long ago, and I'd always figured that one day before very long I *would* be dead. An artillery burst, a skirmisher's bullet, a badly placed shot on a charging buffalo, who knows — a knife fight in a drovers' saloon in some cow town along the railroad? But then I'd just be . . . finished. *Punkt.* Like that. I never even imagined a situation where I'd be alive but incapable of making a living."

"Who says you can't make a living? You can still walk, you have at least one arm, you're educated and intelligent. Think of the wise, wonderful things you could tell your students about the Great West if you taught school."

"Bitter things, Jennchen. Ugly things. How to kill buffalo, how to kill Indians, how to kill soldiers in a war. No, I could never teach, nor will I ever work in a store of any kind. I am a hunter who can hunt no longer. I would rather be dead than live on as an object of pity."

"Otto, Otto," Jenny moaned. "What can I do?"

"Look in that drawer beside the bed."

Jenny opened it and saw the LeMat revolver.

"If you love me, sister, take it and shoot me," Otto said. "It's loaded — I asked the orderly to check before he put it there."

His eyes burned into hers.

She took up the pistol, heavy in her hand. Her heart felt heavier.

But she shook her head. "You know I can't," she said finally. "Anything but that."

He laughed bitterly. "*Ach ja,* I knew you couldn't. Nor will the orderly, much less Dr. Wallace. Maybe Tom will oblige me."

"No," Jenny said. "I'll forbid it."

Otto sighed. "Then I must live with myself," he said. "But I won't be a burden to you. You're young yet, Jennchen, a whole happy life ahead of you — you should marry, have children, but who would marry a woman saddled with a crippled brother? Dr. Wallace was telling me about the

223

new Soldiers' and Sailors' Homes being built by the Grand Army of the Republic. For crippled veterans of the war, he says. The nearest one is in Kansas City. He says that as a decorated veteran of the 2nd Wisconsin, I would qualify for admission, even though my injuries occurred after the end of hostilities. His say-so would guarantee it."

"Who says I even want to get married?" Jenny asked. "I'm your sister, and if I choose to care for you for the rest of our lives, you cannot properly deny me that right. It is my *Pflicht* — my family duty — and I want to discharge it as honorably as you performed yours in the war. No, sending you to a home would be to my dishonor."

The argument went on for days, until one evening Tom Shields interceded.

"Let's go north to my people," he said. "There are many widows among the Sa-sis-e-tas, lonely women who'd be only too happy to provide a wounded warrior with a warm lodge and plenty of meat. My mother will care for you even if no one else does. And . . ."

"I thought you said your mother was dead," Jenny interrupted.

"I lied," Tom said. "My father lives, too."

"Why did you lie about them?"

"I wanted your sympathy," Tom said. "My mother said it would work."

"Well," Jenny said, "she was right. Where are your people right now?"

"Somewhere in what you call the Big Horn Mountains," Tom said. "Don't worry, I'll find them."

"Well, do it," Jenny said. She looked at Otto. He had sunk back into silence and apathy.

PART III

16

On the first day of spring 1874, Jenny and Tom left Fort Dodge and headed north toward the Big Horn Mountains. Otto, still too weak to ride, they carried with them in a light Studebaker wagon Jenny had bought secondhand from the Army, along with two big Missouri mules and a played-out cavalry horse, a fifteen-year-old buckskin called Trooper. She paid for all this with money her brother had saved from the sale of buffalo hides, drawn on a letter of credit from a bank in Leavenworth, Kansas. Otto rarely spoke. He lay red-eyed and haggard, propped up in the back of the wagon under heavy blankets, staring at the horizon or watching the wolves that trailed them whenever Tom or Jenny killed fresh meat. He never complained, not even when the wagon jounced for days over rough, frozen ground. He watched the wolves intently.

They crossed the Saline and Solomon Rivers with little difficulty, for the water was still low, locked up in the icy Rockies, which loomed far and ghostly blue to their west, awaiting the heat of the summer sun before it came crashing down through the rivers of the plains. But the upper Republican was already rising when they got there, nearly in spate. They unloaded the wagon to lighten it. Tom cinched winter-dried cotton-wood logs to the frame which served as floats and they breasted the roaring brown river in a surge of spray. The mules swam strongly. They emerged on the far bank with only an inch of water in the wagonbed. Otto, whom they had wrapped in a tarpaulin, said nothing. Then Tom and Jenny rode back to ferry across on horseback all the goods they'd unloaded earlier — guns, ammunition, blankets, cookware, kegs, crates, and provisions. The transfer took many trips.

Twice as they approached the right-of-ways of railroads they spotted parties of men on horse-back moving swiftly in the distance. Pawnees, Tom said. Looking for trouble. Both times they hid the wagon in a creek bottom and watched from a grassy crest of the prairie, lying on their bellies, rifles locked and loaded, until the dust of the horses faded from sight.

"I thought the Pawnees were friendly to whites," Jenny said. "You hear all sorts of stories back East about Major Frank North and his val-iant Pawnee scouts keeping the railways safe for commerce."

Tom frowned. "We'd be safe enough if either Major North or his brother Lute were leading them, but I could see no spider soldier traveling with those savages. If they caught us, they'd kill me first off, no matter what you said. To them I'm a Cheyenne, not a human being. Then they'd kill you for your horses and your guns and your hair. Trust me. I know them all too well. They love a blond scalp."

And if I were traveling alone, Jenny thought, how well would I fare with a war party of *your* people? Sometimes at night, under the vast, cold prairie sky, she found herself wondering and worrying about the reception she and Otto would receive from the Cheyennes, when and if they got there. Tom made it sound like a family reunion — why sure, they'd be welcomed with open arms. But perhaps he was lying again.

One night, as she lay wrapped in her blankets near the fire, staring up into space and musing on this possibility, Tom asked her what she was pondering.

"Oh, just the stars," she lied quickly. "So many of them, and so beautiful — like sapphires and rubies up there." She rolled over onto an elbow and looked up at him. "If you could have one to wear around your neck, Tom, which would you pick?"

He laughed. "The Cut-Arms have a story about that," he said. "Two girls of the People were sleeping out on the prairie and one of them asked the same question. The other girl looked carefully and found a very bright star — 'That one there,' she said. 'I'd take it for my very own.' Next day they were hunting for food along a creekbank and they spotted a porcupine high in a cottonwood. The girl who'd chosen the brightest star said she'd climb up there and throw the animal down so her friend could kill it. So up she climbed — and climbed, and climbed some more. But the porcupine just kept going higher. It seemed to her that the tree was getting way too tall, that it was growing taller even as she climbed it. The girl on the ground called her friend to come down. But the Bright Star Girl was stubborn and kept on climbing, until she was among the clouds. When she came to the top of the tree, she couldn't find the porcupine. She reached a foot off the branch she was on, reached it out through the clouds, and found herself touching solid ground. She had climbed all the way up into the Sky Land. Then a handsome man came over the Sky Prairie and smiled at her, and his teeth were like starlight, and he took her to his tepee. 'But I must go back to my friend and to my people,' she said. 'Why must you go?' the Sky Man asked. 'Just last night you said you wanted me for your very own.' Of course, she thought, he is the Bright Star."

Tom laughed with delight, and Jenny with him.

"So she stayed in the Sky Land," Tom continued, "and became the wife of Bright Star. Soon she was with child. One day she was out digging roots on the prairie and pulled out a big turnip, of a kind that her husband had warned her not to dig. When she looked into the hole it had left, she saw the earth far below. She widened the hole, and then she could see better — her Cut-Arm People, her ponies, her friends, and her family. And she got very homesick. So she wove a rope of braided grass and began to climb back down to earth. But she was too heavy, what with the baby in her belly, and when she was halfway

232

down, the grass rope broke. She fell faster and faster — so fast that the air started to feel hot, like when you ride your pony hard through a sandstorm. Bright Star Girl got so hot that her hair caught on fire. Then her skin, then her meat, and then finally her bones — all were burning. She fell through the air like a blazing stick. Like this . . ."

He reached into the campfire bare-handed and shied a flaming brand at the wolves that circled them just outside the firelight. Their eyes winked out and they ran off. But a sudden growl from the nearby wagon made Jenny jump.

"Don't worry," Tom said. "It's only Black Hat. He likes to watch the wolves." He shrugged and shook his head.

"Sometimes he talks to them at night, but he doesn't really know their language yet . . . Anyway, when Bright Star Girl hit the ground, still burning, she broke into many pieces, and she was killed. Finished. But the baby in her belly survived — he was made of stone, just like his father, just like I am or any Cut-Arm — like the stars themselves. The People called him Falling Star, and he was a great hero in those days."

A meteor blazed across the night sky.

"Look out," Tom said, laughing. "Here he comes again!"

They finally found Tom's family band, the Suhtaio, camped on the Red Fork of Powder River, up near the headwaters in a rough, broken

233

country that the spiders called Hole-in-the-Wall. It had been a favorite resort of outlaws for more than twenty years. From the east, where the Bozeman Trail ran, there was only one way into Hole-in-the-Wall, through a narrow, easily guarded gap in a scarp of sandstone called the Red Wall. On the sundown side, many trails led west through the high Big Horn country and across a great basin of prairie to the Absarokas and the Wind River Mountains, and to the gold mines of Virginia City. Over the years, the Cheyenne had been forced to kill a few of these spider outlaws, when the men tried to rob their camps or rape Sa-sis-e-tas women.

When Tom located the Suhtaio lodges, he did not reveal himself. He returned quickly to the wagon and told Jenny to wait. Then he stripped off his clothes, bathed in a nearby brook, dressed himself in fringed buckskin leggings, a red breechclout, and a doeskin shirt decorated with porcupine quills. He blackened his face and hands with ashes from the fire, took the scalps — a dozen of them — from his war bag, tied them to a pole in groups of four, and rode off on Wind Blows toward the Cheyenne camp. Black was the color of victory. Jenny hid the wagon in a brush-grown gully — Otto was sleeping — and followed on one of the mules to see what happened. She brought the Henry and a bandolier of bullets, just in case of trouble.

Tom galloped up to the semicircle of lodges, then rode Wind Blows back and forth outside the east-facing entranceway, shaking the scalp pole above his head and singing out in a strange, harsh voice how each scalp had been taken. Everyone in the village came running, the men with guns in hand or arrows nocked on their bows. Jenny began to raise her rifle. But when the Cheyennes recognized Tom, great cries of joy went up.

Two men took the scalp pole from him, while the rest of the people returned hastily to their lodges and began lugging bundles of firewood to the center of the village. A huge cone of firewood rose, underlaid with dried grass to ensure quick ignition. This tepee of wood Jenny later learned was called the *hka-ó,* or "skunk." Drummers and singers, their faces painted red and black, gathered near it. Older men and women stripped to the waist and painted their upper bodies black and stood in a line on one side of the fire cone. The girls and unmarried young women had dressed themselves in long deerskin dresses, their finest outfits, and lined up in a row facing a similar row of young men, their sweethearts. Jenny recognized Crazy for Horses, Cut Ear, and Walks like Badger among them. The two older men who had taken the scalp pole now returned with it and lit the fire.

Tom spotted Jenny standing at the edge of an alder thicket near the stream and walked out to her. He took her by the hand and led her toward the fire. The Indians did not stare, they were too polite for that. They merely glanced at her, some of the girls with unconcealed jealousy. "Don't be

235

nervous," Tom said. "This first dance is the Dance of the Sweethearts. Some of these girls wanted me to pick them for the dance. But I want you to be my sweetheart from now on. Will you?"

"And what would that entail — being your sweetheart?"

"Living in my lodge," he said. "Eating with me, sleeping with me, at least for as long as we're here with my people. Or at least for as long as you can still stand me." He laughed with some embarrassment. "At any rate, it will keep the other girls away from me, and from you as well. They can be quite wicked. I'm certain my mother will welcome you."

It was as close as he would ever come to a proposal of marriage.

"All right," she said, amused and strangely titillated by the exchange. "But what about right now? What will become of Otto? We can't just leave him out there in the wagon."

"I'll send one of my Elk Soldier friends to take care of him," Tom said.

Jenny said, "Good. Now what do I do for this dance?"

"Just follow my steps."

After speaking briefly with Walks like Badger, who walked reluctantly toward the hidden wagon, Tom put his arm through Jenny's as they reached the line of girls. Each of them had been selected by her sweetheart or, if she had none, by her brother, and now they danced forward, arm in arm, toward the fire. The drums beat a fast rhythm, the voices of the Sa-sis-e-tas rose above the crackle and roar of the flames. The stuttering, hard-heeled dance steps were simple once Jenny got into the swing of them, and Tom was a good dancer, easy to follow. His arm was strong and sure. She glanced at him, at the sweat cutting clean stripes of tan on his ash-darkened face, eyes burning green as he chanted the alien words in staccato cadences.

The scalp pole stood behind the fire, its trophies glinting in the random dance of the flames. For an instant it seemed to her that the dead hair of Tom's enemies was alive again and dancing with them. With her free hand Jenny reached up and pulled off her hat, skimming it backward without looking. She untied her braids and shook them out, so that her long blond hair swung wildly. As she warmed to the beat of the dance, she felt her body loosen deliciously, tasted the clean sweat on her upper lip. The rhythms worked into her bones. She heard herself chanting now along with Tom, with her fellow dancers, and though the words were strange, they somehow felt familiar on her tongue. It felt good, dancing this way, wild and free, and suddenly an image formed in her brain — something half remembered, perhaps from a tale her father had read her from one of his many books on the ancient Germans, or perhaps a deep reverberation of folk memory — of painted, half-naked people, white-skinned men and women both, dancing to drums in a fire-lit forest, their long blond hair swinging in ritualistic rhythm to an ancient song of death and new love.

After the dances, which lasted well into the dark of night, an older woman who had been talking to Tom in Sa-sis-e-tas came up to Jenny as she was rebraiding her hair. The woman had washed the black from her face and upper body and put on a deerskin blouse. Her own braids, nearly white, had streaks of yellow in them. Her eyes were as green as Tom's, level and questioning; her cheekbones broad, her nose shorter than an Indian's, though her skin was as dark as any Cheyenne's.

"*Grüss Gott,*" she said in German. "*Ich bin der Two Shield's seine Mutter, heiss' Ulrike Bauer. Die Indianer haben mich 'Starkherz' genennt* — I am Tom's mother, called Strongheart Woman by these people."

Jenny stepped back and put out her hand. "*Sehr gefreut,*" she said formally, with a slight bow. "Very pleased, I'm sure. My name is Jenny Dousmann. And you are a captive, Tom says — Two Shields, that is?"

"Not for a long time already," Strongheart Woman said. "These are my people now, and a much better *Volk* than those I was born among. But we will talk of that later. Now you must be hungry. You and your brother will sleep in my husband, Little Wolf's, lodge tonight, until Two Shields prepares his own tepee for you. Little Wolf is off at war right now, but I am sure he would approve."

In the days that followed, Strongheart Woman taught Jenny much about the ways of the Cheyenne, from the rudiments of their strange, complicated language to the niceties of womanly behavior that Tom could never have explained. Yet it was Strongheart Woman who insisted quite firmly that Jenny not adopt Cheyenne dress.

"They think of you just now as a creature beyond sex," Strongheart Woman said. "If you dress as a woman, they will consider you one, and some of the mystery will be gone. And since you are now with Two Shields, I would not be allowed to speak with you — among these people, a mother-in-law and daughter-in-law are wisely kept apart. But if they should get the idea that you are merely a captive, some of the wilder soldiers — the Kit Foxes or the Crazy Dogs — might take it in mind someday when Two Shields is away to put you 'on the prairie,' as they call it. It is just a fancier term for rape. They do not think of captive women as human beings."

She paused and frowned, perhaps remembering.

"I hear the Old Man Chiefs talking, though," Strongheart continued. "Perhaps you are E-hyoph-sta, they say, come back to test us, to see if we're worthy of your assistance. Even before you came, Two Shields's Elk Soldier friends had described your birth from the belly of the cow buffalo, after the storm. And Two Shields has told us of your hunting skills. Don't misunderstand me, though. The Sa-sis-e-tas treat their own women well enough. We have much influence in the tribal councils. Some women of this tribe have themselves been great soldiers, women who have counted coup in battles with our enemies. I myself have done so. It's how I won my name. But our most important role is the bearing of children, as it is with women everywhere. You mustn't be burdened with that task just now. If by chance you should get with child and you don't want the baby, tell me and I will take care of it. I know the right medicines. Don't tell Two Shields or anyone else. Killing a Cheyenne child either before it is born or afterward is considered a mortal sin by the Old Man Chiefs — you and I would be cast out of the tribe, as would any woman who did so. But our women — all women, I suppose — have ways of getting around the wrongheaded rules of men, as I'm sure you know."

Jenny nodded.

"*Ja, sicher,*" Strongheart continued, smiling. "But truly, you must remain free of womanly obligations until Little Wolf returns and decides how best you might serve the Cut-Arm People."

"And if I don't care to serve them?"

"Then you may leave, but you'll take my son's heart with you."

The Cheyenne camp stood on the edge of the timber, against which the buffalo-hide lodges shone white in the hard morning light, blackened

240

only near their conical tops from the smoke of cookfires. The smoke rose slowly, thin in the cold still air. In front of the lodges a tributary of the Páae-ó'he, or Powder River, raced clear and cold over beds of rattling gravel. The pony herd, more than three hundred strong, grazed in lush meadow grass just downstream from the camp. Each morning when the first rays of the sun warmed the lodges, an old, battle-scarred crier named Tall Meat walked through the camp, relaying the orders of the day from the band's four chieftains.

He might announce that the band would remain in this camp for another two or three days. There were buffalo nearby. No one must make unnecessary or excessive noise for fear of frightening them away. The soldiers of the Kit Fox Society would be in charge of discipline in this regard. The chiefs would decide today when to run the buffalo. Or Tall Meat might tell the camp that someone had misplaced a favorite skinning knife, it had a handle of otter skin and a nick in the blade, and anyone finding it must not claim it for his own but return it at once. The crier's words confirmed ownership of the knife, and had the force of law. No member of the band would now think of keeping it. Nor would any Cheyenne, once warned by the crier — not even the most obstreperous boy — dare to hunt buffalo on his own, against the crier's orders. The Fox soldiers enforced discipline with pony quirts, forcefully and expertly wielded.

241

Already the men and boys of the band had run down from their lodges to the creek, to splash and wrestle in the icy water. Women did not bathe as often, nor were they as vain as the men in their mode of dress and makeup. The women had followed with buckets made from buffalo paunches to replenish the water in their lodges. The Sa-sis-e-tas would not drink "dead water," which had stood overnight in a bucket. It had no strength. Their water must be cold and alive, from the running brooks. In the lodges, cast-iron pots of stew were heating over the fires for the morning meal, sending forth a rich odor of buffalo meat and sliced wild turnips. The turnips and other tubers were gathered daily on the prairie by women and girls with their elkhorn root diggers, while the men hunted meat and scouted for enemies.

Jenny was known throughout the camp as E-hyoph-sta, or Yellow-Haired Woman. The Cheyennes didn't know quite what to make of her. For one thing, she dressed like a white man, in woolen trousers, a man's chambray shirt, and a drover's jacket of tanned sheepskin, wool side in. On her head she wore a flat-brimmed, dark brown beaver-felt hat. She braided her blond hair and pinned it in a knot, under the hat. She carried a nine-shot revolver in a holster on her right hip, and she shot it well. Knee-length boots of black leather covered her man-sized feet. She often hunted alone, carrying a heavy Sharps breech-loading buffalo rifle, returning with wild turkeys, mule deer, antelope, and once a large cow elk which she had quartered expertly by herself and dragged in behind her pony on a travois.

In so many respects she was like a man, yet she was a woman. The Sa-sis-e-tas had seen her bathing. She lived in a lodge with Two Shields, who was not a Contrary — not the sort of man who did everything backward, dressing as a woman and sleeping with men. Perhaps E-hyoph-sta was a Contrary, though among the Sa-sis-e-tas there were no female Contraries. Perhaps it was different with the white spiders, surely the strangest creatures on earth.

With them in their lodge lived E-hyoph-sta's brother, the spider named Black Hat, whom some of the men of the band had seen a few years ago, living alone in a cave near the Mán-oi-o'he, or Burnt Timber River, which the spiders called the Smoky Hill. Black Hat was crippled now. His fingers, toes, and right arm had been cut off by a white spider doctor at Fort Dodge after Black Hat froze them in a blizzard down near the Bull Buffalo River. The Sa-sis-e-tas knew just from looking at him that Black Hat wanted to die. No one would kill him, though they all felt sorry for him. They were afraid of his magic. He had killed many Crazy Knife soldiers in a fight just before he was frozen. Two Shields had told them so, and Two Shields did not lie.

Perhaps because she had spoken both German

and English from childhood, Jenny found the Cheyenne language easy to learn. To her ear, at least, it sounded like German, with a lot of *ch* and *sch* sounds, and the same vowel pronunciations. Like German it also contained many compound words constructed of shorter ones, chained together and subtly altered in combination to create a whole new meaning. Sugar, for instance, was called *ve'kee-mahpe,* or "sweet water," in Cheyenne, just as — say — oxygen in German was *Sauerstoff,* or "sour stuff." She had brought a wheel of cheese with her from Fort Dodge, and learned when she shared it with the Cheyennes that they called it *he'kone-ame,* or "hard grease," while butter — *heóve-ame* — was literally "yellow grease."

Jenny was glad she had also packed the wagon with plenty of coffee, since the Cheyennes were crazy for it. A scarred old warrior might stride up to her at any time of the day or night and declare in a booming voice, *"Na-mane-tano!"* ("I am thirsty"). Then, whipping a horn cup from behind his back and grinning from ear to ear, add, *"Hoseste ne-xohose-metsestse mo'kohtávi-hohpe."* ("Give me some more black soup"). Tea, by contrast, was *vépotsé-hohpe,* or leaf soup.

She especially delighted in the Cheyenne names for certain birds and animals — *heove-se'tave,* or "yellow feet," for the cottontail rabbit; *néschke'ésta,* or "perky ears," for the chipmunk; *no'he'o,* or "brown wings," for the little brown bats that hawked bugs along the river in the dusk. The big, glittering dragonflies which roared in metallic diminuendo over the river meadows were aptly named *hevovetaso*, "the whirlwind." Apt, too, was their word for child, *ka'ischkone*, or "little mind" — but only in the sense of unformed, untutored. The Cheyenne loved their children and took more pride in them than many whites she had known. They answered a child's questions seriously, no matter how foolish, and were rarely too busy to tell a tale out of the past to illustrate a point of behavior or technique. They answered Jenny's questions the same way, and at first it irked her. It smacked of condescension.

Many Cheyenne words were more direct, earthier, like *cháa'e* for weasel, which meant "the pisser," and *heschkó'sema*, or "thorny bug," for cricket. Coffee, which the Cheyenne loved with lots of "sweet water" in it, was called *mo'kohtávi-hohpe*, or "black soup." For some reason, perhaps out of the distant past when the Cheyenne were dwelling elsewhere, their word for dog, *oeschkeso*, translated into English as "small seal." A rifle, *ma'aetano*, meant "iron bowstring," while a bullet, *vé'ho'o-maahc*, was a "spider (or white-man) arrow."

"Why do they call us *vé'ho'e* — 'spider'?" she asked Strongheart one day. "Because we're poisonous?"

The old woman laughed. "I hadn't thought of that, but it makes sense. No, it's actually a compliment. The People believe there are two main gods who control the world — *He-amma-vé'ho'e* and *Akh-tun-o-vé'ho'e*, the Spider Above and the Spider Below. They consider the spider a very clever creature. He spins a web to trap his food, so he must have tools that they cannot see. Other insects get caught in the web and cannot get loose, but the spider runs across it without sticking. He goes up and down through the air with no support. When French traders came down from Canada, nearly a century ago, from what I can make out, they were the first whites the People ever met. They had tools and implements the Cheyenne had never seen before — iron traps and cook pots and axes, magical sticks that roared and threw flames and smoke, and killed their enemies at great distances, leaving holes with no arrows sticking from them. So the People stood in awe of them. They believed those first white men were sent by their gods, and so they called them *vé'ho'e*. No, no, my dear, all the poison came later, when the white men started spreading their steel webs — their railroads — across our land and began killing the buffalo."

For the most part, once she'd gotten through the language barrier, life in the camp was pleasant. Living in skin tents — even in the mud and rain of early spring — was not much different from living under canvas in the buffalo camp. Smudge fires kept off the black flies and mosquitoes that swarmed with the onset of hot weather, and Cheyenne wives were death on lice and fleas, picking them out of the seams of clothing and crushing them with tough-tipped, expert fingers. Food was fairly abundant — elk, deer, antelope meat aplenty, though buffalo were growing ominously scarce. Or so the old people claimed. Still, in any lodge, at any hour of the day or night, a kettle of meat and root vegetables was always simmering. Anyone whose appetite was stirred by the odors wafting from the cook pot, whether a member of that lodge's family or not, was free to step into the tepee and help himself.

All day long the camp was busy — with men making or repairing weapons, if they were not out hunting or scouting or training their horses, while women scraped and tanned hides, or searched in the brushy draws or out on the plains themselves, picking plums and berries, grubbing up edible tubers with root diggers made from the shoulder blades of animals, or else loading their travois with firewood or dried buffalo chips. Cheyenne boys played at war or hunting, and little girls cuddled their dolls or imitated their mothers by trekking around camp with tiny travois loaded with sticks or straw and pulled by the old, calm, slow dogs of the camp. Sometimes the children paired off, playing mother and father, building toy tepees, cooking doll-size meals of mice and songbirds and minnows and weeds, tending mock horse herds that were really just bundles of sticks.

Meanwhile, there were always a few crotchety old women stalking the camp day and night in search of scandal. Old women angry at their lives, looking to make trouble for others wherever it could be snooped out. And the other common coin of any human community: self-important young men who spent more time on their dress and grooming than even the most vain of the Heldendorf belles Jenny had known, hoping to appear cool and brave, but simply looking silly as they strutted through camp in their finery. Harried young mothers scurrying from one task to another, scolding their husband when things went wrong whether it was his fault or not. And always a few pompous old men solemn as parsons, pipe-smoking dotards who leaked adages and homilies day and night. It was probably not unlike life in any village over the past thousand years, Jenny thought — European or American, white or red.

One morning, when Jenny had been admiring an elegantly painted red-and-black tepee that stood alone in the center of the camp, Strongheart suddenly stopped scraping her deer hides and rushed over.

"Don't go in there," she said. "This is the home of Is'siwun, the Buffalo Hat. It is the great Sacred Mystery of these people, their Holy Grail. It brings success in war and the buffalo hunt."

Strongheart explained the origins of the Hat and its counterpart, the Sacred Arrows of the Southern Cheyenne — about the two heroes, Erect Horns and Sweet Medicine, and the woman, E-hyoph-sta, who had brought buffalo and corn to the Cheyenne from the All-God Maheo's Thunder Lodge inside No-wah-wus, the Sacred Mountain in the Black Hills which the whites now casually called Bear Butte. From time to time, over the many years since then, the strength of the Hat and the Arrows had had to be renewed, by painful sacrifice in the "Standing Against the Sun" ceremony and by other, more elaborate rituals, when some Cheyenne had committed a sin against the People or some unforeseen tragedy had befallen the Mysteries themselves.

Such a tragedy had occurred not long before Strongheart had joined the People. In an attack on a Skidi Pawnee village, the Sacred Arrows, all four of them, had been captured by the hated Wolf People. Normally the Hat and Arrows led the attack on an enemy force and, when accompanied by the proper ceremonies, blinded the enemy soldiers to their Cheyenne attackers. This time, because of the rashness of some hot-blooded, coup-crazy young warriors who attacked before the ceremonies had been completed, the Skidis were ready, their eyes wide open. They defeated the Cheyennes easily and stole the Arrows.

"Nothing's been right for us since," Strongheart concluded. "The buffalo grow fewer and wilder on the prairie, we find their skinned carcasses everywhere, killed by the spider hide hunters. The Traveling Houses of the spiders blow black smoke from their Iron Roads, which reach everywhere, clear across the prairie, frightening what game remains and bringing more and more spiders into our country. Diseases I knew as a child among the spiders — measles, whooping cough, pneumonia — now move among the Cut-Arm People and take off not only our children and old ones but even the strong and healthy, men and women alike. We fight the spiders and often win, and then the spider chiefs promise us peace. But a year later they invade the land they had promised was ours forever, and we must fight and die all over again. How can we live now? Everywhere we turn it's sundown. Sundown for the buffalo, sundown for the Cheyenne. Sundown for all of us — Sioux, Pawnee, and Snake, perhaps even for the spiders themselves someday. For who can live in a world without buffalo?"

Late one afternoon, while Jenny was skinning an antelope, Strongheart beckoned to her. Jenny could tell from the old woman's face that it was serious business. She led the way back into the hills surrounding the camp. Magpies were screaming. Strongheart said nothing as they hiked. In tall grass, near a coulee, Strongheart halted. They were still within earshot of the camp. With her right hand alongside her ear, Strongheart made a fist, leaving the index finger and thumb pointing upward — the Plains Indian sign language for "rabbit." But when she rotated the fist from side to side on the axis of her wrist, Jenny knew, that meant: "Listen."

Jenny did so. All she could hear was the screaming of the magpies. They bounced on the branches of the spindly cottonwoods lining the draw. She shook her head in puzzlement.

Strongheart repeated the sign, this time more urgently: *Listen more keenly!*

Jenny concentrated, and finally she heard a false note. Someone was trying to sound like a magpie. She started to pull her sheath knife, but Strongheart grabbed her wrist. Come with me, Strongheart signed.

They walked into the coulee. In the tall grass of a south-facing slope, above a pool of stagnant water left from the winter, they found a young woman in labor. Jenny recognized her as Lame Deer, a short, thin girl whose husband had been killed during a horse-stealing raid on the Crows that past winter. Her skirt was hiked to her hips, her legs spread, and as they watched, her belly heaved with a powerful convulsion. This was the moment, Jenny thought. A baby's head emerged through bulges of blood. It stuck there for a moment. Strongheart signed Jenny for her knife. Jenny handed it over. Strongheart spat on the point of the blade, worked it against a whetstone, wiped it clean against her shirt, and cut the woman just below the birth canal. Lame Deer's belly convulsed once more. The head emerged fully this time.

Lame Deer looked up at Strongheart and said something in Sa-sis-e-tas that Jenny could not understand. Lame Deer's eyes were sad, tired.

Yet they were also strong, Jenny realized, as if she was steeling herself for some new ordeal. Jenny could not see Strongheart's eyes.

The old woman reached down and cupped her hands around the baby's head, pulled, then reached in for the baby's shoulders and snaked them out. Lame Deer heaved once more. Strongheart lifted the baby clear. She bit through the umbilical cord and wiped the blood away with a wisp of dry buffalo grass that lay by Lame Deer's side. The baby was a girl. Strongheart lifted the infant and showed it to the mother. Lame Deer nodded and looked away.

Not once has she screamed, Jenny thought. My God, the women of Heldendorf . . .

Strongheart tucked the newborn into a fold of her hide shirt. Lame Deer reached for the buffalo grass she had picked earlier. She wiped herself clean, then lay back and closed her eyes. Tears glistened in their corners.

Jenny followed Strongheart up into the hills, even farther away from the camp. There, in a grassy hollow, they stopped. A dry wind howled overhead. The old woman placed the baby on a patch of moss, in the shadow of a smooth, weathered boulder.

What now? Jenny wondered. Some strange new Cheyenne ritual?

The baby's face was red and wrinkled, and it cried feebly, grimacing and wriggling its short arms and legs. Blood dried on its eyelids. Jenny's heart went out to it. Then Strongheart placed her

hand over the baby's nose and mouth. It struggled for a minute, while Jenny looked on in horror
— more than a minute; but finally the baby lay
still. Strongheart was staring at her. "Yes," she
whispered harshly, "but it must be done."

"Why?"

"Lame Deer has three sons and a daughter
already, all of them still children. You've seen
them playing around camp. Since her husband
was killed by the Crows, her brother has been
giving her meat. That means taking meat from
his own family. But now another man is interested in her, Old Gland with the withered arm.
He is a poor hunter, Old Gland, and he let it be
known that with another child to feed he could
never marry her." She sighed and smiled ruefully.
"Too few buffalo. Too many people. In German
we call this *Ökonomie*, Lame Deer had no choice.
She is my friend. I helped her."

With her root digger, Strongheart had already
prepared a hole in the ground. She placed the
tiny body in the hole and scraped dirt on top of
it. Jenny found a heavy, flat stone to place over
the grave. Before they left, Strongheart cut a
branch from a nearby osier and brushed out all
signs of their footprints.

"Won't the others know that Lame Deer had
the baby?" Jenny asked, irritated suddenly at all
this secrecy. "Certainly they knew she was with
child, so why won't they suspect that she'd had
it murdered when her belly's flat?"

"They'll know all right," Strongheart said. She

laughed, the dry cough of a crow. "Even the Old Man Chiefs will know. But no one will say anything if we don't. It is one of the Mysteries of the People."

When they passed the spot where Lame Deer had given birth, the young woman was gone. Jenny looked around, searching the hillsides, and finally spotted her down by the river, grubbing for cattail roots. She and Strongheart walked on back toward the tepees.

"Would you have spared the baby if it had been a boy?" Jenny asked.

"No," Strongheart said. "A child is a child, hunger is hunger."

17

Otto hadn't allowed Jenny to bathe or shave him since he'd left the infirmary at Fort Dodge, cursing and weeping whenever she suggested it. "Kill me!" he begged her again and again. "I'm no man at all if I can't keep myself clean!"

"You're a mess all right," she told him, angry in her own turn, fed up with his self-pity. Then: "Oh God, I'm sorry, brother — but you've got to stop feeling so hopeless. You can do things if you'll only try!"

"Like . . . what?"

"Well, you could start by trying to walk."

"And where would I walk to, if I could manage it?"

"You might try the river, it's not twenty steps from this tent. And once you're there, you might take a bath."

Otto looked away, his face sullen beneath his unkempt beard.

"What are you afraid of?" she asked.

"They'd laugh at me," he muttered. "I know the Indian and his wicked sense of humor. And truly I can't blame him. Many's the time I almost laughed at the sight of an old soldier crippled by the war. But only because I couldn't weep anymore."

"What can I do to help you?" she pleaded, nearly frantic with frustration.

"Nothing," he said. "I'm beyond help."

The Elk Sisters took care of that. Tom Shields sent the *noot-uhk-e-a,* the four girl soldiers of the Elk Society, to care for Black Hat. Their names were Crane, The Enemy, Yellow Eyes, and Slick Blue Serpent. All were plump and virtuous. At first the Elk Sisters were repelled by Black Hat's sorry condition. Cheyenne doctors never amputated, not even the most badly mangled limbs, trusting in secret herbal medicines and sacred spells to cure them. If a cure failed, then the All-God Maheo clearly intended that person to die. Black Hat's lack of fingers, toes, and half of one arm was shocking, but the Elk Sisters were positively disgusted by his filth.

They picked him up from his blankets and trundled him down to the river, where they stripped off his clothes and flung him into the water. While Crane and Yellow Eyes scrubbed him with sand and gravel, Serpent and The Enemy boiled his clothes in a bucket over the fire, then hung them over the nearby bushes to dry. With a sharp knife the girls shaved off Otto's beard, so that he would look more human. Otto didn't know which hurt worse, the scrubbing or the shave. But he felt a lot better once he was clean.

The Elk Sisters then sang some songs for him and danced awhile. He said nothing. They decided that the spider was the most stupid animal they had ever seen, since even dogs and horses could understand language. "Let's see if we can teach it to talk," said Yellow Eyes. She picked up a rock. *"Ho'honáa,"* she said, pointing to the rock. She cracked it sharply against Otto's head.

"Ouch!" he said.

"Na-oomo," Yellow Eyes said. *I am hitting!* She tapped him again. *"Na-oomo."*

"Na-oomo," Otto said in self-defense. He rubbed his head with his fingerless hand. *"Ho'honáa,* rock."

The Elk Sisters yipped and clapped their hands. Not only was it clean now, but it *could* speak! Maybe this spider was human, after all.

The Elk Sisters cooked for Otto, teaching him the words for various kinds of food and utensils. Whenever they picked up a tool, they told him its name. They taught him the names of animals, starting with dogs and horses. Each morning they took him to the river and washed him. When E-hyoph-sta and Two Shields went off to hunt, they slept in his lodge.

One night Yellow Eyes woke from a strange, warm dream. The other girls were snoring. So was Black Hat. Yellow Eyes began to massage him gently. He stiffened. He stared into her eyes, there in the warm dark. He caressed her cheek with the glassy-smooth stump of his arm.

"Haáhe," he whispered in his deep spider voice. *"E'peva'."*

Yes, it is good . . .

Jenny had excelled in archery at the academy, but she was awed by the skill of the Cheyenne bowmen. Their bows were short, not more than four and a half feet long. The best of them were made of horn or rib bone from elk, bighorn sheep, or buffalo. They were powerful weapons, recurved at their tips like the illustrations she had seen of Mongol and Turkish bows. Tom's bow, which he carried in a beautifully finished otterskin bow case decorated top and bottom with elaborately braided red-and-black quillwork, had been made from the horn of a mountain sheep, he told her. He had boiled the horn a long time to make it limber, then trimmed and shaved it down and straightened and laboriously flexed the limbs until they had assumed the shape he desired. Finally he had backed it with the glued shoulder sinew of a bull buffalo, to give it more throwing power. It was white on the front — actually the "back" of the bow, in the peculiar parlance of bowyers — with powdered gypsum sprinkled over a thin sizing of glue rendered down from buffalo hide, and was painted an ocherous red on the "belly." Its hand grip was a soft spiral wrap of deerhide. For all her strength, Jenny could draw the bow only a little more than half the length of its two-foot-long hunting arrow, but even that small effort drove the iron-headed shaft through a thick slab of pinewood.

"When I was a boy, our arrowheads were made of stone or bone," Tom told her. "The old men say they killed better than these iron ones." He laughed and threw back his head. "Old folks always like old ways."

He pointed out the lengthwise grooves incised on the arrow shafts — a straight one from fletching to head on the top surface, a sinuous groove on the bottom. "Some say these are to make the blood run more freely, others that they are magic to make the arrow fly straight and hit like lightning. My father laughs at that stuff. He says the grooves are only there to keep the arrow from warping back to its original shape, when it was a green wand of birch." Each arrow had Tom's personal mark on it, two red, shieldlike circles forward of the fletching on either side of the shaft. "That's to see who actually killed the buffalo when they're all down and the hunt is over," he said. "Sometimes there are fights over questions of meat."

Tom had her roll a willow-withe hoop, no more than three feet in diameter and covered with parfleche, across the prairie some sixty paces from where he stood. He zipped five arrows through it before it toppled to the ground, shooting faster and far more accurately than even Duck Bill Hickok could have with a six-shooter at that range. She had seen small boys, little more than toddlers, with tiny bows and arrows shooting at similar hoops around the camp, whooping and screeching whenever they scored a hit. All day long they practiced. Sometimes the more mischievous ones shot their blunt-headed arrows at her tepee when she was inside, then ran off laughing. They're flirting with me, Jenny thought, not unflattered. No better than white boys with their infernal baseballs, knocking a girl's bonnet off just to hear her squeal. But with a more useful purpose to their silly skills. These Cheyenne boys would kill enemies or bring home meat for their families when they grew up. You couldn't bring home meat with a baseball, not yet at least, though before leaving Wisconsin she had read of professional baseball clubs being formed in New York.

At night the white wolves howled, putting Otto in mind of his happy days on the Smoky Hill. Yellow Eyes lived with him now, having surrendered her post as an Elk Sister. The other girls had gone. The sisters of the Cheyenne soldier societies must remain chaste, and Yellow Eyes had relinquished that state. She alone cooked for Otto, helped him to bathe and shave, sewed new clothes of skin for him; she alone slept with him, in a small tepee of their own set apart from the camp circle. Yet still he refused to try walking, unwilling to submit himself to the possible taunts of the young warriors. He would allow her to help him from the tepee only at night when the village slept. Then they would sit together at the entrance to the tent while she washed him and trimmed his beard and he breathed the sweet night air.

She cut him an elegant walking stick of fragrant

cedar, peeled the bark, rubbed the wood with buffalo grease and ocher, and decorated its knurled top with a carefully carved wolf's head. At first he had trouble holding the stick firmly in the clenched cup of hand that remained to him, but Dr. Wallace had left him a small stub of thumb which eventually gave him a suitable grip. With Yellow Eyes at his side, holding his stump to give him support, Otto started walking again, only short distances at first, limping painfully down to the river to bathe, then out into the near hills. Slowly he regained his balance. He began to eye the horse herd and wondered if he could ride again. The Cheyennes rode quite well without using their hands, guiding their mounts with only their heels and knees, but they were centaurs from birth.

One night as the wolves sang and Yellow Eyes snored gently in the resonant dark, Otto rolled out from under his sleeping robe. With the aid of his wolf stick he hoisted himself to his feet and limped to the entrance of the lodge. He was still out of kilter — his toeless feet betraying him into a stumble whenever he forgot himself and tried to walk too fast. The weight of his body on his maimed feet remained painful, though it was beginning to ease.

He hobbled slowly away from the camp and up to the top of a ridge overlooking the river. There he propped himself against a boulder. The moon was nearing its full and he could see white wolves coursing a young elk through the valley below and up toward the opposite height of land. His heart thumped wildly, but more with excitement than exertion. Two of the younger wolves headed the elk and turned it back toward the slower members of the pack. One big lobo snatched at the elk's near hind leg as it galloped past, caught it, and upended the animal. The wolf pack fell on it like a thrashing white blanket. He could hear the crunch of their great jaws half a mile away. He felt a surge of elation. He raised his wolf stick and shook it at the moon.

Then he raised his head as well and howled along with the pack.

One dark and rainy morning Jenny laid an ambush for her pesky bowmen. Three of them were loitering nearby, waiting for her to go into the lodge. She pretended she didn't notice them and dodged under the flap. Then she crawled quietly out the rear of the tepee, having removed a peg for that express purpose only an hour earlier. She dodged around the Buffalo Hat tepee and walked quietly up to the archers just as they were about to shoot.

"Hi-yah!" She charged them. Two of the boys ducked away, but the third she grabbed by his braids. "I count coup on you," she said in Sa-sis-e-tas. She drew her sheath knife. "And now I shall take your scalp!"

The boy — he couldn't be more than ten years old, she thought — turned to her with big black eyes, half smiling, half fearful.

She frowned. "Are you a Cheyenne or a mouse?" she asked. "You should be singing your death song!"

He composed his face stoically, tears gleaming, and began to chant in a broken voice:

> *Rain is falling,*
> *The day is young,*
> *I am taken in battle —*
> *It does not hurt to die!*

"All right," Jenny said. "Now you're brave. Give me your bow and arrows and I'll give you back your life."

The boy grinned and handed her the weapons. The bow was made of a tough wood, probably ash, she thought, and backed, like Tom's, with the carefully cured shoulder sinew of a buffalo. Someone had lavished a lot of care on its making. The length of its back was beautifully painted in lozenges of red and blue, and from the lower limb, tied by strands of dried sinew to a carved plug, trailed a tuft of red-blond hair. At first she thought it might be a scalp, then realized from the coarseness that it was only horsehair. The bow's handle was wrapped with a piece of dark blue wool, probably cut from a captured U.S. Army blanket and sewed neatly up the belly. She nocked an arrow and drew it full-length. The bow pulled about thirty or forty pounds — a heavy draw for such a small boy to master. She aimed at a weather-bleached buffalo skull about twenty paces off and let fly. Because of the sinew backing, the bow released much harder and faster than the yew longbows she'd shot in her archery classes at the academy. The blunt-headed arrow bounced off the skull and sailed out over the tops of the tepees.

She kept the bow, but that night brought to the boy's tepee the hooves and tanned hide of a deer she had killed, along with a hefty load of its salted, sun-dried meat. For the next three days she hunted the brushy draws near camp with her new bow. She killed jackrabbits, a sage grouse, and a yearling antelope buck she lured into range as Tom had taught her, by waving the tuft of horse-hair, tied to the bow's top, over the lip of a ridge behind which she crouched. The antelope seemed mesmerized by the motion, stepping closer and closer on its shiny black toes, until she stood and put an arrow feather-deep into the base of its throat.

When she brought the prongbuck into camp draped across her shoulders, people came running from their tepees to admire her kill. Tom smiled proudly. Strongheart winked at her, and even Pony Quirts, the boy from whom she had taken the bow as her spoils of war, whooped happily in her honor. To kill with an arrow, Jenny reckoned, was to be a Cheyenne. Or at least well on her way to becoming one.

Yellow Eyes sewed moccasins of heavy buffalo hide to cover Otto's tender toe stumps, lining them with moss she gathered from the rocks of the high country. He found he could walk much faster now. She devised pads of supple, wide-cut buffalo leather that fit snugly over Otto's knees, left hand and elbow, and the stump of his right arm, allowing him to stalk game on all fours without being seen from a distance. Every day he walked out with her, mile upon mile, uphill and down, with the hide of a white wolf draped over his back. The Indians, Otto knew, used hides like this to disguise themselves when approaching a herd of feeding buffalo, which paid little attention to wolves until they were quite close. Buffalo, the Indians said, could tell by the way wolves walked when they were about to attack. Cheyenne hunters crawled up obsequiously to within bow range, then killed the fattest cows with ease.

But Otto couldn't use a bow. Nor was he fast enough on his truncated feet to catch even a day-old calf — and if by chance he caught one, how would he kill it? He didn't have the jaws of a wolf and he couldn't wield a knife.

One night, sleepless with the desire to hunt, to provide meat for himself and his woman, it came to him.

A javelin.

He awakened Yellow Eyes and set her to work at once, fashioning a short throwing spear with a shaft of tough ash. For a spearhead of the proper weight she found a double-edged spontoon, an eighteenth-century infantry weapon similar to a pike. The Elk Soldiers had captured it sometime in the dim past, Yellow Eyes said, in a battle with spider soldiers near the great lake where the Sa-sis-e-tas had lived before venturing onto the plains in pursuit of buffalo. Probably Frenchmen, Otto thought, and sure enough found a faint, time-worn fleur-de-lis, the armorial emblem of the Kings of France, engraved on the spearhead. She honed its edges to razor sharpness and bound it to the spear shaft with strands of sinew. A thong of rawhide tied just below the spearhead and then to Otto's left hand allowed him to drag it with him as he stalked. He could untie the thong with his teeth when he was ready to throw. Into the pad of his throwing hand Yellow Eyes sewed a small shallow socket which would accept the butt of the spear. Balancing the shaft with his stump while throwing with his left hand, he found with much practice that he could hit a stationary target hard and accurately up to fifty feet away.

They began hunting at night, for small game at first. Yellow Eyes accompanied him, crawling beside him as he made his careful stalks on graz-ing deer and antelope, then running down the game he hit and finishing it off with a stone-headed war club Crazy had given her. She gutted and skinned their kills, but he insisted on carrying the meat back to camp by himself, lashed over his back. One night a pack of white wolves spotted him stalking a deer and came over to investigate this alien-smelling look-alike. Black Hat faced off against their leader, growling ominously under his visor of dried wolf face. The wolf chief circled cautiously, his heavy neck bowed, his thick gray mane and bushy tail bristling. Slowly, Black Hat got down on his knees and let the wolf approach.

Yellow Eyes noticed that he had not untied the spear, which still lay in the grass behind him.

Man and wolf stood neck to neck, shoulder to shoulder, of a height, and she saw from her own safe distance how the wolf curled his lip, bared long white fangs. Then Black Hat stood and showed his own teeth, rumbling caution deep in his chest. The pack leader, confused by this odd wolf's dangerous posture and smell, finally turned and stalked stiffly away, pretending that Black Hat wasn't there. The other wolves, too, stared off into the distance as if nothing had happened. Then they trotted into the dark.

He is a *maiyun,* Yellow Eyes thought suddenly, one of Maheo's helpers here below. She shook with excitement. From that time on, once she had told the story to the camp, he was no longer Black Hat. Now he was called Hó-nehe Vé-ho — Wolf Chief.

Scouts had located a small herd of buffalo — bulls, cows, and yearlings, all still shedding their winter coats — moving slowly up the river toward the greening meadows on the flanks of the Big Horns. They had herded them with care toward a familiar killing ground not ten miles from the camp, then settled the herd peacefully on a piece of good grazing ground.

On the morning of the hunt, shamans prayed and smoked their long pipes over painted buffalo skulls and fires of white sage. The women sang buffalo songs, the Kit Fox soldiers in charge of hunt discipline smeared their faces with black ash to indicate their authority, while the hunters themselves — only about a dozen of them, Jenny guessed, surprised at how few they were — caught up their prized and pampered buffalo ponies and readied their weapons. Unlike her fellow townsmen at pre-hunt festivities she'd witnessed in Wisconsin, the Cheyennes went about the whole affair quite solemnly. In Heldendorf the eve of a big townwide deer drive was marked with loud roistering and joyous fiddle music; beer flowed freely along with an abundance of brag. A kind of Fourth of July in the fall. But the Indians, unlike the whites, counted on this meat for their very survival. They would take no chance of offending the All-God with their hubris.

Tom came up from the river leading Wind Blows and a second buffalo pony, a tall bay gelding. Jenny noticed a brand on its hip. A U.S. Army horse, and by the look of him a cavalry mount. "We call him *Vé'ho Mo'éhe-no'ha,*" Tom said. "Spider Horse. My father took him in a fight with the cavalry. He's a good buffalo pony — he loves to bite their tails as they run. He rides rough, but he's afraid of nothing."

Both horses were wet. Tom had thoroughly doused them with cold river water to get their blood up, and now they blew and tossed their heads, dancing fretfully as he held them, eager for the hunt.

"They want to run," Tom said. "Get your horse Trooper and let's go."

"I'm going with you?"

"Yes. Don't you want to make some meat?"

"You expect me to hunt?"

"Of course," Tom said. "It's fun."

"I can't ride as well as you or these others, and I've never shot anything from horseback."

"It's easy," Tom said. "Use your Yellow Boy. When you come up on a fat cow, aim for her kidneys — the small of her back. The horse will bring you so close that you can nearly touch her with the muzzle."

"Trooper can't run with the buffalo," she said. "He's too old. Ready for the glue factory."

"You'll only be riding Trooper until we get ready to run the buffalo. Then I'll give you Wind Blows. She's the best buffalo pony in the memory of the Cut-Arm People. She'll put you right on top of the buffalo. She recognizes the fattest cows from the thickness of the roots of their tails and will take you through the herd, straight to them. If a bull hooks at you, she'll dodge away. Come on now, get Trooper and your Yellow Boy and let's make tracks. The buffalo wait to die."

Jenny stared at him. She did not want to hunt buffalo on horseback, not out of any sentiment for the animals — the Cheyennes would make good use of them — or fear of embarrassing herself, but out of sheer funk. She did not want to die under their hooves or on their wicked horns. Tom had told her about friends of his who had met just such a fate. Yet at the same time she was pleased that Tom would allow her to ride Wind Blows. He loves that horse more than most men love a woman, she thought. But can I really ride with them? I've ridden mostly plowhorses so far, except for Vixen. These men — their women and children, too — ride as if they were born on horseback.

But if I beg off hunting, what will they think of me?

Strongheart had told her that when E-hyoph-sta first brought the buffalo to the Cheyenne, the Yellow-Haired Woman's father, Coyote Man — who had generously allowed her to take them to the People from his great cave high on No-wah-wus — warned that if she ever expressed sympathy for the animals while the Indians were killing them, the buffalo would return whence they came. The Cut-Arm People would go hungry again. For eight years after she'd joined the tribe, Yellow-Haired Woman had heeded his warning. Then one day some boys dragged a buffalo calf they'd captured into the camp and started clubbing it to death outside her tepee. Without thinking she cried, "Oh, my poor buffalo!"

With that, the herds had vanished, and for many long years the Cheyenne lived on rabbits and skunks, until the heroes Sweet Medicine and Erect Horns once again brought the buffalo back to them.

They rode to the killing ground leading Wind Blows and Spider. Strongheart rode with them on one of Little Wolf's ponies. Women and children followed the hunting party, carrying knives and hatchets to butcher the kill, trailing their packhorses to bring in the meat. Not one of them laughed or shouted, not even the babies. This was serious business.

"Don't use the Yellow Boy," Strongheart said in a quiet voice as they trotted toward the mountains. "I've brought your bow and some special arrows, ones that belong to my husband."

"I'm not good enough with the bow," Jenny said.

"At close range you are, and Wind will bring you close. It's important you hunt in the traditional manner, a test of the gifts Maheo gave you. Two Shields didn't want you to come on this hunt, he feels you have too much to lose. But the other evening some of the People began questioning whether you were truly our Yellow-Haired Woman. 'She's just another spider,' they said. These critics are the enemies of my husband. They're ambitious. Two Shields told them that as Maheo's daughter you would kill buffalo as you were instructed to do. A wicked old crone named Loon-Eye Woman laughed — the children call her Screech — and said you could not hunt buffalo. Birds and rabbits and antelope and elk, yes, they are easy to kill, even women kill them, but not the buffalo. She said you would feel sorry for the buffalo because of what the other spiders are doing to them. Else why did you leave the hide men? She said you would not kill them, or even if you did, you would only kill them from afar, where you didn't have to see the buffalo's big wet eyes weeping at its death; you would kill with the spider's throat gun. So you must use the bow, my dear, in close."

"Is my bow strong enough?"

"More than enough," Strongheart said, "if you place your arrows in the short ribs, halfway along the buffalo's body. The muscles are thin and widespread down there, and your arrow will hit the lungs. When you see blood begin to blow out the buffalo's nostrils and mouth, then you've killed her. Waste no more arrows, but ride on to the next one. Your pony will know. She's wise in the death of the buffalo."

Strongheart handed over Jenny's bow in its case, and a dozen strangely marked arrows. "The Wolf captured these arrows from a creature who came over the mountains, a thing dressed all in bark and rat skins, with tangled hair hanging to its waist. See how strange it is, the way the feathers are put on — merely tied at the front of the fletching by weed threads, so the vanes fly all floppy. But these arrows hit the mark. My husband was struck by one that swerved in its slow flight, following him wherever his horse ran. You'll see the scar it left on his shoulder when he comes home soon. See the heads of these arrows? All made of stone, as our grandfathers made their arrowheads. But a strange black stone, isn't it,

272

shiny like the mirrors of the spiders? No stone like this in Cheyenne country. You could see your face in it, but this black mirror might steal your spirit."

Not mine, Jenny thought. She took the arrows from Strongheart and brandished one defiantly, then looked closely at its wide, glossy head.

The face that frowned back. . . . It frightened her. Even taking into account the warped, concave surface of the obsidian, the distortions it would provoke, this face was cruel. Her eyes glared dark as death, with only the faintest tinge of green, and that a corpselike shade. Her nose was too long, too strong. Harsh lines furrowed her cheeks, bone-white spokes radiated from the corners of her eyes — spiderwebs, she thought. Her mouth was a scabbed, tight gash, and when she bared her teeth in contempt of her image, they flashed back at her like palings of white-hot steel.

Herr Gott, how can Tom love me?

"There they are," he said, beside her suddenly and pointing to the west. "The buffalo. Now all we must do is kill them."

Wolf Chief lay hidden behind a skull-shaped boulder on the lip of a grassy hollow, high above the slope where the buffalo grazed. His wolf's hide cloak shaded him from the dazzling sun. He saw the long line of hunters approach, slowly and calmly so as not to alarm the herd. The people trailing behind with their scrapers and hatchets and butcher knives stopped and hid themselves in the grass. He saw the hunters rein in when they reached a convenient swale. It would hide them from the herd. They dismounted from their riding horses, stripped off their shirts and leggings for the chase, readied their weapons, and sprang up on their buffalo ponies. The ponies knew the hunt was at hand. They danced and threw their heads, the bright ribbons braided into their manes tossed eagerly.

Jenny did not disrobe but took off her spider hat and let her blond braids swing full-length, nearly to her waist. She strung her bow, drew half a dozen arrows from the quiver, then swung up on Wind's bare back. The Appaloosa curvetted briefly at the unfamiliar weight and balance of a new rider. Tom rode over to reassure his pony.

"If Wind steps in a prairie-dog hole and you happen to be thrown," he said, "stay with the pony. If you run, the buffalo will trample you. Pull Wind down and lie behind her; she won't try to escape and her body will shield you."

The hunters spread out in a wide arc, like the horns of a bull hooking toward the knot of feeding buffalo. No noise, no quick movement, but an ominous aura of calm that pervaded the killing ground. Already, as if they'd been hatched from thin air, vultures circled on tilting wings high overhead.

The hunters walked their ponies slowly toward the herd, slouching low behind their manes to withhold for as long as possible the sight of their own erect and deadly man-posture from the doomed buffalo. Jenny dropped the jaw rein and placed an arrow firmly on the bowstring. She was riding with her knees now, her balance sure and easy. She had tucked the tips of her toes into the rawhide girth that cinched Wind's belly.

As they neared the herd, the buffalo grew restless. An old cow, barren and wise, threw back her head and began to moan low in her chest. She flipped her tail and trotted back and forth, then faced the approaching horsemen. A bull standing near her lifted his heavy head and glared ominously downslope.

I'd kill her first, Wolf Chief thought as he watched from a mile away, then the bull. If I had my Sharps and two loaded cartridges. . . . But I don't have it and I couldn't shoot it if I did. But I'll kill them anyway, or at least the big bull. If he tramples me, so be it. I will kill him anyway.

You will come to me, Old Bull. Come to me — *now!*

Suddenly the old cow spun on her heels and galloped away, uphill toward where Wolf Chief lay. The bull followed. The rest of the herd whirled without looking and charged after them.

Now the distant horsemen slacked their reins, kicked in their heels — their ponies finally free to chase, streaking out on the instant from a walk to a pelting gallop. The grasslands rumbled under clear blue skies.

Jenny rode just behind Two Shields, near the tip of the right horn of horsemen. Crazy led the charge, hawk feathers fluttering in the mane of his pony. Walks like Badger pounded at Jenny's side, grinning wide, braids flapping. She could hear Cut Ear's pony two jumps behind her. Clods of wet dirt and buffalo grass spun back from the hooves of the charging herd, exploding black and green off Wind's shoulders, stinging Jenny's hands and face. She tucked in tight behind Wind's neck for protection. Cold spray flew in her face, the buffalo running full tilt now through pooled rainwater, then the sharp stinging scent of sage crushed under their hooves, spangles of sunlight glancing from the white boulders that studded the slope, and they were up among the trailing buffalo, the hot heavy black-maned bulls grunting as they bucketed along, bringing up the rear, running more slowly and deliberately than the lighter, faster cows, swinging their horned heads from side to side as they ran.

Crazy did not raise his bow at the bulls, nor did Tom, so Jenny rode on through.

She saw a bull glance over at her — fire-red eyes glaring through a mop of wet black wire, silver whips of sputum trailing from his nostrils, from the gaping black-rimmed mouth — swing and aim the blunt, frayed, wicked tips of his horns toward her. Wind Blows veered before the bull could hook.

Then they were into the cows. Crazy's bow bent and twanged simultaneously with Tom's, their arrows disappearing past the fletching into heaving rib cages. Jenny heard Tom whoop and saw bright blood spurt from the nostrils of his first cow. Crazy whooped, too, and thumping along beside her, Walks like Badger was nocking another arrow, swinging his bow up to full draw, loosing a second shaft into the short ribs of the cow to his left. The cow stumbled and coughed blood. The Badger Walker whooped, and Cut Ear whooped almost in echo, close behind Jenny — he, too, had shot; another kill.

Now Wind came up fast behind a plump cow, veering out slightly to the right of her at the last moment, slowing her gallop just enough to take station on the cow's right flank, not a bow length from her racing, pounding, sweat-lathered sides. Fat bulged beneath hair at the root of her tail. Jenny swung upright on Wind's wiry back, drew her bow full-length, the cool obsidian broadhead kissing her knuckles, and loosed the arrow. But it merely wobbled off the string, thwacked weakly into the cow's hump — no good! Jenny fumbled another arrow free from under her bow hand. She tried to nock it, her hands and the bowstring dancing madly against each other, failed the first time. She gripped Wind's barrel more tightly with her shuddering legs, and the mare seemed to sense her difficulty, for she slowed just a bit. Jenny took a deep breath. She nocked the arrow solidly, dug in her heels, and Wind sprinted ahead, back to where she'd been on the racing cow's flank. The pony seemed to be running more smoothly now — almost consciously so, to give her an easier shot — and she drew and shot smoothly this time, a prayer to the pony. The arrow sank into the cow's ribs, feather-deep.

Ten jumps farther on, the cow belched blood. She stumbled and folded at the hocks, skidded around in a half circle, tongue lolling, eyes rolled skyward.

Jenny whooped for joy of the kill!

The black hulks of dead or dying buffalo, most of them cows, lay scattered randomly down the gentle hillside. Already the women, children, and old men were out and at work on them, blades flashing in the sunlight, the puckering rip of hides tearing loose from hot flesh reaching upward to where Wolf Chief lay in ambush. The old cow who'd stampeded the herd lay dead among half a hundred others. But the bull he'd marked for his own was still alive and at bay. Having finished with the serious slaughter, the hunters were now torturing the old bull. They had him surrounded and bristling with arrows; blood from the slashes of their lances ran down his shoulders and flanks. The bull held his head low and ready, and whenever a horse darted toward him, he lurched forward, trying to hook it. But the circle of torturers merely backed off, then regrouped to continue their game.

They were backing slowly toward Wolf Chief's boulder.

Some of the hunters, to show the skill and

deftness of their ponies, dashed in to plant arrows by hand in the bull's hump. Other Indians knelt on their horse's back as they lanced the brave bull. One young warrior tried to rush in mounted backward on his pony but fell at the last moment as the pony balked. The old bull stumbled forward and flashed his short thick horns forward with the full strength of a thick heavy neck. The fallen Cheyenne flew upward trailing a string of glistening intestines from a broad gash in his belly.

The circle of riders paused for a moment in confusion and the bull took advantage of it. He broke toward Wolf Chief's boulder, nearly on top of him now, the arrows in his hump rattling, his breath harsh and hot, bloody spray blowing from his nostrils. Wolf Chief reared and slung his javelin. It took the bull as he passed, deep behind the shoulder, low down, through the heart. The bull turned to stare at this new adversary, and its huge black eyes locked on Wolf Chief's. You too . . .

Wolf Chief heard Jenny's high whoop; then all the hunters were grinning and shaking their weapons over their heads. From the slope below he heard the tremolo of the women, gazing upward to where he stood, all singing their strongheart songs. He checked his impulse to howl. Judged solely by Cheyenne joy, he was a man again.

When the hunting party came home that evening, laden with fresh meat and hides and the body of the horseman killed by the old bull, there was a muted sense of excitement in the camp to offset the formal lamentations over the dead man. Little Wolf and his war party had returned.

With them they brought scalps and horses aplenty, but also grave news.

18

He was a short, scarred, wiry man with the blackest, most ominous eyes Jenny had ever seen. He stared at her as if she were no more than a rock. Yet she could see something of Tom in his father's face, particularly the strong chin and wide cheekbones, the breadth of skull. But there was no sense of fun in Little Wolf's eyes. He spoke in slow cadences, uninflected, in a deep no-nonsense voice. Everyone deferred to him.

Little Wolf's party had ridden south, he told the Old Man Chiefs, with the rest of the band listening in the dark beyond the council fire, through the land of the Pawnee Wolf People, where they had stolen some horses and taken two scalps, but had lost a Crazy Dog soldier named Broken Face. Quiet groans arose from the audience — the mourning would begin later, when the story had ended. They had crossed the War Shield and the Salty Rivers, seeing no great herds of buffalo as in years past, only a few stragglers among the bleaching bones. They had crossed the two Iron Roads of the spiders and been chased by blue soldiers for a day, shot three soldiers and killed one of them, but left him his hair — it was far too short for a trophy.

They had skirted Fort Dodge and crept into

the great spider village that had grown up around it: lodges of wood, each one as big as a hundred tepees, with the sound of singing metal coming out the windows and gunfire in the streets, women courting men brazenly in the doorways. From a corral on the edge of town they had taken twenty-four horses and ridden south for the Flint River. Buffalo hunters everywhere, coming and going, their great wagons creaking along the new, deeply rutted trails, piled high with freshly killed hides. They had encountered three spiders cutting wood along Crooked Creek and killed them, tied them to the wheels of their wagon and shot arrows into them until they resembled *heschkóveto*, hedgehogs. Then they had burned the wagon with the hides and the dead spiders still on it.

Some of the Old Man Chiefs muttered objections at this. They were Peace Chiefs.

"The spiders are killing the buffalo of our Cheyenne brothers, south of the Dead Line set by the Medicine Lodge Treaty," Little Wolf answered them. "The buffalo of our allies the Arapaho, the Comanche, and the Kiowa. They've already killed all the buffalo in our own old hunting country, from the Flint to the Buffalo Bull River. According to the treaty, they had no right to do this. But the spider soldiers won't stop them. Why don't you try to tell them about it and see what they say? They'll just laugh in your face, as they did mine. 'Our orders are to stay here,' they say, safe in their forts. 'We can't go chasing every lawbreaker in the Territory.' "

Later, Little Wolf continued when the muttering had quieted, they had met with a group of spiders — not soldiers but decent fellows who were carrying instruments of metal and glass, tall instruments that stood on three spindly legs of wood, with which they were marking out with string and stakes a series of straight lines across the land. These men had given them black soup and sweet water, even shared their meat with the Cheyennes. Yet one of these men they had killed, when they caught him alone the following day, and smashed his tools. Now he could make no more straight lines.

More muttering from the Peace Chiefs.

"The land was made by Maheo," Little Wolf said calmly, "and surely the All-God did not intend it to be marked with straight lines. It is along these lines that the spiders build their Iron Roads and their villages full of crazy water and unchaste women and singing metal."

They had then reached the camp of Iron Shirt, the great Southern Cheyenne war leader of the Bow String Society. Iron Shirt was living near the Darlington Agency on Red River, which the spiders called the North Canadian. Iron Shirt's people had had no food from the agency in two months, despite the promises of the Spider Father in Washington of beef and corn and blankets in plenty. Yet the Sa-sis-e-tas were forbidden to go away from the agency to hunt buffalo farther west, or else they would be labeled Hostiles and killed by the blue soldiers wherever they were found. Iron Shirt's brother, Medicine Water, was there as well, and he, too, had a bad face for the spiders.

Medicine Water spoke of a new holy man among the Quahadi Comanches, a fat young fellow named I-sa-taí, who urged war on the spiders before all the buffalo were gone and the Indians starved to death or were killed by the spider disease, the coughing of blood. This I-sa-taí, whose Quahadi name translated into Cheyenne as Wolf Shit, claimed the ability to vomit up whole wagonloads of cartridges, and yet to turn the spiders' own bullets to water in the barrels of their throat guns.

"I met with this man," Little Wolf said, with a perfectly straight face, "and his name suits him well."

Jenny laughed. Little Wolf frowned at her.

"I don't believe it's possible for even so plump a Quahadi to hold a wagonload of anything in his belly, or to turn bullets to water in rifle barrels. Yet there's something to be said for a war right now. The spiders are still few in number, especially south of the Dead Line and north of the land of the Tehannas and Meskins. The Treaty of Medicine Lodge forbids these hide killers to hunt on our lands. If we kill enough of them, maybe they'll finally learn how to behave themselves and spare us the rest of our buffalo."

"They aren't killing our buffalo," said a Peace

Chief called No Neck, "not up here in the north, anyway."

"Not yet," Little Wolf said. "But once they've finished the southern herd, they're bound to come here. They love to kill buffalo, just as we love to steal horses."

"If we make war on the spiders," No Neck said, "they'll only send their blue spiders into this country and burn our lodges, kill our women and children and horses, as the spiders under Long Hair Kúh'sta did to Black Kettle's people on the Lodge Pole not long ago, and Chivington before him at Sand Creek."

"Black Kettle believed in peace at any cost," said a young woman named Lance, who had come from the south and was now living with relatives in this band. "Black Kettle didn't make war on the spiders; in fact, at Sand Creek he had a big spider flag flying over the village to show his allegiance to Washington. I was with him there, along with many of you. We were camped near the spider village called Fort Lyon, but Chivington's bad faces came and killed us anyway. And they took not only scalps — they cut the breasts from the women and rode away with them, to make purses." Her children, three boys and a girl, and her husband had died in that fight. "The spiders will kill us whatever we do," she concluded. "War or peace."

"It's better we leave them alone," old Screech said. "Maybe Maheo will send a great plague to kill all the spiders. They're a sickly lot, anyway."

285

"There's no doubt that the buffalo are getting fewer every year," said another Peace Chief, an old man named Chewing Elk. "This never happened before. What we need is a fresh supply of buffalo. I can't believe Maheo has turned his face from us. Perhaps the mouth of the cave on No-wah-wus where the buffalo emerge has been blocked by some obstruction — a huge boulder, maybe. We could send some soldiers to pull the boulder free . . ."

"We passed No-wah-wus on our return," Little Wolf said. "I stopped to pray there. The cave isn't blocked. The reason the buffalo are fewer every year is because the spiders are killing them faster than Maheo can breed new ones. Soon they'll all be rubbed out — buffalo, antelope, elk, and deer, even rabbits and skunks — and our life as a People will end along with them. Soon we'll all be dead, except for a few of us maybe, hanging on as farmers, scratching the dirt like the spiders themselves." He paused to let that thought sink in.

"When the Southerners were here a few years ago to renew the Arrows," No Neck said, "Chief Stone Calf spoke of another cave like the one on No-wah-wus. It's in a butte on the Staked Plain, and it, too, sends forth buffalo. An Old Woman sits in the cave, tending them, and orders them out into the world each spring. Maybe the Old Woman died, or forgot to release them lately, and the buffalo don't know they're supposed to come out. Let's send some soldiers down there to see what's happened. It would be better than war with the spiders, which we cannot win."

"We could send Yellow-Haired Woman," old Screech said. "She claims to have power over the Buffalo People."

"No, I don't," Jenny said. "It's just you people who say that. No matter what you think, I'm just a woman — with no power at all but what's in my own two arms."

"You might be touched by the *maiyun* and not even know it," Chewing Elk said. "It's happened before. And our Elk Soldiers saw you being born from the belly of a buffalo cow. Can you deny that, too?"

"My brother, Wolf Chief, only put me in there to save me from the storm," Jenny said. "He had killed the cow with his throat gun for that purpose. The carcass froze in the cold of the storm and they rode up just as I was breaking out."

"Wolf Chief is a *maiyun*," Screech said. "His own woman says so. Besides, wolves speak to us all the time, in many ways, warning us of dangers or telling us where to find success."

The people around her nodded and said, "*Haáhe!* It's true."

"Let's send her," someone shouted. Others — women and old men mainly — chimed in from the darkness. "Yes, yes — it's better than war!"

"You don't even know where that cave is," Jenny said, angry now. "It's all just hearsay anyway, and based on superstition at that."

"I know where the cave is," Little Wolf said.

"We scouted it on our way back north. It is inside a butte shaped like the head of a buffalo, on the Staked Plain near the canyon the Meskins call Palo Duro. But it would be dangerous for a woman of the spiders to go there, especially traveling with Cheyenne soldiers. There are spider hide hunters all through that country now. They'd think the woman was a captive and kill our soldiers. Maybe the woman, too, if she showed sympathy to the Cheyenne. The spiders have a permanent camp near the Palo Duro now, on Red River across from a creek called White Deer. Two stores and a place to sell spider water, what they call a saloon, also a small tepee where a man puts iron shoes on their horses and repairs their wagons. It's not far from the old trading post called Adobe Walls, the one built by William Bent, where our people fought the blue soldiers in the old days. At the new camp are many spiders we used to steal horses from in the Smoky Hill country — Rath and Leonard and Myers, the one called Hanrahan, young Ogg, and the yellow-haired friend of this man Black Hat, whom you now call Wolf Chief."

"McKay?" Jenny said. "Rides a pretty little chestnut mare?"

"That's the very one," Little Wolf said. "I scouted his camp myself. He has some English with him, rich Long Knife spiders who live in big, striped tepees. They wear strange clothes of velvet, drink spider water all night, and only wake up at noon. Then they go out on their tall horses

with their tall, weak, fast dogs and shoot everything they can find, but take only the heads."

"I'll go to your Buffalo Butte," Jenny said. "Not
that it will do any good, mind you, but that's my
horse McKay's riding. He stole her from me and
I'll have her back."

"That's a laudable attitude," Little Wolf said.
"But it won't be as easy to take ponies from the
spiders as it was in the old days. Too much hair
has been lifted lately, and these English keep close
watch. Their guards shoot at anything that
moves, and the head chief of the Long Knives
has a heavy brass gun that one man can shoot all
day, merely by turning a crank that's mounted
on its side. A gun so heavy that one man alone
cannot lift it. We tried to steal it and take some
of their horses as well, but their dogs were everywhere at night. Strongheart tells me you're a
brave woman, a good shot with throat gun and
bow, not a bad rider. Perhaps you're a good thief
as well, better than a Cheyenne. Take my son
with you, and such of his friends who care to go
along." He waved his hand in dismissal.

"Haáhe!" yelled the friends of Little Wolf. The
Peace Chiefs looked glum but did not object.

They made ready to leave the following morning — Jenny, Tom, Crazy, Walks like Badger,
Cut Ear, and the young Indian boy Pony Quirts.
It was Pony's father who had been killed in the
closing minutes of the buffalo hunt, eviscerated
on the horns of the big bull. The boy was almost

twelve years old, nearly of age for the war trail anyway. He was a good rider and hunter — Jenny had seen him in action. His mother was long dead, she learned — tuberculosis. Pony had been living with a stingy old aunt who was happy to see him leave.

"What will you use for a bow, now that I have yours?"

"I have my father's," Pony said. "Along with his ponies. His moccasins, too, though I'll have to grow into them."

"If you live so long," Jenny said. "You must care for yourself on this trail, for I'll not be a mother to you."

"I can fend for myself," Pony said. She believed it.

As they cinched down the last loads on their packhorses — extra powder and lead, parfleches of pemmican, sleeping robes, cookware — Little Wolf rode over to see them off.

"You've met Quanah?" he asked Tom.

"Yes, two years ago in a spider camp on the Buffalo Bull. He came in to trade hides."

"Quanah's a good man, but he backs this Wolf Shit fellow. They may go to war soon. If so, try to stay out of it. I don't think they can win, much as I hope they will. But I don't want you getting killed down there. We may have plenty of fighting of our own up here before long, and I'll need all the soldiers I can get."

"Yes, Father."

" 'Yes, Father.' " Little Wolf laughed. "I'd

have said the same thing to mine when I was your age — then gone out and counted as many coups as possible. The young don't believe they can die. Well then, I won't order you to stay out of it. But don't get yourself killed needlessly. None of these mad, lone charges against massed rifles. Remember — the buffalo hunters can shoot straight, their bullets respect no Indian's medicine, and they kill at a great distance. But you know that, you've been with them."

"Haáhe."

"The main thing I wanted to tell you, though, was this: While you were away from the People, I made a trip to Washington, along with Morning Star and the Arapaho Little Bear. Yes, 'Wild Indians' in the heartland of the spiders, strange, indeed — but the Army had arranged it. We took the Iron Road, and I'll tell you, it frightened me. Their Traveling Houses move fast as the wind. And the villages — more than you could count in a year of counting, all crooked and crowded together and smelling vilely of spiders, horse dung so deep on the streets you could disappear beneath it and never be missed. Washington is hot, full of horseflies and mosquitoes, big stone carvings of war chiefs and leaders, pillars of marble that reach the sky, gigantic lodges made of white stone, spiders everywhere. Most of them thieves. I developed a great respect for their pickpockets."

Little Wolf paused, shook his head, then spat on the ground as if to erase the memory.

"There we met with the Washington Chief, a

291

great leader of blue soldiers named Grant. Now he is chief of all the spiders. Ugly little bug, hair all over his face. But tough. You remember the Fort Laramie Treaty of 1868, after we killed Fetterman?"

"*Haáhe.*"

"Well, the Washington Chief says we agreed by that treaty to give up all our country north of the Greasy River — what they call the Platte — and move down with the Southern Cheyenne. But we did *not* agree to that, or at least the interpreter didn't mention it, and we told him so. Grant and a subchief of his, a fat man named Columbus Delano, the Secretary of the Interior, they call him, in charge of all the dirt the spiders walk on, tried to make us agree to go south. Grant even said we'd be happier there. That country isn't as cold, he said, and the game is more plentiful. Ha! I've just been there, I know differently."

"*Haáhe.*"

"What he *did not* say is that the country, while it is certainly 'not as cold,' is at the same time *too hot* to live in, at least for our people. What he *did not* say is that the game is disappearing fast, thanks to his hide hunters. We refused to go south. We sat there for a long time, in silence, staring at each other. They finally agreed to let us remain here in the north for a while, until they figured out 'a better solution.' Whatever that means — more tricks, more promises, more lies, no doubt. But you can be sure they will not budge on this business of sending us south. They want our country. They want to make it like their own. All farms and Iron Roads and great ugly villages full of weak ugly spiders. Everyone crazy with working fever. So there will be war, count on it. And I want you alive to help me fight it."

"Then why do you send us south?"

"Yes, your woman is right about this buffalo cave business," Little Wolf answered. "Nothing will come of it. If Maheo is willing to see the buffalo disappear from the south, there is nothing we can do about it. But your going there will allow me to see how I-sa-taí's war develops. You must learn how the blue soldiers fight. They have big guns, what they call cannons. See how they work. They also seem to fight more as groups than as individual soldiers, as we do. Try to figure how they manage that. I could use this knowledge in the war that's coming."

"*Haáhe,* Father."

"But the most important thing is this," Little Wolf said. "Yellow-Haired Woman wants to find the hide man McKay. She has a feeling for him, love or hate, I don't know which. McKay is now with the Long Knife chief, and the Long Knife chief has the Gun-That-Shoots-All-Day. I saw it demonstrated in Washington, as a guest of the blue soldier chief. They call it a Gatling gun. It shoots the same bullets as the spider soldiers shoot, the .45–70 — so we can always get more ammunition if we should need it. I want that gun. It could save us in the war that is sure to come. Imagine the surprise on the faces of the blue spiders if they charged into our camp, only to be met with that gun! This I know — the Long Knife chief keeps the Gatling gun hidden under a stiff black blanket on one of his wagons. But remember, it is loaded all the time, so be careful when you try to take it. It can kill a hundred men in less time than it would take you to count your dead."

Strongheart helped Jenny with the last of the packing.

"Take care of my brother while I'm away."

Strongheart laughed.

"What does that mean?"

"You can take care of him yourself," Strongheart said. "Here he comes now."

She gestured behind her.

Jenny looked over her shoulder. Yellow Eyes and Otto were coming — both mounted on ponies, with a laden packhorse tagging along. Wolf Chief rode without reins, but he seemed well-balanced nonetheless.

"*Herr Gott!*" Jenny said. "What is this?"

"Wolf Chief rides," Otto said. "A little trick I've been practicing for a while. With the aid of Two Shields and Yellow Eyes."

He nudged the horse with his right knee and it turned to the left. Then the other, and it swung right. He whistled through his teeth and the pony stopped in its tracks. He kicked its sides with both knees simultanously and it started forward again.

"A clever little pony," he said.

"You're riding with us?"

"With your permission, sister. For I, too, have scores to settle, particularly with Milo Sykes. I'm sure we'll find him in the Yarner, along with Raleigh McKay."

Little Wolf watched them over the horizon. He was thinking of Grant. A squat, hairy man, plainly dressed and smelling of spider water, but he had a killer's eyes. Little Wolf knew his own eyes were strong, and he used them consciously to keep his people in line. Grant was unconscious of his eyes. When Grant looked straight at him, Little Wolf could not help but look away. How many men had those eyes killed? Little Wolf had killed plenty himself, but he knew his dead would make only an anthill on the slopes of Grant's mountain.

On the Iron Road coming back from the East, the Traveling House had hit a wagon stalled on the tracks. The train came to a halt. Little Wolf and Morning Star got down from the cars and walked back to where the wagon lay in splinters on both sides of the track. A strong west wind blew red and gold leaves from the trees over the tracks. Corn tassels rattled in the fields. Two spiders who had been riding in the wagon lay bloody and dead under the cars, one of them a man with a white beard, cut in half across the belly. A horse was down, its rear legs crushed by the big iron wheels of the House. It was trying to pull itself forward with its front legs, but the steam from the House had glued its hindquarters to the gravel by the juice of its leaking entrails. A big bay mare, in the prime of her life, and she looked at them, pleading for help.

"We should kill her," Little Wolf said.

Morning Star shrugged.

Little Wolf took a pistol from one of the blue soldiers standing nearby and walked over to the mare.

It was the first time he had felt compassion since he was a boy. But it was more than that.

What had happened to the horse could happen to the Sa-sis-e-tas.

PART IV

19

"I say, Blandish, where's my chai? Get your arse over here with it — *chop-chop,* you sorry sodomite!"

"On my way, Your Lordship! Sorry!"

"Christ, what's the bloody world coming to? If I've told that fool once, I've told him a thousand times — I want my tea piping hot, the instant I emerge from my bath."

Lord Malcontent was in one of his moods again.

Raleigh McKay grunted and spat in the fire. Sir Henry Charles Windham Fitzwilliam Malevil, fourth Baron Malcombe, of Malcombe Manor, County of Antrim in northern Ireland, was mighty particular about his "bawth." As indeed he was about many things. He could not begin a day, he often said, without his copy of *The Times,* which he preferred to consult in his morning bath. To that end, before they left England he had had his manservant, Blandish, arrange shipments of the London daily to wherever he happened to be in America. Each month a bundle of papers was rushed to a waiting steam packet in Southampton, whence it was whisked across the Atlantic to New York. There it was transshipped by rail to the End of Track and thence to Fort Lyon on the

Purgatoire River in Colorado. An express rider carried it the rest of the way to Sir Harry's camp, wherever that might be. The newspapers arrived only a month or two out of date, but to His Lordship's way of thinking, the important thing about a newspaper was tone, not timeliness.

Often of a morning Raleigh had seen him submerged to his aristocratic armpits in the canvas tub, clouds of steam rising into the chill, a pair of spectacles perched at the end of his long nose, rattling and turning the crisp, blanket-sized pages of his cherished *Times*, chuckling or clucking or cursing as the news unfolded.

Right now he was following correspondent Winwood Reade's firsthand coverage of the Ashanti War on the Gold Coast of West Africa. A force of British regulars, mainly Black Watch, Welch Fusiliers, and Rifle Brigade, had set out for Kumasi, the Ashanti capital, to teach King Kofi Karikari a lesson. "Ah, there you are, Blandish," Sir Harry cried when that worthy rushed into the bath tent. "Listen to this. Some black scoundrels have abducted our ally the King of Accassi's Queen from her vegetable garden, where she was tending her plantains. 'Fears are expressed for her chastity,' *The Times* says, and quotes from a dispatch sent by an officer on the scene to Colonel Wood: 'Please do what you can to save Her Majesty's honour — or the plantains — for I cannot make out which is rated at the highest figure by the King.' That's niggers for you, what?"

Raleigh had met Sir Harry at Camp Supply back in January. His Lordship was engaged in a two-year sporting tour of the Great West, as were so many monied Englishmen of late. And His Lordship had money to burn — "Sixty thousand pounds sterling per annum from my estates alone," he had boasted to Raleigh in the sutlers' saloon that first night.

"I need a guide for this new, more southerly game country — Tay-Hass, I believe you call it?"

"We call it Texas, suh."

His Nestor on the northern plains, Lord Malcombe said, had been a splendid old trapper and veteran of the Oregon Trail named Henry Chatillon, who had guided such luminaries as the Bostonian scholar Francis Parkman and Sir St. George Gore in decades gone by. Raleigh had heard of neither. Chatillon, though, was pushing sixty years of age and had finally wearied of the swift pace set by His Lordship. He retired from the field, having been compensated handsomely for his labors at the rate of $100 a day.

"Your remuneration would be no less, of course," His Lordship said, "as I'm told you're quite knowledgeable concerning this corner of the country."

McKay looked up from his glass of Bourbon whiskey and studied the man who'd addressed him. A tall, petulant, pigeon-chested fop whose lower lip drooped like a slab of pale liver. Nice hair, though, Raleigh noted with a pang of envy.

Freshly washed, golden yellow, replete with lustrous waves, it hung clear down to His Lordship's sloping shoulders. In the lobe of one ear gleamed a golden ring. A bottle-green shooting jacket, carefully pressed corduroy breeks, and knee-high riding boots of soft black leather completed the ensemble. His Lordship's eyes, magnified by his spectacles, were close-set, pale, and shallow as the Cimarron in high summer.

"Let's reckon, feller," Raleigh said in his best backwoods drawl. He took off his hat, pulled the ivory comb from his hip pocket, and slowly, deliberately, ran it through his own thick mane. "Me and my partner have been killin' up to a hundred buff a day so far this season. Two bucks and a half per hide, today's rate. What does that come to?" He fumbled a stub of pencil from his pocket, wet its point on his tongue, and haltingly scrawled some numbers on the back of his hand. "What's two and a half times a hundred?"

In fact, he'd been shooting no more than twenty or thirty buffalo a day — a slow winter since Otto's departure.

"One hundred and twenty-five," His Lordship countered. "You may add to that a ten-dollar bonus for every cougar, bighorn sheep, royal elk, or grizzly bear we kill, and all the champagne or whiskey you can drink of an evening — unless single-malt Scotch is not to your liking?"

"It'll do."

Sir Harry lived in luxury, even on the prairie. His baggage train alone strung out for a mile along the trail — sixteen newly built Studebaker wagons, drawn by color-matched oxen and mules. One strongly sprung carriage carried nothing but small arms — cutlasses, pikes, Colt's and Webley's revolvers, shotguns by Purdey, Boss, and Dickson in bores ranging from 16 to 8 gauge, and double, single, or repeating rifles by Manton, Gibbs, Holland & Holland, Sharps, Remington, and Winchester.

A separate wagon traveled near the head of the baggage train carrying a long ton of refined bar lead for rifle and pistol bullets, oak-staved barrels of chilled English birdshot, and others of close-grained French gunpowder, as well as case upon case of U.S. Army rifle ammunition, all of it protected from wind and weather by a heavy, leakproof deck of teak planking sealed at its seams with bitumen. Atop the deck, housed beneath a waxed cover of heavy storm canvas, rode Sir Harry's favorite toy, a new, improved model of Dr. Richard J. Gatling's "machine gun," purchased for $1,250 at the Colt works in Hartford, Connecticut, on His Lordship's way west. Mounted on a sturdy, brass-shod tripod, the Gatling was capable of firing more than a thousand rounds of .45–70–caliber center-fire metallic cartridges per minute, Sir Harry said. "It should quickly dissuade any banditti foolish enough to attack us, redskinned or white. The only limiting factor to its use is the amount of ammunition one can carry, and as you see, I have plenty. We'll fire it one day, somewhere down the line, and you'll see how devastating a weapon it is."

"I know already," Raleigh said. "Old 'Beast' Butler's Yanks had a dozen of them at Petersburg back in '64. The .58-caliber model that fired copper rimfire cartridges. Word has it that Butler bought them from the doctor with his own money, $12,000 hard cash, when the Union refused to invest in such newfangled nonsense. They tore us up pretty good."

"Is that why you call him 'Beast'?"

"No. He got that nickname earlier in the war, when he was in command of the Union forces occupyin' New Orleans. I guess he was rude to the ladies."

Lord Malcontent wanted lions, bighorns, and grizz — lots of them. As soon as the snows melted and the trail was hard enough for travel, they fared forth into the Bayou Salado of southern Colorado, hounds howling, servants grumbling, a cavallard of sixteen tall, blooded hunting horses trailing behind under the watchful eyes of three Texas wranglers named Sliding Billy Gomez, Perce Watling, and Sidney Omohundro.

Raleigh didn't know the Rockies all that well, but Milo Sykes had hunted there in the sixties just after the war. It had been Raleigh's plan to dump Milo the moment they reached Camp Supply, but His Lordship's offer changed matters. Milo's knowledge of the country they would be hunting won him a reprieve.

And thanks in large part to Milo, this had proved a good hunt. Fine weather, lush grazing for the cavvy, no Hostiles, and plenty of big game. They made camp in a meadow beside a clear stream bulging with cutthroat trout. Sir Harry had brought along his own English fly tier, and in the mornings on rising, His Lordship and Raleigh caught enough trout for the whole camp's breakfast. Then they ranged out onto the prairie or into the high country in search of trophies. One clear April day above timberline, both men and horses breathless, they came on a herd of bighorn sheep grazing in a boulder-strewn cirque. Sir Harry potted six full-curl rams, all running shots as the sheep scrambled up the far scree slope, his diminutive Welsh gun loader Dai Jones handing him a freshly charged Manton each time another brace of rams fell. The strong brown sheep grunted and flinched as the bullets took them, but leaped on, staggering finally and rolling like dirty snowballs back down the slopes. Rock slides tumbled after them. It was slaughter on a grand scale, the way the English liked it.

Some days they ran wolves or lions with Sir Harry's pack — tireless, long-legged brutes, huge Irish and Russian wolfhounds, mastiffs, burly, bouncy Norwegian elkhounds, slim whippets and greyhounds, and a few rangy Airedales that delighted in tearing the cornered coyotes to pieces when they finally ran them down, the little wolves cowering in submission at last, grinning up with their ears laid back, their bushy tails between their legs, and the Airedales descending upon them with swift, strong, wrathful jaws to rip them limb from limb. The dogs quickly treed the lions, and Sir Harry shot the tawny, long-tailed cats as they crouched on flimsy branches high in the ponderosas. The cats fell twisting and screeching, and the pack had to be whipped off before they ruined the pelts.

"Magnificent," His Lordship said.

On one memorable evening just at dusk, as Raleigh, Milo, Dai Jones, Perce Watling, and His Lordship rode back to camp after a fruitless day in pursuit of Rocky Mountain goats, they suddenly confronted a small, humpbacked, shovel-nosed bear pawing tentatively at a dead mule deer.

"Where's his mama?" Milo whispered.

"Hand me the ten-bore, Dai," said His Lordship in plangent tones.

"We'd better wait a bit, sir," Raleigh said quietly. "That's just a baby bear. He wouldn't be traveling on his lonesome just yet, so there's likely a mother around here somewhere."

"The rifle, please, Mr. Jones."

Dai looked at Raleigh, shrugged his eyebrows and shoulders. "Aye, Your Lordship."

He slapped the rifle into Sir Harry's hand and stepped back respectfully.

The baby bear squinted upward, searching out the sound of their voices. Then it gave up and took another whack at the deer's haunch.

Raleigh said, "You'd better wait, Harry. There's bound to be a bigger one nearby. Best save your lead for the mama."

"I require a family group, Captain McKay," Lord Malcombe said stiffly. "The British Museum have made it quite clear. As you're no doubt aware, I already have a fine male, a fair female, and two cubs from up north. This juvenile will round out my group quite nicely. Should the mother come and by chance prove better than the female now in my possession, all the better. Now let me shoot, and the rest of you keep alert to whatever other bears may be lurking in the vicinity. Leave none of them alive."

He shot.

The baby bear yowled and bit its shoulder.

Sure enough, at her offspring's cry the mother bear materialized from a patch of nearby brush and ran at the party with the speed of a racehorse. Before Perce Watling could raise his rifle, she had crushed his head with one blow of a front paw. As she passed Dai Jones, she slapped him across the belly and he fell. Then she turned toward His Lordship.

Raleigh, ten paces off to one side, shot her behind the left ear, a quick shot with the Sharps. She fell with a thump that frightened the horses and sent pine duff cascading over His Lordship's boots. He stood there with his mouth agape, pale beneath his tan.

"My God, that was fast," he said finally. "Thank you, McKay — not only were you right about the mother bear, but you saved my bloody neck with that shot." He went over to where Dai sat in the dust, looking down at his lap. Blood had soaked the lower front of his shirt and his trousers. "Ah thinks she gutted me, look-you." His Lordship knelt to study the wound, pulling back the torn shirt with hesitant fingers. Gray-green coils of intestine poked through the ragged rips in the loader's abdomen. Sir Harry winced, rose, and walked away to retch behind a nearby sage.

Raleigh and Milo lashed Watling's body to the back of his horse and built a travois for Dai after wrapping his midsection with the remainder of his shirt. They could come back later to skin the bears. It was a long ride to the bivouac. Dai was dead by the time they reached camp, his bristling eyebrows locked in permanent bemusement. They all drank a lot that night and buried their dead at sunup.

Sir Harry insisted that the dead men be interred in proper coffins, which he had his carpenters construct from the floorboards of a broken-down wagon. Then as Perce and Dai were lowered into the rocky ground, His Lordship spoke a few words over them. Teamsters, pastry chefs, muleteers, dog tenders, sommelier, wranglers, grooms, farriers, and half-breed Shawnee trackers looked on solemnly.

" 'They say the Lion and the Lizard keep / The Courts where Jamshyd gloried and drank deep,' " Sir Harry said. " 'And Bahram, that great Hunter — the Wild Ass / Stamps o'er his Head, but cannot break his sleep.' "

"Amen," intoned the mourners.

They hunted slowly south and east, onto the Staked Plain. Summer came sweltering ever more intensely upon them with each day's drop in elevation. Pine and spruce gave way to sage and prickly pear and ocotillo. Spanish bayonet stabbed the horses' legs and they left a blackening trail of blood spattered across that hard-baked, hoof-clanging earth. Mirages plagued them, and one day they saw a great city rise from the plain in the distance, its towers gleaming white as quarried marble, shimmering in the heat, men falling from the parapets as if in the act of mass suicide, falling into the broad avenues below. Closer at hand, the city faded into a band of scrawny, hammerhead ponies cropping panic grass. Many of the wild horses were pintos whose blotchy white markings no doubt accounted for the imagined marble of the dream city.

As the wagon train crossed the prairie one morning, Sir Harry's eye was caught by a band of pronghorn antelope grazing half a mile away. "Good time to try the Gatling," he told Raleigh. "Five years ago in Carlsbad, the Prussian general staff tested one of these guns against a hundred of their best riflemen, all of them armed with the new Dreyse needle gun. The range was 800 meters. Prussian volley fire scored 27 percent hits, the Gatling 88."

With the wagons halted, His Lordship whisked off the gun's canvas cover. *Voilà!* he said, grin-

309

ning. "Behold the true 'Beast.' "

Raleigh had to agree. The Gatling gun was squat, ugly, about as elegant as a cotton gin. Six separate muzzles protruded from its gleaming brass barrel. A dizzying array of knobs, studs, and set screws to control elevation and rate of fire bulged from the contraption, and a crank which both rotated the barrels and fired them protruded from the right side of the breech. Sir Harry pointed to a heavy black drum made of metal attached to the top of the gun.

"This is a new loading device patented by a man named Broadwell," he said. "The drum on this model holds four hundred rounds. It's too heavy for one man to lift, so we have to use a block and tackle. Once it's in place, though, the operator merely has to take aim and turn the crank. Dr. Gatling's ingenious bolt-and-cam mechanism does the rest — loads, fires, extracts the spent shell case, then spits it out and starts all over again, quicker than you can say 'knife.' " He stepped aside. "Here, old man, why don't you have a go?"

Raleigh leaned in behind the gun and aligned the sights, adjusting them to 800 yards. He swung the muzzle to the left-hand side of the antelope band, now standing steadily, their heads up, all of them staring at the wagon train but uncertain of what this strange sight portended. Raleigh took off his hat and waved it back and forth above his head. Three or four bucks stepped quickly toward the wagons, curious as always about the flagging motion. Raleigh took a deep breath and turned the crank handle twice, traversing the gun slowly from left to right as he fired. A near-continuous roar fractured the prairie silence. Clouds of billowing smoke obscured his sight picture. When it blew clear, eight pronghorns lay dead in the sage, while four more struggled feebly to regain their feet. The rest of the band had fled, white rumps bouncing away from the slaughter into the dusty distance.

"Welcome to the Industrial Revolution," Sir Harry said. "Can you imagine what Bonaparte might have done with one of these guns at Waterloo? We'd all be eating snails."

Now they began to cut the trails of many unshod ponies mixed with human footprints, small parties for the most part, but in aggregate a considerable number.

"Mr. and Mrs. Lo on the move to new huntin' grounds," Raleigh said.

"Not a war party?" Sir Harry asked.

"No. See the drag marks left by the travois? The Indians use their tepee poles to haul their goods. If a trail shows lodgepole tracks, it means they're travelin' with women and children. But if you find the tracks of many ponies and no drags, then you'd better look out. War party more than likely. Best thing to do, move out in the opposite direction — fast."

"We have enough men and guns to defeat any Indian tribe in the West," Sir Harry said. "At

311

least on the defensive. Give me a troop of English cavalry and I'd pacify this wilderness in a month's time."

"I doubt it," Raleigh said. "This is Kiowa and Comanche country."

"What does that signify?"

"Persistence."

"Hah!"

"Bloody-mindedness."

"We're bloodier of mind."

I'll agree with you there, Raleigh thought.

"Command of the country — they know every wrinkle in it, every waterhole, every place to lay an ambush. It's their own back yard."

"It's not a difficult country," Lord Malcombe said. "Flat as a billiard table, this terrain. Our horses are longer of limb, sounder of lung; we'd run them down in a mile. From what I've seen of these sorry redskins, they shoot arrows or old muzzle loaders. We have modern repeating rifles and the Gatling. All my men are chosen marksmen. Even McIntosh, my fly tier, is a crack wingshot. Some of these lads, the best of them, were with me in India, fought against *real* Indians — Sikhs and Pathans and British-trained sepoys in the Mutiny. Old Dai, rest his soul, not to mention Bentley, who succeeds him, were with me north of Cape Colony against the kaffirs. Cetewayo's Zulu impis weren't much when faced with a true British square, and your red niggers aren't half the soldiery the Zulus were. Bring them on and I'll show you."

He cantered toward the horizon.

"How old do you reckon that pup to be, Milo?"

"Not yet thirty, I'd say. Twenty-four or -five."

"Hellfire. He'd have still been foulin' his diapers at the time of the Indian Mutiny. Mere bullshit he's givin' us. All blow, no show."

Raleigh drank that night. This country was flat and empty, as Lord Malcontent had said, but both Raleigh and Milo had seen it sprout Kiowas and Cheyennes and Comanches in the wink of an eye, thick and fast as buffalo grass after spring rain.

"I don't like this," Sykes said.

"Me neither."

"What say let's draw our pay first thing tomorrow?"

"He won't give it to us."

"No. But we by God should oughta get out of here anyways. We won't have lost so much on the deal. We can cut out a few of those blood horses, sell 'em at Griffin to the blue shirts for a whole lot more'n he'd pay us."

Raleigh thought about that for a minute. He knew the Limeys would never be able to track them. But His Lordship might possibly report the horse theft to the Army at Fort Griffin, and horse theft was a hanging offense.

"Let's see them as far as the North Canadian anyways," he said. "It's only a few days ahead."

Sykes grunted. Yes or no? Raleigh wondered. But Milo wouldn't go anywhere without Raleigh along for protection. The poor dumb redneck couldn't see a Hostile a quarter mile off, his eyes were that weak. As weak as His Lordship's, but Sykes had no eyeglasses.

In the morning Raleigh rode out ahead of the train toward a butte to the southeast. He'd saddled Vixen because she had the smoothest gait in his remuda, and what old Otto used to call the *Katzenjammer* was on him bad today. He felt fragile and tried heavy breathing. It didn't work. Something had left him during the night. The whiskey had stolen it. Another dream of battle had drained it away. He couldn't remember the dream, but he knew it was awful, as usual, and he knew it was his manhood that had been sapped from him, as usual, but he also knew that it would return as time burned the booze away. That was the thing about whiskey. It gave you time off to confront your woes.

He contemplated the butte. He couldn't very well scale the granite tower, not in this condition, so he circled it. The best way up was from the south. Leaving Vixen to graze near a spring at the shallow base of the butte, he slogged his way to the top through heavy chaparral, lugging the Sharps with him, pausing often to catch his breath. From the high point he scanned the horizon with his field glasses. Nothing. He could just hear the faint, distant boom of buffalo rifles, unless it was his hungover heart pounding in his eardrums.

314

I'm boozin' too much lately, he thought, and not for the first time. But it's the only way I can get rid of it.

Rid of what?

Her, goddamnit, the memory of her, of what we did to her.

He squirmed in his bones as he recalled it.

He'd been surprised to learn, from a cavalryman at Camp Supply, that Jenny and Otto Dousmann were alive. Surprised, at first elated; then, when the fact sank in, the possible repercussions frightened him. The trooper had been up at Fort Dodge and told a sad story of a woman who'd come in after the norther, a yellow-haired woman, with her brother, a hide man so badly froze that the doc had to saw off one of his arms.

Hellfire . . .

You were once an officer and a gentleman, by act of the Congress of the Conflagrated States of America. But you were never a gentleman, or even a very good officer. You're poor white trash, always have been. You killed the best goddamn general officer in the world, Old Blue Light, your own commander, and you killed him at the moment of his greatest triumph. You killed him because you were scared that night — you were pisswilly scared all through the war, admit it, you . . . *poltroon.*

No — those were buffalo rifles, all right. Scattered over the plains ahead of him, to the east and the north and the south. Through the dirty yellow-brown heat haze of the horizon he could see darker clusters, black, slow-moving blotches of living meat — buffalo as far as the eye could see. And the hide camps would be nearby, havens of hope away from this elfin English madness, good solid Americans with real food, buffalo steaks, and corn dodgers, grease over it all, and likker to cut the grease.

Oh yes, the guns were among them now, real sharpshooters making their stands, skinners ripping the hot thick two-dollar hides, oh sure, clawing at the vermin under their greasy shirts, cursing and spitting cotton in the heat of the morn, rotten teeth in hairy faces, bloodshot eyes, the stench of stale sweat and fresh gore, buffalo guts leaking a foul thin gruel from poorly thrown rifle shots, the ugly incessant whine and nip of the buffalo gnats . . .

But do I want to go back to that?

He thought for a long, sorry moment.

I don't want to go back to that.

Raleigh put down the field glasses and fell into the old familiar hunker, butt back on one heel, which all Southerners worthy of the name can hold for hours — our natural posture, he thought, in the plowed red fields or under a tulip tree in the flourlike roadside dust, or whittling and spitting in the cool shade of storefront galleries from Richmond to Savannah to Natchez to Galveston. He felt a sudden pang of homesickness. Why sure, he missed those ugly paintless bare-boards cool shadowed galleries, the leather-faced men squatting there in the shade, straw hats tipped back on their bone-white foreheads, chewing plug, spewing neatly in long dark arcs an artillery of spit into the dust of the street, the long, soft, slow, drawling talk of crops and horseflesh and niggers and womenfolk, the easy circulation of a cool, beaded stoneware jug among the conversationalists, the sharp hot bite of clear corn . . .

He pulled a flat pint bottle from his hunting shirt, drew the cork with his teeth, and took the first grim slug of the morning. Sir Harry's single-malt Scotch. He'd hated it at first, the medicinal odor and taste of it, but he'd grown used to it; indeed, he'd grown to like it. Many things in life were like that. At first he'd hated the scent and taste of his cowardice, woke up sweating the night after a skirmish from which he'd run, but soon he grew accustomed to the familiar feel of funk, it felt natural. Now perhaps he was growing fond of it, perversely so, but fond nonetheless. He took another swallow of whiskey, shuddered, and re-placed the cork, pounding it down with the heel of his hand. Better to save some for the ride back.

As he slipped the bottle back in his shirt, a sudden certainty struck him. *Hostiles out there.* The hair on the back of his neck tingled. He knew they were there, somewhere, as surely as he knew the gripe of his own bowels at the prospect. Raleigh sniffed the air — a faint hot breeze wafted up the face of the butte from the prairie below. No, he couldn't smell them. Maybe he'd seen something from the corner of his eye. He crouched and raised the glasses, remembering to shade the lenses from the high climbing sun with the cupped palms of his hands so they wouldn't throw a giveaway flash.

Only on his third careful sweep of the prairie did he spy them, a dozen riders at least, just slow-moving specks at first, then more clearly; two dozen spotted ponies with skinny men aboard, snaking along the base of a low ridge to the northeast. His eye caught the glint of a weapon — gun barrel or lancehead — that's what gave them away. That's what I must have sensed before, that flash in the corner of my eye. Northeast. The Indians were between Sir Harry's column and the North Canadian River, the safety of the establishment at Adobe Walls where Rath and old Myers had their stores now, and Jim Hanrahan his saloon. To the south lay only sagebrush tangles and alkali pans and prickly pear for a long, long way, until you came to Rio Grande del Norte and Mexico, which wasn't much better than hell.

At this distance, even with the glasses, he couldn't make out what tribe they were, but in this country they'd be Comanche or Kiowa, or possibly Apache, which wasn't much better for the future of a man's hair. He watched them a few minutes more, to make sure of the war party's direction. It was on a collision course with Lord Malcontent's baggage train. Raleigh went over the western end of the butte and scanned his backtrail. He could just make out the canvas of the first wagons emerging through the haze. He started for the edge, to begin the laborious climb back down. Then the worm bit him once more — the old familiar worm of his fear . . .

It would be a whole lot easier, a lot safer, to stay right here. The Indians would have scouts out. They'd surely see him hightailing it back to the wagons. Maybe they'd cut him off — Vixen was a smooth-riding pony but not a fast one, not as fast in a sprint as those quick wiry little war ponies of the Comanche. Surely they'll cut me off, he thought. That's what I'll do, then. Stay put. Let Lord Malcontent have his grand and much desired Armageddon with the redskins, the one he's so confident of winning. And maybe he will win. More power to him: let him win, pray for it. He certainly has men and rifles and powder and ball enough to handle a war party of only twenty or thirty savages. He has the Gatling. What could I do for him, anyway? Hungover like this I couldn't hit my hinder with a hoe handle. Do I owe him anything? I'm no more than another servant to him. And what the hell, he's just another greenhorn, a pampered, pompous foreigner, full of himself to overflowing. Let the Comanches have his hair.

Keeping low so as not to skylight himself, Raleigh went back to his first vantage point. The Indians were closer now, only a mile off. He saw that there were more than he'd counted before. Many more. Perhaps as many as a hundred in the war party. And it certainly was a war party — he could make out the paint now, reds and yellows and sky blues, blacks and bone whites,

319

some of the warriors with blue-white hailstones painted on their chests, others with skulls and leg bones and severed hands in garish yellow. The ponies were painted, too, with spoked red suns and stars and comets and yellow-black lightning flashes. He scanned the column carefully. Mainly bows and arrows, lances, a few rifles. Most of them were Kiowa, he saw from the way they dressed their hair. But also some Cheyenne in there — taller, slimmer, paler-skinned men with long black braids, one carrying the wicked crook-handled lance they favored, and one . . .

Hellfire — it was Jenny Dousmann!

His heart hammered as if it were busting his rib cage. He fumbled the pint out of his shirt, uncorked it, and took a long pull — then another. Then he raised the glasses again.

He'd know that blond hair anywhere, that jounce of bosom beneath the doeskin shirt. And Tom of course, he saw Tom now, riding beside her on that pony of his. All savage now, white man begone, his leggings black along the seams with human hair, a pipe hatchet at his belt, the only thing modern about him the shiny blue-black rifle in the panther-skin boot under his leg — a brand-new Winchester, it looked like. Tom's face was painted red and black, teeth flashing through black lips as he talked animatedly to Jenny.

Her face looked harder than Raleigh remembered, no paint but burned almost black as Tom's from the sun of early summer, the winds of the prairie. She carried a bow case slung across her back and Otto's Sharps across the pommel of her high-ridged Cheyenne saddletree.

And who was that riding just behind her, draped in a wolfskin? Then he recognized the face, the set of the rider's shoulders. It was Otto, by God. With only one arm. Otto dressed as a buffalo wolf. Carrying a spear couched beneath his armpit like some ghostly reincarnation of the Visigoth, come back to purge the plains of Christians, rip raw meat from the bones of the god-fearing, reduce the civilized world to ashes.

God help Sir Harry.

20

Jenny was in control. All the way south from the Big Horns she had felt the doubts falling away, felt the bonds of her upbringing burn away in the fire of a new-sparked passion. Death to the Pale Intruders. At first she tried to keep the attention of the Cheyenne soldiers on their primary mission — get down to the Yarner as quickly and quietly as possible, locate the Buffalo Butte and complete their quest, no fuss, no casualties, no side trips for any purpose, and particularly not for war or thievery. If only one of them was killed, even wounded, their strength would be diminished — certainly they could see that?

But they couldn't. Surely if the mischief they worked was directed at whites, there would just as surely be pursuit and fierce retribution. Yet Tom merely smiled when she urged caution.

"That's not how we play this game," he said.

"Then how do we play it?"

"For fun," he said, laughing.

"For keeps," she said.

He thought about that for a moment. "You're right. The spiders think death is a matter of choice. They all want to live forever." He shook his head, still smiling. "No fun living like that."

"War is fun?"

"Try it. You like to hunt. I've seen you happy with death. Hunt men for a while. They hunt back."

The party had ridden steadily to the south-southwest, crossed the Pawnee Fork, where a large party of Crazy Knives — Kiowas — was camped as if expecting their arrival. An older warrior called Big Face was leading the party. With the Kiowas were a few young Southern Cheyennes. Tom and his Elk brothers knew them from past adventures. One was the son of the famous Peace Chief Stone Calf. The son's name was Red Arm, a handsome young man, though sullen, a look of death in his eyes. He was so ashamed of his father's pleas for peace, Tom said, that he had taken the war trail and vowed not to return alive — a "suicide soldier," Tom called him.

"They're headed to the Yarner to kill spider hide men. Red Arm knows this country, he's been many times to the Buffalo Butte and can take us there. It's as Little Wolf told us — the place where the buffalo come from. We'll travel with them then."

"Don't go haring off on any raids, Tom. We can't afford a costly fight, not until we've completed the task Little Wolf assigned us."

She might as well have cautioned the wind, and she knew it. The Elk Soldiers merely smiled and nodded assent, and raided anyway. She went with them.

Somehow they knew, perhaps by some extrasensory means, when there were people in remote places. She'd seen Tom do the same with animals. Once, while hunting sheep high in the Big Horns, she had spent the better part of an hour scanning a barren cirque for signs of life. Nothing but boulders. Then Tom came up, put a finger to his lips, motioned her to sit, and disappeared over the lip. She heard a shot. Half an hour later he returned with blood beneath his fingernails and the head and hide of a freshly skinned big horn draped over his shoulders.

"How did you know it was there?" she asked.

"I didn't," he said, puzzled for a moment. Then he smiled. "Well, I did, really. I just felt it. Wouldn't you know where your food was in your house, or your money? Wouldn't you know if a thief was in your home?"

The Cheyennes had done the same on the trip south, often sneaking off at night to return in the morning with scalps or ponies or meat. Sometimes all three. The meat was beef from the many herds of cattle being driven up from Texas. She had seen the dust from a few of these herds and thought at first they were buffalo. But there were no buffalo left in that country — not in Nebraska, or Kansas, or even in eastern Colorado. The hide men had done a thorough job.

Toward moonset one evening Jenny rode with the band toward yet another cattle herd. It was full dark when they neared it, riding quietly up a deep coulee. Gnarled mesquite lined the banks, black against the night like hanging trees. Leaving the horses in the care of Yellow Eyes, they crept through the sagebrush toward muttering cattle. A single young cowhand rode watch on the longhorns, singing to them in a sweet choirboy tenor to calm their night fears as he circled the herd.

And when I die, take my saddle from the wall.
Put it on my pony, lead her out of the stall.
Tie my bones to her back,
*   turn our faces to the west,*
And we'll ride the prairies
*   that we love the best . . .*

Tom sent his Elk Soldiers creeping upwind of the herd, signing them to await his cry. Otto disappeared into the sagebrush, down a meandering dry wash.

The cowboy was riding toward Tom and Jenny, slouched in his saddle, swaying rhythmically as he sang, backlit by the dim glow of the drovers' campfire half a mile away. As he approached, Jenny could see his face in the starshine, young and guileless, unsuspecting, dreamy-eyed, half asleep as he rode his round. Tom nocked an arrow to his bowstring, raised the bow, and began his draw. The cowhand was close now, serene in his innocence. Jenny laid a hand on Tom's bow arm — *Wait.* Tom looked at her in puzzlement. He shrugged her off and shot. The cowboy shrieked once, loud, and toppled backward over his pony's rump. Tom yipped. In the near-distance the Elk Soldiers began to howl like wolves, running their ponies forward into the herd, waving their blankets. The longhorns leaped instantly to their deerlike feet, whirled, and pelted away from the threat — back toward the drovers' campfire in full stampede. Tom's bow twanged again and a steer fell, skidding forward on its far shoulder. Then another arrow, and another fell. The Elks ran up and began to butcher the still-quivering cows as Yellow Eyes approached with the pack ponies.

Jenny walked over to where the cowboy lay staring up at the stars in sightless amazement. She wrenched the arrow from his chest and threw it into the darkness.

Later, as they were riding back to the night camp, Otto came up beside her.

"What's the matter?" he asked. "You seem angry."

"Why did they have to kill that young cowhand? Couldn't they just have overpowered him and then stampeded the herd?"

"This is war," Otto said, "and he was an enemy. We kill our enemies before they can kill us, if we plan well and bring it off right. The outrider might have drawn his pistol and fired a warning shot. Then the other drovers would have been on us in an instant and a lot more men would have died, red and white."

"Killing from ambush is a dirty thing," she said.

"*Death* is a dirty thing," Otto countered.

"Death from ambush, when a man is taken completely by surprise, is arguably less awful than death at the end of an infantry charge, with the preparation and worry that precedes it."

"Still, it's an ugly thing."

Otto looked over at her. "Nobody ever said it was pretty."

But war cut both ways, as Jenny learned during a raid on a buffalo camp. As they passed through the broken country near the headwaters of Wolf Creek, a Crazy Knife scout smelled bacon cooking and tracked the scent to an isolated canyon. There he found three well-armed hide men camping. Their horses were not grazing loose or he would have stolen them; the mounts were tied to the wheels of the bullwagon, an indication that these men were wise to the ways of the country. The scout rode back and told Big Face, who without hesitation ordered an attack. As Tom and the other Elks rode off with the Kiowas, Jenny, Otto, and Yellow Eyes trailed behind. Approaching the canyon, they heard war whoops and gunfire — the slow, heavy boom of Big Fifties counterpointing the sharper crack of the Henrys and Spencers of the Indians. Jenny looked down from the canyon's rim. The white men had dived under the wagon and were firing from behind bales of flint hides. Firing accurately. She saw two Kiowas down and dead already, their ponies milling around them in panic, and four more Indians firing at the wagon from behind their dead

327

mounts. Clouds of burned gunpowder, mixed with the tantalizing smell of the bacon still frying over the hide men's cookfire, rose up the canyon walls.

Then, to her horror, Jenny saw Tom and his Elks charging the wagon from the side. Pony Quirts rode with them on his father's buffalo pony. As they swept past the front of the wagon, Tom and the Elks swung themselves sideways and under the bellies of their ponies, their bodies protected from the hide men's gunfire by solid horseflesh, and fired their own rifles one-handed as they passed. Pony Quirts, trailing behind the others and unfamiliar with this maneuver, remained upright. A Sharps boomed and his horse fell. One of the whites dashed out, grabbed Pony by the hair, and dragged him under the wagon.

"That's Lew Winziger down there," said Otto, who had crept up silently beside her. "He's the one who grabbed the boy. I don't know the other fellows."

"Will they kill Pony?"

"Maybe. They might have no other choice if our friends press their attack home. But probably they'll try to use him as a bargaining chip."

Big Face's Kiowas tried one more charge, screaming hideously as they whipped their ponies down the open slope directly into the hide men's guns. More ponies fell, two at the very start of the charge, when the Kiowas were still three hundred yards away, and others halfway down.

As the Indians came closer, two Kiowas themselves were shot. Jenny saw the big bullets tear out of their backs like suddenly blooming red flowers. The remaining Kiowas fled back up the slope.

Then Jenny saw a ramrod poke out from under the wagon with a white handkerchief tied to it. It waggled back and forth, a call for a parlay.

Tom rode alone back down the slope.

A man crawled out from under the wagon. "That's Winziger," Otto said.

Tom and Winziger stood a hundred yards apart, and Jenny could see the muzzles of the two other buffalo rifles aimed square at Tom's chest. Then someone touched her shoulder. It was Yellow Eyes, carrying Otto's big rifle. She pointed downhill at Winziger. Jenny took the Sharps, checked to see that there was a cartridge in the breech, and, resting the heavy barrel on a dry buffalo chip that lay before her, sighted on Winziger's belt buckle.

"You talk English?" Winziger asked.

"Little bit," Tom said.

"We got this young'un of yours. We also got plenty more bullets. You want the boy back in one piece, just call off your wolves."

Tom turned and looked uphill. Big Face stepped into the open. Tom told him in sign language what had been said. The Crazy Knife leader went back to talk to his men.

"You're Lew Winziger, ain't you?" Tom said. "I seen you last year up on the Cimarron."

"That's right. Who are you?"

"Two Shields."

"Cheyenne, ain't ye?"

"Yup."

"What you doin' this far west?"

"Just huntin', like you fellers."

"Huntin' ponies and scalps, more like."

"It's huntin' however you do it," Tom said. "Even better if the game shoots back."

Winziger laughed.

Big Face came back out of the brush at the top of the canyon and made the sign for agreement.

"Okay," Tom told Winziger. "You got a deal. But you let us carry away our dead with their scalps still on, right?"

"Fair enough. No market for Injun hair. We'll finish our breakfast, hitch up our wagon, and take the boy with us till we're clear of the canyon. Then you can have him back."

Tom nodded and rode back to the top.

When the hide men rolled away half an hour later, they had Pony Quirts walking behind the wagon with a noose around his neck and his hands tied. The Indians trailed just out of rifle shot. Once the wagon reached the prairie, Winziger untied Pony, turned him around, and slapped him on the rump.

"Hi-yah! Run, you murderin' little red devil!"

Pony ran. As he rejoined them, Jenny saw tears in his eyes.

That night in the Indian camp there were loud

lamentations for the dead.

One day as they neared the Prairie Dog Fork they spied a lone wagon creeping across the plains. Tom and Crazy rode out to intercept it, while the others circled around concealed by folds in the prairie to cut off escape. Jenny rode after Tom. The wagon was halted when they came up. A frightened, middle-aged man in a dark suit and a bowler derby was driving the team of matched bays. He relaxed a bit when he saw Jenny.

Great shiny coils of wire filled the bed of his wagon.

"What have you got there?" Tom asked.

"Armored fencing," the man said.

"What's that?"

"Oh, it's a new product, sir, brand-new on the market, from De Kalb, Illinois. Finest fencing in the world, sir, lighter 'n air, stronger 'n whiskey, cheaper 'n dirt! All steel and a hundred miles long! Sparks won't set it afire, nor buffler knock it down. It'll keep your cattle from roamin', that it will. The cow ain't been born yet can get through this fence. Notice how sharp and long the prickers?"

He turned in his seat and twanged one of the glittering barbs. It gave forth a muted plink.

"It's bob wire," the man said proudly. "It's the Moultrie Steel Armored Fence. And I'm that very man, J. Eldon Moultrie, who's done gone and invented it. Don't be taken in by inferior products — the weak and paltry strands of Lalor & Slam-

331

mon, Glidden & Vaughn, Kelly or Judson or Haish. 'Moultrie Steel's the Better Deal,' and you'd better believe it!"

Tom translated for Crazy, who laughed and said something Jenny didn't catch.

"My partner here wants to know why you'd fence in your cattle. All that grass out there, everywhere, just for the eating. Why not let 'em roam?"

"Why, it's the wave of the future, my man! Property lines, property lines! You don't want your neighbor's cows trampling your corn, do you? Nor yours theirs. Makes for bad blood in a neighborly community. Ain't that right, ma'am? You don't want Bossy chompin' your peas and beans, or flattenin' your backhouse, do you? The open range — why, it's gonna be closed someday, sooner more likely than later, ma'am, mark my words." He smiled his teeth at them all, but Jenny in particular — eyes pleading, though his cheeks were pink with his vision of the future. She did not reply.

"It's called Progress, ma'am."

Jenny lowered the rifle and shot J. Eldon Moultrie through the chest. The salesman's eyes widened. Crazy reached across and removed the barbed-wire man's long, gray-blond scalp with a quick flashing circle of his knife point. Popped it loose. Shook off the blood. Handed it to Jenny. Moultrie slumped sideways in the wagon, emitting a bubbly sigh as if relieved of a burden. Tom cut loose the frightened horses and herded them off to the west. Looking back as she rode away, Jenny saw Cut Ear, Pony, and Badger rolling the salesman's body in a coil of his own bright wire, then dragging him at a rope's end across the prairie.

"*Haáhe,*" she shouted.

"My God, Jenny," Otto said later as they continued over the prairie, "why did you kill that man?"

"He was the enemy," she said stiffly. "We kill our enemies."

"Oh hell, he was perfectly harmless."

"What he was selling wasn't," she said. "Don't you see what's happening? It's just what General Sheridan told me back at Fort Dodge. The government wants the Indians on reservations, under its control. The hide men are killing off the buffalo to make the Indians dependent on American beef. The drovers are already bringing cattle into the country to replace the buffalo. The cattle all wear brands, and even a white man can be hanged for stealing one. The barbed wire will allow the cattlemen to fence off their ranges and keep out everyone, white or red, who doesn't have money to buy their beef."

"You've got a point," he admitted. "But murder in cold blood — have you become a savage? Aren't you afraid for your . . . well, your *soul?*"

She laughed. "Tom and the others would have killed him anyway. At least he died quickly. Didn't you tell me that a death by surprise is better than the torture of anticipation? When

Pony came back from the buffalo wagon the other day, he told me what he'd do if he ever captured a white man. It was something the Cheyennes worked on a Colorado trooper they captured down in the Big Timbers. They cut the man's belly, pulled out a length of his gut, pegged one end to a tree, then made him walk around it. Later they skinned him and left him to die. Pony said it was revenge for the Sand Creek Massacre."

" 'Revenge is mine, saith the Lord.' "

" 'The Lord works in mysterious ways,' " she countered. "Besides, that barbed-wire salesman presumed on me. You could see in his eyes that he thought a woman, a *white* woman, would surely spare him."

She spurred her horse forward and rode up to Pony Quirts. Otto saw her hand him the white man's scalp.

Two days later they reached the Llano Estacado, a bare, dry, featureless country. The Kiowas knew the waterholes, though, and each night they camped near one spring or another. She kept her eyes peeled for the Buffalo Butte — it shouldn't be hard to spot in this seemingly infinite flatness. Then in the clarity of morning, walking out to bring in the horses one day, she suddenly saw it — bold, horned, and massive, rising above the plain like a ruined god. It must have been visible all yesterday afternoon, she thought, but I couldn't see it for the heat haze and the dust. She felt her heart thump faster.

Tom walked up beside her and laid a hand on her shoulder.

"It *does* look like a buffalo," she said.

"Yes, but we won't be able to go there until tomorrow."

"Why? It's only an hour or two away."

"Well, today we have the battle, you know? You'd better start putting on your paint."

"What battle?"

"Spiders ahead," Tom said. "Those strange ones Little Wolf told us about, with the big pretty horses, the men we call Long Knives — you know, English?"

"Where are they?"

"Straight on in front of us, coming our way. Pony and Badger Walker went out before dawn and saw them. Dozens of ponies, and those big pretty lodges of silk and canvas. They saw your old chestnut pony — you know, from last winter?"

"Vixen?"

"The very one. And they saw Captain McKay, too. He's up on the Buffalo Butte right now, probably having what he calls a 'look-see.' "

Jenny glanced to her left where the butte stood stark on the morning sky, a gaunt black skull against southern brightness. Raleigh McKay was up there. She felt the shame again; it burned in her heart, yes, but more in the pit of her stomach. He was up there with a rifle. Her fingers trembled

335

on the stock of the Sharps. Tom was still smiling, but now he raised his eyebrows.

She had never told him about the rape. She'd told no one, not even her brother or Strongheart. The shame was too great and she was afraid she couldn't speak of it without weeping.

Jenny said, "You're going to fight the English, right? Leave Vixen and Captain McKay to me. But just tell Otto that I'm out hunting. I don't want him worrying or coming with me."

Tom nodded. He didn't laugh this time. He had long suspected, from Jenny's bitterness whenever the captain's name was mentioned, that something shameful had transpired between her and McKay, perhaps that he'd taken her "on the prairie." Though Tom would gladly have killed him for that, not to mention the savage beating he himself had received at McKay's hands, he knew she must exact her own revenge.

"Now you're a Cut-Arm," Two Shields said.

She nodded and rode off toward the Buffalo Butte.

After watching her for a while, Tom turned back to the main group. The Kiowas were talking excitedly among themselves, laying their plan of battle. He called Otto and the Elk Soldiers aside for a Cheyenne council of war. He had to tell them about the Gatling gun.

"We have a special duty in this fight," he told them. "You remember how Little Wolf told us about the many-times-shooting gun these Long Knives have with them? The Gun-That-Shoots-

All-Day, he calls it. Well, he wants us to capture that gun. It will help us when the spiders invade our hunting grounds and attack our camps. The gun lives under a tepee of black canvas on one of the Long Knife rolling things. We will let the Kiowas do most of the killing and dying in this fight, let them count all the coups if necessary . . ."

A groan went up from the Elk Soldiers, and Cut Ear muttered something obscene.

"*Yes,*" Two Shields said, "we will let them take all the horses and lift all the scalps as well! Our job is to get that gun. Now tell me, Badger, did you see a wagon with a black tepee on it when you scouted the train?"

Badger Walker grunted but said nothing, averting his eyes.

"I saw it," Pony Quirts said. "It's at the head of the column, the biggest rolling thing of them all. It is dragged along by many white pulling-buffalo. The animals hitched to the other rolling things are different colors, black, red, blue. Only this one has white buffalo."

"Good. If we move fast the spiders won't have time to uncover the gun and start firing at us. It could kill us all before we get to the spiders. I will ask Big Face to shoot many arrows from cover before we charge. That might throw the spiders into confusion, giving us time to reach the gun before they do. Now tell me truly, will you do as I ask?"

The Elks muttered some more, but finally nodded their heads. Then they ran off to paint their faces for war.

"Will they obey your orders?" Otto asked once the Elks had gone.

Tom shrugged. "I hope so," he said in English. "But it's a strange idea to them, thinking ahead like this. A Cheyenne soldier sees war as a one-man fight, kind of a wild, bloody game to test his courage, show his contempt for death. And it helps that maybe they'll win something special by playing the game — hair, horses, women, honor. Oh sure, they'll get together in a fight sometimes to rescue another Cheyenne, even to retrieve his body under fire, but that's just another way of showing their bravery." He paused, clearly discouraged. "Well," he said at last, "we'll soon have the answer."

"I'll ride with you," Otto told him. "Maybe just the two of us can bring it off. I know from the war that you fire a Gatling by turning a crank, not pulling a trigger. I won't need fingers for that. But you'll have to load and aim it for me."

Two Shields was silent for a moment. Then in Cheyenne he said, *Hó-nehe Vého, tséhe-ve'toveto.* Wolf Chief . . . my brother."

21

Milo Sykes had waited until His Lordship was deep in his bath, engrossed in his newspaper. *The Times* was still following the Ashanti campaign, and the British had finally triumphed. "My God, Blandish," Sir Harry exclaimed. "Listen to this: 'When the Black Watch at long last entered King Kofi's barbarous capital, they found it empty — except for thousands of skulls neatly stacked in a sacred grove, proof positive of human sacrifice.' Ghastly! But then the butcher's bill on our side was only 18 killed and 185 wounded, though another 55 poor sods died of fever. 'The White Man's Grave,' indeed."

Blandish hovered near the tub like a mother hen. "Yes indeed, m'Lord, not at all like this salubrious climate."

As the Limeys babbled on, Sykes eased into the silken cave of His Lordship's sleeping quarters. He knew that Sir Harry had brought many pairs of spectacles with him, redundancy in case of breakage, and that he left them lying all over the place for Blandish to pick up. Sure enough, there were three pairs, in their embroidered cases, on the bedtable beside Sir Harry's couch, along with a stack of leather-bound books. Sykes stepped over, pocketed a pair of the glasses, and walked quietly out of the tent. His Lordship would never miss them, and if he did, he'd blame his flunky.

An hour later the wagon train was creaking southeastward over the prairies, the tents struck and packed, teams harnessed, pickets riding ahead about a quarter of a mile in case of trouble — all of the routines running smoothly now, just another day on the prairie. But Sykes had a crawly feeling in the small of his back, the pit of his stomach. Mister Lo was out there, and McKay, that bastard, had slipped off before dawn "to have a look-see," leaving Milo to fend for himself. Well, he was fending.

He dropped behind the stragglers and pulled out the spectacles case, fumbled it open, and put on the glasses. Thank God, their eyes were the same in their wretchedness! Relief. No — wonderment! It was as he had dreamed — suddenly the world snapped into a clarity of focus it had lost for Milo sometime back around the Battle of Shiloh, where he'd taken a blow upside the head from the steel-shod butt of a Union musket in the confusion of the peach orchard. On sheer reflex he'd managed to bury his bayonet to the hilt, just above the Yankee's belt buckle, but ever since then his vision had been fading. Slowly at first, allowing him to make a living for a time as a wolfer, or meat hunting for the railroad navvies, or finally gambling, but then more swiftly and severely. The bright burning light of the prairie sped it along — at night the sky flamed behind his sore eyelids even in sleep. He tried town for a while, Leavenworth, Hays, Ellsworth, Dodge. Soon he'd been forced to give up cards — he couldn't even count the spots on a deuce accurately. He'd been reduced to skinning shaggies working in filth and grease and the smell of death. The only good thing about his declining vision, he often thought, was that he couldn't see himself clearly in a mirror. What he saw, the dim outline of his face, was as he remembered it. But he was sure now that he was ugly. A man could feel such things — the way that bohunk bitch had recoiled from him whenever he came near her.

Now and then he got letters from his wife, back in Marysville. The young'uns needed this or that, no clothes for the coming winter, the cow died or the sow died, suchlike guff. For a while he'd sent her what money he could, but soon he could spare none and ceased writing entirely. A withered whimpering scold she'd be by now, string-necked and flabby-titted, full of the stink of Jesus, like all married women, the sour smell of sanctity coming off her where once she'd smelled of fire. If he had to, he could go back to her, but he dreaded the thought of the young'uns — the whining and the snot, frail pallid little things that stank of baby shit. Well, they'd be all growed by now, married, with kids of their own — a slew of brats, probably. He'd have to smell 'em. More yet he dreaded the plow — often in his dreams he was plowing a row of heavy red clay that stretched to the dim horizon, staring at the scrawny, dung-caked, high-hipped west end of an

eastbound mule. He'd wake in a sweat, shuddering with fatigue.

But now he felt better than he had in years.
The world was back in focus — clear and crisp,
with all the hairs on it. He hadn't realized how
important clear vision was to a man. Anything
was possible, now he could see. He was awed by
the notion. Anything . . .

At the edge of his vision was movement, and
he turned toward it with newfound delight to see
what forgotten wonders it might reveal. A covey
of quail, buzzing out low and frantic from an
arroyo to his left, one of them breaking away from
the group and flying his way . . . It was an arrow,
winging in hard against the china-blue sky. He
marveled for an instant at the hard-edged clarity
of the image, the red and blue — no, black —
circlets of color just back of the arrowhead, the
snakelike sinuations along its length, the wavelike
motion of the turkey-feather fletches, shimmering
as they caught the sunlight. A cloud of arrows,
he saw, the sky suddenly specked with them.
Arrows about to fall.

He twisted away and kicked his pony.

Something smacked him hard and high, toward
the middle of his back. He looked down. An
arrowhead protruded from the front of his shirt,
below the short ribs, angling earthward. A long,
narrow, black, barbed hunk of iron bound with
sinew to a greasewood shaft and painted near the
binding in circles of red-and-black ocher. The
arrowhead blossomed with gobbets of fat, yellow

fat that shivered like jelly, gleamed like the sun. *His fat.* The horse bucked as another arrow swatted its haunch. Holding on for his life, Milo felt the arrow shaft working in his chest as they bucketed out of the column. Oxen and mules screamed in bouquets, in wreaths of feathery spines. Two men were down, three or four — more. A runaway wagon crushed a fallen man's chest. Horses pelted past with empty saddles. From the coulee to the left of the column rose a cloud of boiling dust, flashing with heat lightning and the flap of red and blue and black blankets, riders jogged crosswise dragging mesquite bushes from the tails of their supernaturally long ponies; other riders raced naked and gaudy across toward them, mirrors flaring, some of them blowing bone whistles high and eerie and the sky filled with a hoarse yipping like the skies of autumn, full of geese. How bad was he hit, he'd be bled out by now if the arrow'd taken lung or heart or a vein: the fat leaking from him gleaming in the light of the sun didn't matter so long as he could tuck it back in, and it'd block the wound better, wouldn't bleed so hard that way, might could make it to the Dobe Walls . . .

From the top of the butte half a mile away, Raleigh watched the attack unfold. It was pitiless. It was masterful. The Indians had hidden themselves well within arrow range in a shallow brush-grown gorge not far from the trail. The first fall of their arrows threw the column into disarray.

343

The dust and the flash of mirrors, the flapping of blankets, the pipes and the war cries only spurred the stock deeper into panic. Malcombe's men were too busy trying to control their teams to think of defensive measures. Why wasn't someone running for the Gatling?

He saw the first painted riders hit the column, bows bent and loosed, lances flashing, hatchets and stone-crowned war clubs swinging. White men sprawled and bled in the dust, brained or speared or shot through and through with arrows fired at point-blank range. The cutting edge of the Indian attack punched through the wagon train in two places, reducing it to three separate, milling, confused, and disconnected parts. He could see Lord Malcombe, his hounds around him, trying to rally his men at the head of the column, draw their wagons into a defensive circle.

The Gatling was still shrouded.

But the Indians were too fast for Sir Harry's men. Too many mules and oxen were down already. Wagon piled on wagon, some tipped sideways, spilling dunnage and boxes into the dirt. The crash and tinkle of shattering china came faintly to his ears. A ragged sputter of gunfire from the midst of the melee, Sir Harry's pistols drawn and bucking. A gaunt mastiff leaped and dragged an Indian from his horse, tore his throat out, looked up red-muzzled and snarling as three arrows sprouted magically from the dog's shoulders. Gouts of thick white gunsmoke rose from the boiling dust and trailed raggedly downwind, obscuring Sir Harry's thin, bespectacled, red-jacketed figure from Raleigh's view.

Where to look, where to look next?

Elkhounds bounded like black rubber balls over the prairie, in pursuit of a belly-ripped ox which trailed both its harness and intestines in a long dusty tangle. He saw a young Cheyenne ride headlong after Blandish as the manservant fled toward an overturned wagon. The warrior swung his hatchet in a bright arc that split his victim's skull to the chin as neatly as a halved melon. An Airedale dashed out of the smoke and howled mournfully. A knot of Indians had found the commissary wagon, skewered its driver, and were helping themselves to whiskey.

Then he saw Otto and Tom Shields fighting their way toward the wagon that held the Gatling gun. Sir Harry saw them, too, and broke away from the main fight, racing them for the prize.

Wolf Chief led the way. *Never been part of a cavalry charge before,* Otto thought, *only on the receiving end.* He was giddy with the thunder of it. As they pounded down on the train, he saw bearded white men gaping at them, some running, others crouched beside the wagon wheels. Their guns spouted smoke, but he couldn't hear the shots for the hoofbeats of the ponies and the whooping of the Kiowas. Then suddenly they were among the wagons. Men and dogs bounced from the shoulders of his horse, sprawling in the dust. He heard Tom yipping behind him, the keening of whistles, grunts and screams, and a low, feral snarling of men and animals locked in mortal combat, all punctuated by the bang and pop of gunfire. The wagon he rode for was on the far side of the tangle. It appeared and disappeared in clouds of dust and gunsmoke. The reek of sulphur filled his mouth.

"There it is," Tom yelled. The black canvas cover of the Gatling loomed straight ahead. No one was in the wagon yet. They dismounted directly into the wagon box. With a whip of his belt knife Tom cut the lashings of the canvas and pulled it clear. The magazine drum was already in place. Bullets snapped close overhead, and looking up, Otto saw two men in cowboy hats kneeling beside an overturned cart, fumbling at cartridge boxes, reloading their fancy double rifles.

"Get those fellows, Tom!" he shouted, pointing with his maimed hand. Tom grabbed up his Yellow Boy from where he'd laid it in the wagonbed and fired twice, dropping one of the shooters. The other man ducked behind the cart.

"All right," Otto ordered. "Point the Gatling toward where that man just hid." Tom swung the gun's heavy brass barrel into line. As the barrel depressed, Otto sighted along it. *On target!* He had never fired a Gatling, only read about the gun. Not knowing what to expect, he stepped to the right of the gun and turned the firing crank with his stubbed left hand. The barrel spun and roared — *Herr Gott,* he thought, *like uncorking a bottle of thunder*. Empty brass clattered in the wagon box, and through the smoke Otto could see bullets rip the bottom of the cart. "Work it from side to side a bit," he yelled over the gun's stutter. They raked the wagon. Then Otto looked for another target.

Two of the wagons, their teams dead in the traces, had halted side by side, leaving an alleyway between them. Otto saw a man dart into the corridor they formed and break in their direction. Blue eyes, blond whiskers. Two heavy revolvers in his hands. A short red jacket, yellow sash, too elegant for the frontier — it must be the Englishman! Tom was firing his Yellow Boy in another direction, so Otto swung the Gatling himself to cover the man, cranked off a dozen rounds. But the gun was aimed too high — Otto saw the bullets rip holes in the canvas top of one Studebaker — and the Englishman dove to his left, under the wagon. Otto pushed the gun barrel down, but it had reached the bottom of its arc. He could depress it no further.

With the Gatling silent, the Englishman quickly rolled out from the far side of the wagon, fired four shots without aiming toward Otto's wagon, and ran to the rear. Then Otto saw Pony Quirts step out from the shadows and swing his war club . . .

Suddenly another white man appeared at the head of the slot between the wagons. It was Milo Sykes. He skidded to a stop, looked wildly around, and Otto saw that he was wearing spectacles now. They flashed in the sun. Blood on his shirt, breathing hard. Otto swung the Gatling on its tripod and hit the crank. For a long thunderous moment gunsmoke erased Milo, but when it cleared he was gone. Nowhere to be seen . . .

By Christ, I'll hunt him down on foot!

From Raleigh McKay's perspective, too, the battle had disappeared in a cloud of smoke and dust. He had seen the Indians picking up guns from the dead. They were well armed now, judging by the sound of it. The bellow of their gunfire began to dominate the fight, a few ragged crackles at first, the pop and thud of different calibers, then rising to a maniacal crescendo as the Gatling entered the fray.

At first Raleigh hoped that His Lordship had reached the gun and turned the tide of battle. Then through rifts in the smoke he could see an Indian standing beside the Gatling — Tom Shields? The firing began dying away in flurries, toward an occasional bang as the redskins tracked down and finished their enemies.

Raleigh looked at the sun.

The whole affair had lasted no more than fifteen minutes.

Already the buzzards were circling.

What had happened to Sir Harry? And Milo? And where in that whole savage scene was Otto? Or Jenny, for that matter? As the dust thinned and settled out and the cries died away, Raleigh searched for them with the glasses.

Milo lay on his side, breathing as shallowly as he could manage in the hot dark beneath an overturned wagon. He'd snapped off the arrow below the fletching and just behind the head, but left the remainder of the shaft in the wound. He'd leak less blood that way. The pain in his chest and belly was intense, but he couldn't allow himself a groan. He could see Indians walking around the wagon from time to time, their ugly bowed legs and beaded moccasins, now and then a lance point thrusting into an already dead man or mule. Beside him under the wagon lay another white man who he'd thought at first was dead. But now the man began to move his head and shoulders, uttered a low groan.

"Easy, partner, easy," Milo whispered. "They're all around us. Jes' keep quiet and mebbe they'll go away."

The other man grunted softly and turned his head toward Milo. Milo could see the pale-blue shine of his eyes, the blond furze of muttonchop whiskers. His Lordship.

Lord Malcombe whispered, "Is that you, Sykes?"

"Jes' pipe down, Sir Harry, please."

They lay there quietly for a while. Then there came a guttural explosion of Indian laughter. Whoops and the sound of open-handed blows. Peering out from under the shattered tailgate of the wagon, Milo saw moccasined feet kicking and stomping a white man — Gomez, he realized. Sliding Billy gritted his teeth. One side of his face was bloody, the right half, blood running down until it was diverted by his mustache to spill off the side of his chin like a lopsided red goatee. A Cheyenne with a blue coat and a crook-handled lance stepped astraddle the Meskin, screamed something hoarse, then with the iron point of the lance began to skin out Billy's face below the cheekbones. Billy seemed unable to move his arms or legs, probably a bullet in the spine, but his belly muscles writhed beneath his bloody shirt. Other muscles danced like snakes in his throat and jaw. Still, he did not scream.

Must have Apache blood in him.

Then another Cheyenne stepped up beside the first and said something. The first Cheyenne laughed and nodded. The other, just a boy, Milo saw, drew aside his breechclout and hauled out his whang. He flourished it and laughed. Then he began pissing on Billy's skinned-out face. A ragged burst of laughter . . .

"Beasts," whispered His Lordship.

Of a sudden Sliding Billy reached up, quick as a cottonmouth, and grabbed the boy by cock and balls. Yanked hard. The boy screamed, and the first Cheyenne plunged his lance into Billy's neck, pinning him to the ground. Immediately the other Indians grabbed Billy by the heels and hauled him out of sight. A few moments later Milo smelled smoke. Over the crackle of flames he heard Sliding Billy's first heartfelt scream.

"Hellfire," Milo whispered. "They're burnin' the wagons."

Pony strutted away from the fire, the spider's scream a scalp song to his ears. At least he strutted as best he could. His groin still ached from the spider's grip. He had counted his first coups on two white men today, taken the hair of the man he pissed on before they threw him on the fire, and he felt proud. He affected a warrior's swagger, his face showing no emotion, his back straight and square-shouldered, walking perhaps a bit more bowleggedly than his limbs demanded, now and then allowing a slight manly sneer to appear on his lips as befit a blooded Elk Soldier. One spider he'd killed at full gallop with the stone-headed war club Two Shields had given him, overtaking the man and reaching across with his empty hand to slap him on the back before swinging the long, whippy-handled club with his other hand in an upward sweep that connected squarely with the base of the spider's jouncing skull. The satisfying crump of stone on bone still felt sweet up the length of his arm.

The second spider he confronted on foot, a hairy-faced man with two empty revolvers and a red jacket and huge, desperate eyes, crazy eyes, pale blue behind the spectacles that covered them, the spider running out of the smoke and dust toward another rolling thing, away from the one with the black tepee on it. Pony had seen him coming, though, and stepped from the con-

351

cealment of the wagon with the club dangling at his side. The spider saw his club, but also saw Pony's youth. He pointed one of the six-shooters at him, pulled the trigger, then stopped when he heard the futile clack of hammer on empty chamber. Pony walked toward him until he was within arm's reach and stuck out his hand and pulled the spider's long yellow sidewhiskers. The crazy-eyed spider swung the barrel of his pistol at Pony's head, but Pony ducked and with the club knocked the spider's legs from under him. Crazy Eyes fell, staring up into Pony's face. Pony leaned over, plucked the spectacles from the spider's nose, crushed them, and placed the palm of his hand on the man's fragile chest. He could feel the man's heart thumping. He seemed paralyzed except for his racing heart, his rapidly blinking ugly white eyes.

Pony swung the club and smacked Crazy Eyes on the side of his head, a glancing blow, then spun on his heel and strode away without looking back. Later, when he returned to the spot to pick up the spider's revolvers, he could not find them, nor even the body. Perhaps he hadn't hit Crazy Eyes hard enough to kill him and the spider had crawled away, maybe under this very wagon.

He turned and saw Two Shields approaching on foot, leading his horse. Pony smiled and started to speak. But Two Shields did not smile back. Blood streaked his red-and-black paint from a bullet gouge on his cheekbone that had left the flesh ridged and ragged at the edges. Burned gunpowder from a close discharge had stippled his chest, throat, and chin with black dots like those on a trout. He dropped the reins of his horse and stepped up to Pony still unsmiling and punched him in the mouth, hard. Pony fell back, on his rump. Tears sprang to his eyes, blood from his lips.

"I saw you make water on that man whose scalp you carry. Never do that again," Two Shields said. "An Elk Soldier does not humiliate a brave enemy, even in defeat. That spider was brave, he wouldn't cry out even when Crazy was skinning his face. You'd have seen that if you'd bothered to look. But you wanted to make a big show in front of your brothers. That's no way for a man."

He reached down and took the limp, dripping scalp from where it dangled on Pony's belt and slung it into the fire of a burning wagon.

"There's still one spider left," Pony said, "maybe more than one, alive and hiding beneath this rolling thing."

Two Shields listened, heard spider voices arguing under the wagon. He smiled at last. "Then let's get them out, into the light of this wonderful day."

Pony yipped, reprieved. Before Two Shields could stop him, he had ducked down to peer under the back of the upside-down rolling thing.

"Don't look yet!" Two Shields yelled. "He may have a . . ."

But his warning came too late.

"What's that?" Lord Malcontent whispered. He had been slipping cartridges into the empty chambers of his pistols. Now he was staring at Milo with a look of madness in his eyes.

"What?"

"Shining there on your face, Sykes. Is it a pair of specs?"

"So what?" Milo said. "Let's keep quiet or they'll have us out of here for the chop."

"You don't even wear spectacles," Lord Malcontent hissed. "Those are *my glasses*." He grabbed for them. Milo slapped his hand away and stifled a groan. The arrow shaft was working in his chest.

"Give them over, you swine!"

"No. Without them I can't see to shoot."

"So what? You've no bullets to shoot with, anyway."

"Give me some of yours. We're both shooting .44s."

"Give me the spectacles, then maybe I'll give you some bullets."

"*Shut up!* Here they come."

Moccasined feet rushed up to the open end of the overturned wagon. A young Indian face appeared, staring into the dark. It saw them and grinned.

Lord Malcontent fired at point-blank range . . .

The red devil fell backward and kicked in the dirt.

I warned him not to look under there, Two Shields thought.

Then he and Cut Ear, on horseback, roped the rear axle of the overturned wagon with their riatas and pulled it up on its side. Another pull and it toppled upright.

Sir Harry stood quickly out of the dust and fired twice in rapid succession. One shot knocked Cut Ear backward. He blinked rapidly as he toppled, dead when he hit the ground.

The other hit Two Shields. He jolted to the hit but did not fall. A black hole below his collarbone began to well with blood. He couldn't raise his arm. On his bare back a fist-sized hole had appeared, opposite the first, raggedly fringed with meat and fragments of his shoulder blade.

Otto, crouched beneath the wolfskin not five paces away, whipped his spontoon and skewered Sir Harry through the belly.

Two Shields watched and tried to say something. He couldn't speak. He slid to the ground, then sat down and laid his head on his knees.

Now Milo staggered to his feet, blood trickling from the corners of his cracked lips, glasses gleaming in the smoke. He threw his empty pistol into the flames. A tall, gaunt figure stepped up to him, limping, a one-armed man clad in a wolfskin, his face sun-blackened except for his eyes. They were blue-green as the lakes of Wisconsin. Otto Dousmann.

Milo couldn't look at him.

A mirror dangled from a rawhide thong on the

chest of the dead Indian boy Sir Harry had killed.
Milo reached down and removed it. He raised his
eyebrows, grinned, looked into the mirror. Then
he laughed, a wheezing liquid sound. He spat
blood and phlegm into the dust.

"I ain't seen nothin' but ugly since I put these
things on," he said.

He plucked the spectacles from his face and
threw them into the smoke, after the empty revolver.

"Come on and kill me, ye red nigger lover."

Otto stuck the spear point first into the ground,
then reached forward and placed his maimed
hand over the stub of the arrow shaft protruding
from Milo's chest.

"You're dead already," he said.

Milo looked down and laughed again.

Then Wolf Chief smiled, took up his weapon,
and killed Milo Sykes with one hard upward
thrust of the spear.

A moment later the flames of the burning wagons reached the gunpowder stowed with the Gatling. The explosion threw the gun high into the
sky, where it twirled brightly in the sunlight before falling, broken, back to the smoke below.

22

Viewed from the flats as Jenny approached, the butte more and more closely resembled the head, hump, and shoulders of some mythic buffalo bull, thrust upward from a cruel and ageless captivity in the depths of the earth to erupt onto the freedom of the plain. Misshapen to be sure, stained yellow in leprous blotches across its craggy face and the sides of a great bulging hump, the entire massif torqued and skewed, frozen in mid-thrust at the very climax of that effort, with one horn truncated as if snapped off just below its tip in that final battle. He hadn't quite made it. The shoulders and neck of the bull sloped upward more gradually than its steep, bulging face or the vertical sides. Raleigh would certainly have climbed the more gradual slope.

She found Vixen standing in short hobbles, still saddled but grazing near a spring at the base of the butte. The mare raised her head as Jenny approached, her nostrils flaring to taste the air, then nickered in recognition. Jenny dismounted from her Indian pony, slapped it on the rump to send it back to the herd. She laid a palm on Vixen's soft, damp muzzle and kneaded gently. "*Na ja, mein Pferdchen*, I've got you back now, my good pony, and in a while we'll ride away from all this. We'll go someplace quiet and green and peaceful where it's never winter and the grass grows deep." She loosed the hobbles. Vixen tossed her head and nickered again, then resumed grazing.

From his vantage point at the top of the butte, Raleigh had watched her ride up, first through the field glasses, then over the sights of his rifle. It would have been easy to kill her, and he knew he should. But he also knew that if he bushwhacked her, what lingering grip he maintained on his self-respect would slip away entirely. Maybe she'll just take the horse and go, he thought. But he knew she wouldn't be content with that. She was out to find him. Maybe to kill him. He pressed the set trigger until it clicked, then snugged down over the comb of the stock, held her in the sights, the bead in the middle of her chest, his trigger finger still resting on the guard. One touch on the hair trigger and she would die.

How many buffalo had he killed this way? Two thousand, three thousand, no, more like five . . . Don't even try to count them. Too many.

He was sick unto death of killing.

Leaving the mare on faith and green grass, Jenny studied the rock face. If he's smart, he'll be covering the route of his own climb, she thought. He could drop me from up there near the horns before I heard the shot. I've got to find a better way up.

She walked around the butte looking for it, and found a route on the far, sheer side of the buffalo's neck — a steep and dangerous climb, but safe at least from Raleigh's rifle. Or so she hoped.

This climb would require both hands. Jenny cut a length of rawhide from the riata looped over her shoulders and knotted it securely, top and bottom, to the wrist and barrel of the Sharps, slung the rifle across her back, and confronted the cliff. The Sharps weighed nearly eleven pounds, the bandolier of spare ammunition another five, and although at first the added weight threw her off balance, she learned to lean forward in compensation. The entire base of the cliff was sharp, shifting rubble, tumbled scree rattling under her feet as she started up the slope. He'll hear me, she thought, and shoot down from the lip. She picked her way more carefully, her moccasins sensitive to the give and play of the rocks beneath her feet.

When she reached the top of the scree, she gazed for a long time upward. A groove seemed to run down from the stone bull's earhole to where she stood, a wind- and rain-worn channel eroded over the eons into the shape of a shallow S, about two or three feet deep, as best she could see. Seams and crevices — black lines and bruises of purple shadow under the noonday sun that now glared down on the prairie — would provide hand- and toeholds for her ascent.

Picking her way carefully from seam to bulge

to fissure, she climbed toward the buffalo's head. Now and then, as the sun worked hot on the rock face, stones fell free above her and came rattling down the chute with murderous speed. A few of the smaller ones hit her. The bigger ones, those which might have smacked her like a fly from the face of the cliff to fall — probably dead before she hit the ground — bounced clear and missed her. She timed her climb in spurts, from one protective outbulge on the channel's route to the next, resting for minutes sometimes between bulges. The feature which represented the buffalo's ear was a tall, lichen-grown outcropping of extruded granite that stuck out a good three feet from the vertical wall, angling upward from the channel she'd just climbed. Out of breath from the climb, shoulders bruised, blood from a rock cut trickling down through her hair into her eyebrows, her toes and fingertips raw, she crouched beneath it and tried to compose her thoughts.

Would Raleigh still be up there when she reached the top? She was on the far side of the butte from the battle. She had heard no heavy gunfire for a long while now, only a few sporadic shots. McKay might well have departed, gone back down the gentle slope of the buffalo's neck and shoulders and remounted Vixen, be on his way to God knows where. I should have waited for him by the horse, laid an ambush for him there, instead of climbing a cliff I'm incapable of climbing, risking my life in a fool's game.

She squinted upward at the sun. Calm down,

she thought. The sun hasn't moved a handspan since you've been climbing — not fifteen minutes yet. You've made good time, with a heavy load at that. She breathed deeply for a minute or two. In the shadow of the overhang, her blood cooled. She looked downward. She had climbed a long way. The height did not frighten her. Rather, it elated her. She had always been easy with altitude. As a girl in Wisconsin she had scaled the tallest white pines on the farm, in search of birds' eggs or nestlings or glossy pinecones, often staying up there for hours on end in the silken green heights, cool in the breezes and the astringent perfume of pine, watching the busy flights of the mother birds feeding their young, quite to Mutti's earthbound consternation. She had enjoyed the view from the top of those trees, from the top of anything, for that matter, and often she'd thought back then as a girl that she would be happy to have been born an eagle. She had watched a nest of eaglets pip out of their shells one afternoon, scrawny, unfeathered, big-headed, clumsy, quite ugly — but in many ways people were uglier.

Make no mistake, though, girl. You are not an eagle. Don't fall.

She worked her way up onto the overhang, almost losing her grip once, pulled backward for a frightful instant by the sudden, shifting weight of the Sharps, but caught herself by the tips of her bleeding fingers. On the ledge of the buffalo's ear she saw a cave leading in and down into the bowels of the butte. She stuck her head in the

cave opening and heard what sounded like a bur-
ble of water coming from within. She tossed a
pebble in. It skidded across the rock and fell,
clattering, for a long time before she heard the
splash.

Yes, the spring rose inside the butte, as the
Cheyennes had said.

From the buffalo's ear to the top of his steeply
crowned skull was only a short climb. She scrambled to the base of the bull's truncated right horn
and looked carefully around, toward the skyline.
The "wool" of this granite buffalo consisted of
mesquite, cholla, ocotilla, and prickly pear.
Everything lay in shadows, every shadow moved
with the wind. But then she saw something that
did not move. It was linear, blue-black — the
barrel of a rifle.

Suddenly, as with animals she had hunted,
Raleigh sprang clear to her eyes against the background. His fringed deerskin hunting shirt
blended smoothly with the sun-blanched vegeta-
tion. He was lying on his belly, the rifle beside
him, its action oddly enough open, peering
through field glasses away from her toward the
battle. Slowly she rose to her feet. She brushed a
trickle of blood from her eyes. She was drenched
in sweat. Her knees trembled, whether from the
climb or the imminence of her final confrontation
with this long-sought enemy she did not know.
Don't worry about it. You've got him now.

She unslung the Sharps, eased the loading lever
forward to lower the breechblock and ensure that

there was indeed a round in the chamber, saw the welcome gleam of the brass cartridge, then cocked the hammer all the way back. The sear clicked. Raleigh did not seem to notice. She reached her trigger finger backward carefully and pressed the set trigger. It clicked, too, but less sharply than the hammer. The rifle was ready to fire. Just the touch of her finger on the hair trigger now would drop the hammer with explosive force.

She walked toward him, slow and Cheyenne-quiet.

Then from the killing ground half a mile away came the sound of a great explosion.

As he saw the mushroom cloud rise from the blast and a moment later felt the slap of the shock wave, Raleigh felt a nudge between his shoulder blades. He started to put down the field glasses.

"Keep them up there near your eyes, Captain McKay," Jenny said. "I wouldn't think twice about touching this trigger." He lowered the glasses despite her words, rolled over into a recumbent position, and grinned up at her. She did not shoot. But the rifle was still aimed squarely at his chest, her forefinger near the hair trigger.

"Jenny, ol' gal, I been expectin' you, saw you nosin' around down there by the pony half an hour ago. You must've come the long way up the mountain." He looked toward the cliff and nodded admiringly. "Stiff climb, too tough for an ol' bag o' bones like me. Say, it's sure good to see you." Raleigh offered her the field glasses. "Lie down here next of me and take a gander at this. Your Hostiles've won the battle."

Insouciant as ever.

"Damn you, Captain McKay!"

"Hey, come on, ol' gal," he said, still grinning, his bright blue eyes all atwinkle. "Let's let bygones be bygones. There's redskins killin' white folks down there, we gotta pull together, forget our petty squabbles of the past. Here, look . . ." He pointed to his own rifle, lying well away out of arm's reach, action open and its chamber empty. "I knew you were comin' and left my piece unloaded — on purpose, so you wouldn't think I was layin' for you. Come on, Jenny, now be a good sport, won't you?"

"I came here to kill you."

"Aw, hell," he said, and the grin began to lose its luster. "Look, I'm damn sorry for . . . what happened that day. I was way out of line, I know it. Eaten up with regret, that's what I been ever since, Jenny. I was hungover and skunk-mean stupid is all I can say. And I'll make it up to you, I promise. I'll take the Pledge, I swear, won't never touch nary a drop again, long as I live. I been all messed up in my thinkin', you know, the war and all, too much killin', men and buffalo both, and if I never hold another rifle in my hands it'll be too damn soon. I've been overlong in the wilds, this country gets to a fellow he's out in it too long, so empty, nothin' but wolf howl for company, wolves and bufflers and buzzards and

364

alkali dust and the sun shinin' clear ever' day you wake up, no drop of rain, the stink of dead meat, it gets to you, it sure does; and I been thinkin', it'd be nice to go back East for a while, ol' gal, I got enough money saved up now, we could buy us a real nice little farm I know up there in the foothills of the Blue Ridge, the old Catawba, the war passed it by and Reconstruction's hardly touched it, I've had my eye on her quite some whiles now, just you and me, Jenny, put out the land on shares, raise us some tabacca, good cash crop that, good rich soil for it back there in the Piedmont, good climate too, none of these damn winters that bite so fierce, good folks thereabouts, you wouldn't even have to keep house, Jenny, hire us a couple niggers for that, why, you'd be a *lady* — think of it, ridin' out of the mornin' on blooded stock, tall bays, and us ridin' easy in the dew, lookin' over the holdin's, we can get a start on our horse herd soon's the Injins clear out here now. That Lordship I been workin' for has good horses: we'll rope a few and head back East, grow watermelons . . . Why, I could do with a nice cool slice of watermelon right now, couldn't you, Jenny? . . . A big nice formal flower garden. Not too far from town, a pretty town at that, Tulip-tree, North Carolina, three churches, the court-house, railroad station, a bell tower, even a playhouse where the minstrel show holds forth when they comes through, seminary school for the young'uns. Why, I might could run for judge, McKay is a name well known in those parts, the

Honorable Judge McKay and His Ladywife. Hellfire, gal, I *love* you, don't you see? — and I'll love
you through all eternity." He paused for the
clincher. *"Will you marry me?"*

He watched her eyes.

He did not like what he saw there. A hard face,
sun-seared. A cruel face, like a red nigger's . . .
Tears welled and spilled down his cheeks. Slowly,
smiling weakly up at her in apology, he reached
back to his hip pocket and withdrew the ivory
comb. He began fussily to reshape his wind-
snarled hair.

As if that would help.

God, what a weakling! Jenny thought, sudden
rage boiling hot in her belly. She remembered
it all now: *Raleigh standing over her, undoing his
belt, then Milo pinning her arms as Raleigh fell on
her, tore down her trousers, forced her legs up and
back — his face close to hers, the stench of stale
booze on his hot, fast breath, his face sagging as he
penetrated her, the face of an elderly bloodhound —
pinned down, restrained, skewered, hurting and helpless no matter her strength — his weak rebel yell as
he spasmed and rolled away. Then Milo was on top
of her, even worse, and Raleigh watching and cheer-
ing him on — Raleigh, spent, combing his hair with
the ivory comb, grinning as he watched . . .*

*Lieber Gott mach mich fromm das ich in dein
Himmel komm'.*

"Not in a million years," she said, as coolly as
she could muster. "But I'll take a lock of your
hair as a keepsake of your gracious proposal —

your kind ministrations of the past."

Raleigh reached behind him as if to repocket the comb. From under his hunting shirt where it had been tucked in his waistband he drew the Whitney. A well-practiced draw.

Jenny was quicker. She swung the heavy butt of the Sharps and caught him flush on the chin. He fell back, his eyes rolling upward, unfocused, unconscious. Jenny retrieved the pistol and stuck it in the belt at the small of her own back. Then she pulled McKay's rifle out of reach and laid the Sharps next to it. She had plans for him. From the sheath at her hip she withdrew her skinning knife.

23

Jenny rode into the swirling smoke. Raleigh McKay's reddish-blond scalp flapped in the wind, drying on the muzzle of her rifle. She stared around her at the carnage. Flames flickered on burned-out wagons. Bodies everywhere. The scream of dying horses. In the near-distance she saw some Kiowas stripping and mutilating the bodies of men they had slain. Pony Quirts lay dead, his face blown away. Was that Cut Ear, lying so flat, so still beside the wagon wheel? She recognized Milo Sykes's body in the dust, his belly ripped open. In the smoke a wounded dog yowled. She looked down at Otto. The explosion had burned his face. A long, bright sliver of brass protruded from his left eye, blown there by the blast like a spear point. His other eye stared upward. She saw a flake of hot soot land on it, but he did not blink.

Gott im Himmel, are they all dead? Sheer chaos — the deepest recess of hell. For a moment she almost collapsed. Then she saw Tom, propped on one elbow in the lee of a burning wagon, and her heart leaped up when he looked at her and tried to smile. But blood spilled slowly from his mouth and nostrils, bubbling as he breathed. Yellow Eyes sat beside him, singing to herself and distractedly jabbing at her bare, bloody legs with the point of a knife. Already she had cut off her braids in mourning, and her hair fell raggedly, uneven, across her wet face. Jenny dismounted as Crazy for Horses and Walks like Badger rode up. Tom raised his head again, but his eyes seemed focused far in the distance, blinking reflexively from time to time. She untied the scalp from her rifle and tossed it into his lap. Feeling it hit, he looked down, then up at her.

He smiled.

"Kuh-kuh-kuh," he said, then shook his head in embarrassment and coughed blood. Oh Christ, she thought, a lung shot. But not too bad yet, maybe I can save him. He picked up the scalp with his left hand and gave it back to her, shaking his head: No. He wanted her to have it. She picked it up, spat on it, and threw it into the nearest fire. She pulled McKay's pistol from her belt and tossed it on the ground. His buffalo rifle she consigned to the flames.

Tom closed his eyes and nodded.

She lifted him onto Vixen's back, stuck his feet in the stirrups. He swayed back against the cantle, then steadied himself. But he reeled again and she held him for a minute, placing his hands on the saddlehorn. He could not speak, but he looked at her and nodded his thanks.

She lifted Otto's body, strangely light, draped it head down over the back of Tom's pony. She remounted Vixen behind Tom and rode out of the smoke. Crazy, Badger, and Yellow Eyes followed, trailing her, with the bodies of Pony and Cut Ear lashed head down across the backs of their horses. They rode toward the Buffalo Butte.

Red Arm, son of Stone Calf, the Southern Cheyenne Peace Chief, watched them depart. He was sad, not because of their leaving, but because he had not died in the fight just ended. He had made his vow. These spiders died too easily. Many of them wept and pleaded before dying. Others went mad and shot themselves before the Indians could get to them. But now they would ride north and east, to the Adobe Walls, where the main group of spider hide hunters had their headquarters. They would rendezvous there with I-sa-taí and the Comanches and make another fight. This one would not be so easy. The spiders had walls to hide behind, their rifles killed far. Surely there Red Arm would fulfill his vow and regain his family's honor.

When they reached the Buffalo Butte, Jenny dismounted and helped Tom down to the spring. She scooped water in her hands and gave him a drink. Then she washed his wounds. The exit wound on his back was ugly, but the bleeding had nearly stopped. At least the bullet wasn't still in there. She wouldn't have to probe for it and worsen his injuries — a small blessing. She placed an ear against his chest and listened to his breathing. A rale, yes, but not as severe as she had feared.

Nearby Yellow Eyes sat beside Otto's body,

singing death songs. Jenny noticed blood on one of her hands. She had cut off the tip of a finger in mourning. Tom sighed and tried to sit up.

"I think you might live," she told him. "You know?"

He smiled and tried to laugh. She could tell, if only from his eyes, that it hurt. He would never moan. Unable to speak, he signed her for more water. She brought a bucket from her packhorse, filled it at the spring, and set it beside him along with a tin cup. He reached for it with his wounded arm, flexing the fingers slowly. They worked. The shock of the bullet was wearing off. He filled the cup and drank.

"E-hyoph-sta," he croaked. "Jenny Dousmann." Then chuckled at the way he sounded.

She felt relief for the first time in hours.

"You were right," he whispered. "The fight was foolish. It was too easy." He gasped for breath. "Wolf Chief fought beside me. He killed both Sykes and the Englishman. He was brave. He called me his brother." He rested awhile, then frowned.

"But we didn't get what we came for."

"What was that?" Jenny asked absently, searching through her war bag.

"My father wanted the Gatling gun — the Gun-That-Shoots-All-Day. Wolf Chief and I captured it, killed with it. But then he went after Sykes and the fire blew up the wagon with the Gatling." He gestured to the sky. "Gone."

In the war bag Jenny found a parfleche sack of

371

Cheyenne medicines Strongheart had given her. She packed Tom's wounds with moldy moss, then cut a strip of buckskin and bound it on as a bandage. She could do nothing about the lung, but if it was only a nick, as she hoped, it might heal by itself, with plenty of rest and no movement.

The other Elk Soldiers cut saplings from the grove of cottonwoods growing beside the spring and built a rough wickiup. She helped Tom inside, out of the afternoon sun, and covered him with a saddle blanket, setting the cup and bucket beside him. She propped his head and shoulders on a folded buffalo robe.

"Rest now," she said. "Lie still, to keep the blood from your mouth. We must ride north as soon as possible."

"But you've got to go into the butte," Tom whispered. "Maheo's buffalo are in there. You must bring them out, and we'll take them north with us. At least I can bring my father some prize."

"They won't be in the butte," she said. "But I'll go there, anyway. I found a spring at the foot of it and a passageway through the water that leads to a cavern inside. That's where I'll bury Wolf Chief."

"The buffalo will be there," Tom assured her. "I know you'll find them. You should have kept McKay's scalp for an offering." He coughed, breathed cautiously, but no blood came to his lips. "Or are you still a spider at heart?"

"I'm enough of a Cut-Arm to know that I couldn't keep McKay's hair. He didn't die bravely. He wept at the fear of death. I only took his hair to show you I had avenged myself."

Tom nodded.

"And his body — did you bury him as the spiders do?"

She laughed and shook her head.

"Let's just say that I left him as he left so many buffalo — hairless and cold, good only to feed the wolves."

That night she slept close beside Two Shields, naked under a buffalo robe. Her body kept him warm in the prairie chill. He was still sleeping, breathing easily, when she went into the butte the next morning just at dawn. She swam into the rocks from the spring pool, through a reed-masked crevice in the sandstone wall. The water was cold, but she did not feel it. She had brought Otto's body, trailing behind her, with one hand locked in his hair. Between her teeth she carried a knife.

There was, as she'd figured, a big cave inside the butte, and a pool with the morning light flooding red from the hole in the wall where she'd skidded the rock. The channel widened out into a pool, shelved at one end with flat sandstone. She climbed out of the water and dragged Wolf Chief's body up onto the cold rough rock.

As the light strengthened, she saw that there were offerings in the cave, the horned skulls of buffalo arrayed around the pool, some of them painted in cryptic designs of ocher, red and yellow, black and white, wood-ash and marl. One great skull — so old it was furred in luminous mold — had long, long horns, longer even than those of the Texas cattle she'd seen driven north. A giant buffalo from the dawn of time. The cave had been a place of worship since the beginning. She thought of the song the young cowboy had been singing when they killed him — *Tie my bones to her back,* he had mourned — and she felt the depth of that time, along with the infernal chill, a time when the buffalo blanketed the Great West and the People lived happily among them, killing and eating and dying and being born again, over and over through unnumbered eons.

Her brother would be another offering to the spirit of the buffalo. Perhaps the last vain prayer for peace.

She sat with him for a long time on the cold wet rocks beside the pool and thought long thoughts, of Tom and the Sa-sis-e-tas, of Raleigh McKay, but mostly of the buffalo. She saw them moving across the plains as she'd first seen the great herds, traveling against the wind, an undulant black blanket, roaring in high summer like thunder from a cloudless sky. She saw them in winter, digging through the snow for the wind-dried grass. She saw the bulls battling, their heads thudding together and their curved black horns searching for one another's vitals. Then the titanic mating. Then yellow calves tottering to their feet for the first time, their mothers licking them dry. For a moment she even imagined she could hear them answering her silent call — E-hyoph-sta's prayer — and the buffalo coming at her bidding from the depths of the earth, the rattle of their dewclaws, the bulls roaring, cows chuffing, the yellow calves bawling as they ran to keep up, a huge herd, many thousands upon thousands of buffalo, Maheo's cattle in their millions, coming up from the bowels of the earth, out of the water, to erupt onto the prairie and spread themselves again, unending, until the world was covered once more with buffalo. For one thrilling minute she believed . . .

She laughed again, the short, bitter laugh of an Elk Soldier.

There were no buffalo coming. It was only the dawn wind.

You can't get them back, she thought, not by magic — not even you, E-hyoph-sta — from the belly of the earth. You have to fight to keep them, for otherwise the spiders will kill them all.

She rose and walked over to where she'd laid Wolf Chief's body. He stared up at the vaulted ceiling of the cave, sightless yet fierce of visage, his one remaining eye hard as a spear point, the hole in the other reaching toward the center of the earth. A warrior to the end, she thought. *Yes, but also my brother.* And now at last she wept, remembering Otto Dousmann as once he was. Young, strong, calm, loving. Impervious to peril. She remembered their hunting trips together, up north in the big woods, and her fears for him during the long years of the war. She remembered the farm, the sweet-smelling cow byres, the songs at night when Vati played his violin and she and Mutti washed dishes, while the cold of winter creaked outside the window. But the cold had caught up with them at last. She remembered how it took Vati and Mutti, then Otto — first his heart, then his limbs, then his mind, then finally his eye, and with them all his life itself.

She closed his eyelids and found pebbles to keep them sealed. She leaned over and kissed his cold, hard mouth. Then she picked up her knife from where she had laid it on the edge of the rocks. With one strong stroke she cut off the tip of a finger. It would remain with her brother in the buffalo cave, an offering to whatever gods might be.

She turned and dove back into the spring.

24

Alone on the empty prairie, Raleigh Fitzroy McKay, Esq., late Captain of Infantry, 18th North Carolina regiment, C.S.A., marches un-armed toward the moonrise. His face sags away from the severed wires of his skull. In a slurred, dry voice he sings a song of defiance.

> *Oh, I'm a good old Rebel*
> *Now that's just what I am*
> *And for this Yankee nation*
> *I do not give a damn.*
> *I'm glad we fought agin her*
> *I only wish we'd won*
> *And I won't ask no pardon*
> *For anything I done.*
>
> *Three hundred thousand Yankees*
> *Is stiff in Southern dust.*
> *We got three hundred thousand*
> *Before they conquered us.*
> *They died of Southern fever*
> *And Southern steel and shot.*
> *I wish they were three million*
> *Instead of what we got.*
>
> *I won't be reconstructed*

I'm better now than them
And for a carpetbagger
I do not give a damn.
So I'm off for the mountains
As soon as I can go
To find myself a rifle and start for Mexico.

He walks through an endless boneyard —
horned skulls, vaulting rib cages, the warped sine
curves of chained vertebrae. The scattered hooves
of countless dead buffalo. Vultures disturbed by
his passage flap up from the carcasses that loom
to the horizon, translucent against the evening
light. Others, less timid, hold their ground. They
spread their wings and hiss at him.

On his spoor the white wolves follow, lured yet
lulled by his voice, hungry, timid, working up
courage — biding their time.

Awaiting their moment.

Bibliographical Note

In writing this story, the author gained valuable insights and information from many works, most especially:

W. Philo Clark. *The Indian Sign Language, with Brief Explanatory Notes of the Gestures Taught Deaf-Mutes in Our Institutions for Their Instruction, and a Description of Some of the Peculiar Laws, Customs, Myths, Superstitions, Ways of Living, Code of Peace and War Signals of Our Aborigines* (1885).

John R. Cook. *The Border and the Buffalo* (1907).

Olive K. Dixon. *The Life of "Billy" Dixon* (1927).

English–Cheyenne Student Dictionary. The Northern Cheyenne Language and Cultural Center (1976).

Shelby Foote. *The Civil War: A Narrative*, 3 vols. (1974).

George Bird Grinnell. *The Cheyenne Indians*, 2 vols. (1925).

———. *The Fighting Cheyennes* (1915).

William T. Hornaday. *The Extermination of the American Bison: Report of the National Museum, 1887* (1889).

James I. Merritt. *Baronets & Buffalo* (1985).

Alan T. Nolan. *The Iron Brigade: A Military History* (1961).

George F. Ruxton. *Adventures in Mexico and the Rocky Mountains* (1847).